A TEXT BOOK OF

BASIC ELECTRONICS ENGINEERING

FOR
SEMESTER – I

FIRST YEAR DEGREE COURSES IN ENGINEERING

**Strictly According to New Revised Credit System Syllabus
of Savitribai Phule Pune University
(Effective from Academic Year – June 2015)**

COMMON FOR ALL DEGREE ENGINEERING BRANCHES

S. R. DESHPANDE
ME (Electronics), FE Co-ordinator,
Assistant Professor, E&TC Department,
Sinhgad Institute of Technology & Science,
Narhe (Ambegaon), Pune

R.C. JAISWAL
ME (E&TC)
Assistant Professor, E&TC Department
Pune Institute of Computer Technology,
Katraj, Dhankawadi, Pune

M. D. PATIL
ME (VLSI Tech.)
Assistant Professor, E&TC Department
Sinhgad Institute of Technology & Science,
Narhe (Ambegaon), Pune

NIRALI PRAKASHAN
ADVANCEMENT OF KNOWLEDGE

N2755

BASIC ELECTRONICS ENGINEERING (FE)   ISBN 978-93-82448-15-0

Second Edition   :   **July 2017**

©   :   **Authors**

Published By :   Polyplate

NIRALI PRAKASHAN

Abhyudaya Pragati, 1312, Shivaji Nagar,
Off J.M. Road, Pune – 411005
Tel - (020) 25512336/37/39, Fax - (020) 25511379
Email : niralipune@pragationline.com

☞ **DISTRIBUTION CENTRES**

PUNE

Nirali Prakashan   **:**   119, Budhwar Peth, Jogeshwari Mandir Lane, Pune 411002, Maharashtra
Tel : (020) 2445 2044, 66022708, Fax : (020) 2445 1538
Email : bookorder@pragationline.com, niralilocal@pragationline.com

Nirali Prakashan   **:**   S. No. 28/27, Dhyari, Near Pari Company, Pune 411041
Tel : (020) 24690204 Fax : (020) 24690316
Email : dhyari@pragationline.com, bookorder@pragationline.com

MUMBAI

Nirali Prakashan   **:**   385, S.V.P. Road, Rasdhara Co-op. Hsg. Society Ltd.,
Girgaum, Mumbai 400004, Maharashtra
Tel : (022) 2385 6339 / 2386 9976, Fax : (022) 2386 9976
Email : niralimumbai@pragationline.com

☞ **DISTRIBUTION BRANCHES**

JALGAON

Nirali Prakashan   **:**   34, V. V. Golani Market, Navi Peth, Jalgaon 425001,
Maharashtra, Tel : (0257) 222 0395, Mob : 94234 91860

KOLHAPUR

Nirali Prakashan   **:**   New Mahadvar Road, Kedar Plaza, 1st Floor Opp. IDBI Bank
Kolhapur 416 012, Maharashtra. Mob : 9850046155

NAGPUR

Pratibha Book Distributors   **:**   Above Maratha Mandir, Shop No. 3, First Floor,
Rani Jhanshi Square, Sitabuldi, Nagpur 440012, Maharashtra
Tel : (0712) 254 7129

DELHI

Nirali Prakashan   **:**   4593/21, Basement, Aggarwal Lane 15, Ansari Road, Daryaganj
Near Times of India Building, New Delhi 110002
Mob : 08505972553

BENGALURU

Pragati Book House   **:**   House No. 1, Sanjeevappa Lane, Avenue Road Cross,
Opp. Rice Church, Bengaluru – 560002.
Tel : (080) 64513344, 64513355,Mob : 9880582331, 9845021552
Email:bharatsavla@yahoo.com

CHENNAI

Pragati Books   **:**   9/1, Montieth Road, Behind Taas Mahal, Egmore,
Chennai 600008 Tamil Nadu, Tel : (044) 6518 3535,
Mob : 94440 01782 / 98450 21552 / 98805 82331,
Email : bharatsavla@yahoo.com

niralipune@pragationline.com | www.pragationline.com

Also find us on [f] www.facebook.com/niralibooks

PREFACE TO THE SECOND EDITION

We are glad and excited to announce that the First Edition of this book received an overwhelming response from the engineering student community, compelling us to release its New Edition within a very short period of time.

This New Edition has been updated with including all University Question Papers from May 2015 to November 2016 (Including In Sem. Question Papers also).

Special care has been taken to maintain high degree of accuracy in the theory and numericals throughout the book.

We take this opportunity to express our sincere thanks to Dineshbhai Furia of Nirali Prakashan, a reputed pioneer in the publication field. Our special thanks to Jignesh Furia for their effective cooperation and great care in bringing out this revised edition. We also appreciate the efforts of M. P. Munde and the entire staff of Engineering Books Deptt. of Nirali Prakashan namely Mrs. Deepali Lachake (Co-ordinator) for bringing this book to the students in a timely manner.

We sincerely hope that this "Second Edition" will also be warmly received by all concerned as in the past.

Valuable suggestions from our esteemed readers to improve the book are most welcome and highly appreciated.

Pune   **Author**

PREFACE TO THE FIRST EDITION

It gives us great pleasure in publishing this text book on **"Basic Electronics Engineering"** for the Students of First Year Degree Courses in Engineering. This book is strictly written According to New Revised Credit System Syllabus of Savitribai Phule Pune University (2015 Pattern).

As per the policy of the University, Engineering Syllabi is revised every five years. Last revision was in the year 2012. New revision is coming little earlier, as university has introduced **Online** system of examination from year 2012.

In New Credit System, there will be two online examinations conducted at the end of first and second month in every semester. The first online (Phase I – 25 Marks) examination will be based on units I and II and the second online (Phase II – 25 Marks) examination will be based on units III and IV. Both the online examinations will be based on Multiple Choice Questions. End Semester Examination (Theory - 50 Marks) will be based on all six units and will be descriptive type and theory course will have 4 credits.

We have given Free Separate book of Multiple Choice Questions (MCQ's) which will be very useful to the students, especially for Online Examinations.

The subject matter is presented in a lucid, fluent and comprehensive manner. All efforts have been taken to present the text matter in Simple & Lucid Language, Illustrative Figures, University Question Papers and Solved Problems with Answers have been added. **Also, Solved University Question Papers (New Pattern) have given (Dec. 12 to May 16) at the end of the Book**, and it will help student to understand nature of questions that could be asked in the final examination.

We take this opportunity to express our sincere thanks to Shri. Dineshbhai Furia, Shri. Jignesh Furia, Mrs. Nirali Verma and Shri. M. P. Munde and entire team of Nirali Prakashan namely Mrs. Deepali Lachake (Co-ordinator) who really have taken keen interest and untiring efforts in publishing this text.

Finally, we express our gratitude to our family members for their continuous support and encouragement, thanks to all.

We have no doubt that like our earlier texts, student's community will respond favourably to this new venture.

The advice and suggestions of our esteemed readers to improve the text are most welcomed, and will be highly appreciated.

Pune   **Authors**

SYLLABUS

Unit 1: Diode Circuits   (6 Hours)

Half wave rectifiers, Full wave rectifiers, Power supply filters and Capacitor filters, Diode limiting (Clippers) and Clamping circuits, Voltage multipliers, Zener diode and its applications, LEDs and Photodiodes.

Unit 2: Bipolar Junction Transistor (BJT) Circuits   (6 Hours)

BJT Structure and its operation with normal biasing, Transistor characteristics and parameters, DC operating point, Transistor as an amplifier, Transistor as a switch, Enhancement-type MOSFET.

Unit 3: Linear Integrated Circuits   (6 Hours)

Introduction to operational amplifiers, Op-amp input modes and parameters, Negative feedback. Op-amp with negative feedback, Comparators, Summing amplifiers, Integrators and Differentiators. IC 555 timer as an oscillator, Voltage regulation, IC voltage regulators (Three pin).

Unit 4: Digital Electronics   (6 Hours)

Introduction, Digital signals, Basic digital circuits-AND, OR, NOT, NAND, NOR, EX-OR, Standard and representation for logic functions, Half adder, Boolean algebra, Examples of IC gates, Full adder, Multiplexers, De-multiplexer, Flip-flops, 1-bit memory cell, D flip-flop, Shift registers, Counters, Block diagram of Microprocessor and Microcontroller and their applications.

Unit 5: Industrial Electronics   (7 Hours)

Power Devices : Basics of 4-layer devices : Silicon Controlled Rectifier (SCR), Diac and Triac.

Transducers : Introduction, Electrical transducer, Selecting a transducer, Resistive transducer, Thermistor, Inductive transducer, Linear Variable Differential Transducer (LVDT), Load cell, Phototransistor, Temperature transducers, Flow measurement (Mechanical transducers) Application of transducers : Digital Thermometer, Weighing machine (Block diagrams).

Unit 6: Electronic Communication   (7 Hours)

Importance of Communication System, The elements of a Communication System, Bandwidth requirement, IEEE frequency spectrum, Transmission media: Wired (Twisted pair, Coaxial and Optical fiber Cables) and Wireless, Need for modulation, Analog modulation schemes AM and FM, Mobile communication system: Cellular concept, Simple block diagram of GSM system.

CONTENTS

DIODE CIRCUITS

1.1 DIODE FUNDAMENTALS

1.1.1 Classification of Materials

- Materials can be classified in many ways. Here we shall consider the property of conduction of electricity for classification of materials. Some materials like copper, aluminium, silver etc. are good conductors of electricity, whereas materials such as plastic, rubber, wood etc. are bad conductors of electricity. They are called insulators.

- Also, there are some materials, like Silicon and Germanium, whose conductivity lies between conductors and insulators. Such materials are called semiconductors. These materials have 4 electrons in the outermost shell of their atomic structure. These four electrons are called valance electrons. They form a bond with another valence electron of the neighbouring atom. These bonds are called covalent bonds. The energy levels associated with the valance electrons merge into each other. This merging forms a valance band.

1.1.2 The Energy Band Theory

- Energy band diagrams for conductors, insulators and semiconductors are as shown below in Fig. 1.1.

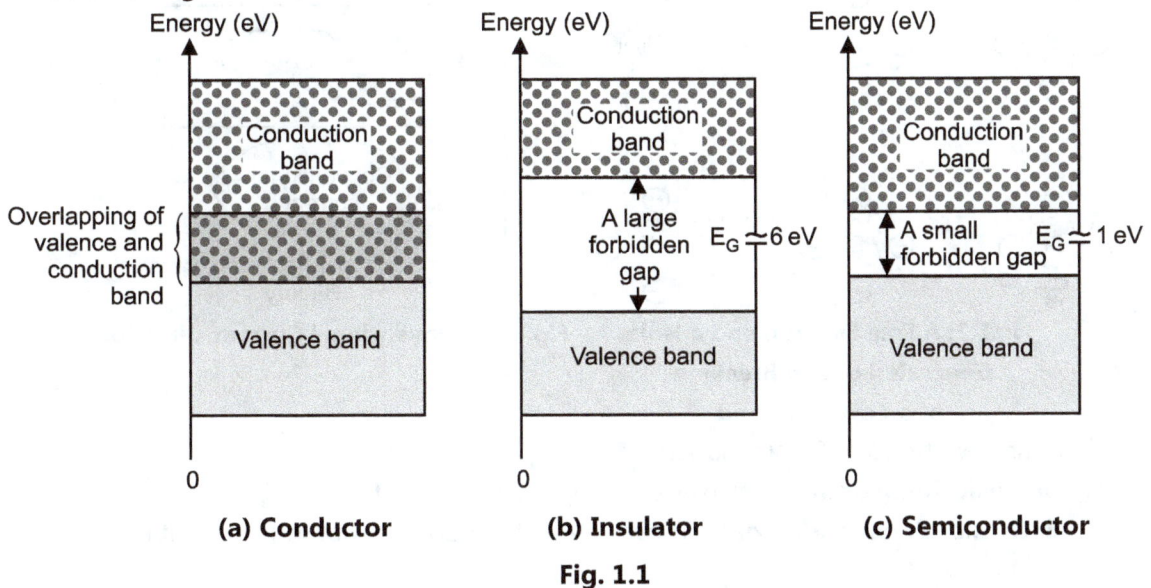

(a) Conductor   **(b) Insulator**   **(c) Semiconductor**

Fig. 1.1

- The energy band formed due to merging of energy levels associated with the free electrons is called as the conduction band.
- When the valance electron gets energy, it jumps from the valance band to the conduction band and becomes free. While jumping it has to cross the energy gap (E_G).
- The energy gap is the gap separating the valance band and the conduction band and is called the forbidden gap.

1.1.3 Classification of Materials Based on Energy Gap (E_G)

- **Conductors:** As shown in Fig.1.1, in conductors like copper, aluminium etc. the valance band and the conduction band overlap and there are large number of electrons available for conduction at room temperature.
- **Insulators:** As shown in Fig. 1.1, in insulators like plastic, wood etc. there is a large forbidden gap (approx. 6 eV) between the valance band and conduction band and so these materials cannot conduct the electricity.
- **Semiconductors:** As shown in Fig. 1.1, in semiconductors the forbidden gap is much smaller (approx. 1 eV) than insulators. At absolute zero temperature, these materials behave as perfect insulators. But at room temperature, the value of E_G is 0.72 eV for Germanium and 1.12 eV for Silicon. As the temperature increases, these materials can conduct heavily.

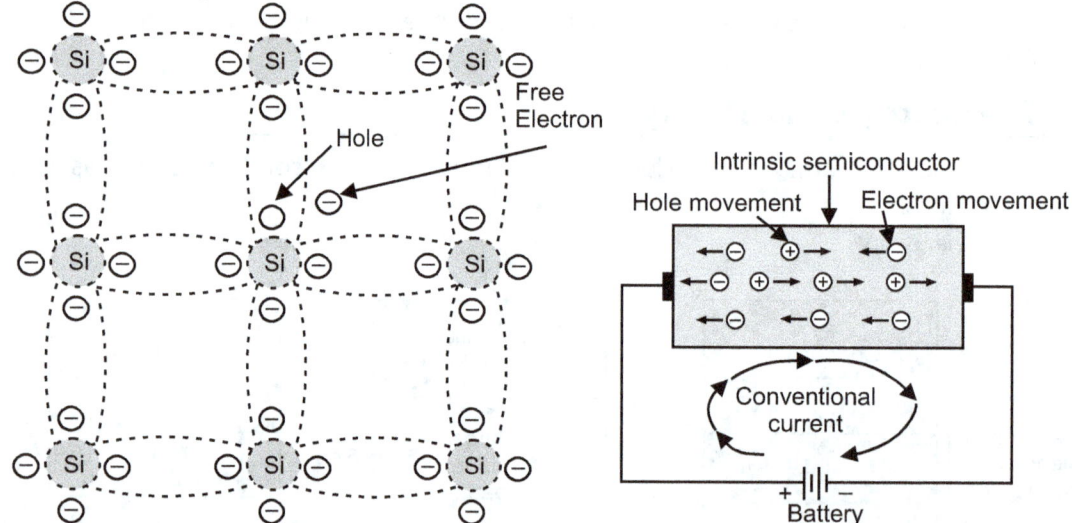

Fig.1.2: A Free Electron and a Hole Generated due to Breaking of a Covalent Bond

Fig. 1.3: Conventional Current Direction

- There are two types of Semiconductors:
  1. **Intrinsic Semiconductors:** These are pure semiconductors.
  2. **Extrinsic Semiconductors:** These are obtained by adding impurities to pure semiconductors.

1.1.4 Effect of Temperature on Conduction of Semiconductors (Intrinsic)

- As we have seen earlier, at absolute zero temperature, in intrinsic semiconductors, the outermost shell of all the atoms is completely filled and valence electrons are tightly bound to the parent atoms. Due to this, no free electrons are available at absolute zero temperature and the semiconductor behaves as a perfect insulator.

- However at room temperature, some of the covalent bonds break because of the heat energy. These electrons, which break the bond and come out as free electrons are available for conduction.

- The empty space left behind by the electrons makes an incomplete covalent bond and is called a **hole.**

- A valance electron from a neighbouring atom can fill up this hole and create another hole. So each valance electron leaves behind a hole which is occupied by another valance electron and the process continues. Thus, holes can be considered as carriers of electricity.

- An electron is negatively charged particle and hole is positively charged. The overall concentration of free electrons and holes is always equal in an intrinsic semiconductor.

- If external voltage is applied to an intrinsic semiconductor, free electrons move towards the positive terminal of the battery and the holes move towards the negative terminal of the battery, as shown in Fig. 1.3.

- The current which flows from the positive to the negative terminal of the battery, and external to the battery is called as conventional current.

- The conventional current direction is thus opposite to the direction of the electron flow.

- Intrinsic semiconductors are never used independently.

- In order to change the properties of intrinsic semiconductors, a small amount of some other material is added to it. The process of adding some selected impurity to the crystal of intrinsic semiconductors to improve the conductivity is called doping. A semiconductor thus formed is called an Extrinsic semiconductor.

- There are two types of impurities, donor impurities and acceptor impurities and hence there are two types of extrinsic semiconductors as 'P' type or 'N' type semiconductors.

- By adding a small amount of pentavalent impurity (having five valance electrons) or donor impurity to a pure semiconductor, an N-type semiconductor is formed as shown (free electrons are created) in Fig. 1.4. Examples of donor impurities are arsenic, phosphorous etc. This type of semiconductor has a large number of free electrons.

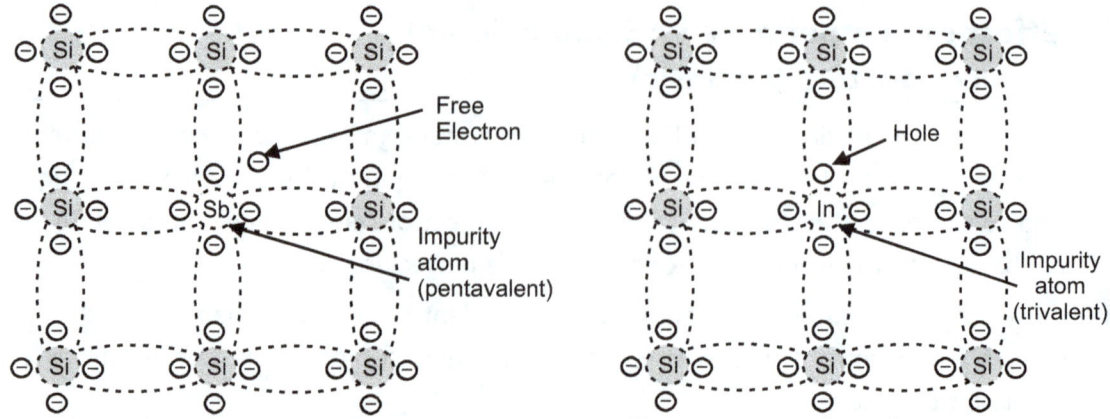

Fig. 1.4: Formation of N-type Material   **Fig. 1.5: Formation of P-type Material**

- By adding a small amount of trivalent impurity (having only three valance electrons) or acceptor impurity to a pure semiconductor, a P-type semiconductor is formed (free holes are created) as shown in Fig. 1.5. Examples of trivalent impurity are Gallium, Boron etc. This type of semiconductor has a large number of holes.

- **Drift Current:** When a voltage is applied to a semiconductor, the free electrons try to drift towards the positive terminal of the battery. This drift causes a current to flow in the semiconductor which is called drift current and the velocity with which the electrons drift is called drift velocity.

  Note: The direction of conventional current is always opposite to the direction of drifting electrons.

- **Diffusion Current:** In semiconductors it is possible to have a non-uniform concentration of the charged particles due to non-uniform doping. For example, the concentration of electrons on one side of the surface is more than the density on the other side. So the electrons will move from the side of greater concentration to the side of lower concentration. This transport of electrons results into a flow of current which is called diffusion current.

1.2 P-N JUNCTION AND ITS CHARACTERISTICS

> **❖ Important Questions Related to this Topic ❖**
> 1. Explain how a P-N junction and the depletion region are formed in an unbiased p-n junction.
> 2. What is barrier potential? On which factors, it depends? State the values of barrier potential for Si and Ge P-N junctions.
> 3. What is P-N junction diode? Draw its symbol. What is function of ohmic contacts.

- The two 'P' type and 'N' type materials are chemically combined with a definite fabrication technique to form a p-n junction which is called a diode.

- As we have seen earlier, the movement of charge carriers from high concentration to low concentration area to achieve uniform concentration over the material is called as a diffusion process.

- In P-N junction, there is large number of electrons on the N side, whereas on the P side the concentration of electrons is very low.
- Due to this non-uniform concentration, diffusion starts and electrons start moving from N side towards P side. Similarly the holes from p-region diffuse into the N-region across the junction. This is shown in the Fig. 1.6 below.

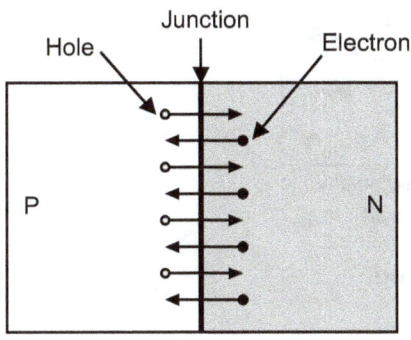

When the P-N junction is formed, the N-side donor atoms accept additional holes and they become positively charged immobile ions. Similarly, P-side acceptor atoms accept additional electrons and they become negatively charged immobile ions. The formation of immobile ions near the junction is shown in Fig. 1.7. In this region, there exists a wall in which there are no mobile charge carriers. Such a region is depleted of the free mobile charge carriers and hence is called as depletion region or depletion layer.

Fig. 1.6: Initial Diffusion in P-N Junction

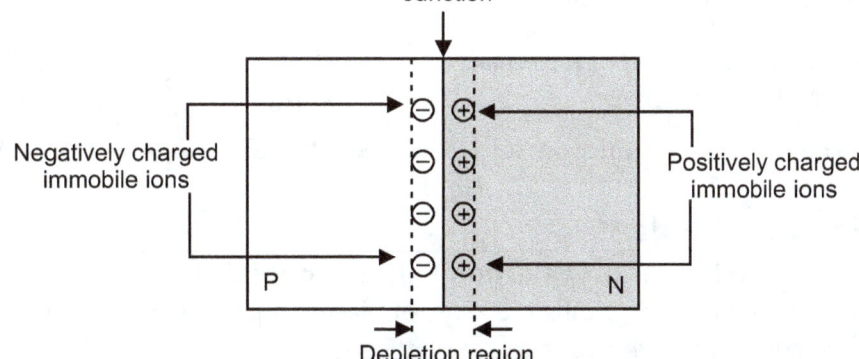

Fig. 1.7: Formation of Depletion Region

- Thus, under thermal equilibrium, the depletion region gets widened up to an extent where no more electrons or holes can cross the junction. This depletion region acts as the barrier due to which the hole and electrons cannot diffuse further. This condition is shown in Fig. 1.8.
- Thus at the junction, there are immobile positive and negative ions, due to which an electric field called barrier potential or cut-in voltage is created at the junction.

The Barrier Potential Depends on Different Factors Like:

- Type of semiconductor,
- The donor impurity added,
- The acceptor impurity added,
- The surrounding temperature.

The barrier potential for Silicon is 0.7 V and the barrier potential for Germanium is 0.3 V.

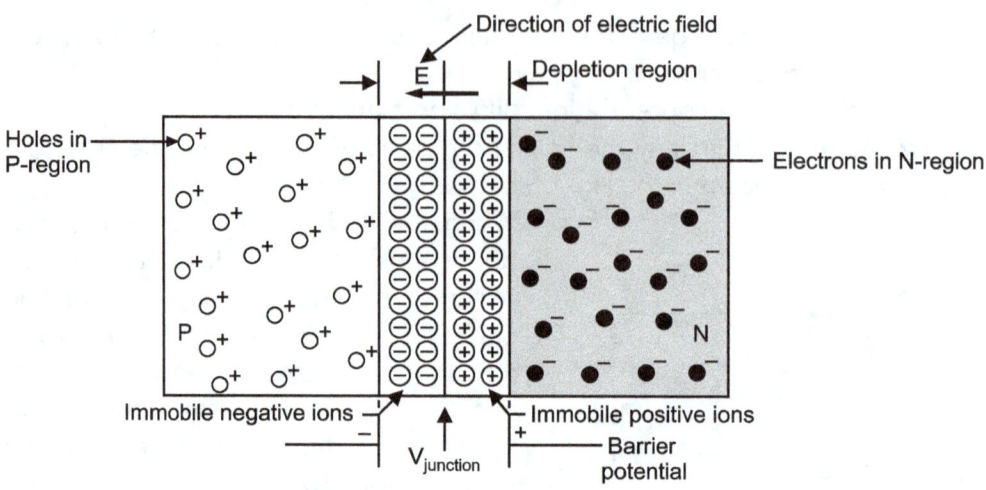

Fig. 1.8: Depletion region

1.2.1 P-N Junction Diode

- The P-N junction forms a device which is known as Diode. The symbol of a diode is shown below. The P-type electrode connection is called as **Anode** and N-type electrode connection is called as **Cathode**.

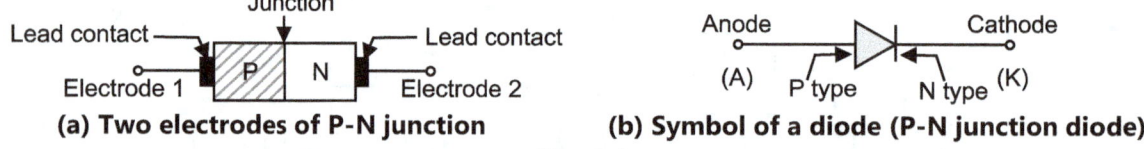

(a) Two electrodes of P-N junction   **(b) Symbol of a diode (P-N junction diode)**

Fig. 1.9

1.2.2 Biasing of a Diode

> **❖ Important Question Related to this Topic ❖**
> Explain with diagrams and graphs the ways of biasing a p-n junction diode and variation of the diode current with the voltage across the diode.

- Biasing means applying an external DC voltage to a device. The P-N junction diode can be reverse biased or forward biased depending upon the polarity of the battery connected across it. The forward biasing of a P-N junction diode is shown below.

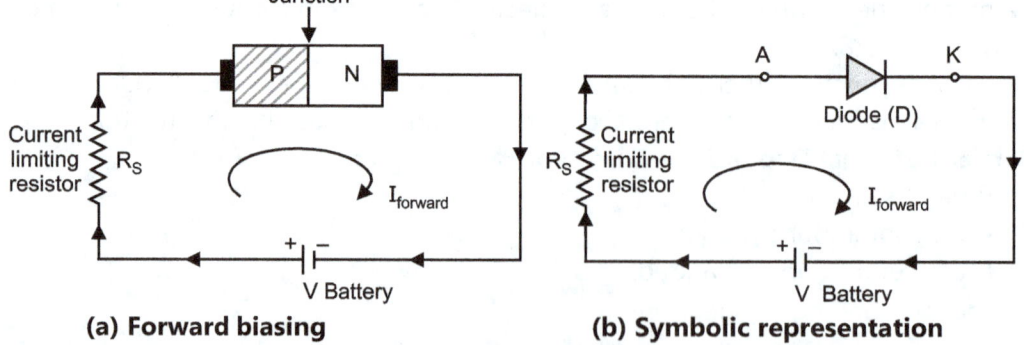

(a) Forward biasing   **(b) Symbolic representation**

Fig. 1.10: Diode in forward bias condition

- The conduction is not possible as long as the applied forward voltage is less than the barrier potential.

- When the applied voltage becomes more than the barrier potential, the negative terminal of the battery pushes free electrons from N to P region and positive terminal of the battery pushes the holes from P to N region.

- If the applied forward voltage is further increased, it overcomes the barrier potential. The depletion region gets reduced and majority carriers can pass through the junction which causes a current to flow. Refer Fig. 1.11. This current is called as the forward current I_F.

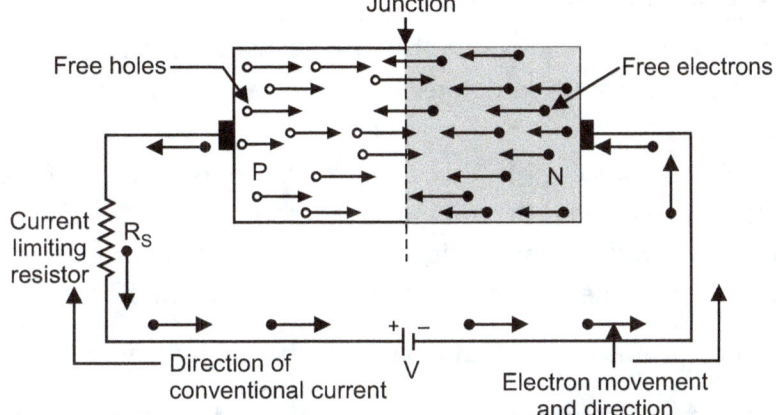

Fig. 1.11: Forward current in a P-N junction diode

1.2.3 Forward V-I Characteristic of P-N Junction Diode

- The V-I characteristics and the circuit for forward biased diode are as shown in Fig. 1.12.

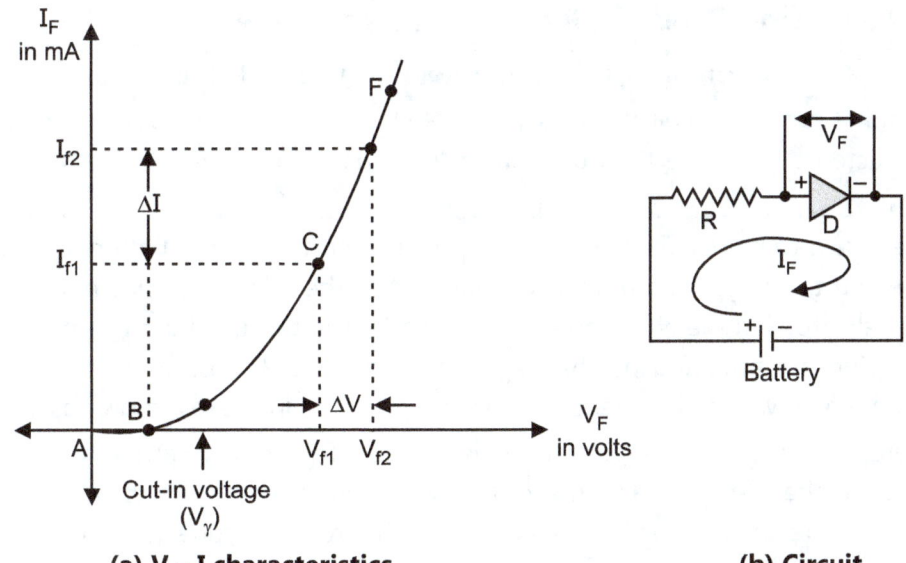

(a) V – I characteristics   **(b) Circuit**

Fig. 1.12: Forward biased P-N junction diode

The forward characteristic may be divided into two parts:

- **Region A to B:** This is the region where V_F is less than the cut-in voltage and the current flow is very small, so I_F is assumed to be zero. (The cut-in voltage is 0.3 V for Germanium diode and for Silicon diode it is 0.7 V).

- **Region B to F:** As the applied forward voltage (V_F) increases, at point B it exceeds the cut-in voltage V_γ the depletion region reduces to zero and there is a sudden increase in I_F. As shown in the Fig. 1.12 (a), the curve B to F is exponential in nature.

1.2.4 Forward Resistance of Diode

- The resistance offered by the diode in the forward biased condition is called as forward resistance, which is very small in nature. There are two types of forward resistances viz. static and dynamic.

- **Static Forward Resistance (R_f):** This is the forward resistance offered by the P-N junction diode when a forward DC voltage is applied to it. The static forward resistance R_f at a point on the forward characteristic, can be calculated by taking the ratio of the DC voltage applied across the P-N junction to the DC current flowing through the P-N junction at that point. Thus, $R_f = \dfrac{V_{dc}}{I_{dc}}$ at a particular point on the forward characteristic.

- **Dynamic Forward Resistance (r_f):** This is the forward resistance offered by the P-N junction diode when a forward AC voltage is applied to it. The dynamic resistance 'r_f' is the reciprocal of the slope of the forward characteristic. Thus, $r_f = \dfrac{\Delta V_f}{\Delta I_f}$.

1.2.5 P-N Junction Diode in Reverse Biased Mode

❖ **Important Question Related to this Topic** ❖

Show with a suitable circuit diagram, how a P-N junction can be reverse biased. Draw the V-I characteristics for the P-N junction in this circuit and define the reverse saturation current.

- A diode is said to be reverse biased when positive terminal of the battery is connected to cathode and the negative terminal is connected to the anode, as shown in the Fig. 1.13. The free electrons in the N region are attracted by the positive terminal and the holes in the P region are attracted by the negative terminal of the battery, due to which the depletion region widens and hence the barrier potential increases, shown as in Fig. 1.14.

- Therefore very small reverse current flows due to the minority carriers which constitute the holes in the N-region and the electrons in the P-region. As they are very less in amount, the reverse current is very small. The reverse current depends upon the temperature and not on the reverse voltage applied. It is represented as I_o. It is few micro amperes in Germanium and few nano amperes in Silicon.

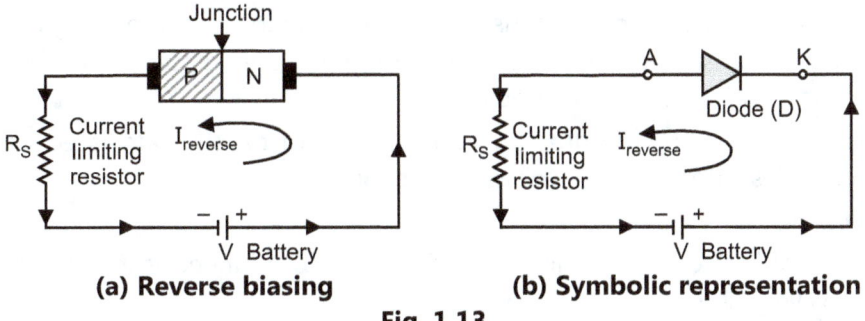

(a) Reverse biasing   **(b) Symbolic representation**

Fig. 1.13

- The reverse biased diode current flow is shown in Fig. 1.14.

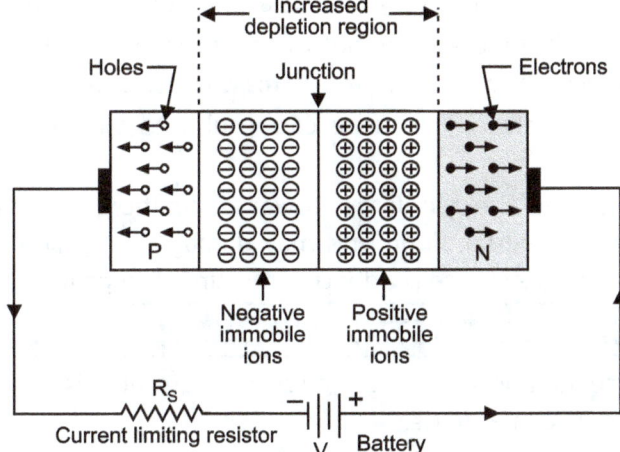

Fig. 1.14: The depletion region widens in reverse biased diode

1.2.6 Breakdown in a Reverse Biased Diode

- Though we have mentioned earlier that the reverse current is independent of the value of the applied reverse voltage, if this applied reverse voltage is increased beyond a particular value, it may damage the diode. It is called reverse breakdown of the diode which is caused due to the following two effects: (a) Avalanche breakdown (b) Zener breakdown.

(a) Avalanche Breakdown:

- As the magnitude of the reverse bias voltage is increased, the kinetic energy of the minority carriers gets increased. While travelling, the minority carriers collide with the stationary atoms, which in turn results in breaking some of the covalent bonds and generating free electrons.
- These electrons act as minority carriers. Again they get accelerated by the strong reverse bias field, thereby increasing the collision and also the number of free electrons. This is known as carrier multiplication.
- This process continues leading to a very swift multiplication effect and giving rise to a large reverse current in just a few picoseconds. This effect is called as "Avalanche breakdown effect".

- Avalanche breakdown effect causes reverse breakdown in the p-n junction. Due to large power dissipation, the junction temperature increases and may destroy the semiconductor device permanently.
- To limit this reverse current, a series resistance of exactly calculated value must be used in series with the diode for its protection.

(b) Zener Breakdown:

- This type of breakdown occurs in heavily doped p-n junctions in which the depletion region is very narrow.
- All the applied reverse voltage appears across the depletion layer. The electric field is voltage per unit distance. It is very intense at the depletion region.
- Therefore it can pull the electrons out of the valance band by breaking the covalent bonds and producing the free electrons. This process is known as Zener effect.
- A large number of such free electrons can result into a large reverse current through the diode.
- Due to large current, there is large power dissipation. This increases the junction temperature beyond certain limit and may damage the diode permanently. To limit the current, a series resistance is added in the circuit to protect the diode.

1.3 REVERSE CHARACTERISTICS OF DIODE

- The graph of reverse voltage V_R verses the reverse current I_R is shown in Fig. 1.15(a). It is the reverse characteristic of a diode.
- As we can see from the Fig. 1.15 (a), at constant temperature, if the reverse voltage is increased the reverse saturation current (I_o) remains constant showing that it is independent of the reverse voltage.

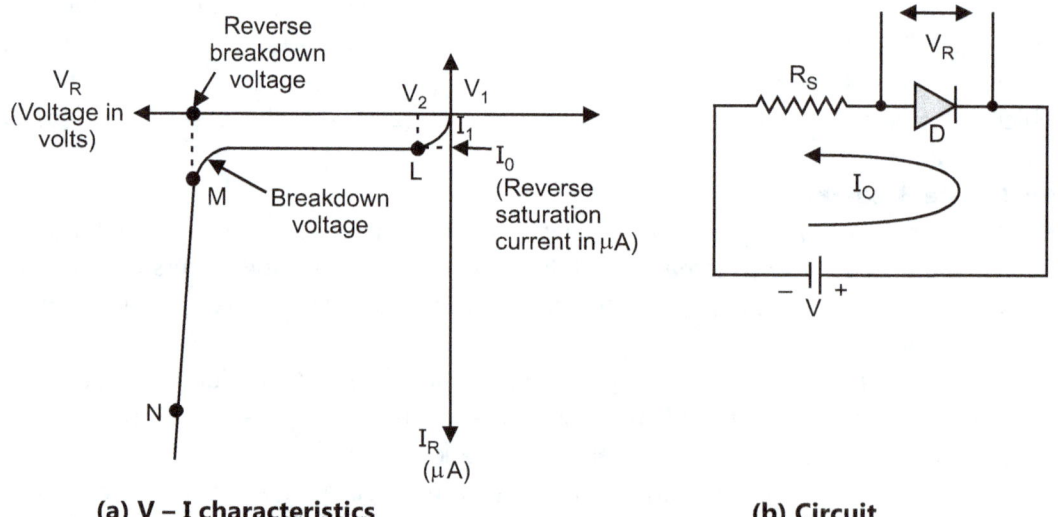

(a) V – I characteristics   **(b) Circuit**

Fig. 1.15: For reverse biased P-N junction diode

- But if the reverse voltage is increased beyond the breakdown voltage, a large current flows through the diode. Typically, the breakdown voltage is about 50 V to 100 V.

- A very high resistance of about few hundred kilo ohms is connected in series with the diode for protection.

1.3.1 Reverse Resistance of Diode

- **Reverse Static Resistance (R_r):** It is equal to 'the ratio of applied reverse DC voltage to the reverse DC saturation current I_0'. It is very large in Mega ohms.

- **Reverse Dynamic Resistance (r_r):** Under AC conditions, r_r is defined as 'ratio of change in reverse voltage applied to the corresponding change in the reverse current'.

$$\text{Reverse resistance} = \frac{\Delta V_f}{\Delta I_f} = \frac{1}{\text{Slope of graph}} = \frac{V_2 - V_1}{I_0 - I_1} = \frac{V_2}{I_0}$$

1.4   V-I CHARACTERISTICS OF THE TYPICAL SILICON AND GERMANIUM DIODES

❖ **Important Question Related to this Topic** ❖

Draw and explain the V-I characteristics of Ge and Si diodes. Give reasons for variations in the characteristics.

- The combined forward and reverse V-I characteristics of the typical Silicon and Germanium diodes are as shown in Fig. 1.16.

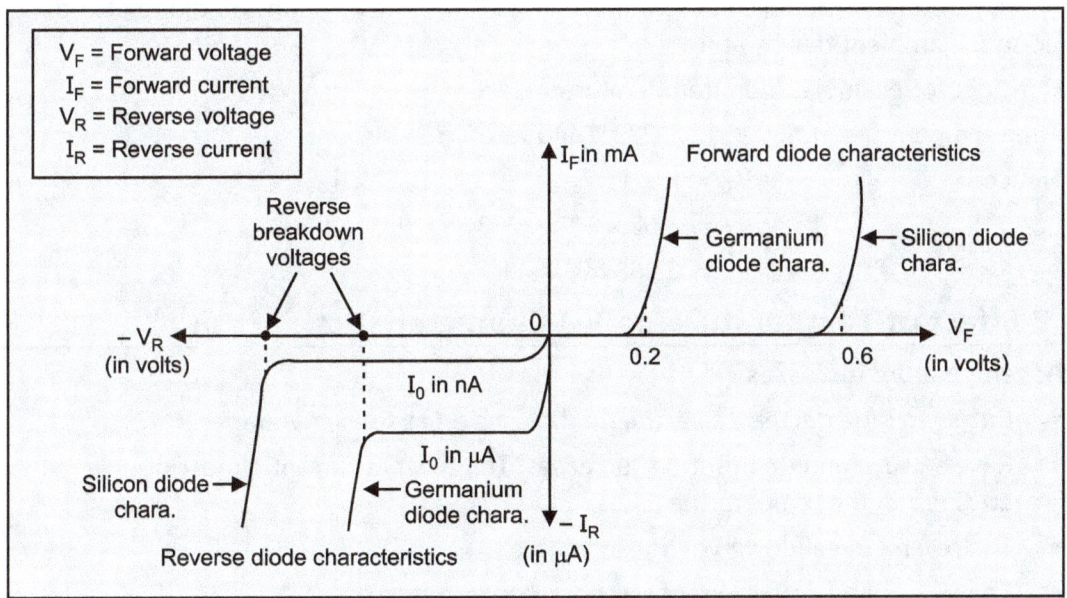

Fig. 1.16: V-I characteristics of typical Ge and Si diodes

1.4.1 Diode Current Equation

> **❖ Important Question Related to this Topic ❖**
> Write the V-I equation for a p-n diode. Explain the meaning of each symbol.

- The relation between the applied voltage 'V' across the diode and current 'I' flowing through the diode can be expressed mathematically by the diode current equation which is given as,

$$I = I_o [e^{V/\eta \, V_T} - 1] \text{ amperes}$$

where,

V = Applied voltage across the diode in volts

I = Current flow through the diode in amperes

η = 2 for Silicon P-N junction diode

= 1 for germanium P-N junction diode

I_o = Reverse saturation current flow through diode in amperes

- The term 'e' indicates that the diode current equation is exponential in nature and is applicable for all the conditions of the diode operating modes (i.e. whether diode is forward biased, reverse biased or in unbiased condition).

- V_T is the voltage equivalent of temperature in volts. It is given by following equation.

$$V_T = K \times T \text{ volts}$$

where,

K = Boltzman's constant = 8.62×10^{-5} eV/°K.

T = Temperature in °K (°Kelvin)

- The equation $V_T = K \times T$ indicates that the current flow through the diode also depends upon the ambient temperature.

- Consider for example, room temperature = 25°C.

Then temperature in °K= 25°C + 273. Therefore T= 298°K

Hence, $V_T = K \times T$

∴. $V_T = 8.62 \times 10^{-5} \times 298 \text{ K}$

∴. $V_T = 25.68 \text{ mV}$

1.4.2 Effect of Temperature on V-I Characteristics

As the temperature **increases**,

- Cut-in voltage decreases i.e. the diode turns on at smaller voltages.
- Reverse saturation current (I_0) increases. The reverse current almost doubles at every 10°C rise in the temperature.
- The reverse breakdown voltage increases.
- The V_T (voltage equivalent of temperature) also increases.

These effects are shown in Fig. 1.17.

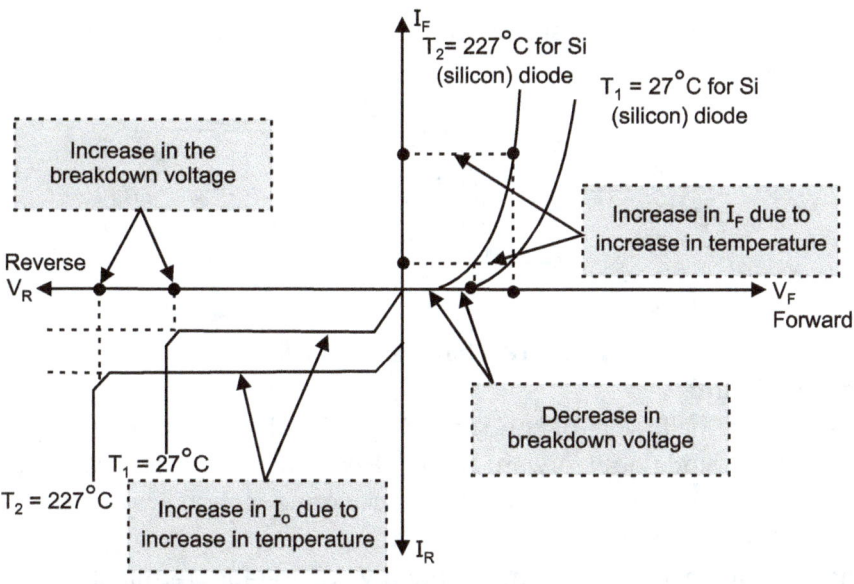

Fig. 1.17: Effect of temperature on P-N junction diode

1.5 TYPES OF DIODE RECTIFIER

❖ Important Questions Related to this Topic ❖

1. For a halfwave rectifier, define and derive an expression for the following parameters:
   (a) I_{DC}
   (b) V_{DC}
   (c) Ripple factor
   (d) Rectifier efficiency

2. For a half wave rectifier, derive an expression for the following:
   (a) I_{DC}
   (b) V_{DC}
   (c) Ripple factor
   (d) P_{DC}

3. Derive an expression for T.U.F. and voltage regulation for a half wave rectifier.

- A device which converts AC voltage to a pulsating DC voltage using p-n junction diodes is called a rectifier. Rectifier circuits may be classified as we will see below.
  1. Half-wave rectifier,
  2. Full-wave rectifier (center tap),
  3. The full-wave bridge rectifier.

1.5.1 The Half-Wave Rectifier

- A half wave rectifier uses a step down transformer, a diode and a load resistor R_L. The AC line voltage (230 V, 50 Hz) is lowered by a step down transformer that provides lower AC voltage at the secondary in order to increase compatibility.

- The rectifying element diode D shown in the Fig. 1.18 conducts only for the positive half cycle of the input AC supply.

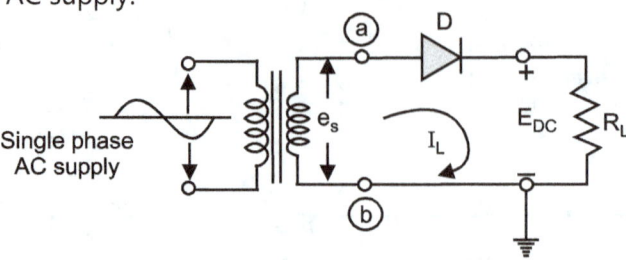

Fig. 1.18: Half-wave rectifier

Operation of the Circuit:

- During the positive half cycle of the secondary AC voltage, terminal 'a' is positive w.r.t. terminal 'b', so the diode gets forward biased. Hence the current flows through the diode and through the load resistor R_L in the clockwise direction, which develops positive voltage across load resistance.
- During the negative half cycle of the secondary AC voltage, terminal 'b' is positive w.r.t. terminal 'a', so the diode gets reverse biased. Hence, the current cannot flow through the circuit. Hence, the value of output voltage is zero.
- Refer the waveforms shown in Fig. 1.19. The waveforms show that the output of a rectifier is not exactly a DC It is called a **pulsating DC.**

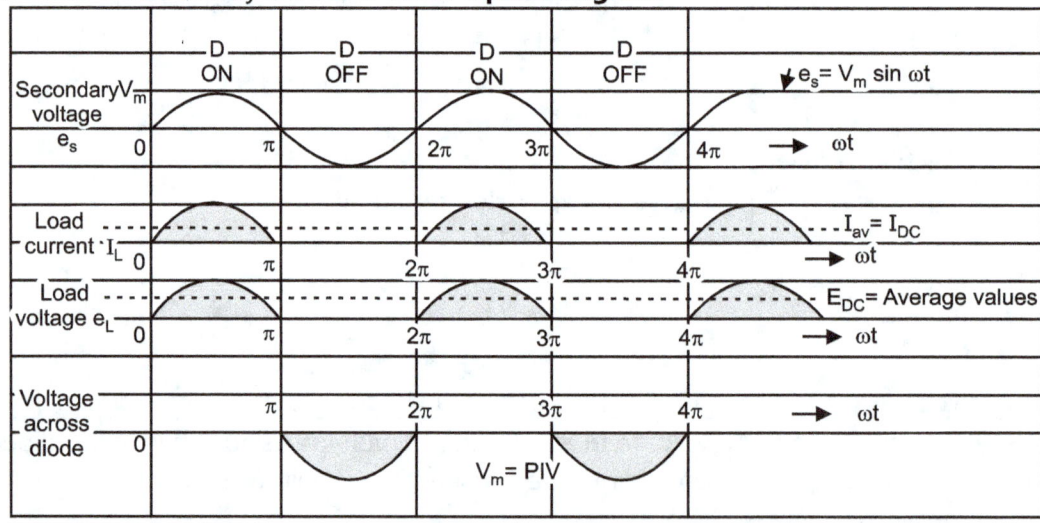

Fig. 1.19: Load current and load voltage waveforms for half wave rectifier

1.5.2 Detail Analysis of Half-Wave Rectifier

1. DC or Average Load Current (I_L dc)

- To find the average value of a periodic function, we determine the area under the curve over one cycle of the function divided by the period. Refer to Fig. 1.19, if we observe the waveform of load current, we see that no current flows during negative half cycle of the AC input. Therefore we take integration over the period 0 to π.

$$\therefore \qquad I_{L\,dc} = \frac{1}{2\pi} \int_{0}^{\pi} I_m \sin \omega t \, d\omega t = \frac{-I_m}{2\pi} [\cos \omega t]_{0}^{\pi}$$

where, $\qquad I_m$ = Peak amplitude of the load current

$$I_{L\,dc} = \frac{-I_m}{2\pi} [\cos \pi - \cos 0] = \frac{-I_m}{2\pi} [-1 - 1]$$

$$\therefore \qquad I_{L\,dc} = \frac{I_m}{\pi} = \text{Average load current}$$

where, $\qquad I_m = \dfrac{V_m}{(R_S + R_F + R_L)}$, it is the peak load current

By Kirchhoff's law,

$$V_m = \text{Maximum or peak secondary voltage}$$

$$R_S = \text{DC resistance of transformer secondary}$$

$$R_F = \text{Forward resistance of Diode}$$

2. DC or Average Load Voltage ($V_{L\,dc}$)

The average load voltage for the resistive load, is given by

$$V_{L\,dc} = I_{L\,dc} \times R_L$$

Substituting the value of $I_{L\,dc}$ we get,

$$V_{L\,dc} = \frac{I_m}{\pi} \times R_L = \frac{V_m}{\pi (R_S + R_F + R_L)} \times R_L \qquad \text{... (exact value)}$$

Practically, R_S and R_F are considered to be very small as compared to R_L.

$$\therefore \qquad (R_S + R_F) << R_L$$

$$\therefore \qquad V_{L\,dc} \approx \frac{V_m}{\pi} \qquad \text{(where } V_m = \text{peak secondary voltage)}$$

3. AC or RMS Value of the Load Current ($I_{L\,rms}$)

• We refer to the load current waveform shown in Fig. 1.19. Consider one complete cycle of the load current waveform (0 to 2π) to write the following equation:

$$I_{L\,rms} = \left[\frac{1}{2\pi} \int_{0}^{\pi} I_m^2 \sin^2 \omega t \, d\omega t \right]^{1/2} = \left[\frac{I_m^2}{2\pi} \int_{0}^{\pi} \left(\frac{1 - \cos 2\omega t}{2} \right) d\omega t \right]^{1/2}$$

$$I_{L\,rms} = \frac{I_m}{2} \left[\frac{1}{\pi} \left(\pi - \frac{1}{2} \sin 2\pi \right) \right]^{1/2} , \text{ But } \sin 2\pi = 0$$

$$\therefore \qquad I_{L\,rms} = \frac{I_m}{2}$$

This is the rms value of the load current.

4. AC or RMS Value of Load Voltage ($V_{L\,rms}$)

- The rms value of load voltage for purely resistive load is given by,

$$V_{L\,rms} = I_{L\,rms} \times R_L = \frac{I_m}{2} \times R_L$$

$$V_{L\,rms} = \frac{V_m}{2\,(R_S + R_F + R_L)} \times R_L$$

But $(R_S + R_F) <<< R_L$;

$$\therefore \quad V_{L\,rms} \approx \frac{V_m}{2} \qquad \text{... (approximate value)}$$

5. Ripple Factor (r)

- The output of a rectifier is not pure DC. Some AC component is present alongwith the DC. The ripple factor (r) is a measure of the percentage of AC component present in the output. It is denoted by "r".

- Ideally the ripple factor should be zero. Practically it should be small, as it indicates the output close to pure DC.

- Mathematically, ripple factor is defined as the ratio of 'the R.M.S. value of the AC component in the output to the average or DC component present in the output'.

$$\text{Ripple factor} = \frac{\text{RMS value of the AC component of output}}{\text{DC or average value of the output}}$$

$$\therefore \quad r = \frac{\left[V_{L\,rms}^2 - V_{L\,dc}^2\right]^{1/2}}{V_{L\,dc}}$$

Substituting the values for half wave rectifier, we have

$$r = \frac{[\,(V_m/2)^2 - (V_m/\pi)^2\,]^{1/2}}{V_m/\pi}$$

$$\therefore \quad r \approx 1.21 \text{ or } 121\%$$

- From the above equation we can conclude that the ripple content in the output voltage of a half wave rectifier is 1.21 times the DC component. It can be reduced by using filters at the output of the rectifier to get a pure DC output.

6. Voltage Regulation

- Voltage regulation is a measure of the change in DC output voltage with the load change from no load to full load condition.

- The average output voltage of a rectifier should be ideally constant, but practically it varies with changes in load current.

$$\text{Voltage regulation} = \frac{V_{NL} - V_{FL}}{V_{FL}} \times 100\,\%$$

where, V_{NL} = Average load voltage at no load i.e. when R_L = infinity

$\therefore$ For half-wave rectifier,

$$V_{NL} = \frac{V_m}{\pi}$$

and $\qquad V_{FL}$ = Average load voltage at full load $= \dfrac{V_m}{\pi} \dfrac{R_L}{(R_S + R_F + R_L)}$

Substitute the values for V_{NL} and V_{FL} to get

$$\text{Load regulation} = \frac{\left(\dfrac{V_m}{\pi}\right) - \left(\dfrac{V_m}{\pi} \cdot \dfrac{R_L}{R_S + R_F + R_L}\right)}{\left(\dfrac{V_m}{\pi} \cdot \dfrac{R_L}{R_S + R_F + R_L}\right)} = \frac{\dfrac{V_m}{\pi}[R_S + R_F + R_L - R_L]}{\dfrac{V_m}{\pi} \cdot R_L}$$

$\therefore$ Voltage regulation $= \dfrac{(R_S + R_F)}{R_L} \times 100\%$

Ideally the value of load regulation should be 0%. Practically it should be as low as possible.

- **Regulation Characteristics:**

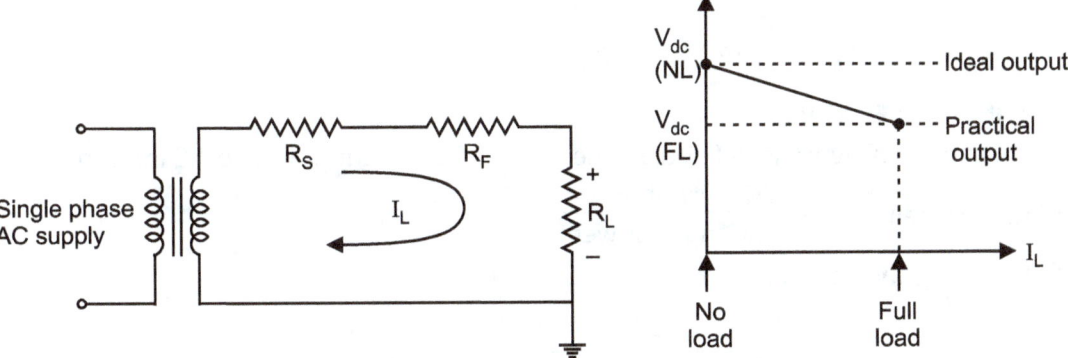

(a) **Equivalent circuit of HWR**   (b) **Regulation characteristics**

Fig. 1.20: **Decrease in the output voltage V_{dc} due to drop across $(R_F + R_S)$**

As the load current (I_L) increases, the voltage drop across R_F (diode forward resistance) and R_S (secondary resistance) increases, thus decreasing the output DC voltage.

7. **DC Output Power ($P_{L\,dc}$)**

The DC or average output power delivered to the load is given by,

$$P_{L\,dc} = I_{L\,dc}^2 \times R_L = \left[\frac{I_m}{\pi}\right]^2 R_L = \frac{I_m^2}{\pi^2} R_L$$

Substituting the value of I_m, we get,

$$P_{L\,dc} = \frac{V_m^2}{\pi^2 (R_S + R_F + R_L)^2} \times R_L$$

If $R_L >> (R_S + R_F)$ then we may write the expression for $P_{L\,dc}$ as,

$$P_{L\,dc} \approx \frac{V_m^2}{\pi^2 R_L}$$

But $\qquad \frac{V_m}{\pi} = V_{L\,dc}$ Therefore, $\quad P_{L\,dc} \approx \frac{V_{L\,dc}^2}{R_L}$

8. AC Input Power (P_{ac})

- The AC input power to a rectifier is the power supplied by the secondary winding of the transformer. It is given by,

$$P_{ac} = I_{S\,rms}^2 \times (R_S + R_F + R_L)$$

where, $\qquad I_{s\,rms}$ = RMS value of the secondary current.

- For Half Wave Rectifier, the secondary current is the same as the load current.

$$\therefore \qquad I_{S\,rms} = I_{L\,rms} = \frac{I_m}{2}$$

$$\therefore \qquad P_{ac} = \left(\frac{I_m}{2}\right)^2 (R_S + R_F + R_L)$$

$$\therefore \qquad P_{ac} = \frac{I_m^2}{4} (R_S + R_F + R_L)$$

9. Rectification Efficiency

- Rectification efficiency is defined as 'the ratio of DC output power to AC input power'.

Mathematically, $\quad \eta = \dfrac{\text{DC output power}}{\text{AC input power}} = \dfrac{P_{L\,dc}}{P_{ac}}$

- Substituting the values of $P_{L\,dc}$ and P_{ac} we get

$$\eta = \frac{I_{L\,dc}^2 R_L}{I_{s\,rms}^2 (R_S + R_F + R_L)}$$

$$\eta = \frac{(I_m/\pi)^2 R_L}{(I_m/2)^2 (R_S + R_F + R_L)} = \frac{4}{\pi^2} \frac{R_L}{(R_S + R_F + R_L)}$$

If $R_L \gg (R_S + R_F)$, we get the maximum rectification efficiency as

$$\eta_{max.} = \frac{4}{\pi^2} = 0.405 \text{ or } 40.5\%$$

1. Ideally the efficiency should be 100%. Practically it should be as high as possible.
2. From the above equation, we say that rectification efficiency of a half-wave rectifier is small. Only 40% of the applied AC input power actually gets converted into the average load power. The remaining 60% is present in the form of ripple in the output.

10. Transformer Utilization Factor (TUF)

- Transformer utilization factor is defined as 'the ratio of DC output power to the AC power rating of the transformer'. TUF indicates how well the input transformer is utilized.

Mathematically, $\text{TUF} = \dfrac{\text{DC output power } (P_{dc})}{\text{AC power rating of the transformer}} = \dfrac{V_{L\,dc}\,I_{L\,dc}}{V_{s\,rms}\,I_{s\,rms}}$

If $R_L >> (R_S + R_F)$, we get

$$\text{TUF} = \dfrac{[V_m/\pi]\,[I_m/\pi]}{[V_m/\sqrt{2}]\,[I_m/2]} = \dfrac{2\sqrt{2}}{\pi^2}$$

Thus $\text{TUF} = \mathbf{0.287 \text{ or } 28.7\%}$

1. Ideally TUF should be 100% and practically it should be as high as possible.
2. In half-wave rectifier, the value of TUF is very low which indicates that only 28.7% of its total capacity the transformer is being utilized.

11. PIV (Peak Inverse Voltage)

*   The Peak Inverse Voltage is the maximum peak negative voltage that appears across the diode in the reverse biased condition i. e. when the diode is not conducting.

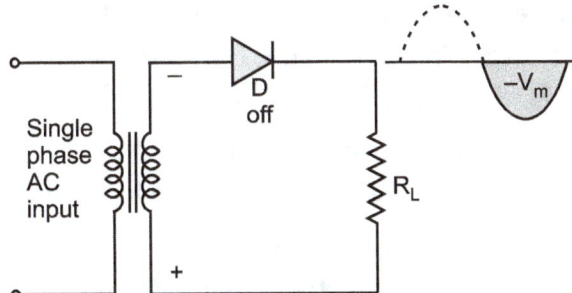

*   Thus, $\text{PIV} = V_m$ volts
*   Thus, while selecting a diode, PIV rating must be taken care of. It should be higher than the maximum possible reverse voltage to prevent the diode from getting damaged.

Fig. 1.21: PIV of the Diode = V_m

Advantages of Half-wave Rectifier:

*   Uses less number of components so there is reduction in the size of the circuit and less cost.
*   It is simple in construction.

Disadvantages of Half-wave Rectifier:

*   Rectification efficiency is low = 40.5%.
*   Ripple factor is high = 121%.
*   Due to high ripple, large filter components are required.
*   TUF is low = 28.7%

Due to the drawbacks mentioned above, the HWR is usually not used for rectification.

1.6 THE FULL-WAVE RECTIFIER

❖ **Important Question Related to this Topic** ❖

For a center-tapped full wave rectifier, derive the expression for:

(i)   DC load current,   (ii)   Ripple factor,

(iii) V_{DC},   (iv) P_{DC}.

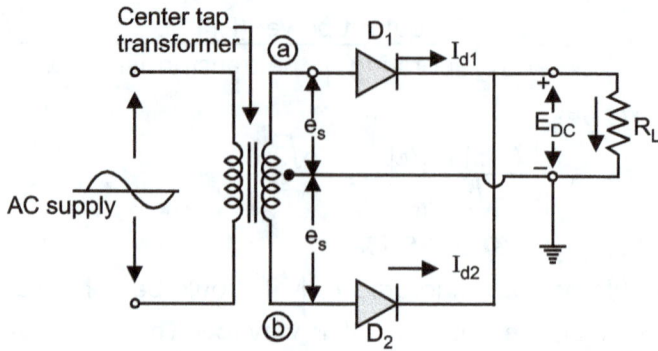

Fig. 1.22: Full-wave rectifier with center tapped transformer

- In half-wave rectifier only half of the incoming AC cycle is utilized and all the energy associated with the other half cycle is wasted. Thus, it is not very efficient.

- Fig 1.22 shows center tapped full wave rectifier circuit with input 230V, 50Hz at primary of transformer. Circuit uses two diodes D_1 and D_2 connected across secondary of transformer. Center-tapped is taken as zero reference point.

- For greater efficiency, we need to utilize both halves of the incoming AC. Here only one diode conducts in one half cycle of the AC input, thus giving full-wave rectification.

- However, for proper operation, it is necessary to ground the center connection of the secondary winding.

Operation of the Circuit:

- Refer Fig. 1.22 shown above.

- During the positive half cycle of the AC input, terminal **'a'** is positive w.r.t. terminal **'b'**. Diode D_1 is forward biased and D_2 is reverse biased. Ideally D_1 acts as closed switch and D_2 as open switch. So current cannot flow through D_2. The current flows through D_1 and the load resistor R_L through the upper half of the secondary winding, thus providing the load current which develops positive voltage across load resistance.

- During the negative half cycle of the AC input, terminal **'b'** is positive w.r.t. terminal **'a'**. Therefore diode D_2 is forward biased while D_1 is reverse biased. Ideally D_2 acts as closed switch and D_1 as open switch. So current cannot flow through D_1. The current flows through D_2 and the load resistor R_L through the lower half of the secondary winding, thus providing the load current which develops positive voltage across load resistance.

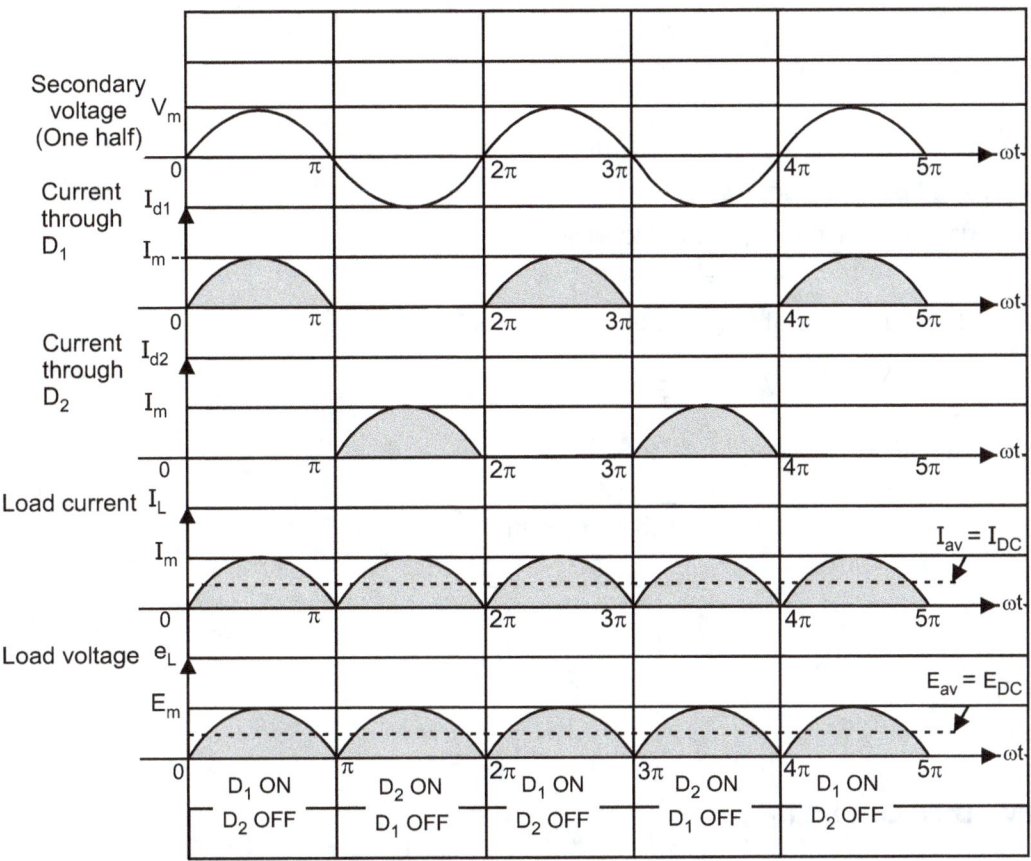

Fig. 1.23: Load current and voltage waveforms of full wave rectifier

1.6.1 Detail Analysis of Full-Wave (center-tapped) Rectifier

1. Average Load Current ($I_{L\,dc}$)

- In full-wave rectifier,

Peak load current, $I_m = \dfrac{V_m}{(R_S + R_F + R_L)}$

where, V_m = Peak secondary voltage for half the secondary

                  R_S = DC resistance of half of secondary

                  R_F = Forward resistance of a diode

- Referring to the load current waveform shown in Fig. 1.23, we see that the waveform repeats itself after the period 0 to π.

- Therefore we take integration over 0 to π. The average value of load current is given by,

$$I_{L\,dc} = \frac{1}{\pi} \int_0^\pi I_m \sin \omega t \, d\omega t$$

$$= \frac{-I_m}{\pi} [\cos \omega t]_0^\pi = \frac{-I_m}{\pi} [\cos \pi - \cos 0]$$

$$\therefore \qquad I_{L\,dc} = \frac{2I_m}{\pi}$$

where, $\qquad I_m = \dfrac{V_m}{(R_S + R_F + R_L)}$

2. Average Load Voltage ($V_{L\,dc}$)

For purely resistive load, the DC load voltage is,

$$V_{L\,dc} = I_{L\,dc} \times R_L$$

Substitute the value of $I_{L\,dc}$ we get

$$V_{L\,dc} = \frac{2I_m}{\pi} \times R_L$$

Substituting the value of I_m we get

$$V_{L\,dc} = \frac{2V_m}{\pi\,(R_S + R_F + R_L)} \times R_L$$

$$= \frac{2V_m}{\pi \left[1 + \dfrac{(R_S + R_F)}{R_L} \right]}$$

If $R_L >> (R_S + R_F)$, we get

$$V_{L\,dc} \approx \frac{2V_m}{\pi}$$

3. RMS Load Current ($I_{L\,rms}$)

$$I_{L\,rms} = \left[\frac{1}{\pi} \int_0^\pi I_m^2 \sin^2 \omega t \, d\omega t \right]^{1/2}$$

$$I_{L\,rms} = \left[\frac{I_m^2}{\pi} \int_0^\pi \left(\frac{1 - \cos 2\omega t}{2} \right) d\omega t \right]^{1/2}$$

$$= \frac{I_m}{\sqrt{2}} \left[\frac{1}{\pi} \left(\pi - \frac{1}{2} \sin 2\pi \right) \right]^{1/2}$$

But $\sin 2\pi = 0 \qquad I_{L\,rms} = \dfrac{I_m}{\sqrt{2}}$

4. RMS Load Voltage ($V_{L\,rms}$)

The rms value of the load voltage for resistive load is given by,

$$V_{L\,rms} = I_{L\,rms} \times R_L$$

Substituting the value of $I_{L\,rms}$ we get

$$V_{L\,rms} = \frac{I_m}{\sqrt{2}} \times R_L$$

Substituting the value of I_m we get

$$V_{L\,rms} = \frac{V_m}{\sqrt{2}\,(R_S + R_F + R_L)} \times R_L$$

$$= \frac{V_m}{\sqrt{2}\left[1 + \dfrac{(R_S + R_F)}{R_L}\right]}$$

If $R_L >> (R_S + R_F)$

$$V_{L\,rms} \approx \frac{V_m}{\sqrt{2}}$$

5. **Ripple Factor (r)**

$$\text{Ripple factor (r)} = \frac{\left[V_{L\,rms}^2 - V_{L\,dc}^2\right]^{1/2}}{V_{L\,dc}}$$

Substituting the values, we get

$$r = \frac{\left[(V_m/\sqrt{2})^2 - (2V_m/\pi)^2\right]^{1/2}}{2V_m/\pi}$$

$$r = \left[\frac{\pi^2}{8} - 1\right]^{1/2} = 0.48$$

This value of ripple factor is much less as compared to that of half-wave rectifier (which is 1.21).

6. **DC Output Power ($P_{L\,dc}$)**

The DC output power $\quad P_{L\,dc} = I_{L\,dc}^2 \times R_L$

Substituting the value of $\quad I_{L\,dc} = \dfrac{2I_m}{\pi}$

We get $\qquad P_{L\,dc} = \dfrac{4I_m^2}{\pi^2} \times R_L \qquad$ But $\quad I_m = \dfrac{V_m}{(R_S + R_F + R_L)}$

$\therefore \qquad\qquad P_{L\,dc} = \dfrac{4V_m^2}{\pi^2\,(R_S + R_F + R_L)^2} \times R_L$

7. **AC Input Power (P_{ac})**

The AC input power is given by,

$$P_{ac} = I_{S\,rms}^2 \times (R_S + R_F + R_L)$$

$$= \left[\frac{I_m}{\sqrt{2}}\right]^2 \times (R_S + R_F + R_L)$$

$\therefore \qquad\qquad P_{ac} = \dfrac{I_m^2\,(R_S + R_F + R_L)}{2}$

Substituting the value of I_m we get

$$P_{ac} = \frac{V_m^2 (R_S + R_F + R_L)}{2 (R_S + R_F + R_L)^2}$$

$$\therefore \quad P_{ac} = \frac{V_m^2}{2 (R_S + R_F + R_L)}$$

8. Rectifier Efficiency

$$\eta = \frac{P_{L\,dc}}{P_{ac}} = \frac{I_L^2\,dc \times R_L}{(I_{S\,rms})^2 (R_S + R_F + R_L)}$$

Substitute the values of $I_{L\,dc}$ and $I_{S\,rms}$ as,

$$I_{L\,dc} = \frac{2I_m}{\pi} \quad \text{and} \quad I_{S\,rms} = \frac{I_m}{\sqrt{2}}$$

$$\therefore \quad \eta = \frac{(2I_m/\pi)^2 R_L}{(I_m/\sqrt{2})^2 (R_S + R_F + R_L)} = \frac{8R_L}{\pi^2 (R_S + R_F + R_L)}$$

If $R_L >> (R_F + R_S)$, we get the maximum theoretical value of efficiency as,

$$\eta_{max} = \frac{8}{\pi^2} = \textbf{0.812 or 81.2\%}$$

9. Transformer Utilization Factor (TUF)

- As the center tapped connection is used, the secondary current flows through each half separately whereas the primary carries the current continuously. Therefore, TUF is calculated separately for each winding and then average TUF is calculated.

1.   TUF of secondary winding $= \dfrac{\text{DC load power}}{\text{Power rating of secondary}}$

$$= \frac{V_{L\,dc} \times I_{L\,dc}}{V_{S\,rms} \times I_{S\,rms}}$$

Substituting the values, we get

$$\text{TUF of secondary winding} = \frac{(2V_m/\pi)\,(2I_m/\pi)}{(V_m/\sqrt{2})\,(I_m/\sqrt{2})} = \frac{8}{\pi^2}$$

$$\text{TUF} = 0.812 \text{ or } 81.2\%$$

$$\therefore \quad \text{Secondary TUF} = \textbf{0.812 or 81.2\%}$$

$$\text{Primary TUF} = 2 \times \text{TUF of HWR}$$

$$\text{Primary TUF} = 2 \times 0.287 = \textbf{0.574}$$

$$\text{Average TUF} = \frac{\text{TUF}_{(secondary)} + \text{TUF}_{(primary)}}{2} = \frac{0.812 + 0.574}{2}$$

$$\text{Average TUF} = \textbf{0.693 or 69.3\%}$$

10. Peak Inverse Voltage (PIV)

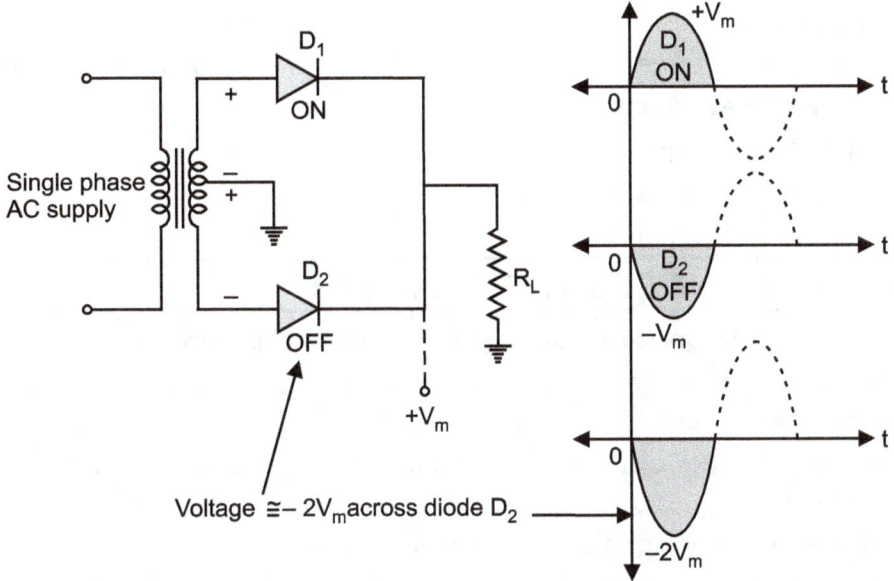

Fig. 1.24: PIV for full-wave rectifier

Thus, PIV of diode D_2 = $2V_m$ volts

11. Voltage Regulation

$$\text{Voltage regulation} = \frac{V_{NL} - V_{FL}}{V_{FL}} \times 100\%$$

We know

$$V_{NL} = \frac{2V_m}{\pi}$$

and

$$V_{FL} = \frac{2V_m}{\pi} \times \frac{R_L}{(R_S + R_F + R_L)}$$

Substituting these values in the actual equation,

$$\text{Voltage regulation} = \frac{(2V_m/\pi) - [2V_m R_L/\pi \, (R_S + R_F + R_L)]}{2V_m R_L/\pi \, (R_S + R_F + R_L)} \times 100$$

$$\text{Voltage regulation} = \frac{(2V_m/\pi) \, (R_S + R_F + R_L - R_L)}{(2V_m/\pi) \, R_L} \times 100$$

$$\text{Voltage regulation} = \frac{R_S + R_F}{R_L} \times 100$$

Advantages of Full Wave Rectifier:

- Better rectification efficiency = 81.2%.
- Low ripple factor (48%) better than half-wave rectifier.
- Increased $V_{L\,dc}$ and $I_{L\,dc}$ values.
- No transformer saturation because of bi-directional current in the secondary of the transformer.
- Better TUF = 69.3%.

Disadvantages of Full Wave Rectifier:
- The cost increases because diodes of high PIV ($2V_m$) are required.
- A center tapped transformer is required which is costlier and complicated to design.

Applications of Full Wave Rectifier:
- It is used in battery chargers.
- Also used in power supplies in laboratory.
- In high current power supplies.

1.7 THE FULL-WAVE BRIDGE RECTIFIER

❖ Important Questions Related to this Topic ❖

1. Draw the circuit diagram and output voltage waveform of a bridge rectifier. Also derive the expression for V_{dc} and V_{rms}.
2. Compare the two types of full wave rectification: using center-tapped transformer and using bridge circuit.
3. Give peak inverse voltage of diode of the following circuits:
   (i) Half-wave rectifier without filter
   (ii) Half-wave rectifier with capacitor input filter
   (iii) Full-wave rectifier
   (iv) Bridge rectifier

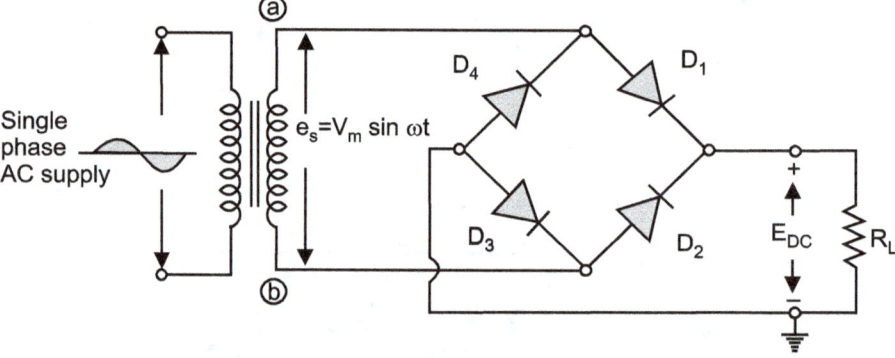

Fig. 1.25: Full-wave bridge rectifier

- The circuit shown above (Fig. 1.25) is the four-diode rectifier circuit that provides full-wave rectification of the AC input 230V, 50Hz, using a transformer without centertapped connection. This is the main advantage of the four diode bridge circuit.
- This rectifier circuit is known as a *bridge rectifier*.

Operation of the Circuit:
- During the positive half cycle of the AC input voltage, terminal 'a' of the secondary is positive with respect to terminal 'b'. Therefore, diodes D_1 and D_3 get forward biased, ideally acts as closed switch. Diodes D_2 and D_4 are reverse biased and hence they do not conduct during the positive half cycle, ideally acts as open switch.

- The load current flows through $D_1 \rightarrow$ the load resistor R_L and then through diode $D_3 \rightarrow$ to terminal 'b' which develops positive voltage across load resistance.

- During the negative half cycle of the AC input voltage, terminal 'b' of the secondary is positive with respect to terminal 'a'. Therefore, diodes D_2 and D_4 get forward biased. Diodes D_1 and D_3 are reverse biased and hence they do not conduct during the negative half cycle.

- The load current flows through $D_2 \rightarrow$ the load resistor R_L and then through diode $D_4 \rightarrow$ to terminal 'a' again there is development of positive voltage across load resistance.

- Note that the current always flows in only one direction through the load resistor. The diodes keep switching the transformer connections to the load resistor.

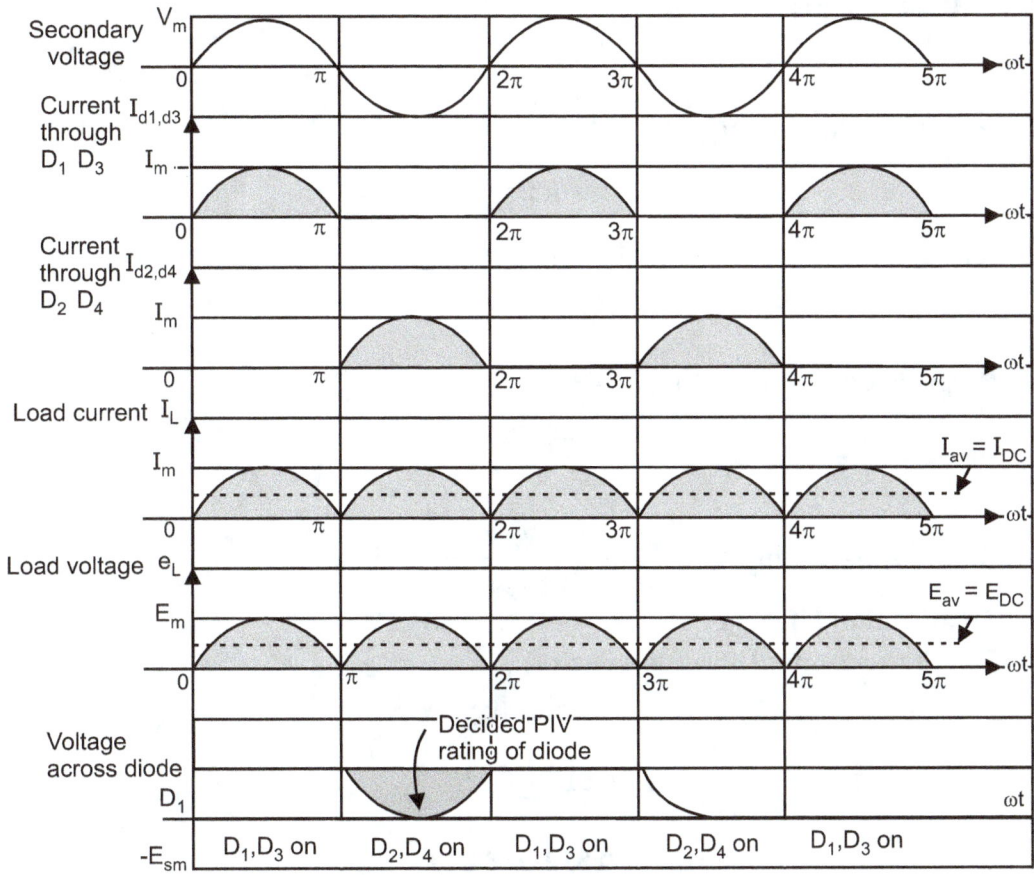

Fig. 1.26: Waveforms of bridge rectifier

1.7.1 Detail Analysis of Bridge Rectifier

- The bridge rectifier is basically a full-wave rectifier, therefore its analysis remains the same as that of the full-wave rectifier.

- Only here instead of one diode two diodes are conducting simultaneously, so R_f is replaced by $2R_f$.

1. **Average Load Current ($I_{L\,dc}$):**

$$I_{L\,dc} = \frac{2I_m}{\pi}$$

2. **Average Load Voltage ($V_{L\,dc}$):**

$$V_{L\,dc} = \frac{2V_m}{\pi} \times \frac{R_L}{R_S + 2R_F + R_L}$$

for $\qquad R_L >> (R_S + 2R_F)$

$$V_{L\,dc} = \frac{2V_m}{\pi}$$

3. **RMS Load Current ($I_{L\,rms}$):**

$$I_{L\,rms} = \frac{I_m}{\sqrt{2}}$$

4. **RMS Load Voltage ($V_{L\,rms}$):**

$$V_{L\,rms} = \frac{V_m}{\sqrt{2}} \times \frac{R_L}{R_S + 2R_F + R_L}$$

for $\qquad R_L >> (R_S + 2R_F)$

$$V_{L\,rms} = \frac{V_m}{\sqrt{2}}$$

5. **Ripple Factor (r):** $r = 0.48$ or 48%

6. **DC Output Power ($P_{L\,dc}$):** $P_{L\,dc} = \dfrac{4I_m^2 R_L}{\pi^2}$

7. **AC Input Power (P_{ac}):** $P_{ac} = \dfrac{V_m^2}{2(R_S + 2R_F + R_L)}$

8. **Rectification Efficiency (η):** $\eta = 0.812 = \mathbf{81.2\%}$

9. **TUF (Transformer Utilization Factor):**

$$\text{Average TUF} = \frac{TUF_{(secondary)} + TUF_{(primary)}}{2}$$

$$\text{Average TUF} = \frac{0.812 + 0.812}{2} = 0.812$$

$$\text{Average TUF} = \mathbf{0.812 \text{ or } 81.2\%}$$

10. **PIV (Peak Inverse Voltage):** $PIV = V_m$

11. **Peak Load Current (I_m):** $I_m = \dfrac{V_m}{(R_S + 2R_F + R_L)}$

As two diodes conduct simultaneously, instead of R_F, we take $2R_F$.

As two diodes conduct simultaneously, instead of R_F, we take $2R_F$.

Advantages of a Bridge Rectifier:

- Does not require center-tapped transformer therefore cost is less.
- Increased TUF because the transformer used is not center-tapped.
- High rectification efficiency.
- The cost gets reduced as the diodes with less PIV rating are required.
- Both output voltage and current are higher.

Disadvantages of Bridge Rectifier:

- As the circuit requires four diodes, there is additional voltage drop across them which reduce the output voltage.

Applications of Bridge Rectifier:

- Used to convert AC to DC in power circuits.
- Used in power supplies.

SOLVED EXAMPLES

Example 1.1: *Fig. 1.27, shows a half wave rectifier circuit with a transformer coupled input.*

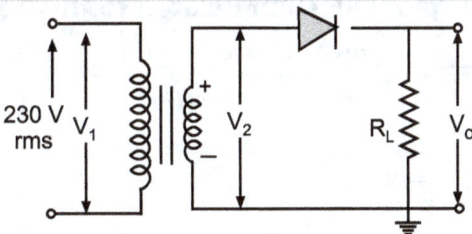

Fig. 1.27

Determine the maximum and average values of power delivered to the load. Take R_L equal to 200 Ω..

Solution:
$$V_1 = 230 \text{ V}$$
$$\frac{N_2}{N_1} = \frac{1}{2} = 0.5$$
$$R_L = 200 \ \Omega$$

(a) RMS value of secondary voltage:
$$V_2 = V_1 \times \frac{N_2}{N_1} = 230 \times \frac{1}{2} = \textbf{115 V}$$

(b) Maximum value of secondary voltage:
$$V_m = \sqrt{2} \times V_2$$
$$= \sqrt{2} \times 115 = \textbf{162.6 V}$$

(c) Maximum value of load current:
$$I_m = \frac{V_m}{R_L} = \frac{162.6}{200} = \textbf{0.813 A}$$

(d) Maximum value of load power:

$$P_m = I_m^2 \times R_1 = (0.813)^2 \times 200 = 132.19 \text{ W}$$

(e) Average value of load power:

$$V_{dc} = 0.318 \times V_m$$
$$= 0.318 \times 162.6 = 51.7 \text{ V}$$

(f) Average value of load current:

$$I_{dc} = \frac{V_{dc}}{R_L} = \frac{51.7}{200} = 0.26 \text{ A}$$

∴ Average value of load power

$$P_{dc} = I^2_{dc} \times R_L$$
$$= (0.26)^2 \times 200 = 13.4 \text{ W}$$

1.8 COMPARISON OF THREE RECTIFIER CIRCUITS (HWR, FWR, AND BRIDGE RECTIFIER)   [Dec. 14, Nov. 15]

❖ **Important Question Related to this Topic** ❖

Give comparison between half-wave, full-wave and bridge rectifiers.   **[Dec. 12]**

Sr. No.	Parameter	HWR	FWR	Bridge Rectifier
1.	Circuit diagram	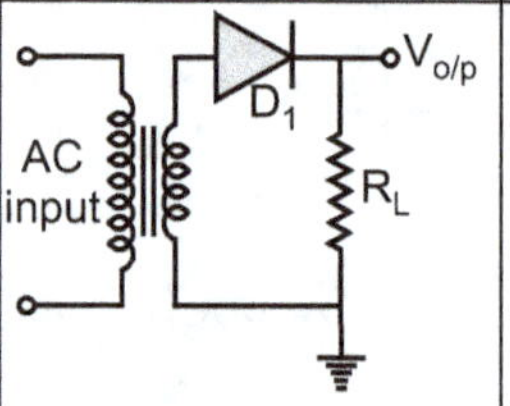	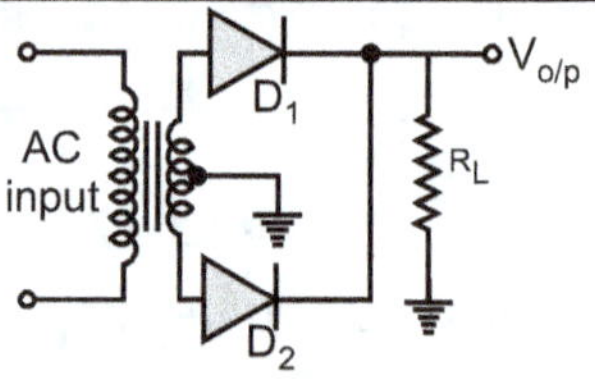	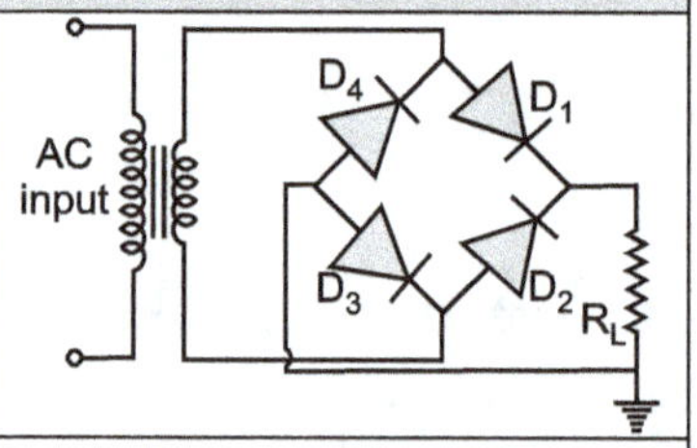
2.	Center-tapped transformer	Not required	Required	Not required
3.	DC or average load current ($I_{L\,dc}$)	$\dfrac{I_m}{\pi}$	$\dfrac{2I_m}{\pi}$	$\dfrac{2I_m}{\pi}$
4.	Maximum average load voltage $V_{L\,dc}$	$\dfrac{V_m}{\pi}$	$\dfrac{2V_m}{\pi}$	$\dfrac{2V_m}{\pi}$

...Conti.

5.	RMS load voltage $V_{L\,rms}$	$\dfrac{V_m}{2}$	$\dfrac{V_m}{\sqrt{2}}$	$\dfrac{V_m}{\sqrt{2}}$
6.	RMS load current $I_{L\,rms}$	$\dfrac{I_m}{2}$	$\dfrac{I_m}{\sqrt{2}}$	$\dfrac{I_m}{\sqrt{2}}$
7.	DC load power $P_{L\,dc}$	$\dfrac{I_m^2}{\pi^2}R_L$	$\dfrac{4I_m^2 R_L}{\pi^2}$	$\dfrac{4I_m^2 R_L}{\pi^2}$
8.	Expression for the peak load current	$I_m = \dfrac{V_m}{(R_S + R_F + R_L)}$	$I_m = \dfrac{V_m}{(R_S + R_F + R_L)}$	$I_m = \dfrac{V_m}{(R_S + 2R_F + R_L)}$
9	PIV	V_m	$2V_m$	V_m
10	Ripple factor	(1.21) or 121%	(0.48) or 48%	(0.48) or 48%
11	Maximum rectification efficiency (η)	(0.40) or 40%	(0.812) or 81.2%	(0.812) or 81.2%

Solved Examples on FWR

Example 1.2: *For center-tapped full wave rectifier circuit voltage across complete secondary of transformer is 30 V_{ac} and if R_L = 5.1 kΩ, calculate DC output voltage and the average load current.*

Solution: Given: V_2 = 20 V_{ac}, R_L = 5.1 kΩ = 5100 Ω.

(1) DC output voltage:

$$V_s = \frac{V_2}{2} = \frac{30}{2} = \mathbf{15\ V_{ac}}$$

Maximum value of this voltage

$$V_m = \sqrt{2} \times V_s = \sqrt{2} \times 15 = \mathbf{21.2\ V}$$

∴ DC output voltage

$$V_{dc} = 0.636 \times V_m$$
$$= 0.636 \times 21.2 = \mathbf{13.5\ V}$$

(2) Average or DC load current:

$$I_{dc} = \frac{V_{dc}}{R_L} = \frac{13.5}{5100}$$
$$= 2.647 \times 10^{-3}\,A = \mathbf{2.647\ mA}$$

Solved Examples on Half-Wave Rectifier

Example 1.3: *A voltage V = 300 cos 100 t is applied to a half-wave rectifier with R_L = 5 kΩ. The rectifier may be represented by an ideal diode in series with a resistance of 1 kΩ.*

Calculate: (1) I_m, (2) DC power, (3) AC power, (4) Rectifier efficiency, (5) Ripple factor.

Solution: Given: V_m = 300 V, R_F = 1 kΩ, R_S = 0 Ω (transformer is not used)

(1) Peak load current:

$$I_m = \frac{V_m}{(R_S + R_F + R_L)}$$

$$= \frac{300}{(0 + 1\ k\Omega + 5\ k\Omega)} = 0.05\ A$$

$$= \textbf{50 mA}$$

(2) DC power:

$$P_{L\ dc} = I^2_{L\ dc} \times R_L = \left[\frac{I_m}{\pi}\right]^2 \times R_L = \left[\frac{0.05}{\pi}\right]^2 \times 5 \times 10^3$$

$$= \textbf{1.2655 W}$$

(3) AC input power:

$$P_{ac} = I^2_{S\ rms}(R_S + R_F + R_L)$$

$$= [I_m/2]^2 \times (R_F + R_L) = [0.05/2]^2 \times 6 \times 10^3$$

$$= \textbf{3.75 W}$$

(4) Rectifier efficiency:

$$\eta = \frac{P_{L\ dc}}{P_{ac}} \times 100\% = \frac{1.2665}{3.75} \times 100$$

$$= \textbf{33.77\%}$$

(5) Ripple factor:

$$r = \left[\frac{I^2_{L\ rms} - I^2_{L\ dc}}{I^2_{L\ dc}}\right]^{1/2} \times 100$$

Therefore first we find,

$$I_{L\ rms} = \frac{I_m}{2} = 25\ mA$$

and

$$I_{L\ dc} = \frac{I_m}{\pi} = 15.91\ mA$$

∴

$$r = \left[\frac{(25)^2 - (15.91)^2}{(15.91)^2}\right]^{1/2} \times 100$$

$$= \textbf{121.13\%}$$

Example 1.4: *A half-wave rectifier with R_L = 1 kΩ is given an input of 10 V peak from a step-down transformer. Calculate the DC voltage and load current for an ideal and silicon diode.*

Solution: Given: R_L = 1 kΩ, V_m = 10 V, R_S = 0 Ω

(a) Calculations assuming ideal diode: For an ideal diode, drop across the diode V_F = 0 V. Therefore, DC voltage is given by,

(1) $\qquad\qquad\qquad V_{L\,dc} = \dfrac{V_m}{\pi} = \dfrac{10}{\pi} = $ **3.18 volts**

(2) $\qquad$ Load current, $I_{L\,dc} = \dfrac{I_m}{\pi} = \dfrac{V_m}{\pi\,(R_S + R_F + R_L)}$

But for an ideal diode $R_F = 0$

$\therefore \qquad\qquad I_{L\,dc} = \dfrac{V_m}{\pi R_L} = \dfrac{3.18}{1\ k\Omega} = $ **3.18 mA**

(b) Calculations with silicon diode: For a silicon diode, forward voltage drop across the diode $(V_F) = 0.7$ V.

(1) DC output voltage, $\ V_{L\,dc} = \dfrac{(V_m - 0.7)}{\pi} = $ **2.96 V**

(2) Load current, $\qquad\qquad I_{L\,dc} = \dfrac{V_{L\,dc}}{R_L} = \dfrac{2.96}{1\ k\Omega} = $ **2.96 mA**

Solved Examples on Full-Wave Center-Tapped Rectifier

Example 1.5: *A full-wave rectifier using two diodes has a maximum voltage of 18 volts, across the full secondary winding as an input. Calculate the peak inverse voltage for the diodes.*

Solution: Given: The maximum voltage across the full secondary voltage is $2V_m$.

$\therefore \qquad\qquad\qquad 2V_m = 18$ V

$\qquad\qquad\qquad\quad$ PIV $= 2V_m$ volt for center-tapped FWR

$\therefore \qquad\qquad\qquad$ **PIV $= 18$ V**

Example 1.6: *In a center-tapped full-wave rectifier, the rms half-secondary voltage is 9 V. Assuming ideal diodes and load resistance $R_L = 1\ k\Omega$, find: (1) Peak current, (2) DC load voltage, (3) RMS current, (4) Ripple factor, (5) Efficiency.*

Solution: Given: Given parameters are: $V_{S\,rms} = 9$ V, $R_L = 1\ k\Omega$, $R_F = R_S = 0$.

(1) Peak current (I_m):

$$I_m = \frac{V_m}{R_S + R_F + R_L} = \frac{\sqrt{2}\,V_{S\,rms}}{R_L}$$

$$= \frac{\sqrt{2} \times 9}{1 \times 10^3}$$

$$= \textbf{12.72 mA}$$

(2) DC load voltage ($V_{L\,dc}$):

$$V_{L\,dc} = I_{L\,dc} \times R_L$$

$$= \frac{2 \times 12.72 \times 10^{-3} \times 1 \times 10^3}{\pi}$$

$$= \textbf{8.1 volts}$$

(3) RMS load current: $\qquad I_{L\,rms} = \dfrac{I_m}{\sqrt{2}} = \dfrac{12.72}{\sqrt{2}}$

$$= \textbf{8.994 mA}$$

(4) Ripple factor:

$$r = \frac{[V_{L\,rms}^2 - V_{L\,dc}^2]^{1/2}}{V_{L\,dc}} = \frac{[I_{L\,rms}^2 R_L^2 - V_{L\,dc}^2]^{1/2}}{V_{L\,dc}}$$

$$r = \frac{[(8.994 \times 1)^2 - (8.1)^2]^{1/2}}{8.1}$$

$$= 0.4827 \text{ or } 48.27\%$$

(5) Efficiency:

$$\eta = \frac{8R_L}{\pi^2 (R_S + R_F + R_L)} = \frac{8R_L}{\pi^2 (R_L)} = \frac{8}{\pi^2}$$

$$= 0.8105 \text{ or } 81.05\%$$

Example 1.7: *What is the necessary AC input power from the transformer secondary used in a half rectifier to deliver 500 W of DC power to the load? What would be the AC input power for the same load in a full-wave rectifier?*

Solution: Given: $P_{L\,dc} = 500$ W

(1) To find P_{ac} for half-wave rectifier:

We know, Rectifier efficiency, $\eta = \dfrac{P_{L\,dc}}{P_{ac}}$

$\therefore$ $P_{ac} = P_{Ldc} / \eta$

We know, for a HWR, $\eta = 0.4$

$\therefore$ $P_{ac} = \dfrac{500}{0.4} = \textbf{1250 W}$

(2) To find P_{ac} for full wave rectifier:

As we know, for FWR, $\eta = 0.812$

$\therefore$ $P_{ac} = \dfrac{500}{0.812} = \textbf{615.76 W}$

Solved Examples on Bridge Rectifier

Example 1.8: *For a bridge rectifier, the RMS secondary voltage of a transformer is 12.7 volts. Assume ideal diodes and $R_L = 1$ kΩ.*

Find: (1) Peak current, (2) DC load current and DC load voltage, (3) RMS current, (4) Peak inverse voltage of diodes.

Solution: Given: $V_{S\,rms} = 12.7$ volts, $R_L = 1$ kΩ, $R_S = 0$ Ω, $R_F = 0$ Ω.

(1) Peak current: $I_m = \dfrac{V_m}{R_L + 2R_F + R_S}$

But $V_m = \sqrt{2}\, V_{S\,rms} = \sqrt{2} \times 12.7 = 17.96$ volts

$\therefore$ $I_m = \dfrac{17.96}{1 \times 10^3}$

$$= \textbf{17.96 mA}$$

(2) DC load current: $\quad I_{L\,dc} = \dfrac{2I_m}{\pi} = \dfrac{2 \times 17.96 \times 10^{-3}}{\pi}$

$$= \mathbf{0.1143\ mA}$$

(3) DC load voltage: $\quad V_{L\,dc} = I_{L\,dc} \times R_L = 11.43 \times 10^{-3} \times 1 \times 10^3$

$$= \mathbf{11.43\ volts}$$

(4) RMS current: $\quad I_{L\,rms} = \dfrac{I_m}{\sqrt{2}} = \dfrac{17.96 \times 10^{-3}}{\sqrt{2}}$

$$= \mathbf{12.69\ mA}$$

(5) Peak inverse voltage: $\;\; PIV = V_m$

$$= \mathbf{17.96\ volts}$$

Example 1.9: *Find out the rms value of the secondary voltage of a transformer which provides 9 V DC output voltage when connected to a bridge rectifier. If the secondary winding resistance is 3 Ω and the diode forward resistance is 1 Ω, what will be the output voltage when a 90 Ω load is connected to the power supply?*

Solution: Given: $V_{L\,dc} = 9$ V, $\;R_S = 3\ \Omega$, $R_F = 1\ \Omega$, $R_L = 90\ \Omega$.

(1) To calculate rms secondary voltage ($V_{S\,rms}$):

Given: $V_{L\,dc} = 9$ V

Assuming that no load was connected, the expression for average load voltage is,

$$V_{L\,dc} = \frac{2V_m}{\pi}$$

where $\qquad\qquad V_m$ = Peak secondary voltage

$\therefore \qquad\qquad \dfrac{2V_m}{\pi} = 9$

$\therefore \qquad\qquad V_m = \dfrac{9\pi}{2} = 14.14$ volt

$\therefore \qquad\qquad V_{S\,rms} = \dfrac{V_m}{\sqrt{2}} = \dfrac{14.14}{\sqrt{2}} \approx \mathbf{10\ V}$

(2) To calculate DC output voltage ($V_{L\,dc}$):

Given: $V_m = 14.14$ V, $\;R_L = 90\ \Omega$, $R_S = 3\ \Omega$, $R_F = 1\ \Omega$.

Peak load current, $\qquad I_m = \dfrac{V_m}{(R_S + 2R_F + R_L)} = \dfrac{14.14}{(3 + 2 + 90)}$

$$= 0.1488\ A$$

$$= \mathbf{148.8\ mA}$$

$\therefore$ DC load current, $\qquad I_{L\,dc} = \dfrac{2I_m}{\pi}$

$$= \mathbf{94.75\ mA}$$

$\therefore$ DC load voltage, $\qquad V_{L\,dc} = I_{L\,dc} \times R_L = 94.75 \times 10^{-3} \times 90$

$$= \mathbf{8.528\ volts}$$

Example 1.10: *A bridge rectifier is applied with input from a step-down transformer having turns ratio 1: 8 and input 230 V, 50 Hz. If the diode forward resistance is 1 Ω, secondary resistance is 10 Ω and load resistance connected is 2 kΩ, find: (1) DC power output, (2) PIV across each diode, (3) % efficiency.*

Solution: Given: $N_P : N_S = 8 : 1$, $R_S = 10\ \Omega$, $R_F = 1\ \Omega$, $R_L = 2\ k\Omega$.

RMS secondary voltage, $V_{S\,rms} = \dfrac{N_S}{N_P} \times 230 = 28.75\ V$

Peak secondary voltage, $V_m = \sqrt{2}\ V_{S\,rms} = \sqrt{2} \times 28.75 = 40.65\ V$

Peak load current, $I_m = \dfrac{V_m}{(R_S + 2R_F + R_L)} = \dfrac{40.65}{(10 + 2 + 2000)} = 20.2\ mA$

DC load current, $I_{L\,dc} = \dfrac{2I_m}{\pi} = \dfrac{2 \times 20.2}{\pi} = 12.86\ mA$

(1) DC load power: $P_{L\,dc} = I_{L\,dc}^2 \times R_L = (12.86 \times 10^{-3})^2 \times 2 \times 10^3$

$= \mathbf{331\ mW}$

(2) PIV across each diode: $V_m = \mathbf{40.65\ V}$

(3) AC input power: $P_{ac} = I_{S\,rms}^2 (R_S + 2R_F + R_L)$

$= \left[I_m/\sqrt{2}\right]^2 (R_S + 2R_F + R_L)$

$\therefore$ $P_{ac} = \dfrac{(20.2 \times 10^{-3})^2}{2} \times 2012 = 410\ mW$

$\therefore$ $\%\ efficiency = \dfrac{P_{L\,dc}}{P_{ac}} \times 100 = \dfrac{331}{410} \times 100$

$= \mathbf{80.63\%}$

1.9 TYPES OF RECTIFIER FILTERS

- As we have seen earlier, the rectifier circuitry converts the AC sine wave to a pulsating DC That is, the output is not pure DC, it contains ripple. To reduce the ripple factor, a filter circuit is introduced before the load resistor.
- Usually a filter circuit uses components like a capacitor and inductor.
- As we know that reactance of capacitor is given by $X_C = 1/2\pi fC$ for low frequency reactance is very high hence ideally capacitor acts as open circuit (DC) and for high frequency reactance is very low hence ideally acts as a short circuit (AC). It is always connected in parallel with the load; whereas an inductor acts as short for DC and so it is always placed in series with the load (Because $X_L = 2\pi fL$).
- Any given filter may involve capacitors, inductors, and/or resistors in some combination. Each such combination has both advantages and disadvantages, and its own range of practical application.
- Inductor filters are bulky, costly and consume a lot of power and hence are not popular. We will examine the operation of the capacitor filter in this section.

1.9.1 Half-Wave Rectifier With Capacitor Filter

- Half-wave rectifier with capacitor filter is as shown below.

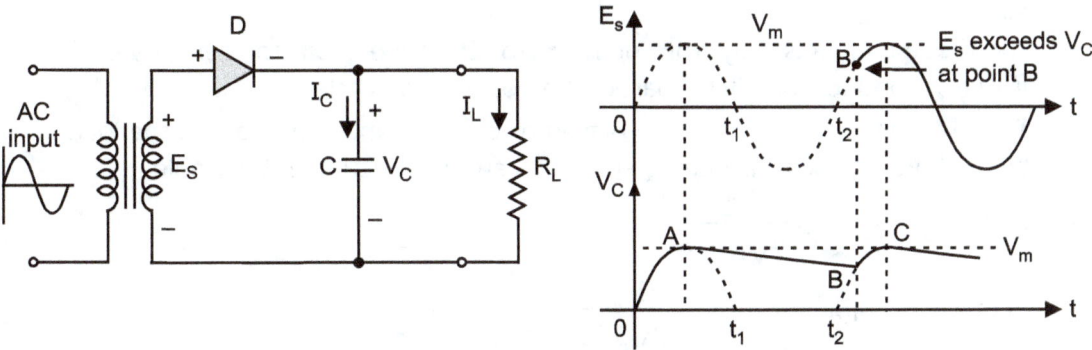

Fig. 1.28: Half-Wave Rectifier with Capacitor Filter

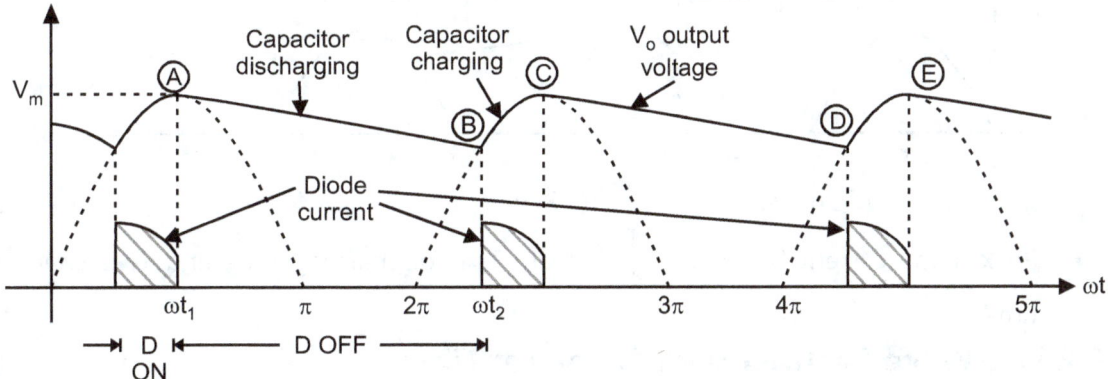

Fig. 1.29: Diode Conducts only for Part of Positive Cycle

- Refer Fig. 1.28, we can see that a capacitor is connected as a filter, in parallel with the load resistor R_L, to minimize the ripple.

- During the positive quarter cycle of input E_S, the diode gets forward biased and charges the capacitor C to peak value V_m. Practically, the capacitor charges to $(V_m - 0.7)$ if the diode voltage drop is considered. This initial charging is done once when power is turned-on.

- As the input voltage starts to decrease below its peak value, the diode gets reverse biased, the capacitor remains charged at V_m. Thus, during the entire negative half cycle and some part of the next positive half cycle, the capacitor discharges slowly through R_L because of the large time constant R_LC. Thus, point 'A' $\rightarrow$ 'B' is the discharging period of the capacitor as shown in Fig. 1.29.

- In the next positive half cycle when E_S becomes greater than the capacitor voltage V_C, i.e. at point 'B' the diode gets forward biased and charges the capacitor 'C' back to V_m.

- The diode conducts only from point 'B' to 'C' till the capacitor gets charged back to V_m. i.e. it conducts only for a part of the positive half cycle.

- Thus, when the diode is reverse biased or off, the capacitor supplies the load current by discharging itself through R_L slowly. It causes reduction in the ripple.

- Ripple factor 'r' $= \dfrac{1}{2\sqrt{3}\ fCR_L}$

- RMS ripple voltage $V_{r\,(rms)} = \dfrac{I_{L\,dc}}{2\sqrt{3}\ fC}$

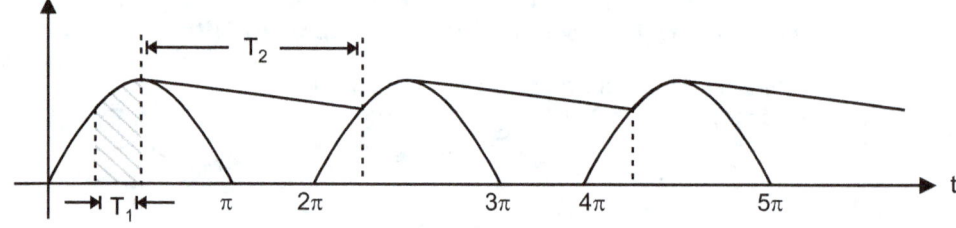

Fig. 1.30

- Peak diode current $I_P = I_{L\,dc} = \dfrac{T_2}{T_1}$, where T_2 is discharging time and T_1 is charging time.

1.9.2 Full-Wave Rectifier with Capacitor Filter   [May 2016]

- Full-wave rectifier with a capacitor filter is as shown below. Also the diode currents are indicated in Fig. 1.31, 1.32, 1.33. From the figures you can clearly tell about the switching ON and OFF of diodes D_1 and D_2 and the corresponding charging and discharging of the capacitor.

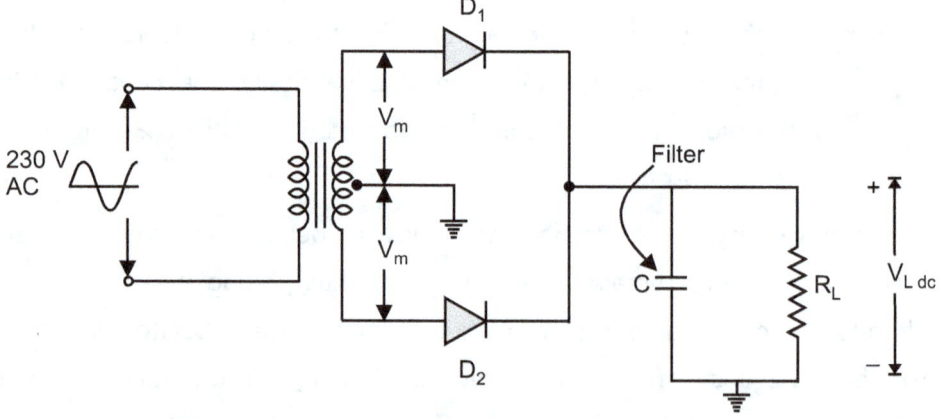

Fig. 1.31: Full-wave rectifier with capacitor filter

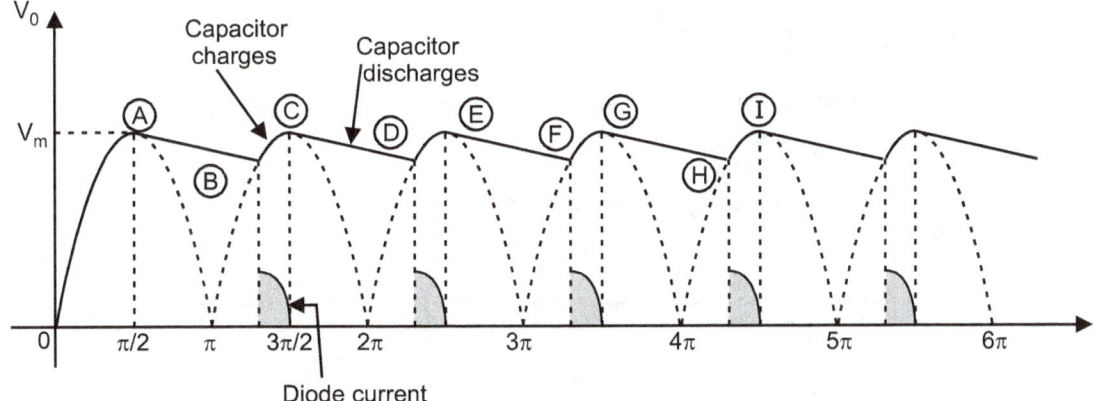

Fig. 1.32: Output voltage and diode currents shown

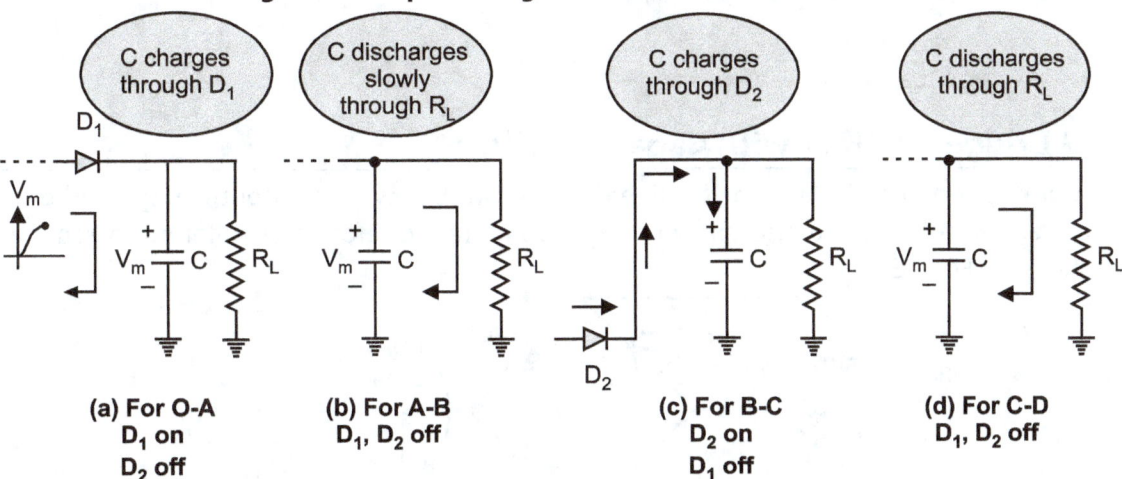

Fig. 1.33: Capacitor charging and discharging instants in FWR circuit

- As soon as when the power is switched on, the capacitor gets charged to V_m through diode D_1 from the period $\pi/2$ to π, as shown in the Fig. 1.32 from point 0 to A.

- At $\pi/2$, diode D_1 becomes reverse biased. So, from instance $\pi/2$ to $3\pi/2$ (i.e. from A to B) the capacitor start discharging through R_L, thus providing the load current.

- At instance B the capacitor voltage becomes less than the input voltage V_m. Therefore D_2 becomes forward biased and starts charging the capacitor again to the peak value V_m.

- At point C, the diode gets reverse biased and the capacitor starts discharging from point C to D, thus providing the load current.

- The cycle repeats. The time required by the capacitor to charge is very less; whereas its discharge is very slow due to large time constant. Hence, there is considerable reduction in the output ripple.

Ripple factor, 'r' = $\dfrac{1}{4\sqrt{3}\,FCR_L}$

- Peak diode current $I_p = I_{L\,dc} \cdot \dfrac{T_2}{2T_1}$

  where T_1 = charging time, T_2 = discharging time.

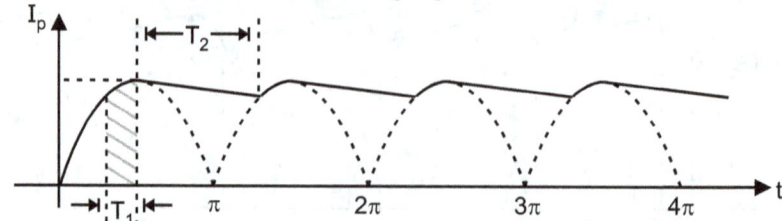

Fig. 1.34

- RMS value of ripple voltage, $V_{r\,(rms)} = \dfrac{I_{L\,dc}}{4\sqrt{3}\ FC}$

- Average load voltage, $V_{L\,dc} = V_m - \dfrac{I_{L\,dc}}{4FC}$

1.9.3 Bridge Rectifier with Capacitor Filter

- A bridge rectifier with a capacitor filter is as shown below. The output voltage and diode current waveforms are also shown in Fig. 1.34. The waveforms at different instants are shown in Fig. 1.35.

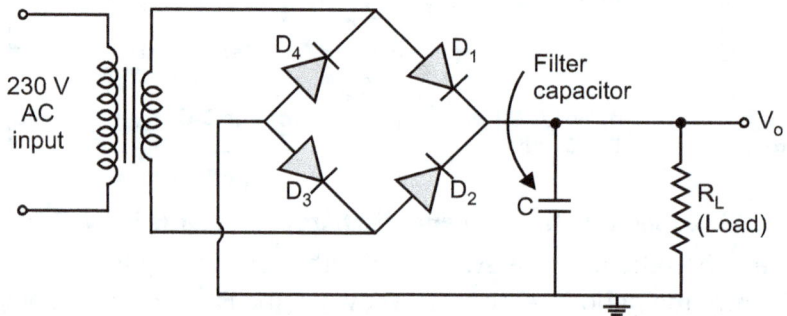

Fig. 1.35: Bridge rectifier with capacitor filter

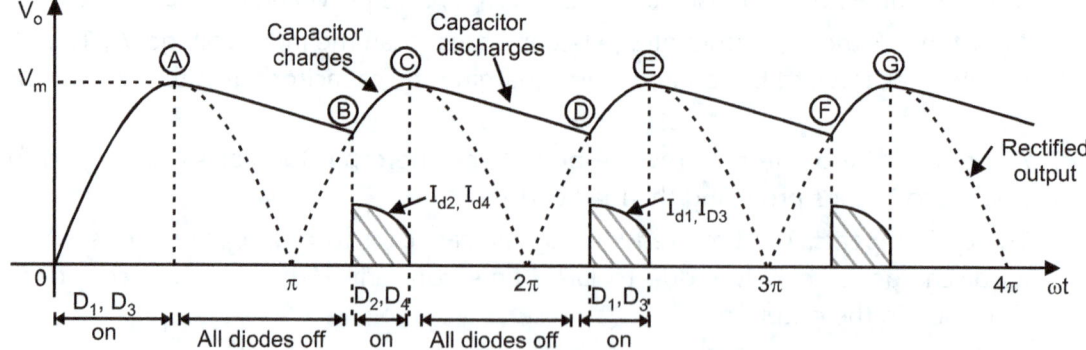

Fig. 1.36: Diode currents and the output voltage of the above circuit

1.9.4 Surge Currents in Capacitor Filter

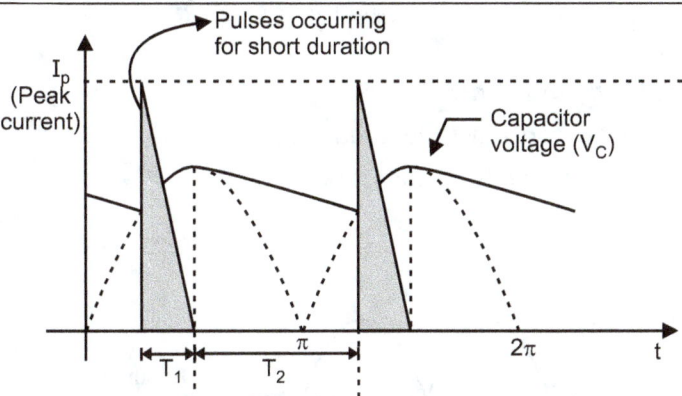

Fig. 1.37: Surge current in diodes

- We know the property of capacitor that it acts as short circuit initially when there is a sudden input pulse. Momentarily the capacitor offers zero resistance when the power is switched on.
- Therefore very large current may flow through the forward biased diode at start. This current is called surge current. It may destroy the diode permanently if the current rating of the diode is not high enough.
- By connecting a resistor in series with the capacitor, the surge current can be limited, thus protecting the diode.

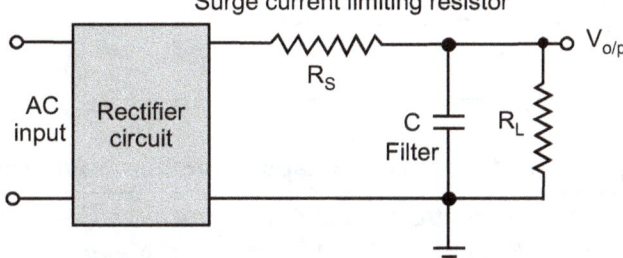

Fig. 1.38: Limiting the surge current by resistor R$_S$

Advantages of Capacitor Filter:
- Decrease in the ripple factor.
- Increase in the average load voltage ($V_{L\,dc}$).

Disadvantages of Capacitor Filter:
- Ripple factor (r) depends upon the load resistance (R_L).
- Protection from surge current is a must.

Example 1.11: *If a circuit of a full-wave center-tapped rectifier with a capacitor filter has a load R_L = 100 Ω and C = 1050 µF, calculate the ripple factor.*

Solution: Given: R_L = 100 Ω, C = 1050 µF

$$r = \frac{1}{4\sqrt{3}\, fC\, R_L} = \frac{1}{4\sqrt{3} \times 50 \times 1050 \times 10^{-6} \times 100} = 0.027 = \mathbf{2.74\%}$$

Example 1.12: *Draw the circuit diagram of a full-wave center-tapped rectifier with a capacitor shunt filter. If the input of the rectifier is a sine wave, draw the nature of the output waveforms for the following:*

(i) Rectifier output without filter.

(ii) Output with capacitor only, without load resistance.

(iii) Output with capacitor filter, with load resistance.

Solution:

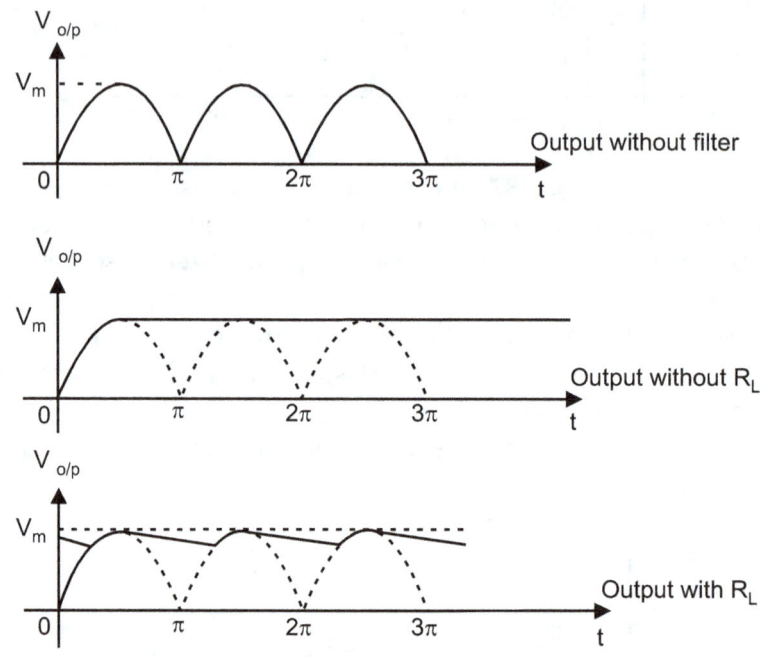

Fig. 1.39: Full-wave center-tapped rectifier waveforms

Example 1.13: *A full-wave centre-tapped transformer rectifier is supplied from 230 V, 50 Hz with $N_P : N_S/2 = 15/1$. It has $R_L = 50\ \Omega$. Calculate the load voltage and ripple voltage. Recalculate these values if a condenser of 470 µF is connected across the load.*

Solution: Given: Turns ratio = $N_P : N_S/2 = 15/1$, $R_L = 50\ \Omega$, C = 470 µF.

Without a capacitor filter:

(1) RMS secondary voltage:

$$V_{S\,rms} = \frac{1}{15} \times 230$$

$$= \mathbf{15.33\ V}$$

∴   Peak secondary voltage,

$$V_m = \sqrt{2}\,V_{S\,rms} = \sqrt{2} \times 15.33$$

$$= \mathbf{21.7\ V}$$

(2) Assuming $R_S = 0 \, \Omega$ and $R_F = 0 \, \Omega$

Maximum load current:

$$I_m = \frac{V_m}{(R_S + R_F + R_L)} = \frac{21.7}{50}$$

$$= \textbf{0.4337 A}$$

(3) Load voltage:

$$V_{L \, dc} = I_{L \, dc} \times R_L = \frac{2I_m}{\pi} \times R_L = \frac{2 \times 0.4337}{\pi} \times 50$$

$$= \textbf{13.8 Volts}$$

(4) Ripple voltage = Ripple factor $\times V_{L \, dc}$ = $0.482 \times 13.8 = \textbf{6.65 Volts}$

(Since the ripple factor for FWR = 0.482)

(5) The average load current:

$$I_{L \, dc} = \frac{V_{L \, dc}}{R_L} = \frac{13.8}{50}$$

$$= \textbf{0.276 Amp}$$

With the capacitor filter

(1) Load voltage:

$$V_{L \, dc} = V_m - \frac{I_{L \, dc}}{4fC} = 21.7 - \frac{0.276}{4 \times 50 \times 470 \times 10^{-6}}$$

$$= \textbf{18.76 volts}$$

(2) Ripple factor:

$$'r' = \frac{1}{4\sqrt{3} \, FCR_L} = \frac{1}{4\sqrt{3} \times 50 \times 100 \times 10^{-6} \times 2.5 \times 10^3}$$

$$= \textbf{0.01154}$$

Example 1.14: *A 100 μF capacitor when used as a filter has 12 V DC across it with a terminal load resistor of 2.5 kΩ. If the rectifier is full wave with center tapped, and supply frequency is 50 Hz, what is the % of ripple in the output ?*

Solution: Given: C = 100 μF, R_L = 2.5 kΩ, $V_{L \, dc}$ = 12 V, F = 50 Hz

$$\% \text{ ripple} = \frac{\text{RMS output ripple voltage}}{\text{Average load voltage}} \times 100$$

$$r = \frac{V_{rms}}{V_{L \, dc}}$$

$\therefore$

$$V_{rms} = \frac{V_{L \, dc}}{4\sqrt{3} \, R_L} = \frac{12}{4\sqrt{3} \times 50 \times 100 \times 10^{-6} \times 2.5 \times 10^3}$$

$$= \textbf{0.138 volts}$$

$$\therefore \qquad \% \text{ ripple} = r = \frac{0.138}{12} \times 100$$

$$= \mathbf{1.154\%}$$

Example 1.15: *Determine the peak to peak ripple voltage and the ripple factor for a bridge rectifier using a capacitor input filter. The load resistance is 2 kΩ while the DC voltage across the load is 12 V. Assume the supply frequency to be 50 Hz and ideal diodes. The capacitor of 100 μF is used in the filter circuit.*

Solution: Given: R_L = 2 kΩ, E_{DC} = 12 V, f = 50 Hz, C = 100 μF.

(1) Peak to peak ripple voltage:

$$V_r = \frac{V_{L\,dc}}{2fCR_L}$$

$$\therefore \qquad V_r = \frac{12}{2 \times 50 \times 100 \times 10^{-6} \times 2 \times 10^3}$$

$$= \mathbf{0.6\ V}$$

(2) The ripple factor:

$$r = \frac{1}{4\sqrt{3}\ fCR_L}$$

$$= \frac{1}{4\sqrt{3} \times 50 \times 100 \times 10^{-6} \times 2 \times 10^3}$$

$$= 0.0144$$

$$= \mathbf{1.44\%}$$

1.10 CLIPPING CLAMPING CIRCUIT

1.10.1 Clipper Circuits

- The basic action of clipper circuits is to remove certain portions of the input waveform above or below a certain level without distorting remaining part of applied waveform.

1.10.2 Positive Clipper   [Dec. 13]

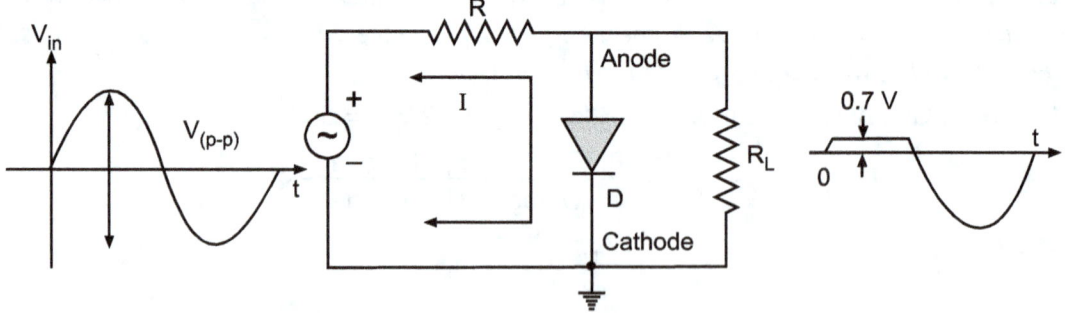

Fig. 1.40: Positive Clipper Circuit

- Fig 1.40 shows a positive clipper circuit. Here diode is connected in parallel with load.
- In positive half cycle of input, as cathode is at ground and when input voltage exceeds

0.7 V, diode turns ON. In this condition voltage drop across silicon diode is 0.7 V and this is the output voltage of circuit. So output voltage is limited to 0 + 0.7 V even when the input exceeds 0.7 V.

- When input voltage goes below +0.7 V the diode is reverse biased and ideally appears as a open switch and output is like the negative part of input voltage. Magnitude of this voltage is dependent on voltage divider formed by R and load resistance R_L as follows :
$$V_{out} = (R_L/R + R_L).V_{in}$$
If R_1 is smaller compared to R_L, then $V_{out} = V_{in}$

1.10.3 Negative Clipper   [Dec. 13]

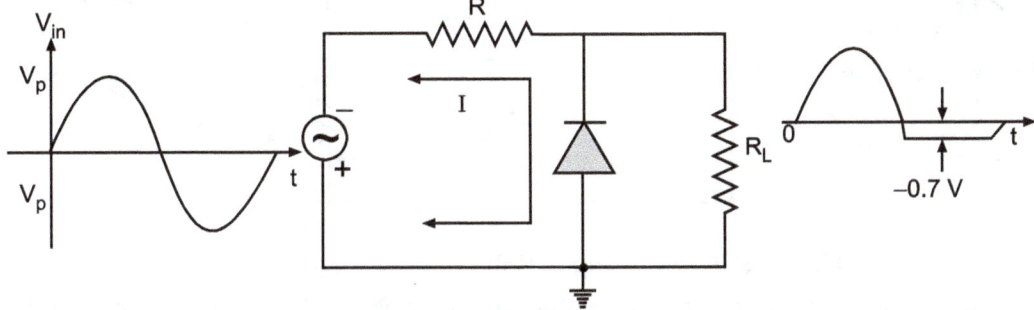

Fig. 1.41 : Negative Clipper Circuit

- Fig 1.41 shows a negative clipper circuit here diode is connected in parallel with load but here diode is connected in reverse direction. So negative part of the input voltage is clipped off.
- When the input voltage goes above –0.7 V the diode is no longer forward biased, and a voltage appears across R_L is proportional to the input voltage.
- When the input voltage goes below –0.7 V the diode is forward biased because anode cathode terminal is at ground potential-anode voltage does not exceeds –0.7 V. So anode voltage is limited to –0.7 V even when the input goes below –0.7 V.

1.10.4 Biased Clipper

- The level to which an AC voltage is limited can be adjusted by adding a DC bias voltage (VBIAS) in series with diode.

1. **Positive Clipper using V$_{BIAS}$**   [May 15]

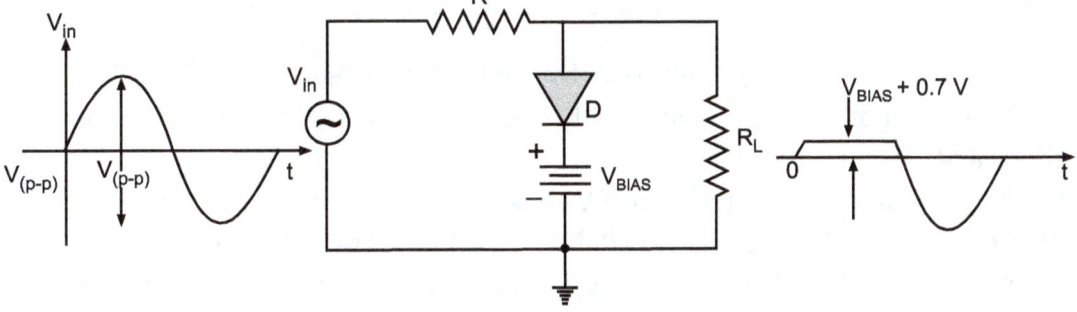

Fig. 1.42: Positive Clipper Using V$_{BIAS}$

- Fig 1.42 is positive clipper circuit with bias voltage is in series with diode.
- Before the diode is forward biased the voltage at anode terminal is V_{BIAS} + 0.7 V. Once the diode is forward biased, the voltage at anode terminal is limited to V_{BIAS} + 0.7 V. So all voltage above this level is clipped off.
- During negative half cycle the diode is reversed biased and negative voltage appears across load resistance. Magnitude of this voltage is decided by Voltage divider formed by R and R_L.

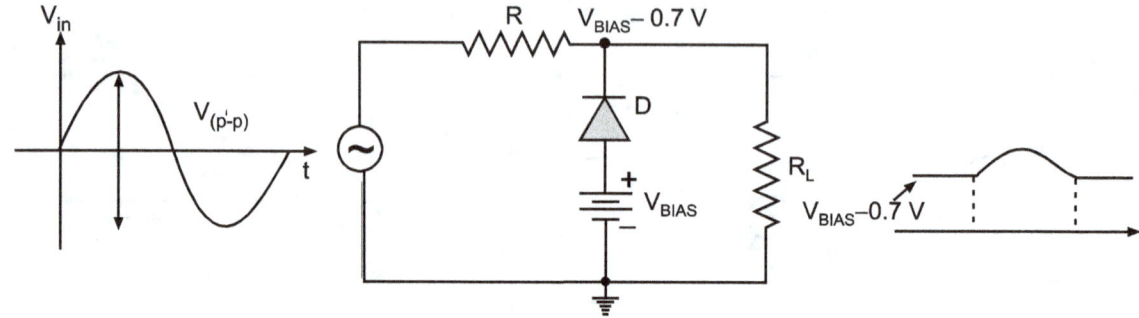

Fig. 1.43: To Limit Input Voltage below V_{BIAS} – 0.7 V

- Fig. 1.43 is modification of positive limiter shown in Fig. 1.42 to limit the output voltage to the portion of the input voltage waveform above V_{BIAS} – 0.7 V.
- When V_{in} greater than V_{BIAS} – 0.7 V, diode is reversed biased and we get positive part of the input above V_{BIAS} – 0.7V.
- When V_{in} is below V_{BIAS} – 0.7 V, diode is forward biased and below this voltage part of input waveform is clipped off.

2. **Negative Clipper using V_{BIAS}**

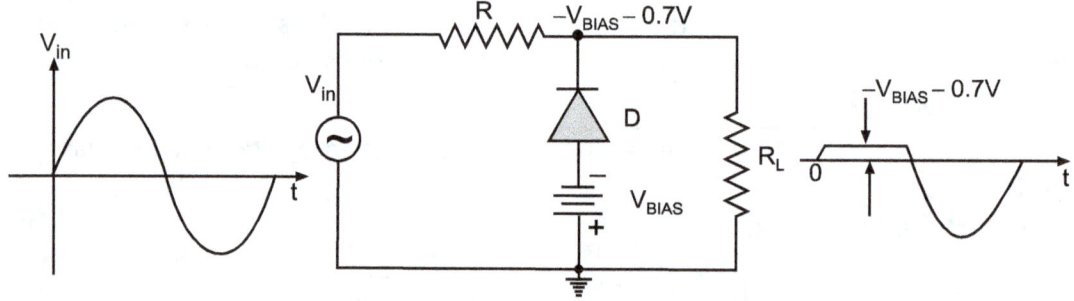

Fig. 1.44: Negative Clipper Using V_{BIAS}

- Fig 1.44 is negative clipper circuit with bias voltage in series with diode with battery connected in reverse direction.
- For input voltage V_{in} greater than $- V_{BIAS}$ – 0.7 V, diode is reverse biased and output follows the input, but magnitude is limited by voltage divider formed by R and R_L.
- When input voltage is below $- V_{BIAS}$ – 0.7 V, diode is forward biased and limiting action is achieved as shown in Fig. 1.45.

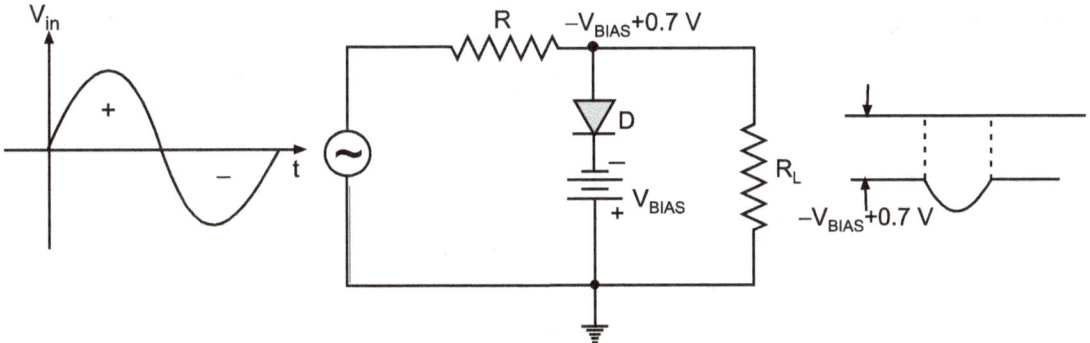

Fig. 1.45: To Limit Input Voltage above – V_{BIAS} + 0.7 V

- Fig 1.45 is modification of negative limiter shown in Fig. 1.44 to limit the output voltage to the portion of the input voltage waveform below $-V_{BIAS}$ + 0.7 V.
- When V_{in} is above $-V_{BIAS}$ + 0.7 V diode is forward biased and above this voltage part of input waveform is clipped off.
- When V_{in} is below $-V_{BIAS}$ + 0.7 V diode is reversed biased and output follows the input but magnitude is limited by voltage divider formed by R and R_L.
3. Diode Clipper Implemented with the Help of Voltage Divider Bias
- Here direct DC voltage source is replaced by voltage divider circuit and bias voltage is set by resistor values according to the voltage divider formula.

$$V_{BIAS} = (R_3/R_2 + R_3).V_{supply}$$

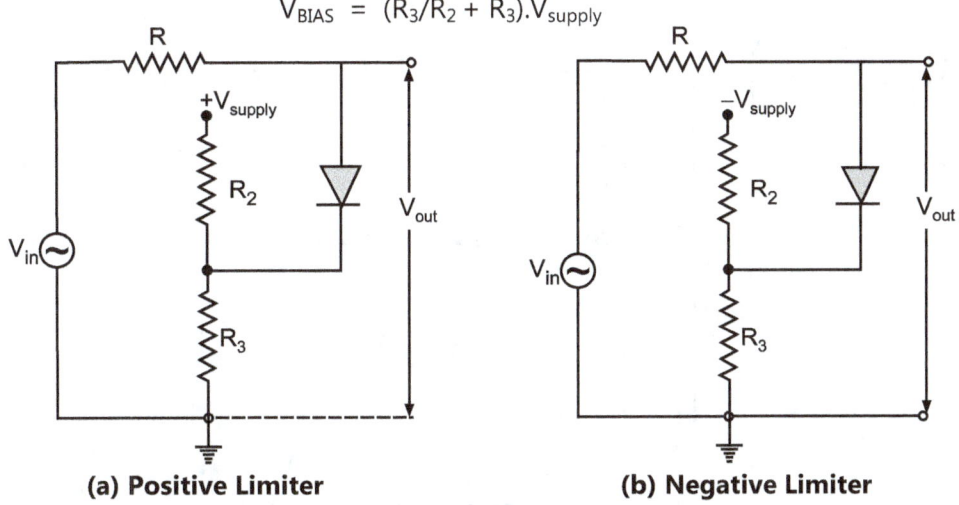

    (a) Positive Limiter   **(b) Negative Limiter**

Fig. 1.46

1.10.5 Diode Clampers

- A clamper adds a DC level to an AC voltage. Clampers are also known as DC restorers. It is a network constructed of a diode, a resistor, and a capacitor that shifts a waveform to a different DC level without changing the appearance of the applied signal. The chosen resistor and capacitor of the network must be selected such that the time constant is determined by RC is sufficiently large to ensure that the voltage across the capacitor does not discharge significantly during the interval when diode is non-conducting.

1. Positive Clamper

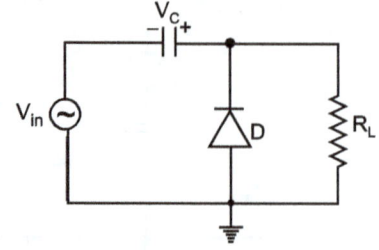

(a) Positive Clamper

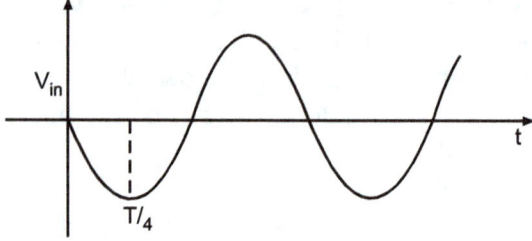

(b) Input Voltage Waveform

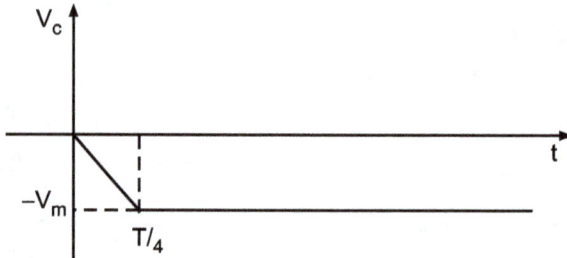

(c) Voltage Across Capacitor

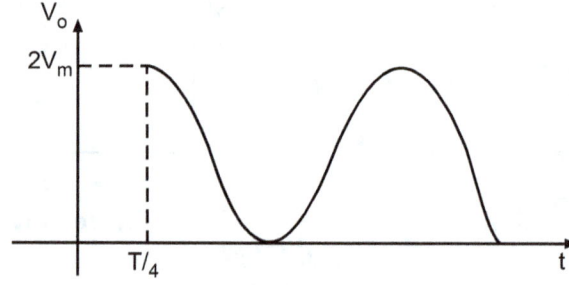

(d) Output Voltage

Fig. 1.47

- Positive clamper is a circuit which clamps the input signal waveform positively. Fig. 1.47 shows circuit diagram of positive clamper. The clamping output is obtained across resistor R_L.

Operation of the Circuit:

- The sinusoidal input voltage signal is applied as shown in Fig. 1.47 and assume that capacitor is uncharged.

- During first 90° negative cycle of input waveform the voltage across capacitor follows the input and capacitor voltage is equal to input voltage i.e. $V_{in} = V_c$ (assuming that $r_f = 0$ and cut in voltage = 0 V).

- After V_{in} and V_c reaches their peak values. V_{in} begins to decrease and diode becomes reversed biased. Ideally voltage across capacitor remains constant at $V_c = V_m$. By Kirchhoff's voltage law

$$V_o = V_c + V_{in} = V_m + V_m. \text{Sin wt}$$

- The capacitor and output voltages are shown in Fig. 1.47.

2. Negative Clamper

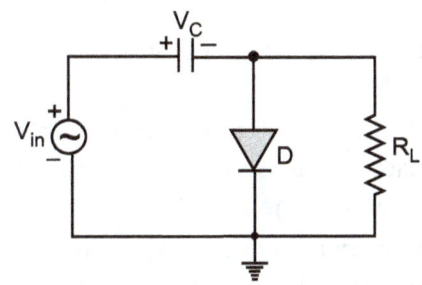

(a) Negative Clamper

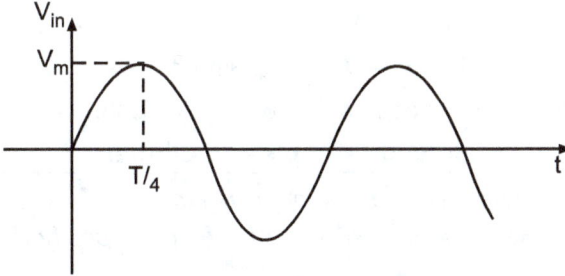

(b) Input Voltage Waveform

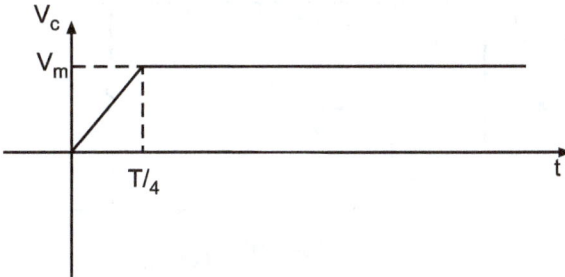

(c) Voltage Across Capacitor

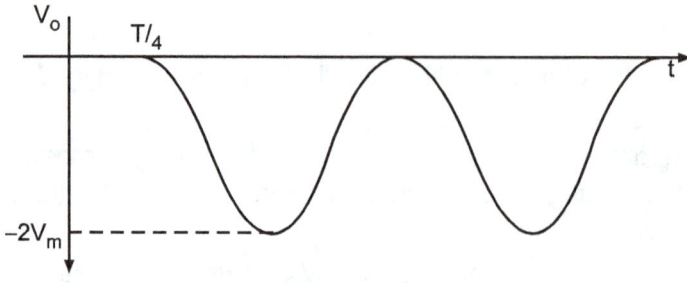

(d) Output Voltage

Fig. 1.48

- Negative clamper is a circuit which clamps the input signal waveform negatively. Fig. 1.48 shows circuit diagram of negative clamper. The clamping output is obtained across resistor R_L.

Operation of the Circuit:

- The sinusoidal input voltage signal is applied as shown in Fig. 1.48 and assume that the capacitor is uncharged.

- During the first 90° positive cycle of input waveform, the voltage across the capacitor follows input and capacitor voltage is equal to input voltage i.e. $V_{in} = V_c$ (assuming that $r_f = 0$ and cut in voltage = 0 V)

- After V_{in} and V_c reaches their peak values, V_{in} begins to decrease and diode becomes reversed biased. Ideally voltage across capacitor remains constant at $V_c = V_m$. By Kirchhoff's voltage law

$$V_o = -V_c + V_{in}$$
$$= -V_m + V_m. \text{ Sin wt}$$

- The capacitor and output voltages are shown in Fig. 1.48.

Solved Examples on Clipper

Example 1.16 : *The negative clipper shown in Fig. 1.49 has ± 9V input and zero load current. Determine a suitable value of resistance for R_1 and specify diode forward current and reverse voltage.*

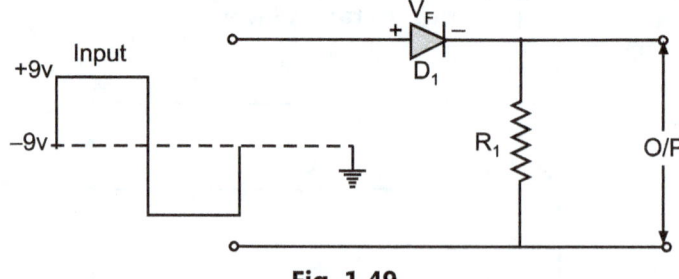

Fig. 1.49

$$V_o = V_{in} - V_F$$
$$= 9V - 0.7 = 8.3 \text{ V}$$

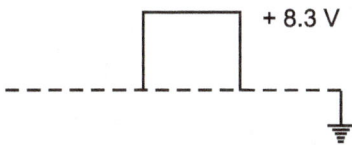

Fig. 1.50: Output Waveform

Select I_F = 1 mA

$$R_1 = \frac{V_o}{T_F} = 8.3\ V\ \mathbf{= 8.3\ k\Omega}$$

Diode specifications: V_R = E **= 9 V**

I_F = **1 mA**

Example 1.17: *For a circuit shown below, draw the output waveform for the given input.*

[Nov. 2015]

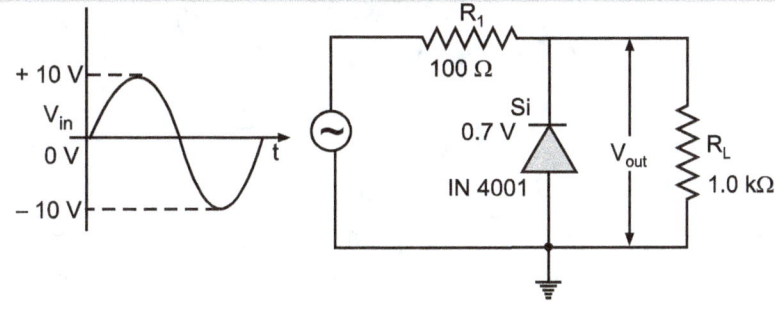

Fig. 1.51

Solution: The diode is forward biased and conducts when input goes below – 0.7 V and peak output voltage across R_L is given by

$$V_{m(out)} = \left(\frac{R_L}{R_1 + R_L}\right) \cdot V_{m(in)} = \frac{1.0\ k\Omega}{1.1\ k\Omega} \times 10\ V = 9.09\ V$$

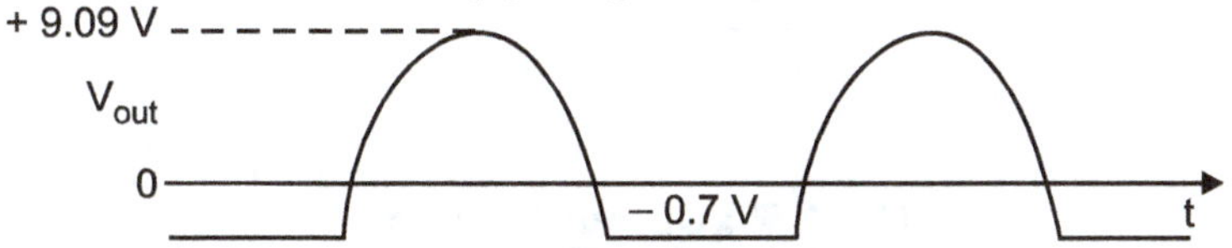

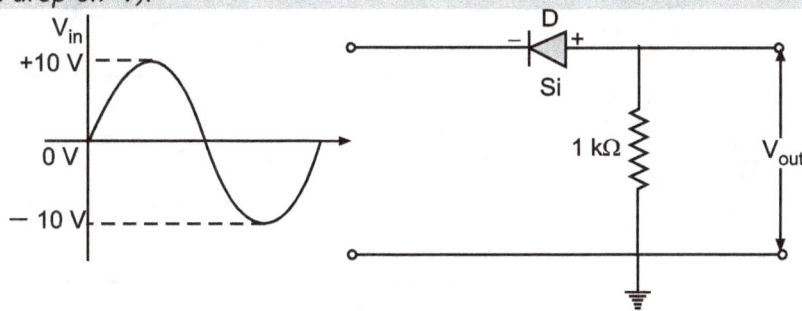

Fig. 1.52: Output Waveform

Example 1.18: *Determine the output voltage waveform for each circuit shown below (Assume diode drop 0.7 V).*

Fig. 1.53 (a)

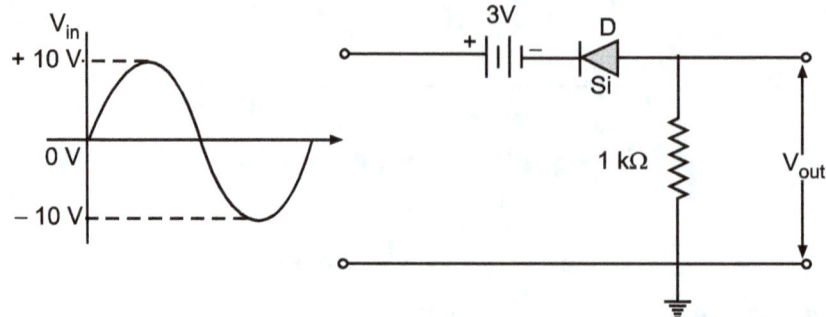

Fig. 1.53 (b)

Solution: For Fig. 1.53 (a) diode D is forward biased when input voltage is below – 0.7 V and it is reverse biased for input voltage above – 0.7 V.

For Case I: $V_{out} = V_{in} - V_F = -10 - (-0.7\ V)$

∴ $V_{out} = -\mathbf{9.7\ V}$

Case II: $V_{out} = \mathbf{0\ V}$

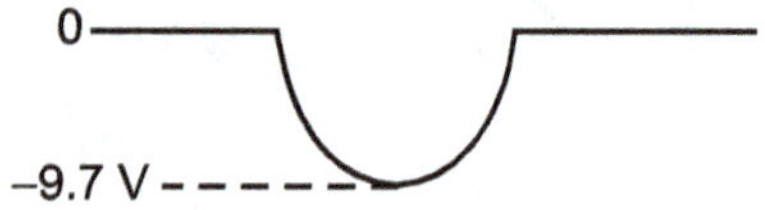

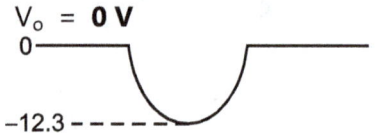

Fig. 1.54: Output Waveform

For Fig. 1.53 (b), diode is connected in reverse direction. So when diode is forward biased voltage across it is – 0.7 V.

Addition of battery voltage and diode drop is 3 – 0.7 V **= 2.3 V**

When diode is reverse biased it acts as open switch for input voltage less than **2.3 V.**

For Case I: $V_o = -10 - 2.3\ V = -\mathbf{12.3\ V}$

Case II: $V_o = \mathbf{0\ V}$

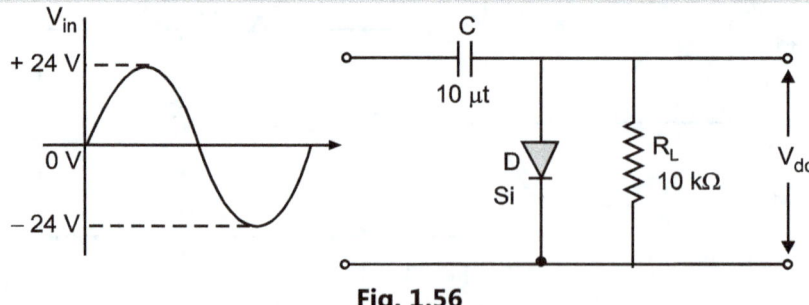

Fig. 1.55: Output Waveform

Solved Examples on Clamper

Example 1.19: *For Fig. 1.56 shown below draw the waveform across R_L in the clamping circuit.*

Fig. 1.56

Solution: Ideally, negative DC value equal to the input peak (less) the diode drop inserted by clamping circuit is:

$$V_{dc} = -(V_{m(in)} - 0.7 \text{ V})$$
$$= -(24 \text{ V} - 0.7 \text{ V}) = -23.3 \text{ V}$$

Actually, capacitor will discharges slightly between peaks and as a result, the output will have an average value of slightly less than calculated above, the output waveform goes approximately + 0.7 V as shown in Fig. 1.57.

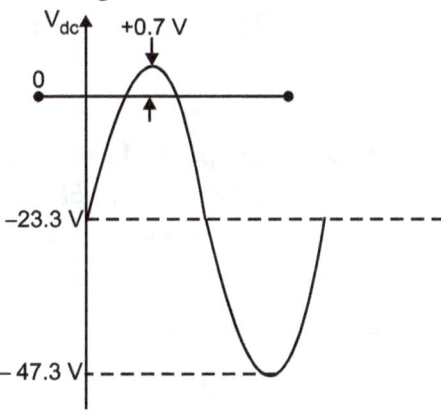

Fig. 1.57: Output Waveform

1.11 VOLTAGE MULTIPLIERS   [May 2014]

- The basis of voltage multiplier is clamping action which is used to increase the magnitude of peak rectified voltages without increasing the voltage rating of transformer. Multiplication factors of two, three or four may be achieved.

Voltage Doubler:

(a) Half Wave Voltage Doubler:

Half wave voltage doubler is having multiplication factor of two as shown in Fig. 1.58.

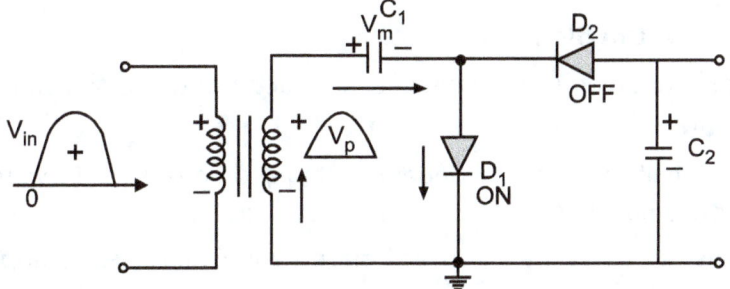

(a) Half Wave Doubler Operation during Positive Half Cycle

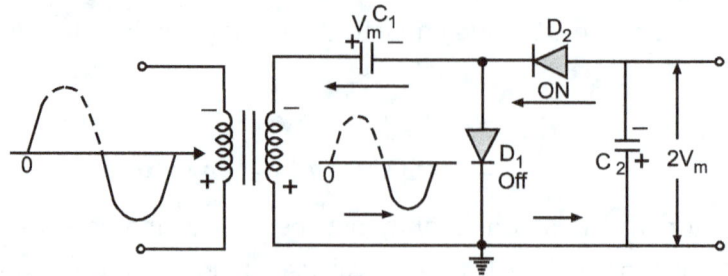

(b) Half Wave Voltage Doubler Operation during Negative Half Cycle

Fig. 1.58

Operation of Circuit:

- During positive half cycle the secondary voltage, diode D_1 is forward biased and D_2 is reverse biased. Capacitor C_1 charge to the peak of the secondary voltage (V_p) (Assuming that $r_f = 0$ and cut in voltage = 0 V) as shown in Fig. 1.58 (a).

- During the negative half cycle, diode D_2 is forward biased and D_1 is reverse biased, as shown in Fig. 1.49 (b).

- Since C_1 cannot discharge, the peak voltage of C_1 adds to the secondary voltage C_2 to approximately $2V_m$.

- Applying Kirchhoff's law around the loop in Fig. 1.58 (b),

$$\therefore \qquad V_{C_1} - V_{C_2} + V_m = 0$$

$$V_{C_2} = V_m + V_{C_1}$$

Neglecting the diode drop $V_{C_1} = V_m$. Therefore, $V_{C_2} = V_m + V_m = 2V_m$

- With no load condition, C_2 remains charged to approximately $2V_m$.

- If load resistance is connected across the output, C_2 discharges slightly through the load on the next positive cycle and is again recharged to $2V_m$ on the following negative half cycle.

- The resulting output is a half wave, capacitor filtered voltage. And peak inverse voltage across each diode is $2V_m$.

(b) Full Wave Voltage Doubler:

Full wave voltage doubler having multiplication factor of two is shown in Fig. 1.59.

Operation of Circuit:

- During positive half cycle of secondary voltage, diode D_1 is forward biased and C_1 charges to approximately V_m, as shown in Fig. 1.59 (a).

- During negative half cycle, D_2 is forward biased and C_2 charges to approximately V_m, as shown in Fig. 1.59 (b).

- The output voltage $2V_m$, is taken across two capacitors in series.

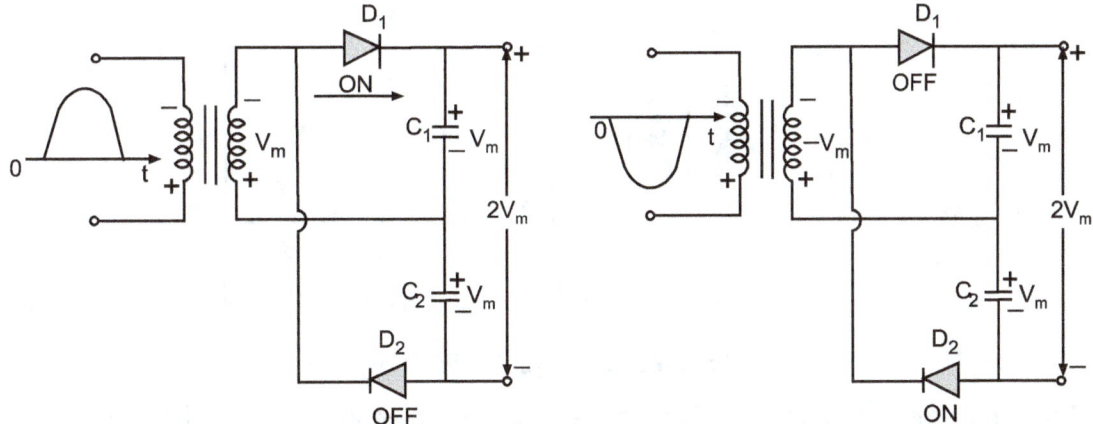

(a) Full Wave Voltage Doubler Operation during Positive Half Cycle

(b) Full Wave Voltage Doubler Operation during Negative Half Cycle

Fig. 1.59

(c) Voltage Tripler :

In half wave voltage doubler if we add one diode and capacitor it forms voltage tripler, as shown in Fig. 1.60.

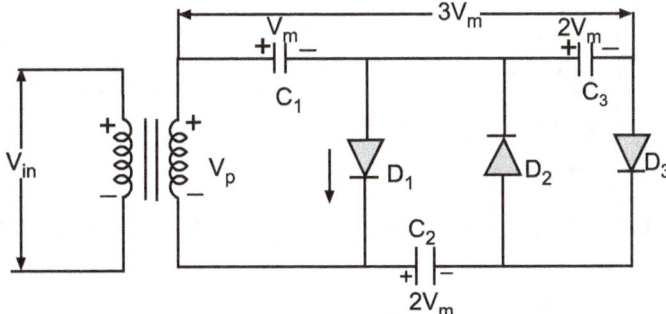

Fig. 1.60: Voltage Tripler

Operation of Circuit:

- During positive half cycle of secondary voltage across transformer, C_1 charges to V_m through diode D_1 because it is forward biased.

- During negative half cycle, C_2 charges to $2V_p$ through diode D_2 as described in voltage doubler circuit.

- During next positive half cycle C_3 charges to $2V_p$ through D_3.

- The tripler output is taken across C_1 and C_3 as shown in Fig. 1.60.

(d) Voltage Quadrupler:

In voltage tripler if we add one diode and capacitor it forms voltage quadrupler, as shown in Fig. 1.61.

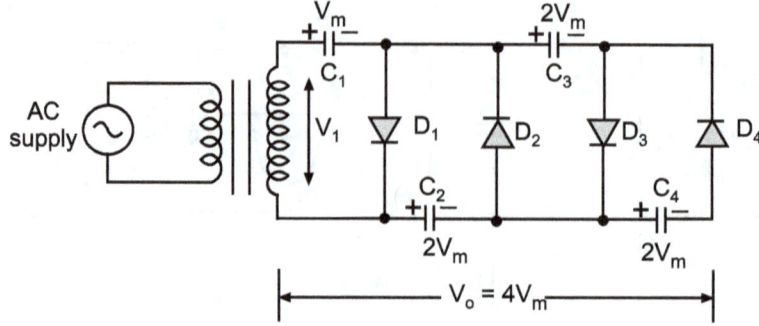

Fig. 1.61: Voltage Quadrupler

The capacitor C_4 charges to $2V_m$ with the polarity shown in a negative half cycle though D_4 is making the total voltage $4V_m$.

1.12 ZENER DIODE

❖ **Important Question Related to this Topic** ❖

Draw and explain the V-I characteristics of a zener diode. What are the two breakdown mechanisms in a zener diode ?

Zener diode is a special silicon P-N junction diode, which is specially designed to operate in **reverse breakdown region**.

- During manufacturing of the zener diodes, the doping level is controlled in such a way that their breakdown voltage ranges from 3 V to 210 V.

- The symbol of zener diode and its forward and reverse biased configurations are as shown in Fig. 1.62.

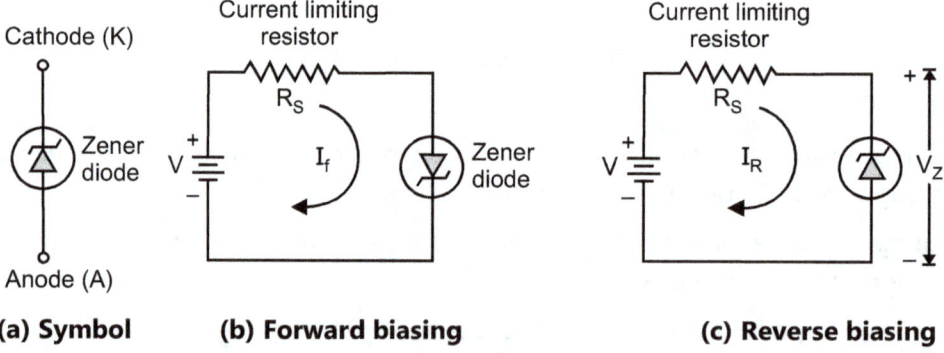

(a) Symbol   **(b) Forward biasing**   **(c) Reverse biasing**

Fig. 1.62

- In the forward biased condition, zener diode operates like a normal P-N junction diode.

- In reverse biased condition, initially, the current through zener diode is very small in micro amperes. (Same as the reverse leakage current I_o of the diode).

- As the reverse voltage is gradually increased, at a particular point, the zener diode breaks down and current through it increases rapidly. This is known as the breakdown voltage **or knee voltage** of a zener diode. It is denoted as V_Z. It is different for different zeners and is decided by the doping level during the manufacturing.

- The current through the zener diode at this time is known as the **knee current** and is denoted as I_Z.

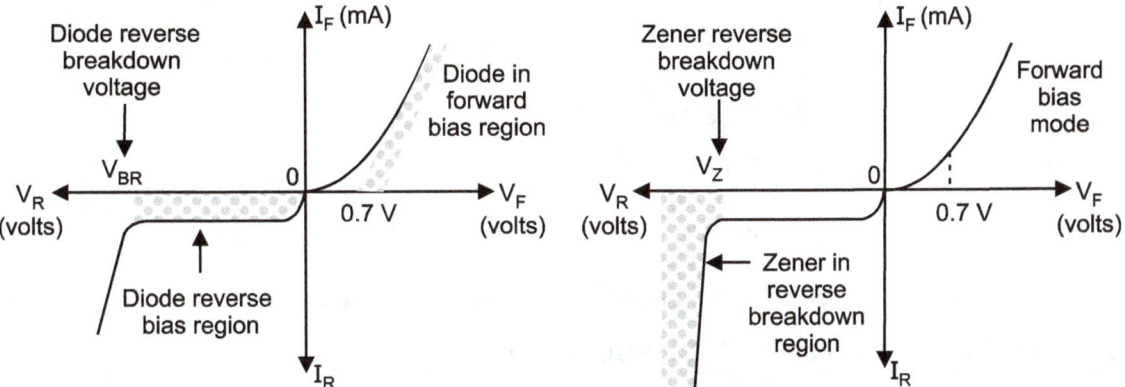

(a) V-I Characteristics of normal diode   **(b) V-I Characteristics of zener diode**

Fig. 1.63

- The reverse breakdown voltage is fairly independent of the reverse current flowing. This property makes it ideal as a voltage reference.

- The characteristics of normal P-N junction diode and the zener diode in reverse biased mode are as shown in Fig. 1.63.

1.12.1 V-I Characteristic of the Zener Diode   [May 13, 16]

- The important voltage and current terms of the zener diode in reverse biased condition are: (a) I_o, (b) V_Z, (c) I_{Zmin}, (d) I_{ZT}, (e) I_{Zmax}, (f) P_Z.

> **❖ Important Question Related to this Topic ❖**
>
> Give and explain any three specifications of a zener diode.

- **Reverse Leakage Current (I_o):** It is the current that flows through the zener diode when reverse bias is applied.

- $I_{Z\,min}$ and $I_{Z\,max}$ are the current operating regions of the zener diode.

- I_{ZT} is the zener test current at which the nominal zener breakdown voltage is specified.

- Every zener diode has a capacity of carrying current. As current increases, $P_Z = V_Z I_Z$, P_Z i.e. power dissipation in the zener diode increases and beyond a certain value the zener diode may get damaged (or burnt).

- $I_{Z\,max}$ is the maximum current that can be carried safely by a zener diode. All these parameters are shown in the zener diode characteristics in Fig. 1.64.

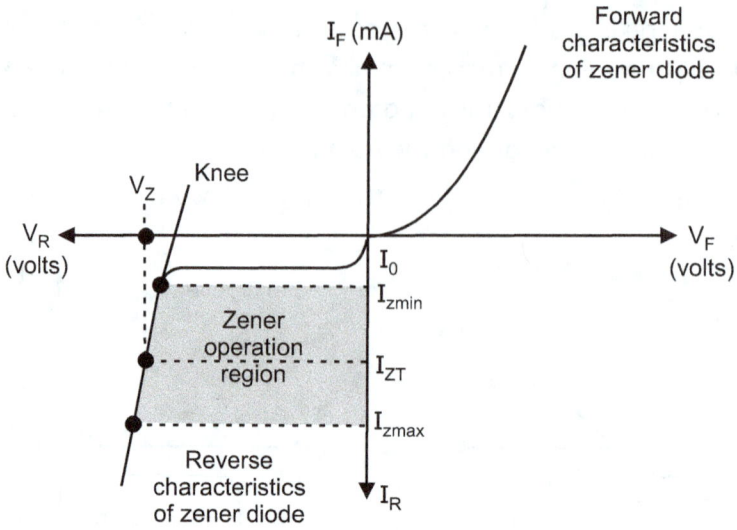

Fig. 1.64: V-I Characteristics of Zener Diode

1.12.2 Equivalent Circuit of a Zener Diode

- Ideally the equivalent circuit of a breakdown zener is indicated by a battery of voltage V_z which remains almost constant in the zener region.

- Practically, small internal zener resistance, r_z does exist, it is known as dynamic resistance of the zener diode. Therefore the practical equivalent of the zener diode is indicated by a battery source V_z along with a series resistor r_z as shown in 1.65 (b).

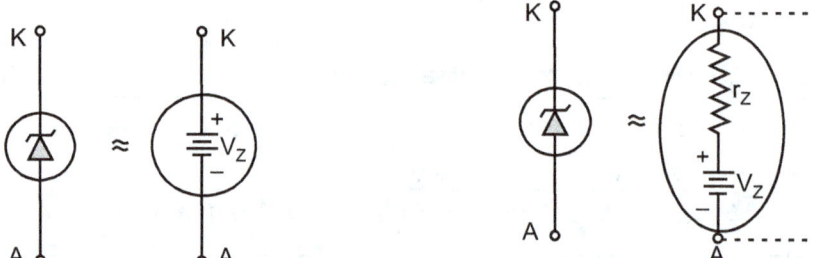

(a) Ideal Equivalent Circuit of Zener Diode   (b) Practical Equivalent Circuit of Zener Diode

Fig. 1.65

- r_z is the dynamic resistance of the zener diode and is given as

$$r_z = \frac{\Delta V_Z}{\Delta I_Z} = \frac{1}{\left[\dfrac{\Delta I_Z}{\Delta V_Z}\right]} = \frac{1}{\left[\begin{array}{c}\text{Slope of the reverse} \\ \text{characteristics in} \\ \text{zener region}\end{array}\right]} = \frac{1}{\left[\dfrac{I_{Z2}-I_{Z1}}{V_{Z2}-V_{Z1}}\right]}$$

- This value is specified at I_{Zt} and represented as shown in Fig. 1.66.

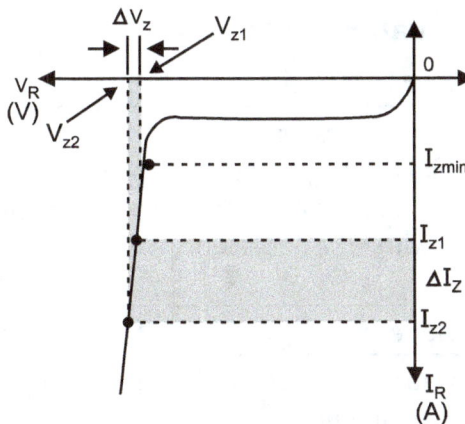

Fig. 1.66: Dynamic Resistance r_Z of Zener Diode

1.12.3 Breakdown Mechanism of Zener Diode

❖ **Important Question Related to this Topic** ❖

Differentiate between Zener breakdown and Avalanche breakdown.

- There are two different breakdown mechanisms in zener diode viz. Zener breakdown and Avalanche breakdown. Usually the zener breakdown is observed at voltages less than approximately 6 V (5 V to 8 V) and avalanche breakdown is observed at voltages greater than 8 V.

1. **Zener Breakdown:**
   o When a reverse voltage (< 6 V) is applied across the zener diode, an intense electric field, of the order of 3×10^5 V/cm, appears across the narrow depletion layer.
   o This strong electric field is capable of breaking the covalent bond and generating the free electrons available for conduction.
   o A large number of such free electrons cause heavy reverse current through the diode. This is called zener breakdown which occurs only for heavily doped diodes.

2. **Avalanche Breakdown:**
   o Avalanche breakdown is due to collisions when a reverse voltage > 6 V is applied across the zener diode.
   o As the magnitude of the reverse bias voltage is increased, the kinetic energy of the minority carriers gets increased. While travelling, the minority carriers collide with the stationary atoms, which in turn results in breaking some of the covalent bonds and generating free electrons.
   o These electrons act as minority carriers. Again they get accelerated by the strong reverse bias field thereby increasing the collision and also the number of free electrons. This is known as carrier multiplication.
   o This process continues leading to a very swift multiplication effect and give rise to a large reverse current in just a few picoseconds. This effect is called as "Avalanche breakdown effect".

1.12.4 Zener Diode Vs Avalanche Diode

Sr. No.	Avalanche breakdown	Zener breakdown
1.	The breaking of covalent bonds is due to the carrier multiplication process in which the highly accelerated free electrons collide with the adjacent atoms.	The breaking of covalent bond is due to intense electric field across the narrow depletion region generating a large number of free electrons to cause breakdown.
2.	Occurs for zener diodes with $V_z > 6$ V.	Occurs for zener diodes with $V_z < 6$ V.
3.	The breakdown voltage increases with increasing junction temperature.	The breakdown voltage decreases with increasing junction temperature.
4.	The temperature coefficient is positive.	The temperature coefficient is negative.

1.12.5 Zener Shunt Voltage Regulator   [May 2013, 2016]

❖ **Important Questions Related to this Topic** ❖

1. With the help of a neat circuit diagram, explain how you will use the zener diode as a regulator. What is the minimum and maximum limit for the load current?
2. Describe with the help of a neat diagram the operation of zener voltage regulator.
3. Draw the circuit diagram of a zener voltage regulator and explain how it gives line and load regulation.

- The reverse characteristic of a zener diode shows that, over the breakdown region, voltage across the zener diode remains constant irrespective of the current that is flowing through it. Therefore the zener diode is used in the reverse biased region for voltage regulation. It is connected in shunt to the load. The circuit diagram of the zener shunt regulator is as shown in Fig. 1.67.

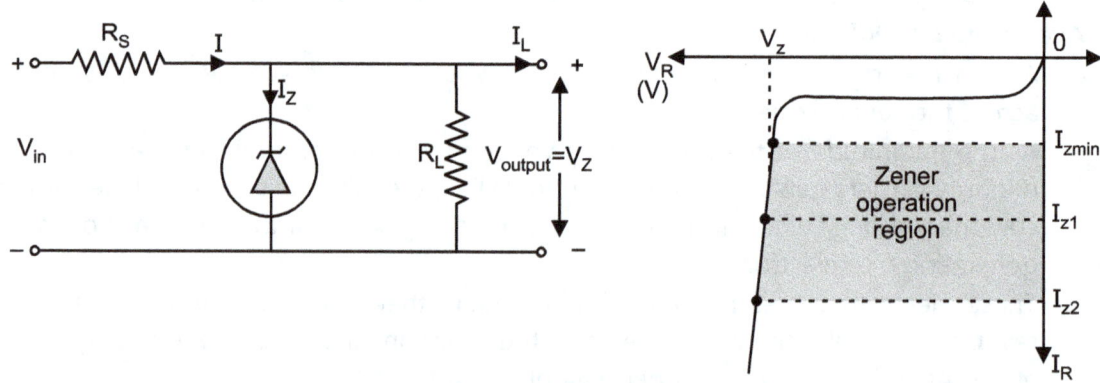

Fig. 1.67: Zener Shunt Regulator

- This circuit is called zener shunt regulator because the controlling element i.e. the zener is connected in parallel with the load.

- As seen from the reverse characteristic of the zener, under reverse biased condition, the current through the zener is very small, of the order of few micro amperes.
- When a sufficient reverse voltage is applied, the electrical breakdown of the zener diode occurs and a large current flows through the diode.
- Resistance R_S is used to limit the reverse current.
- Under breakdown condition, the voltage across zener remains constant equal to V_Z, independent of the variations in the input voltage. Thus, zener diode acts as ideal voltage source which maintains a constant load voltage independent of the current.

1.12.6 The Regulating Action in Zener Shunt Regulator with Varying Input Voltage (R_L Constant)

- We know the output of the zener regulator $V_O = V_Z$ = constant is, $I_L = \dfrac{V_O}{R_L} = \dfrac{V_Z}{R_L}$

- We can say from the above equation, if R_L and V_z are constant; the load current always remains constant $I = I_z + I_L = \dfrac{V_{in} - V_z}{R_S}$.

- From the above equation, we can say that, if the input voltage V_{in} increases, the current through R_S increases. I_L cannot increase as V_z and R_L are constant.
- As the zener diode resistance is much smaller than R_L when it is conducting, this extra current flows through the zener diode to keep the load current constant as long as $I_Z < I_{Zmax}$.
- Therefore, I_L remains constant and so V_O remains constant.

$$I_{max} = I_{Zmax} + I_L$$
$$I_{min} = I_{Zmin} + I_L$$

1.12.7 Regulating Action with Varying Load (Keeping V_{in} Constant)

- Here we consider that R_L is variable and V_{in} is constant.
- $I = \dfrac{V_{in} - V_z}{R_S}$, where I is the total current.
- If the load resistor R_L decreases, load current I_L increases, the current flow through R_S is constant. Hence, the current through the zener diode decreases to keep the output voltage V_O constant.

1.12.8 The Limitations of Zener Regulator

- Overall regulation is poor.
- The output voltage remains constant only when the input voltage is sufficiently large.
- Most of the power is dissipated across R_S therefore the efficiency of the circuit is low.
- If V_i is increased a lot, I_Z may increase beyond limit and hence break down will occur.
- Voltage regulation can be maintained only between the limits typically from 10 mA to 1 A.

Example 1.20: *Design a zener diode shunt regulator to have an output voltage 7.3 V and load current is changed from 25 mA to 110 mA. The input voltage applied to the regulator is 12 V.*

Solution: Given: V_o = 7.3 V, $I_{L\,min}$ = 25 mA, $I_{L\,max}$ = 110 mA, V_{in} = 12 V. The circuit diagram of the zener diode shunt regulator is shown in Fig. 1.68.

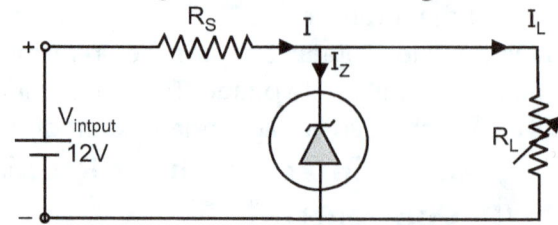

Fig. 1.68: Zener Diode Shunt Regulator

1. Assume $I_{Z\,min}$ = 10% $I_{L\,max}$ and $V_Z = V_O$

$$I_{Z\,min} = 11 \text{ mA and } V_Z = \textbf{7.3 V}$$

2. Select the resistance R_S $R_S = \dfrac{V_{in} - V_Z}{I}$

where

$$I = I_{Z\,min} + I_{L\,max} = 11 \text{ mA} + 110 \text{ mA}$$

$$= \textbf{121 mA}$$

$$R_S = \frac{12 - 7.3}{121 \times 10^{-3}} = 38.84\ \Omega \approx \textbf{39 } \boldsymbol{\Omega}$$

$$P_{R_S} = I^2 R_S = (121 \times 10^{-3})^2 \times 39$$

$$= \textbf{0.56 W}$$

Select the resistance R_S such that the value of R_S = 39 Ω and power rating ≥ 0.56 W.

3. Selection of zener diode:

$$V_O = V_Z = 7.3 \text{ V}$$

$$I_{Z\,max} = I - I_{L\,min} = (121 \text{ mA} - 25 \text{ mA})$$

$$= \textbf{96 mA}$$

Select the zener diode such that V_Z = 7.3 V and current rating ≥ 96 mA.

4. Selection of load resistance:

$$R_{L\,max} = \frac{V_O}{I_{L\,min}} = \frac{7.3}{25 \times 10^{-3}}$$

$$= \textbf{292 } \boldsymbol{\Omega}$$

5. $$R_{L\,min} = \frac{V_O}{I_{L\,max}} = \frac{7.3}{110 \times 10^{-3}} = \textbf{66.36 } \boldsymbol{\Omega}$$

6. $$P_{R_L} = I^2_{L\,max}\,R_{L\,min} = (110 \times 10^{-3})^2 \times 66.36 = \textbf{0.803 W}$$

Select the potentiometer such that the resistance will be changed from 66 Ω to 292 Ω and power rating should be ≥ 0.803 W.

Example 1.21: *For a zener regulator, input voltage varies from 22 V to 28 V, V_O = 18 V. The load current varies from 200 mA to 2 A. Design the suitable zener regulator.*

Solution: Given: V_O = 18 V, $I_{L\,min}$ = 200 mA, $I_{L\,max}$ = 2 A, $V_{in\,min}$ = 22 V and $V_{in\,max}$ = 28 V. The circuit diagram of zener diode shunt regulator is shown in Fig. 1.69.

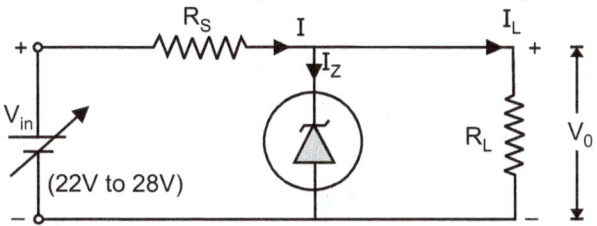

Fig. 1.69: The Circuit Diagram of Zener Diode Shunt Regulator

1. Assume $I_{Z\,min}$ = 10 % $I_{L\,max}$ and $V_Z = V_O$

$$I_{Z\,min} = 0.2 \text{ A and } V_Z = 18 \text{ V}$$

2. **Selection of the resistance R_S:**

$$R_S = \frac{V_{in\,min} - V_Z}{I}$$

Where,

$$I = I_{Z\,min} + I_{L\,max} = 0.2 \text{ A} + 2 \text{ A}$$

$$= \textbf{2.2 A}$$

$$R_S = \frac{22 - 18}{2.2} = 1.82 \ \Omega \approx \textbf{2 } \boldsymbol{\Omega}$$

Find

$$I_{max} = \frac{V_{in\,min} - V_Z}{R_S} = \frac{28 - 18}{2}$$

$$= \textbf{5 A}$$

$$P_{R_S} = I_{max}^2 \ R_S = 5^2 \times 2$$

$$= \textbf{50 W}$$

3. **Selection of zener diode:**

$$V_O = V_Z = 18 \text{ W}$$

$$I_{Z\,max} = I - I_{L\,min} = 5 \text{ A} - 2 \text{ A}$$

$$= \textbf{3 A}$$

Select the zener diode such that V_Z = 18 V and current rating ≥ 3 A.

4. **Selection of load resistance:**

$$R_{L\,max} = \frac{V_O}{I_{L\,min}} = \frac{18}{2} = 9 \ \Omega$$

$$R_{L\,min} = \frac{V_O}{I_{Lmax}} = \frac{18}{200 \times 10^{-3}} = 90 \ \Omega$$

$$P_{R_L} = I_{L\,max}^2 \ R_{L\,min} = (2)^2 \times 9 = \textbf{36 W}$$

Solved Problems on Zener Regulator

Example 1.22: *A zener diode has a Z_Z of 3.5 Ω, V_{ZT} = 6.8 V, I_{ZT} = 37 mA, I_{ZK}= 1 mA. What is voltage across zener terminal when current is 50 mA and 25 mA.*

Solution:

(a) For 50 mA:

$\therefore$
$$\Delta I_Z = I_{given} - I_{ZT} = 50 \text{ mA} - 37 \text{ mA}$$
$$= 13 \text{ mA}$$

$\therefore$
$$\Delta V_Z = \Delta I_Z \times Z_Z$$
$$= 13 \times 10^{-3} \times 3.5 \ \Omega$$
$$\Delta V_Z = + 45.5 \text{ mV}$$
$$V_{Z \text{ total}} = V_{ZT} + \Delta V_Z$$
$$= 6.8 + 45.5 \text{ mV}$$
$$= \mathbf{6.85 \text{ V}}$$

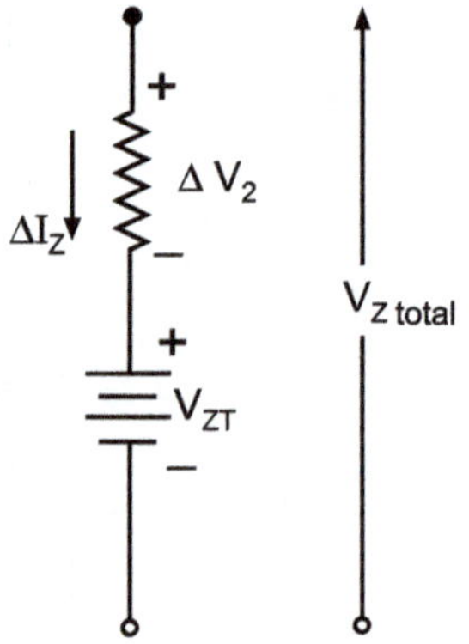

Fig. 1.70

(b) For 25 mA:

$$\Delta I_Z = I_{Z \text{ given}} - I_{ZT}$$
$$= 25 \text{ mA} - 37 \text{ mA}$$
$$\Delta I_Z = -12 \text{ mA}$$
$$\Delta V_Z = \Delta Z_Z \times \Delta I_Z$$
$$= 3.5 \ \Omega \times -12 \times 10^{-3}$$
$$\Delta V_Z = -42 \text{ mV}$$
$$V_{Z \text{ total}} = V_{ZT} + \Delta V_Z$$
$$= 6.8 + (-42 \text{ mV})$$
$$V_{Z \text{ total}} = \mathbf{6.76 \text{ V}}$$

Example 1.23: *For 10 V zener diode shown in Fig. 1.71, calculate range of input voltage over which zener diode will maintain constant voltage across its terminals, I_{ZK} = 0.25 mA and 1_{ZM} = 100 mA.*

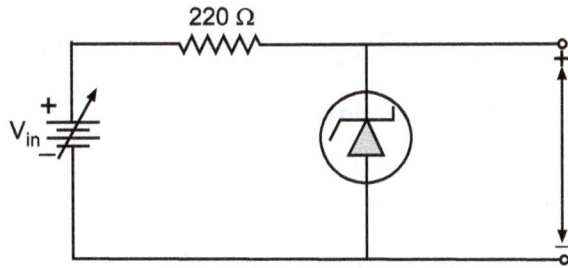

Fig. 1.71

Solution:

(a) V_R for minimum zener current:

$$V_R = I_{ZK} \times R$$
$$= (0.25 \text{ mA}) (220 \text{ } \Omega) \textbf{ = 55 mV}$$
$$V_R = V_{in} - V_Z$$
$$\therefore \quad V_{in \, min} = V_R + V_Z$$
$$= 55 \text{ mV} + 10 = \textbf{10.055 V}$$

(b) V_Z for maximum zener current:

V_R for maximum zener current

$$V_R = I_{ZM} \times R$$
$$= (100 \text{ mA}) \times (220 \text{ } \Omega)$$
$$\therefore \quad V_R \textbf{ = 22 V}$$
$$V_{in \, max} = V_R + V_Z$$
$$= 22 + 10 = \textbf{32 V}$$

10.055 V to 32 V is range of input voltage to be regulated and output is approximately 10 V.

Example 1.24: *Determine minimum and maximum load current for which zener diode will maintain its regulation. What is minimum R_L used. V_Z = 12 V, I_{ZK} = 1 mA, I_{ZM} = 50 mA. Assume Z_Z = 0 Ω.*

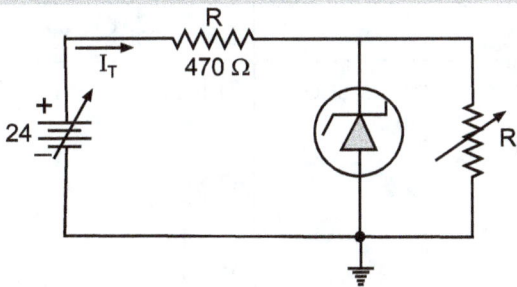

Fig. 1.72

Solution: (a) To find total current:

$$I_T = \frac{V_{in} - V_Z}{R}$$

$$= \frac{24-12}{470} = 25.5 \times 10^{-3} A = \textbf{25.5 mA}$$

(b) For minimum load current: Assume $I_L = 0$

$$I_T = I_{Z(max)}, \text{ for } I_L = 0$$

$$R_L = \infty$$

$$I_{Z(max)} = I_T = \frac{V_{in} - V_Z}{R} = \frac{24-12}{470}$$

$$\therefore \qquad I_{Z\,max} = \textbf{25.5 mA}$$

As $I_{Z\,max} < I_{ZM}$, $I_L = 0$ is acceptable minimum value because zener can handle 25.5 mA, if R_L is removed from circuit.

(c)
$$I_{L\,max} = I_T - I_{ZK}$$
$$= 25.5 \text{ mA} - 1 \text{ mA} = \textbf{24.5 mA}$$

(d)
$$R_{L\,min} = \frac{V_Z}{I_{L\,max}} = \textbf{490 } \Omega$$

Applications of Zener Diode:

- Zener diodes are used in voltage regulators.
- It is used in various protection circuits.
- It is used in clipping circuits.

1.13 COMPARISON OF RECTIFIER AND REGULATOR

❖ Important Question Related to this Topic ❖

Compare rectifier circuit with regulator.

Sr. No.	Regulator	Rectifier
1.	Converts the pulsating DC input into constant DC output.	Converts alternating input into pulsating DC output.
2.	The ideal output should be as shown below. 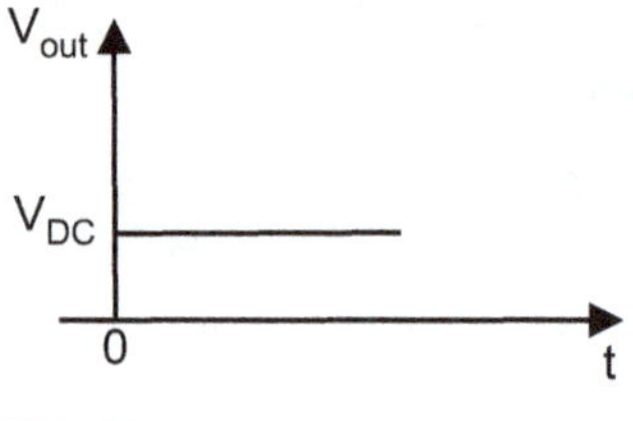	The output of rectifier is as shown below. 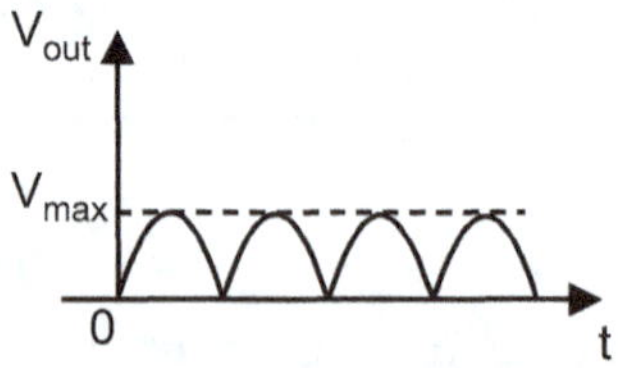
3.	The output is ripple free.	The output contains ripples.

...Conti.

4.	Ideally the output voltage should be independent of changes in load current, input voltage and temperature.	As the diode characteristics change with changes in load current, input voltage and temperature, the output voltage keeps changing.
5.	Uses devices such as transistors, op-amps etc.	Uses diodes.
6.	The examples are zener regulator, transistorized regulator etc.	The examples are half-wave, full-wave and bridge rectifiers.

1.14 LED (LIGHT EMITTING DIODES) DEVICE STRUCTURE

❖ Important Question Related to this Topic ❖

Explain the principle of operation of LED. State the various materials used to fabricate LEDs.

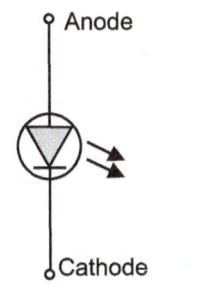

Fig. 1.73: Symbol of LED

- An LED emits light when forward biased. So it is an optical device.

- In Light Emitting Diodes (LEDs), light is produced by a solid state process called **electroluminescence**. When a free electron recombines with a hole, it falls from the conduction band to the valance band. Therefore the energy level associated with it changes from a higher value to a lower value. The energy associated with it is released in the form of heat in case of normal diodes whereas; in LEDs, this energy is given out in the form of photons which emit the light energy.

- The efficiency of a device in converting electrical power to visible light is called "luminous performance" and is measured in lumens/watt.

1.14.1 Construction of LED

- LED can be constructed by depositing three semiconductor layers on a substrate as shown in Fig. 1.74. Light is emitted in the active region, between p-type and n-type semiconductor layers, when an electron and hole recombine.

- When the diode is forward biased, holes from the p-type material and electrons from the n-type material are both driven into the active region. The light is produced by a solid-state process called **electroluminescence**.

- The LED structure is placed in a tiny reflective cup to emit the light from the active layer. In this particular design, the layers of the LED emit light all the way around the layered structure.

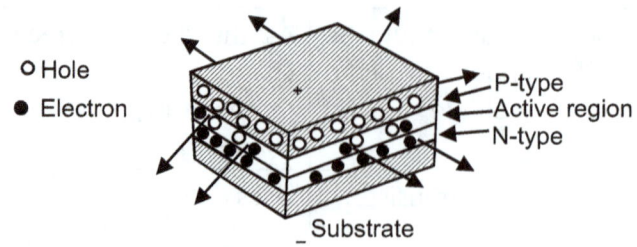

Fig. 1.74: Typical LED Device Structure

1.14.2 Colours and Materials

> ❖ **Important Question Related to this Topic** ❖
>
> List different materials used in LEDs alongwith the colour of light emitted.

- The colour of the emitted light is decided by its wavelength which depends on the forbidden energy gap. This gap differs from material to material. Hence, we get different colours from different materials. Conventional LEDs are made from a variety of inorganic semiconductor materials. The following table shows the available colours with wavelength range, voltage drop and material.

Colour	Semiconductor Material
Infrared	Gallium arsenide (GaAs),Aluminium gallium arsenide (AlGaAs).
Green	Indium gallium nitride (InGaN), Gallium(III) nitride (GaN), Gallium(III) phosphide (GaP), Aluminium gallium indium phosphide (AlGaInP), Aluminium gallium phosphide (AlGaP).
Red	Aluminium gallium arsenide (AlGaAs), Gallium arsenide phosphide (GaAsP), Gallium(III) phosphide (GaP).
Orange	Gallium arsenide phosphide (GaAsP), Aluminium gallium indium phosphide (AlGaInP), Gallium(III) phosphide (GaP).
Yellow	Gallium arsenide phosphide (GaAsP), Aluminium gallium indium phosphide (AlGaInP), Gallium(III) phosphide (GaP).

1.14.3 The Characteristic of LED

> ❖ **Important Questions Related to this Topic** ❖
>
> Justify the following in one sentence:
> 1. In what bias condition is an LED normally operated?
> 2. What happens to the light emission of LED as the forward current increases?

- When an LED is forward biased, as shown in Fig. 1.75 (b), to the threshold of conduction, its current increases rapidly and must be controlled to prevent destruction of the device. So a resistor is connected in series with the LED to limit the current. As seen from Fig. 1.75, the light output is quite linearly proportional to the current within its active region, i.e. as the forward current increases, the light output also increases. So the light output can be precisely modulated to send an undistorted signal through a fiber optic cable.

- When forward biased, the voltage drop across the conducting LED (V_D) is about 2 to 3 volts which is much greater than that across Si or Ge. The reverse breakdown voltage of LED is about 3 to 10 volts.

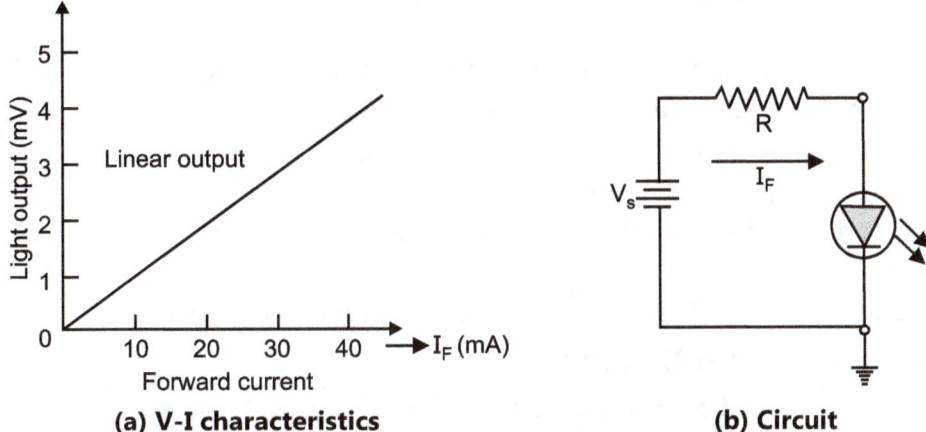

(a) V-I characteristics   **(b) Circuit**

Fig. 1.75: LED in Forward Biased Condition

Advantages of Using LEDs:

- LEDs are light in weight and small in size. Hence, a large number of LEDs can be packed together in a small space.
- They have longer life.
- They are available in various colours.
- Can be turned on and off at a high speed.
- The brightness of the emitted light of the LEDs can be changed by controlling the current passing through them.
- LEDs can be interfaced with the electronic circuits easily.
- They do not contain any toxic material.
- They are shock resistant.

Disadvantages of using LEDs:

- **Temperature Dependence:** LED performance largely depends on the ambient temperature of the operating environment.
- **Voltage Sensitivity:** LEDs must be supplied with the voltage above the threshold and a current below the rating. This can involve series resistors or current-regulated power supplies.
- **Luminous Efficiency:** Luminous efficiency of the LEDs is low, about 1.5 lumen/watt.
- **Power:** Needs large power for the operation compared to normal p-n junction diode.

Applications of LEDs:

> **❖ Important Question Related to this Topic ❖**
>
> State applications of LEDs.

- Used in visual signal applications where the light goes more or less directly from the LED to the human eye, to convey a message or meaning e.g. alphabetical displays at railway stations.
- Used where LED light is reflected from the object to give visual response.
- LEDs are also used to generate light for measuring and interacting with processes.
- Used in opto-isolators.
- Used in fiber optic data transmission.
- Used in remote controls of most of the home-entertainment units to transmit data to the main unit.
- Specialized white LEDs are used in flat-panel computer displays.

1.14.4 Seven Segment Display

> **❖ Important Questions Related to this Topic ❖**
>
> 1. Write a note on seven segment display.
> 2. What are the two types of seven segment display ?

- LED displays are packages of many LEDs arranged in a pattern, the most familiar pattern being the 7-segment displays for showing numbers (digits 0-9).
- The 7 segment display is used in many types of test equipments as a numerical indicator.
- The arrangement and labeling of the segments is as shown in Fig. 1.76. It is an assembly of light emitting diodes which can be powered individually. Most commonly they emit red light.

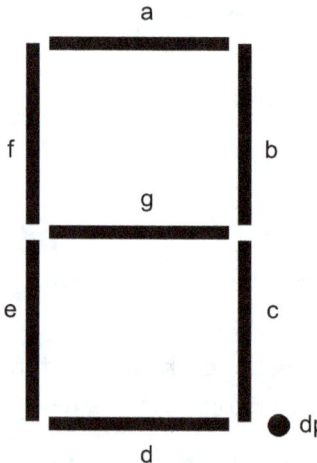

- Numbers from 0 to 9 can be displayed on the display. Depending upon the number to be displayed, corresponding segments are powered. E.g. powering all the segments simultaneously displays the number 8. To display the number 3, the segments a, b, c, d and g are powered. The 'dp' represents a decimal point.
- A current limiting resistor must be placed in series with each diode to limit the current through it to a safe value.

Fig. 1.76 (a) : Basic Seven Segment LED Display

- **The Two Types of Seven Segment Display are:**
  1. Common anode type,
  2. Common cathode type.

1. **Common Anode Type Seven Segment Display:**

   In this type, all anodes of LEDs are connected together to $+V_{cc}$ and the cathodes are connected individually to zero volts. A current limiting resistor is connected between the cathode and ground. To activate a particular segment, in this type of connection, the particular digit must go low. So this type of display is called active low display. The connections are as shown below:

   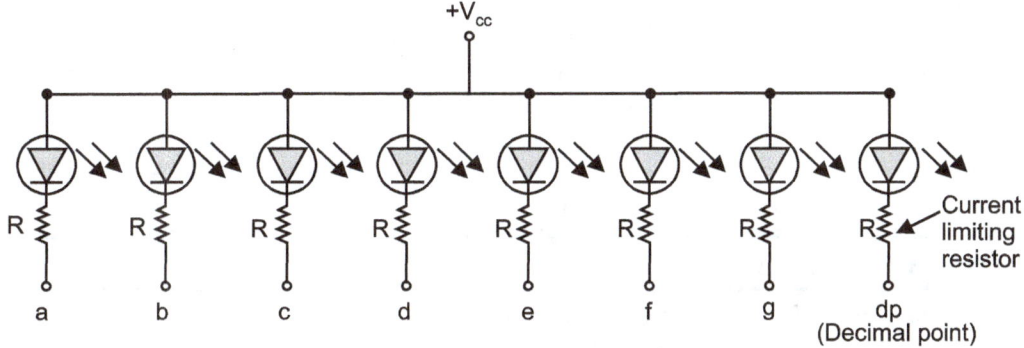

   Fig. 1.76 (b) : Common Anode Type

2. **Common Cathode Type Seven Segment Display:**

   In this type, all cathodes of LEDs are connected together to the ground. And a current limiting resistor is connected between the anode and $+V_{cc}$. To activate a particular segment, in this type of connection, the particular digit must go high. So this type of display is called **active high** display. The connections are shown below:

   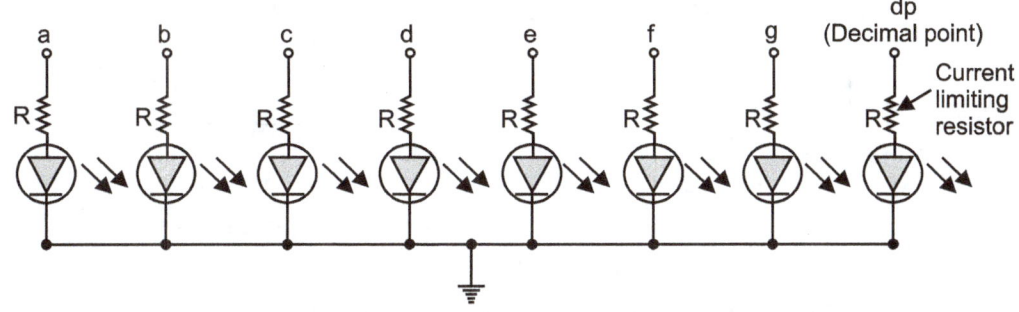

   Fig. 1.77: Common Cathode Type

- Various digits can be displayed by illuminating individual segments as shown below in the table:

Digits Can Be Shown By Illuminating The Individual Segment As Shown

Digit Shown	Illuminated segment (1 = illumination)						
	a	b	c	d	e	f	g
0	1	1	1	1	1	1	0
1	0	1	1	0	0	0	0
2	1	1	0	1	1	0	1
3	1	1	1	1	0	0	1
4	0	1	1	0	0	1	1
5	1	0	1	1	0	1	1
6	1	0	1	1	1	1	1
7	1	1	1	0	0	0	0
8	1	1	1	1	1	1	1
9	1	1	1	1	0	1	1

1.15 PHOTODIODE   [May 2016]

- Photodiodes are efficient light detectors and working function of a photodiode is just opposite to the working function of LED in a sense that photodiode converts light into an electrical signal.
- The photodiode is a device that operates in reverse bias as shown in Fig. 1.78 (a), where Iλ is the reverse current.
- The photodiode has a small transparent window that allows light to strike the PN junction.
- An alternate symbol of photodiode is shown in Fig. 1.78 (b).

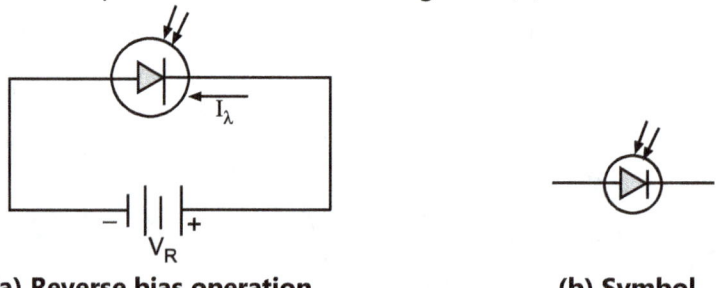

(a) Reverse bias operation   **(b) Symbol**
Fig. 1.78: Photodiode

- In P-N junction diode reverse leakage current flows in reverse bias condition. The same is true for a photodiode.
- The reverse current is produced by thermally generated electron-hole pairs in depletion region which are swept across the PN junction by the electric field created by the reverse voltage.

- Difference between PN junction diode and photodiode is, when junction is exposed to light, the reverse current increases with the light intensity.
- When there is no incident light the reverse current Iλ is very small, it may be neglected and is called as dark current.
- An increase in amount of light intensity, expressed as irradiance (mW/cm^2), produces an increase in the reverse current as shown by graph in Fig. 1.79.

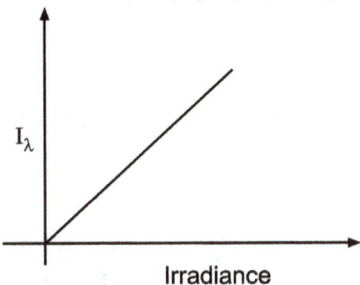

Irradiance

Fig. 1.79: Graph of Reverse Current Vs Irradiance

QUESTIONS

1. Explain with diagrams and graphs, the way of biasing a P-N junction diode and variation of the diode current with the voltage across the diode.
2. Draw and explain the V-I characteristics of Zener diode. What are two breakdown mechanisms in a zener diode?
3. Differentiate between Zener breakdown and Avalanche breakdown.
4. Explain principle of operation of LED. State various materials used to fabricate LEDs.
5. What is rectification? With the help of neat circuit diagram and waveforms explain the operation of a half wave rectifier circuit.
6. Define the following terms and explain their significance in relation with rectifying circuit:
   (a) Ripple factor
   (b) Rectification efficiency.
7. What is Voltage Regulation of a rectifier? Explain line regulation using zener diode.
8. Compare FWR with center tapped transformer and HWR.
9. With the help of neat circuit diagram and waveforms, explain the operation of a FWR using two diodes. Why is it called as a full wave circuit?
10. State the expression for ripple factor of a capacitor input filter with HWR and FWR and explain its significance.
11. What is a filter? Explain its necessity in the rectifier circuits.
12. List demerits of unregulated power supply.
13. Draw a neat circuit diagram of bridge rectifier with capacitor filter and explain its operation, with appropriate waveforms.

14. For a center-tapped full wave rectifier without filter, derive the expression for:
    (a) DC load current
    (b) Ripple factor.

15. With the help of a neat circuit diagram, explain how you will use zener diode as a regulator. What is minimum and maximum limit of load current.

16. Draw the circuit diagram and output voltage waveform of bridge rectifier. Also derive expression for V_{dc} and V_{rms}.

17. Write short note on Photodiode.

18. Explain the working of common cathode 7-segment LED display with the status of each segment for the digits from 0 to 9.

19. Justify:
    (a) In what biasing condition LED is normally operated?
    (b) What happen to the light emission of an LED as the forward current increases?

20. For a Bridge Wave Rectifier derive the expression for following parameters:
    (a) I_{dc}
    (b) V_{dc}
    (c) P_{dc}
    (d) Ripple factor

21. List different materials used in LEDs alongwith the colour of light emitted.

22. Explain how the DC output voltage of a Full Wave Rectifier is improved when capacitor filter is used? Draw waveforms of the load voltage and diode currents.

23. What is clipper? Describe the operation of positive and negative clippers with the help of circuit diagrams.

24. Explain the operation of biased clipper and combination of clipper.

25. What is clamper? Explain the operation of a clamping circuit with the help of circuit diagram and waveforms.

26. Differentiate between positive clamper and negative clamper.

27. Draw and explain voltage doubler using P-N junction diode.

28. Explain the working of Voltage tripler with neat circuit diagram.

29. Draw and explain the working of Voltage quadrupler with neat circuit diagram.

30. Explain clipping and clamping circuits in detail.

31. What are clippers? Explain.

32. What are clampers? Explain.

33. What is Voltage doubler? Explain.

34. Draw and explain working of Photodiode. Also give its applications.

UNIVERSITY QUESTIONS

Dec. 2012

1. Compare performance of half-wave rectifier and full-wave rectifier with respect to following parameters.

    (1) I_{DC}, (2) V_{DC}, (3) I_{rms} (4) Rectifier efficiency, (5) TUF, (6) PIV of diodes used, (7) Ripple factor. **[6]**

May 2013

1. Explain with V-1 characteristics the working of zener diode as voltage regulator. **[6]**

Dec. 2013

1. Draw the circuit of series negative clipper and explain its operation along with the waveform. **[6]**

2. Draw the waveform across R_L in clamping circuit. **[6]**

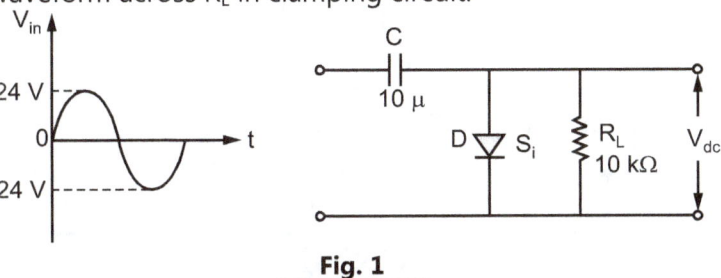

Fig. 1

May 2014

1. Explain Voltage tripler and quadrupler circuit. **[6]**

2. Explain working principle of photo diode with characteristics. Why photodiode is operated in reverse biased mode when used as a optical detector. **[6]**

Oct. 2014

1. Compare performance of half wave rectifier and full wave rectifier with respect to following parameters: **[6]**

    (1) IDC, (2) Irms, (3) Rectifier efficiency, (4) Ripple factor, (5) PIV, (6) TUF.

2. Determine the O/P waveforms for the circuit shown in Fig. **[6]**

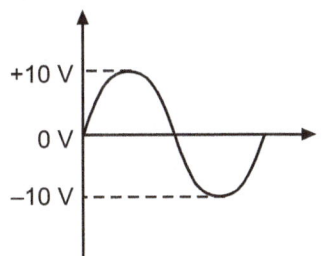
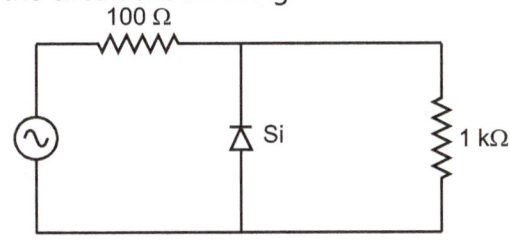

Fig. 2

May 2015

1. Explain the working of positive biased shunt clipper with its input and output waveforms. **[6]**

2. Explain the working of positive clamper with its waveforms. **[6]**

Nov. 2015

1. Compare half wave and full wave rectifier. **[6]**

2. Determine output waveform for the circuit shown in Fig. 1 : **[6]**

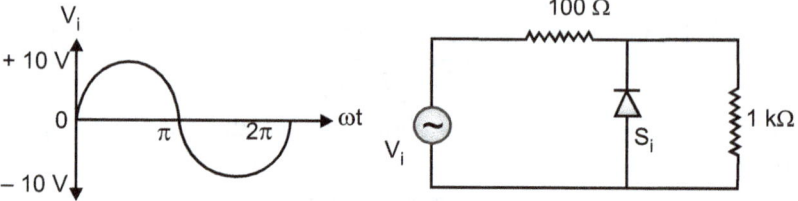

Fig. 3

May 2016

1. Draw and Explain full wave rectifier with capacitor filter. **[6]**

2. Explain with V-I characteristics the working of Zener diode as a voltage regulator. **[6]**

◈ ◈ ◈

BIPOLAR JUNCTION TRANSISTOR (BJT) CIRCUITS

2.1 INTRODUCTION

❖ **Important Question Related to this Topic** ❖

1. What is a transistor?
2. Explain: Transistor means "transfer-resistor".

- As we have studied in the last chapter, a diode is mainly used for rectification. It cannot be used for amplification of the input signal. A **transistor** is a semiconductor device that can **amplify** electronic signals. It is also used as a **switch** in digital electronics. Transistor was first invented by William Shockley in 1951. Transistor is the fundamental building block of modern electronic systems. It is also used in integrated circuits.
- The main advantages of transistor are low cost, small size, flexibility and reliability.
- A transistor has three terminals viz. Base, Emitter and Collector. It can be operated in three different configurations as, Common Base, Common Emitter and Common Collector.
- In a transistor, amplification is achieved by passing input current signal from a region of low resistance to a region of high resistance. Hence the name Transfer-resistor, that is a transistor.

2.2 FEATURES OF BIPOLAR JUNCTION TRANSISTOR (BJT)

- BJT is a bipolar active device. The current in a transistor flows due to both, majority and minority charge carriers (i.e. holes and electrons) and hence the name Bipolar Junction Transistor.
- It is a current operated device. (The output current is controlled by input current).
- BJTs are basically of two types: N-P-N and P-N-P.
- The unique feature of BJT is that it provides high bandwidth.

2.3 CONSTRUCTION OF BIPOLAR JUNCTION TRANSISTOR (BJT)

❖ **Important Questions Related to this Topic** ❖

1. Why is the collector region greater than the emitter region?
2. Give reasons: A transistor cannot be replaced by two back-to-back connected diodes.

- An NPN transistor is formed by sandwiching a single p-type semiconductor between two n-type semiconductors (i.e. N-P-N).

- And a PNP transistor is formed by sandwiching a single n-type semiconductor between two p-type semiconductors (i.e. P-N-P) as shown in Fig. 2.1.

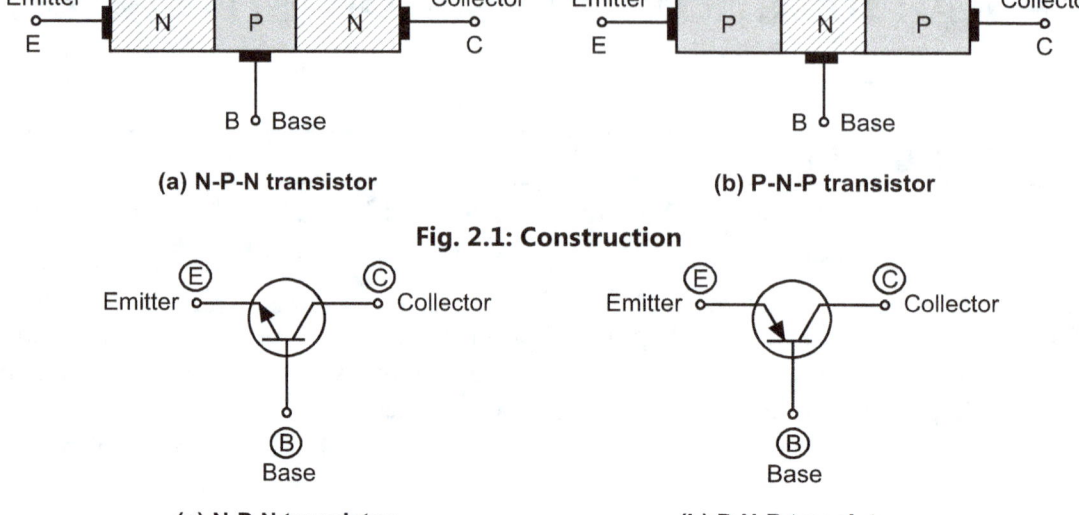

(a) N-P-N transistor   (b) P-N-P transistor

Fig. 2.1: Construction

(a) N-P-N transistor   (b) P-N-P transistor

Fig. 2.2: Symbol

Few Important Properties of a Transistor:

- We have seen in chapter 1, that the process of adding impurities to a pure Semiconductor is called **doping**. In transistors,

- The emitter and collector layers are heavily doped and are much wider than the base region.

- The middle region is called the base. It is lightly doped.

- The emitter doping level is greater than the collector doping level.

- As the collector has to handle more power than the emitter, therefore its area is greater than the area of the emitter, for proper heat dissipation.

- As shown in the Fig. 2.3 below, the two p-n junctions present in a transistor are **base-emitter junction** and **collector-base junction**.

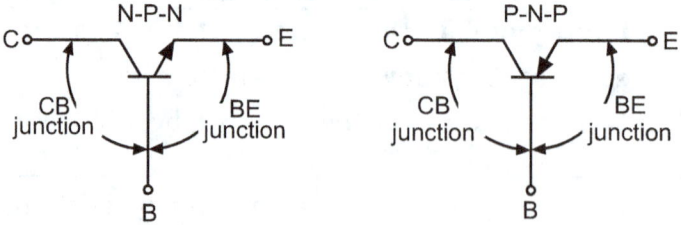

Fig. 2.3: Two Diode Equivalent of Transistor

2.3.1 Transistor Analogy by Two Diodes

❖ **Important Question Related to this Topic** ❖

Explain why depletion layer width at the collector junction is more than the depletion layer at the emitter junction.

- As shown in the Fig. 2.4, two diodes connected back to back, cannot work as a transistor due to the unique properties of a transistor mentioned earlier. i.e.

- Doping levels of the base, emitter and collector regions are different; which cannot be achieved by connecting two diodes back-to-back.

- Also a transistor works due to the diffusion process which occurs in between the forward biased emitter-base junction and reverse biased base-collector junction. Such diffusion process cannot take place in two different diodes connected together.

- The collector region is greater than the emitter region. This condition also cannot be achieved in two different diodes.

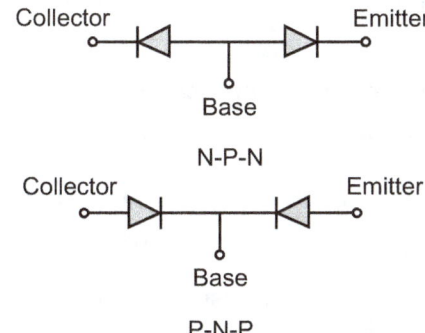

Fig. 2.4: Two Diode Transistor Analogy

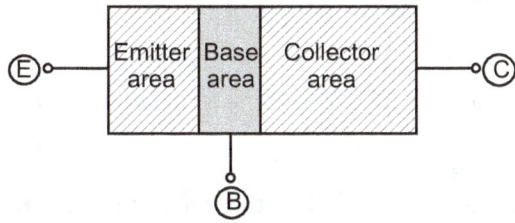

Fig. 2.5: Practically The Area of Base < Emitter < Collector

2.3.2 An Unbiased Transistor

- The two junctions formed in a transistor are **collector-base** (also known as **collector junction**) and **emitter-base** (also known as **emitter junction**).

- Unbiased transistor means a transistor without any external applied voltage or biasing. In this condition two different depletion regions are formed due to **diffusion** process at the two junctions' viz. the collector junction and the emitter junction.

- Due to **heavy doping of the emitter as compared to the collector,** the depletion region across the C-B junction is larger than the depletion region across the B-E junction. Refer Fig. 2.6.

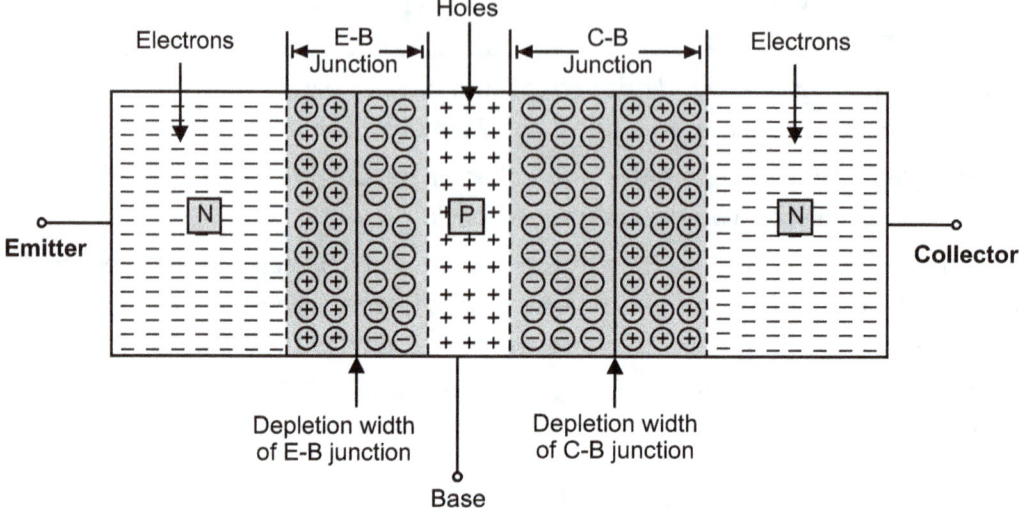

Fig. 2.6: Width of Depletion Region Across C-B Junction > B-E Junction

2.3.3 Biasing of a Transistor

❖ Important Question Related to this Topic ❖
State the biasing conditions required for the three regions of operations of a BJT.

- Applying proper external voltage to a transistor is known as **biasing**. A biased transistor can be operated in two modes:

  1. Transistor as an amplifier.

  2. Transistor as a switch.

- A transistor can be operated in three different regions viz. **Active, Saturation and cut-off.**

Region	Base-emitter junction	Collector-Base junction	Mode of Transistor
Active	Forward biased	Reverse biased	Amplifier
Saturation	Forward biased	Forward biased	Switch is closed
Cut-off	Reverse biased	Reverse biased	Switch is open

- Fig. 2.7 shows the biasing circuit for both N-P-N and P-N-P transistors to operate it in active region. The base-emitter junction is forward biased and the base-collector junction is reverse biased.

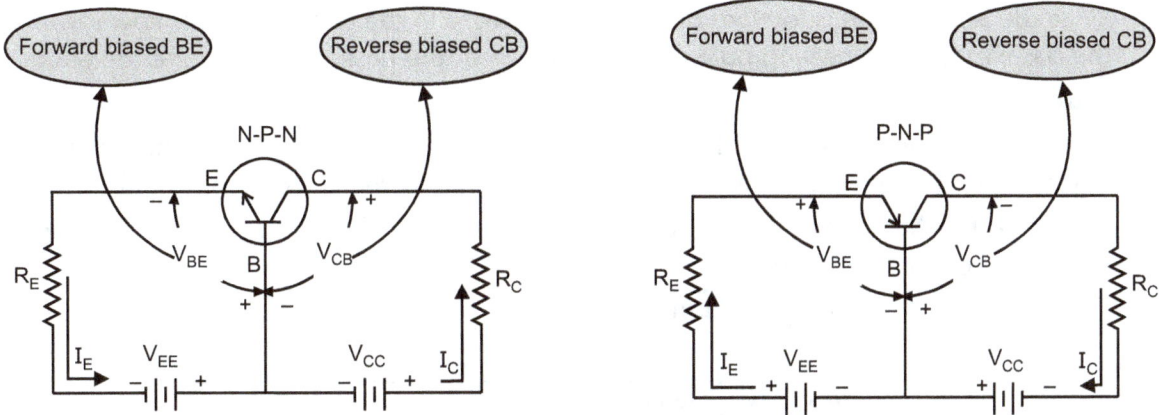

(a) Biased N-P-N Transistor (b) Biased P-N-P Transistor

Fig. 2.7: Transistor in The Amplifier Mode (Active Region)

2.4 WORKING OF N-P-N TRANSISTOR IN ACTIVE REGION

❖ **Important Questions Related to this Topic** ❖

1. Explain the working of a NPN transistor.
2. Explain the working of a PNP transistor.

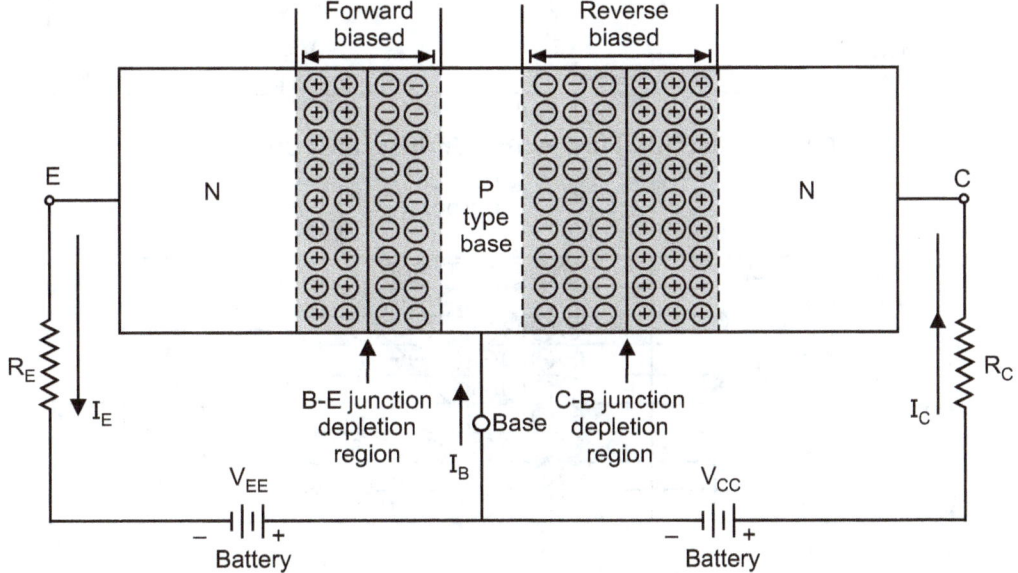

Fig. 2.8: Representation of NPN Transistor Internal in Active Region

The D.C. sources V_{EE} and V_{CC} are applied in such a way that, they **forward bias the B-E junction** and **reverse bias the C-B junction**. Therefore, the depletion region of B-E junction is less than that of the C-B junction as shown in Fig. 2.8 above.

Since the B-E junction is forward biased, the electrons in the N-type emitter flow towards the base; they combine with holes in the P-region of the base and constitute the emitter current I_E.

As the base region is thin and lightly doped, it has less number of holes, therefore very few electrons get injected into the base from the emitter; they recombine with holes and constitute the base current I_B as shown in Fig. 2.9. Therefore base current is small as compared to emitter current.

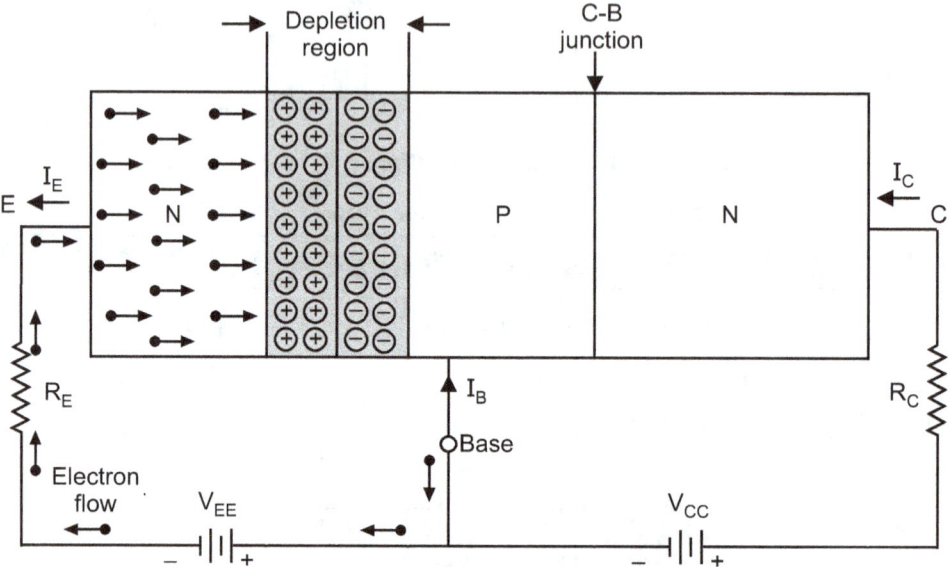

Fig. 2.9: Electron Flow Across Emitter-Base Junction

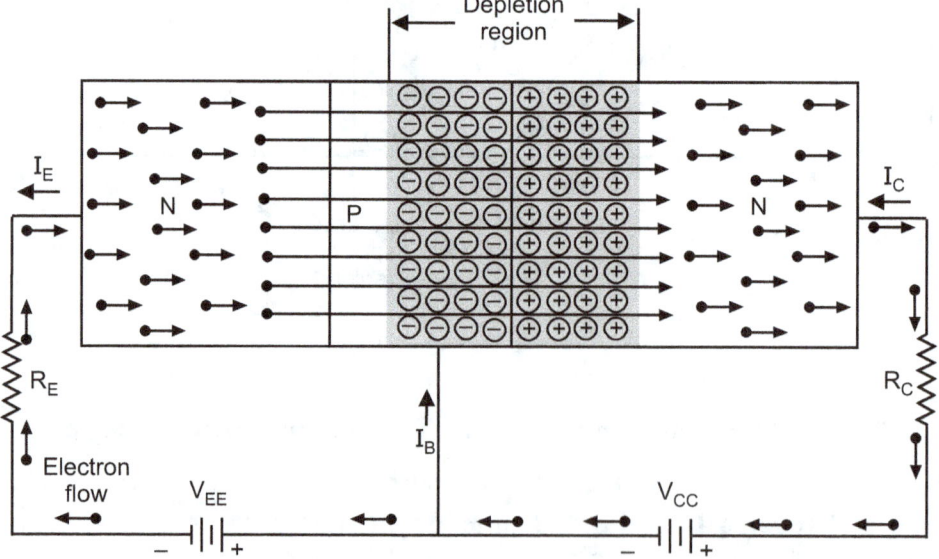

Fig. 2.10: Large Collector Current Due to Large Number of Electrons

The remaining large number of electrons cross the base region, the C-B depletion region and move through the collector region to the positive terminal of the external battery and constitute the collector current I_C as shown in Fig. 2.10. Thus most of the electrons from the emitter flow in the collector region hence the collector current I_C is always greater than the base current I_B.

Thus, we can say that: $I_E = I_B + I_C$ Where $I_C >> I_B$. Hence $I_E \approx I_C$

The current gain of a transistor is $\beta = \dfrac{I_C}{I_B}$, $I_C >> I_B$.

2.5 WORKING OF P-N-P TRANSISTOR IN ACTIVE REGION

- In P-N-P transistor, the majority charge carriers are holes instead of electrons.

- Here, we should note that, the only difference made is, the polarities of V_{EE} and V_{CC} are reversed. Remaining operation remains exactly the same as compared to the operation of NPN transistors.

- The B-E junction is forward biased and the C-B junction is reverse biased. Therefore the depletion width of the B-E junction is less than that of the C-B junction as shown in Fig. 2.11.

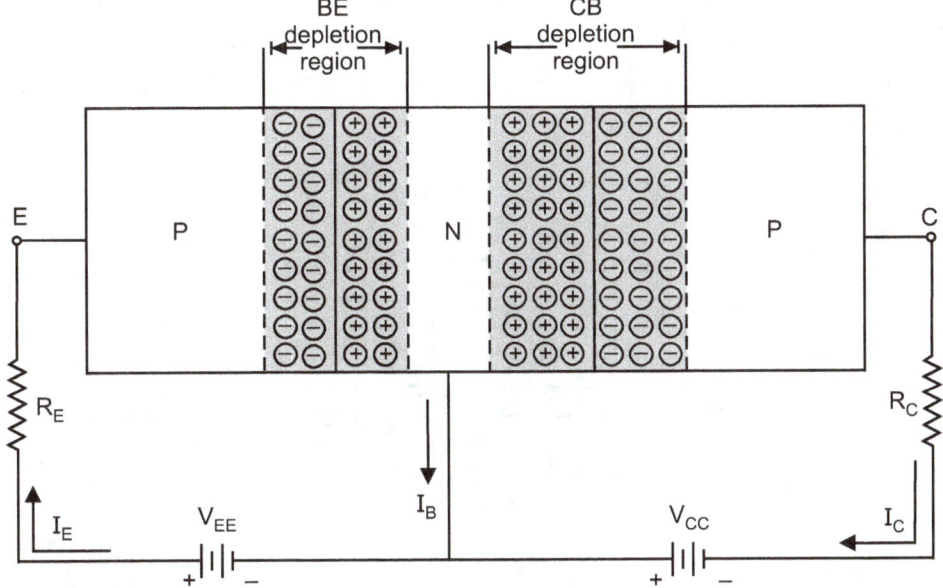

Fig. 2.11: Representation of P-N-P transistor Internal in Active Region

- The forward biased B-E junction causes the holes in the P-type emitter to flow towards the base, these holes combine with electrons in the N-region of base and constitute the emitter current I_E.

As the base region is lightly doped and is very thin, there are very few electrons. So very few holes get injected into the base and recombine with the electrons, to constitute the base current I_B as shown in Fig. 2.12.

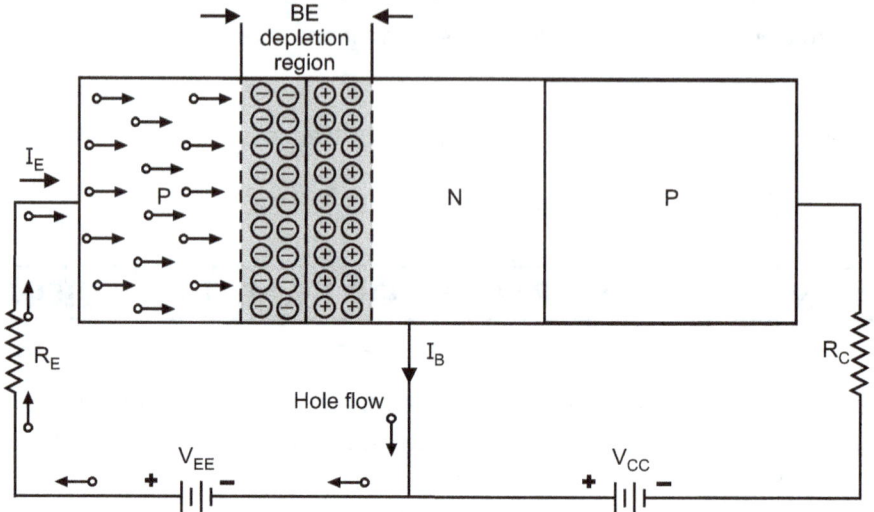

Fig. 2.12: Holes Flow Across Base-Emitter Junction

- The remaining large number of holes cross the base region, the C-B depletion region and move through the collector area to the negative terminal of the external battery and constitute the collector current I_C as shown in Fig. 2.13. Thus, most of holes from the emitter flow in the collector hence the collector current I_C is always greater than the base current I_B.

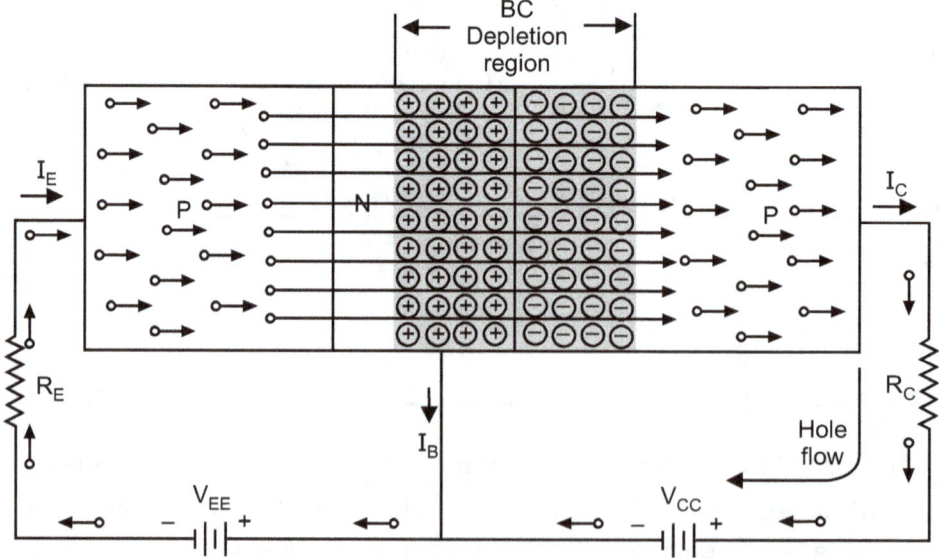

Fig. 2.13: Large Collector Current due to Large number of Holes

2.6 CONVENTIONAL CURRENT DIRECTIONS IN THE N-P-N AND P-N-P TRANSISTORS

- As shown in Fig. 2.14, the base current flows into the terminal of NPN transistor; whereas in PNP transistor, the base current flows away from the base terminal. Similarly note all the current directions from the figure below.

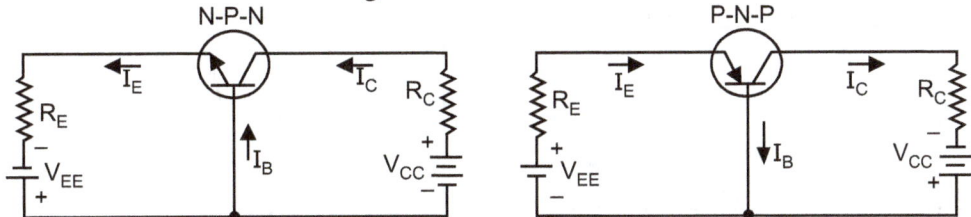

Fig. 2.14: Conventional Current Directions

2.7 CONFIGURATIONS OF BJT

- BJT can be configured in three different operating modes, depending upon the terminal that is made common for both input and output, as below:

  Common base configuration in which base is common to input and output.

  Common emitter configuration in which emitter is common to input and output.

  Common collector configuration in which collector is common to input and output.

- We should always remember that, regardless of the configuration used, for a transistor to operate as an amplifier, in the active region, B-E junction is always forward biased, and C-B junction is always reverse biased.

2.8 COMMON BASE CONFIGURATION   [Dec. 2013]

❖ **Important Questions Related to this Topic** ❖

1. Draw and explain the input and output characteristics of a transistor CB configuration.
2. Explain the transfer characteristics of CB configuration.
3. What is early effect? How can it account for the CB input characteristics?
4. What is punch through effect?
5. Sketch the CB output characteristics for a transistor. Indicate the active, cut-off and saturation regions. Explain the shapes of the curve qualitatively.

- In common base configuration, the input is applied between Base-Emitter and output is taken from Base-Collector, i.e. keeping the Base common to both input and output.

- As shown in the figure above, V_{EE} and V_{CC} are the external D.C. sources for biasing the transistor in active region i.e. to keep B-E junction forward biased and C-B junction reverse biased. R_E and R_C are the current limiting resistors.

- The input voltage is V_{BE} and input current is I_E, whereas output voltage is V_{CB} and output current is I_C.

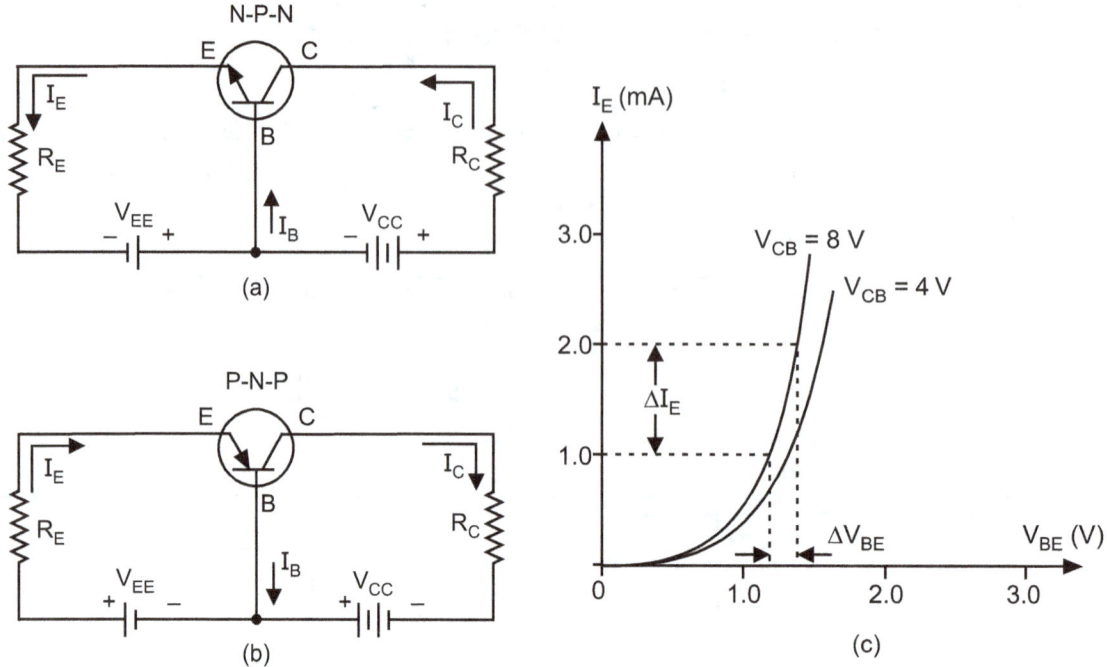

(a & b): Common Base Configuration   **(c): Input Characteristics of Transistor**

Using NPN and PNP   **in CB Configuration**

Fig. 2.15

2.8.1 Input Characteristics of Common Base Configuration

- The input characteristic of the common base configuration is, the plot of V_{BE} and I_E keeping V_{CB} constant. It is as shown in Fig. 2.15 (c).

- This characteristic is similar to that of a forward biased diode. As the input voltage V_{BE} is increased gradually, after cut-in voltage i.e. 0.3 V for germanium and 0.7 V for silicon, we see a rapid increase in the input current I_E with a small increment in V_{BE}.

- That means the input resistance is very small. It is called the Dynamic input resistance of a transistor and is given by

$$r_{i/p} = \left. \frac{\Delta V_{BE}}{\Delta I_E} \right|_{\text{at } V_{CB} = \text{constant}}$$

- Also, we can observe that, there is a slight increase in I_E with increase in V_{CB}. This is due to increase in the width of the depletion region at the base in reverse biased condition.

- With increase in the reverse bias voltage V_{CB}, the width of depletion region also gets increased, reducing the electrical base width. This increases the concentration of charge carriers, which causes more diffusion of electrons from N-type of emitter to

P-type of base, in turn slightly increasing I_E. This is known as **'Early effect'**. It is also known as **'Base Width Modulation'.** It is shown in Fig. 2.16.

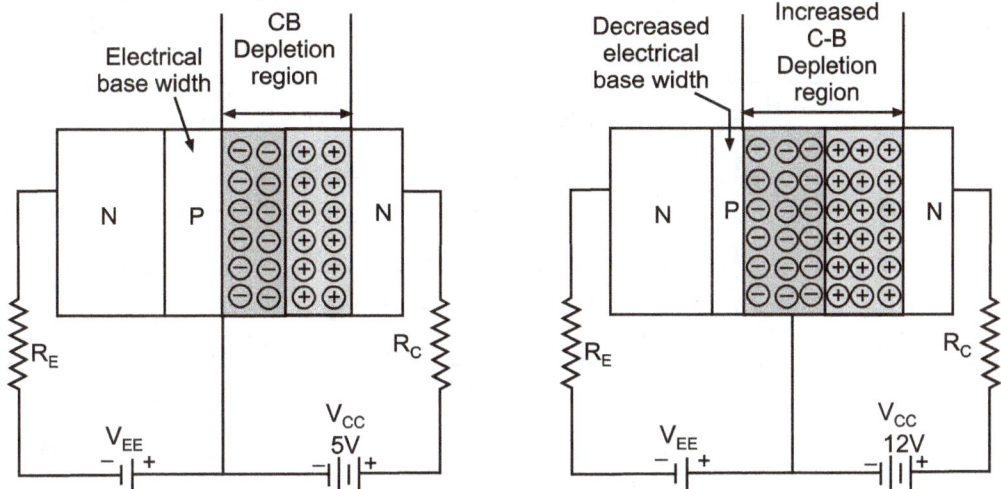

Fig. 2.16: 'Early Effect' in CB Configuration

2.8.2 Output Characteristics in CB Configuration

- The plot of the output current I_C and the output voltage V_{CB} keeping I_E constant, is the output characteristic of the common base configuration.

- Typically it is as shown in Fig. 2.17 for NPN transistor.

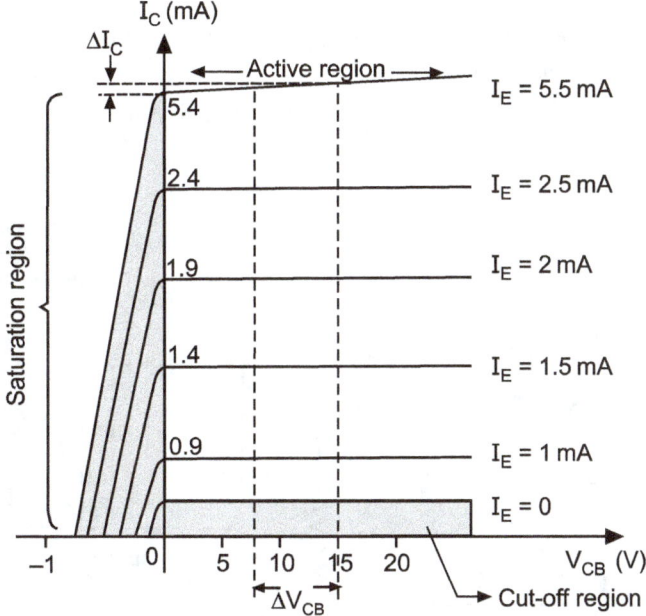

Fig. 2.17: CB Output Characteristics for NPN Transistor

- The output characteristic has three operating regions: Active region, saturation region and cut-off region. Table given below explains the different regions of operation.

Region of operation	B-E junction	C-B junction	Details	Application
Active	Forward biased	Reverse biased	$I_E \approx I_C$ and remains almost constant even if V_{CB} is changed	Amplifier
Saturation	Forward biased	Forward biased	I_C increases exponentially with increase in V_{CB}.	Switch
Cut-off	Reverse biased	Reverse biased	$I_E = 0$, transistor is off, reverse leakage current flows $I_C = I_{CBO}$	Switch

In the CB configuration, the dynamic output resistance ($r_{o/p}$) of transistor is given as

$$r_{o/p} = \frac{\Delta V_{CB}}{\Delta I_C}\bigg|_{I_E} = \text{constant}$$

The C-B configuration is used as preamplifier because the current gain $\alpha_{dc} = \dfrac{I_C}{I_E} > 1$.

- **'Punch through effect'** or **'Reach through effect':** We know that, the CB junction is reverse biased in active region. Fig. 2.18 shows Punch through effect in CB configuration in output characteristic. As V_{CB} is increased, the width of depletion region at the junction increases. The dotted line represents V_{CBmax}, it is the voltage above which breakdown occurs because, the CB depletion region penetrates into the base until it makes contact with the Base-Emitter depletion region and a large collector current I_C flows which damages the transistor.

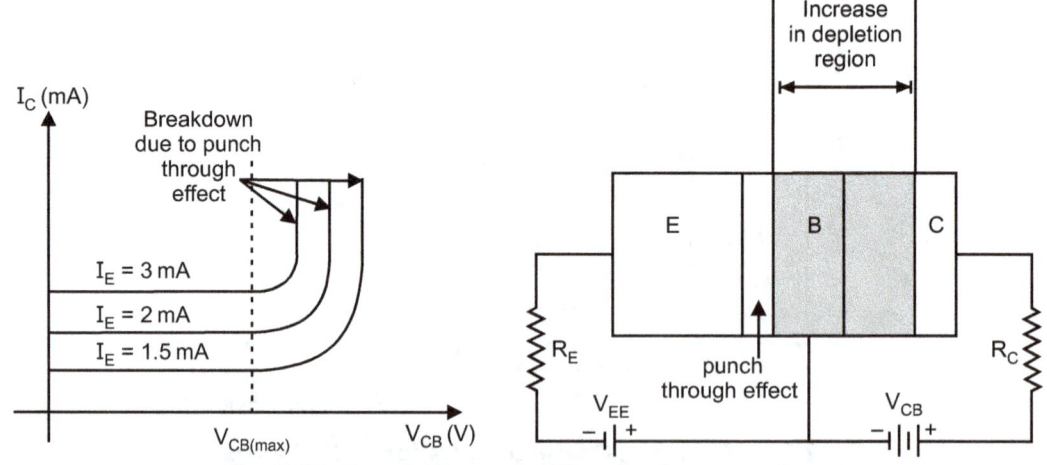

Fig. 2.18: Punch Through Effect in Common Base

2.9 COMMON EMITTER CONFIGURATION   [Dec. 13, 12, May 14, 16]

❖ Important Questions Related to this Topic ❖

1. Draw the output characteristics of BJT in CE configuration. Indicate all the three regions of operation on it.

2. Draw and explain the input and output characteristics for transistor CE configuration.

- In the common emitter configuration, the input is applied between Base-Emitter and the output is taken from Collector-Emitter, as shown in Fig. 2.19, thus the emitter is common to the input and output.

- As shown in the Fig. 2.19, V_{BB} and V_{CC} are the external D.C. sources for biasing the transistor in active region i.e. to keep B-E junction forward biased and C-B junction reverse biased. R_B and R_C are the current limiting resistors.

- The input voltage is V_{BE} and input current is I_B whereas output voltage is V_{CE} and output current is I_C.

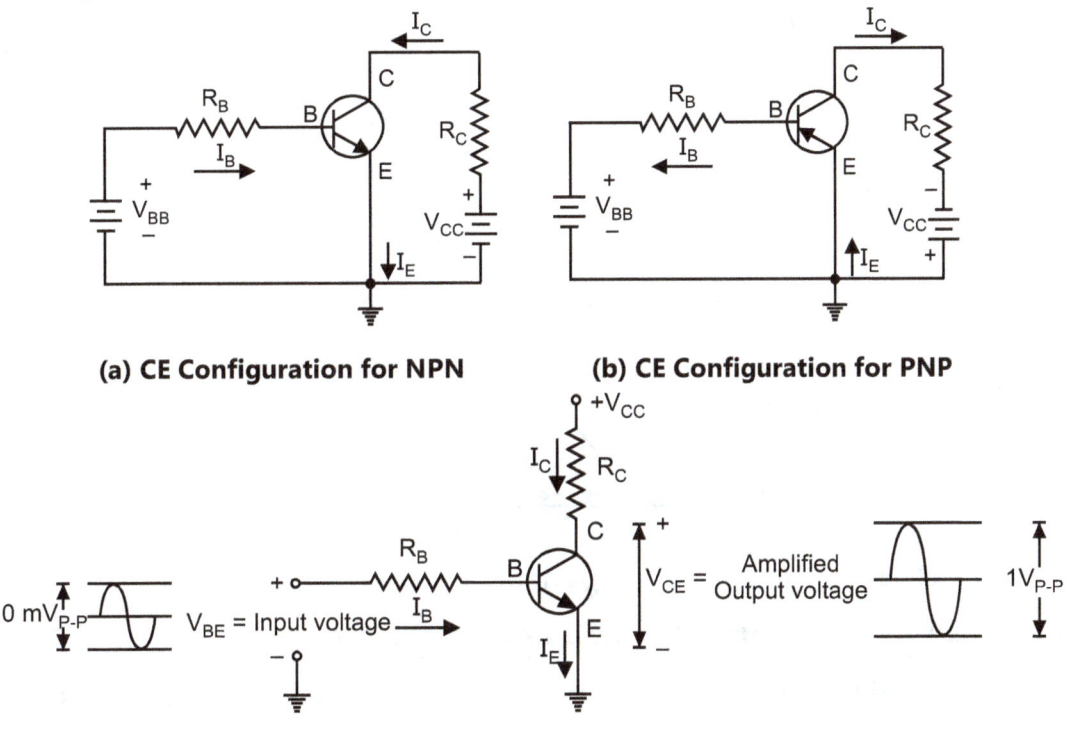

(a) CE Configuration for NPN   **(b) CE Configuration for PNP**

(c) Common Emitter Amplifier

Fig. 2.19

2.9.1 Input Characteristics of Common Emitter Configuration

- The plot of the input voltage V_{BE} and the input current I_B keeping V_{CE} constant is the input characteristics of common emitter configuration. It is as shown in Fig. 2.20.

- This characteristic is similar to that of a forward biased diode. As the input voltage V_{BE} is increased gradually, after cut-in voltage i.e. 0.3 V for germanium and 0.7 V for silicon, we see a rapid increase in the input current I_E with a small increment in V_{BE}.

- That means the input resistance is very small. It is called the Dynamic input resistance of a transistor and is given by

$$r_{i/p} = \left. \frac{\Delta V_{BE}}{\Delta I_B} \right|_{\text{at } V_{CE} \,=\, \text{constant}}$$

- Also, we can observe that, there is a slight decrease in I_B with increase in V_{CE}. This is due to increase in the width of the CB depletion region in reverse biased condition. It reduces the effective width of base, causing decrease in I_B due to fewer re-combinations in the base region.

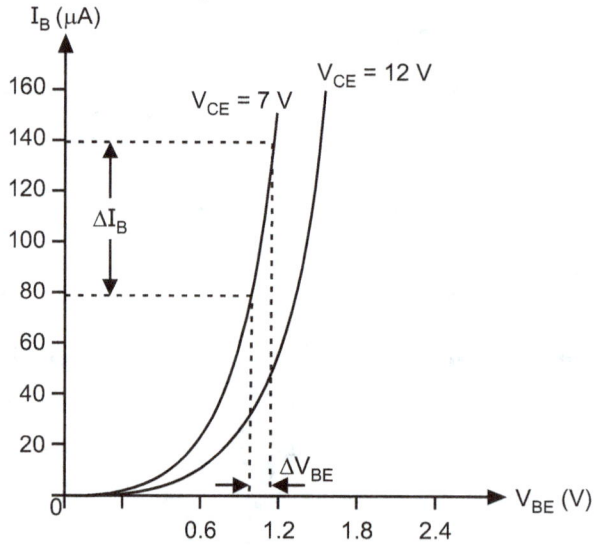

Fig. 2.20: Input Characteristics of the Transistor in CE Configuration

2.9.2 Output Characteristics in CE Configuration   [Nov. 15]

- The plot of the output current I_C and the output voltage V_{CE} for various fixed values of the input current I_B, is the output characteristic of the common emitter configuration as shown in Fig. 2.21.

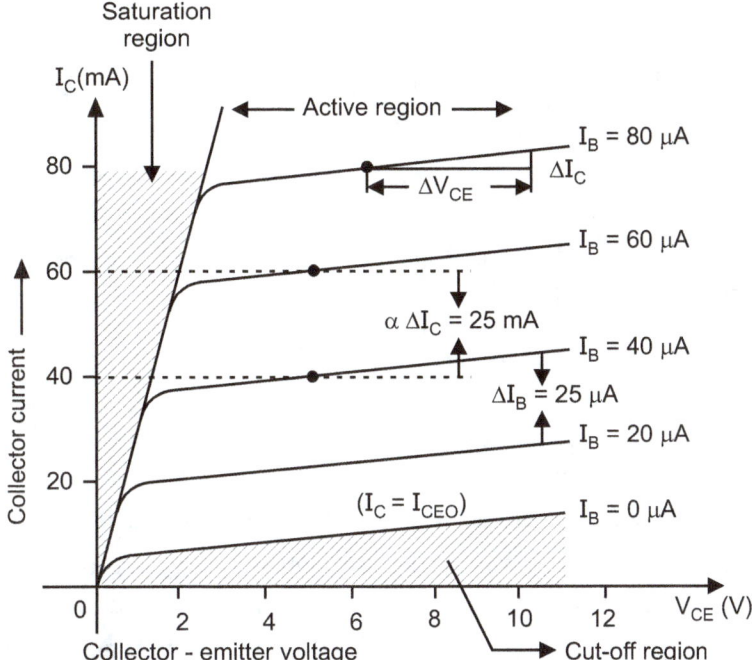

Fig. 2.21: Output Characteristics of the Transistor in CE Configuration

- There are three different regions of operation, as seen from the characteristics, viz. Active, saturation and cut-off.

Region	B-E junction	C-B junction	Details	Application
Active	Forward biased	Reverse biased	I_C increases slightly with increase in V_{CE}. Value of I_C depends on I_B because $I_C = \beta I_B$	Amplifier
Saturation	Forward biased	Forward biased	$V_{CE\,sat}$ = 0.1 to 0.3 V.	Switch
Cut-off	Reverse biased	Reverse biased	I_B = 0, transistor is off, reverse leakage current flows $I_C = I_{CBO}$	Switch

- In the C-E configuration, the dynamic output resistance ($r_{o/p}$) of transistor is given as

$$r_{o/p} = \left.\frac{\Delta V_{CE}}{\Delta I_C}\right|_{I_B = \text{constant}}$$

- **"Punch through effect" or "Reach through effect"**: As shown in Fig. 2.22 punch through effect is observed in C-E configuration in output characteristics.

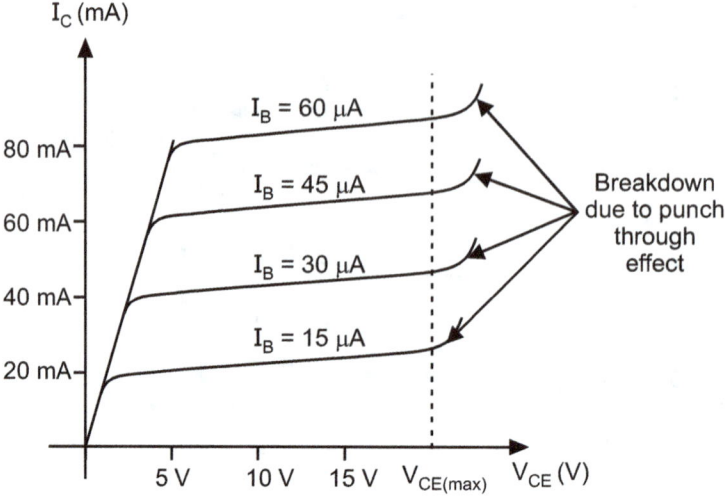

Fig. 2.22: Demonstration of Punch Through Effect

- If V_{CE} is increased above the maximum limit $V_{CE\ max}$, the CB depletion region penetrates into the base until it makes contact with the Base-Emitter depletion region and large collector current I_C flows which damages the transistor. This is known as "punch through effect". (Refer Fig. 2.22)

- C-E configuration can be used as a pre-amplifier and a high gain amplifier, as the

$$\text{Current gain } \beta_{dc} = \frac{I_C}{I_B} > 1 = \left.\frac{\Delta I_C}{\Delta I_B}\right|_{\Delta V_{CE}\ =\ 0}.$$

2.10 RELATIONSHIP BETWEEN α_DC AND β_DC   [May 16]

❖ Important Questions Related to this Topic ❖

1. Derive the expression for α in terms of β.
2. Derive the relationship between α_{dc} and β_{dc}.

We know that,

$$\beta_{dc} = \frac{I_C}{I_B} \text{ and } \alpha_{dc} = \frac{I_C}{I_E}$$

We know, $I_E = I_C + I_B$ or $I_B = I_E - I_C$

$$\beta_{dc} = \frac{I_C}{I_E - I_C}$$

Divide the numerator and denominator of R.H.S. of the above equation by I_E,

we get, $$\beta_{dc} = \frac{I_C/I_E}{I_E/I_E - I_C/I_E}$$

∴ $$\beta_{dc} = \frac{\alpha_{dc}}{1 - \alpha_{dc}}$$ (Since $\alpha_{dc} = I_C/ I_E$)

Divide the R.H.S. and L.H.S. by $1 + \beta_{dc}$,

we get,
$$\frac{\beta_{dc}}{1 + \beta_{dc}} = \frac{\dfrac{\alpha_{dc}}{1 - \alpha_{dc}}}{1 + \beta_{dc}}$$

$$\frac{\beta_{dc}}{1 + \beta_{dc}} = \frac{\dfrac{\alpha_{dc}}{1 - \alpha_{dc}}}{1 + \dfrac{\alpha_{dc}}{1 - \alpha_{dc}}}$$

$$\frac{\beta_{dc}}{1 + \beta_{dc}} = \frac{\dfrac{\alpha_{dc}}{1 - \alpha_{dc}}}{\dfrac{1 - \alpha_{dc} + \alpha_{dc}}{1 - \alpha_{dc}}}$$

Cancel the common denominator terms,

We get
$$\frac{\beta_{dc}}{1 + \beta_{dc}} = \frac{\alpha_{dc}}{1 - \alpha_{dc} + \alpha_{dc}} = \alpha_{dc}$$

$$\therefore \qquad \alpha_{dc} = \frac{\beta_{dc}}{1 + \beta_{dc}}$$

2.11 COMMON COLLECTOR CONFIGURATION [Dec. 13]

❖ Important Question Related to this Topic ❖

Draw and explain the input and output characteristics of a transistor in CC configuration.

- In common collector configuration, the input is applied between Base-Collector and the output is taken from the collector-emitter, thus the collector is common to the input and output. This configuration is also known as **emitter follower**. Fig. 2.23 shows the common collector configuration for both the types of transistors.

- This configuration has high input impedance and low output impedance, therefore it is mainly used for impedance matching.

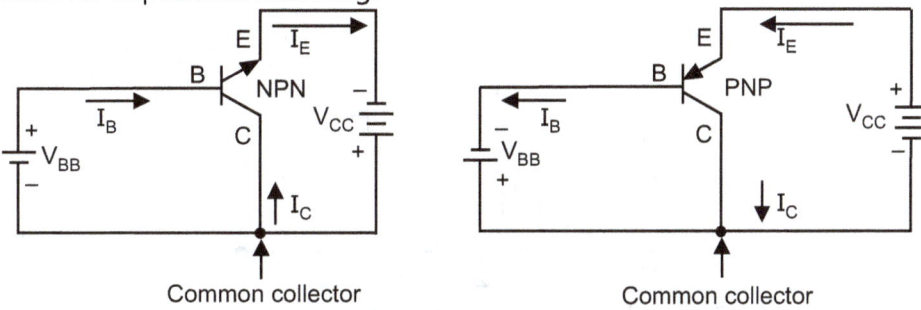

Fig. 2.23: Common Collector Configuration

- As shown in the Fig. 2.23, V_{BB} and V_{CC} are the external D.C. sources for biasing the transistor in active region i.e. to keep B-E junction forward biased and C-B junction reverse biased.

- The input voltage is V_{BC} and input current is I_B, whereas output voltage is V_{CE} and output current is I_E.

- Fig. 2.24 shows the practical way of drawing C-C configuration. Even though the collector is connected to $+V_{CC}$, it is a dc voltage. For A.C. analysis, the D.C. sources are treated as ground. So we can say that the output is measured with respect to ground that is collector. So now, the common collector configuration is similar to common emitter configuration, only the load resistance RE is connected in the emitter lead rather than the collector.

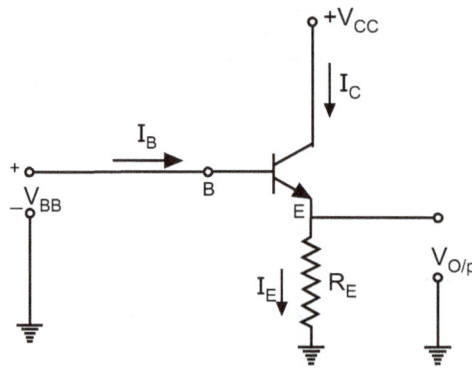

Fig. 2.24: Practical way of showing C-C configuration

2.11.1 Input Characteristics of C-C Configuration

- The plot of the input current IB and the input voltage VCB for a given values of V_{CE} is the input characteristics of common collector configuration. It is as shown in Fig. 2.25.

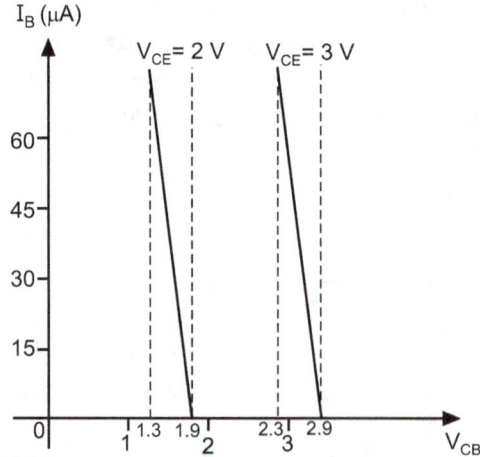

Fig. 2.25: Input Characteristics of Transistor in CC Configuration

- From Fig. 2.24, $V_{CE} = V_{CB} + V_{BE}$. Example, $V_{CE\ constant} = 2V$ and collector to base voltage $V_{CB} = 1.3\ V$ then from above equation $V_{BE} = 2 - 1.3 = 0.7\ V$. Hence for this case base current is high, because B.E. junction is forward biased.

- If $V_{CB} = 1.9$, $V_{BE} = 0.1\ V$. Base current is reduced to zero, since base to emitter junction no longer forward biased.

2.11.2 Output Characteristics of C-C Configuration

- The plot of the output current I_E and the output voltage V_{CE} for various fixed values of the input current I_B, is the output characteristic of the common emitter configuration shown Fig. 2.26.

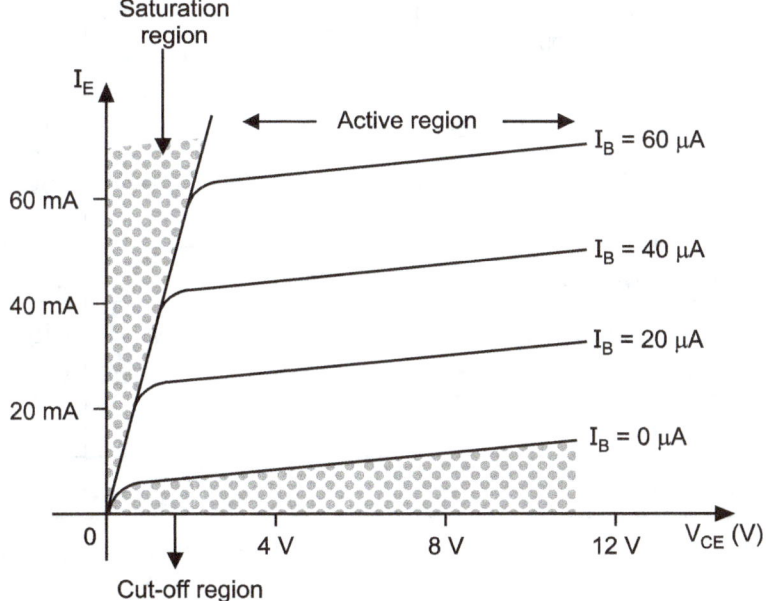

Fig. 2.26: Output Characteristics of Transistor in CC Configuration

- Since I_E is almost equal to I_C, the output characteristic of CC configuration is similar to that of CE configuration.

- Current gain,

$$\gamma\ (gamma) = \frac{I_E}{I_B}$$

$$= \frac{I_C + I_B}{I_B}$$

$$= (1 + \beta_{dc})$$

2.12 COMPARISON OF CB, CE AND CC CONFIGURATIONS [May 15]

❖ **Important Question Related to this Topic** ❖

Compare CB, CE and CC amplifiers.

Sr. No.	Characteristics	Common Base	Common Emitter	Common Collector
1.	Circuit diagram			
2.	Input resistance	Very low (20 Ω)	Low (1 kΩ)	High (500 kΩ)
3.	Output resistance	Very high (1 MΩ)	High (40 kΩ)	Low (50 Ω)
4.	Voltage gain	Medium	Medium	Less than unity
5.	Current gain	Less than unity	High (25 to few hundred)	High (25 to few hundred)
6.	Input current	I_E	I_B	I_B
7.	Output current	I_C	I_C	I_E
8.	Input voltage applied between	Emitter and Base	Emitter and Base	Base and Emitter
9.	Output voltage taken between	Collector and Base	Collector and Emitter	Across emitter resistor
10.	Current amplification factor	$\alpha_{dc} = \dfrac{I_C}{I_E}$	$\beta_{dc} = \dfrac{I_C}{I_B}$	$\gamma = \dfrac{I_E}{I_B}$
11.	Applications	Pre-amplifier and in HF application	Voltage amplifier	For impedance matching and current amplification

2.13 WHY CE CONFIGURATION IS WIDELY PREFERRED?

Common Emitter configuration is widely used because of the following advantages:

- It provides high voltage gain and high current gain and hence high power gain.
- As the input and output resistances have moderate values, the common emitter amplifier stages are more suitable for cascading without any additional impedance matching circuits. Maximum power gets transferred from one stage to another due to this automatic impedance matching.

2.14 TRANSISTOR BIASING AND DC ANALYSIS

❖ **Important Questions Related to this Topic** ❖

1. State the biasing conditions required for the three regions of operation of BJT.
2. Why is biasing needed in a transistor?

- We have seen earlier that a transistor can work as an amplifier or as a switch.
- To achieve amplification, a transistor must be biased in the active region, whereas to operate it as a switch it is biased either in the saturation or in cut-off region.

Sr. No.	Region	Base-Emitter junction	Collector-Base junction	Application
1.	Active	Forward bias	Reverse bias	Amplifier
2.	Saturation	Forward bias	Forward bias	Close switch
3.	Cut-off	Reverse bias	Reverse bias	Open switch

- To operate a transistor in desired region, two external D.C. sources of proper magnitude and polarity are required to bias the two junctions of transistor.
- Proper biasing of the transistor sets the operating point also called quiescent point (Q point) of the transistor. Using the biasing circuits the quiescent point is made stable by establishing certain voltage and current conditions.

2.14.1 The D.C. Operating Point and D.C. Load Line   [May 15, Dec. 14]

❖ **Important Question Related to this Topic** ❖

1. What is a D.C. load line? Derive its equation for a CE amplifier.
2. What do you understand by a D.C. load line and D.C. bias point? Explain their significance.

- Consider a common emitter circuit, biased to operate in active region as shown in Fig. 2.27. The external voltage is applied so as to forward bias the base-emitter junction and reverse bias the collector-base junction. So the circuit behaves as an amplifier.

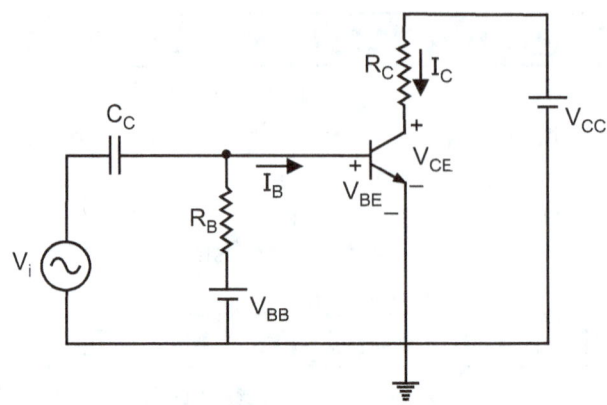

Fig. 2.27: Common Emitter Amplifier

- For D.C. conditions, the coupling capacitor C_C acts as open circuit. Applying Kirchhoff's voltage law to the output circuit, we get

$$V_{CC} - I_C R_C - V_{CE} = 0$$

$$I_C = \frac{V_{CC} - V_{CE}}{R_C} \quad \text{(zero signal collector current)}$$

Rearranging the terms in the above equation, we get,

$$I_C = \left(-\frac{1}{R_C}\right) V_{CE} + \frac{V_C}{R_C}$$

- Comparing the above equation with the equation of a straight line,

$$y = mx + C$$

where,   m = Slope of line

and   C = Y Intercept on Y-axis.

So we can draw a straight line on a graph of I_C versus V_{CE} which is having:

Slope = $(- 1/R_C)$ and Y intercept= $I_{C(max.)} = V_{CC}/R_C$

Now we determine two points on this straight line with $V_{CE} = V_{CC}$ and $V_{CE} = 0$

When $V_{CE} = V_{CC}$, $I_C = 0$ i.e. saturation and

When $V_{CE} = 0$, $I_C = \dfrac{V_{CC}}{R_C}$ i.e. cut-off

- Locate these two points on the output characteristic of CE (i.e. I_C versus V_{CE}) as points A and B as shown in Fig. 2.28. The line joining points A and B is called the D.C. load line. Note that the input signal is assumed to be zero.

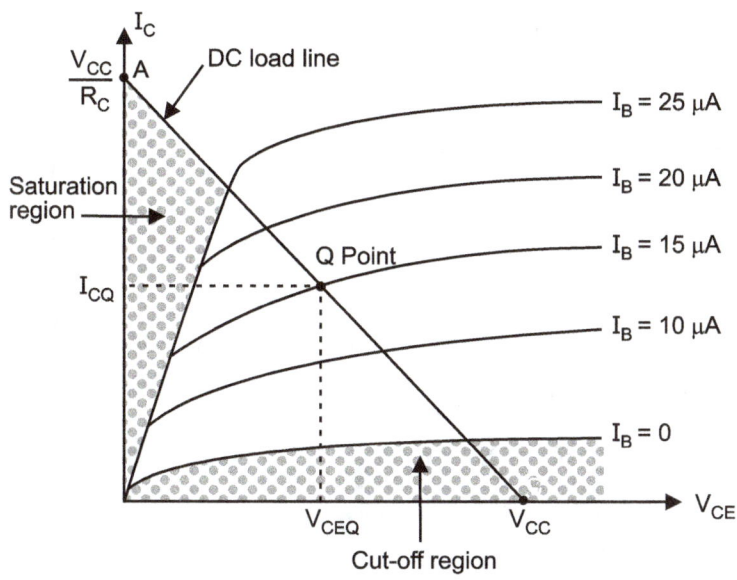

Fig. 2.28: D.C. Load Line and Operating Point on CE Characteristics

- The points A and B give the extreme values of D.C. current and voltage in the circuit respectively.
- Now applying KVL to the input circuit,

  We get, $V_{BB} - I_B R_B - V_{BE} = 0$

$$I_B = \frac{V_{BB} - V_{BE}}{R_B}$$

- If we draw the characteristic curve with this value of base current; the intersection point of it, with the D.C. load line, is known as the Q point.

SOLVED EXAMPLES

Example 2.1: *Calculate the values of I_C and I_E for a BJT with $\alpha_{dc} = 0.97$ and $I_B = 50\ \mu A$. Determine β_{dc} for the device.*

Solution:

1. $\beta_{dc} = \dfrac{\alpha_{dc}}{1 - \alpha_{dc}} = \dfrac{0.97}{1 - 0.97} = 32.33$

2. $I_C = \beta I_B = 32.33 \times 50\ \mu A = 1.61\ mA$

3. $I_E = I_B + I_C = 50\ \mu A + 1.61\ mA = 1.66\ mA$

Example 2.2: *Determine whether or not be the transistor shown in the following figure is in saturation. Assume $V_{CE\ (sat)} = 0.2\ V$.*

Solution:

1. Assuming that the transistor is in saturation,

    We have $V_{CE\ (sat)} = 0.2\ V$ and $V_{BE\ (sat)} = 0.8\ V$.

2. Apply Kirchhoff's voltage law to the collector circuit:

$$V_{CC} - V_{CE} - I_C R_C = 0$$

$$\therefore \quad I_C = \frac{V_{CC} - V_{CE}}{R_C} = \frac{10 - 0.2}{1K} = \textbf{9.8 mA}$$

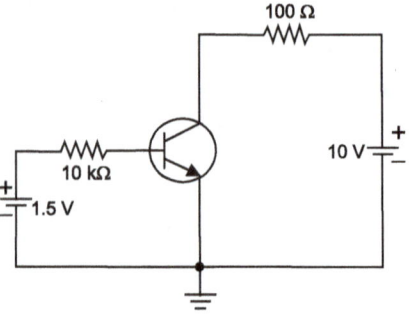

3. Now apply KVL to the base circuit,

$$V_{BB} - I_B R_B - V_{BE} = 0$$

$$\therefore \quad I_B = \frac{V_{BB} - V_{BE}}{R_B} = \frac{3 - 0.8}{10K} = \textbf{220 μA}$$

4. We know, $I_C/\beta = 9.8$ mA/100 = **98 μA**

   i.e. $I_B >> I_C/\beta$. Thus our assumption is true.

Example 2.3: *Determine I_B, I_C, I_E, V_{CE} for the circuit shown below. The transistor has a β = 150. Assume V_{BE} = 0.7 V.*

Solution:

1. Apply KVL to the base circuit:

   We get, $1.5 - I_B R_B - V_{BE} = 0$

$$\therefore I_B = \frac{1.5 - V_{BE}}{R_B} = \frac{1.5 - 0.7}{10 \times 10^3} = \textbf{80 μA}$$

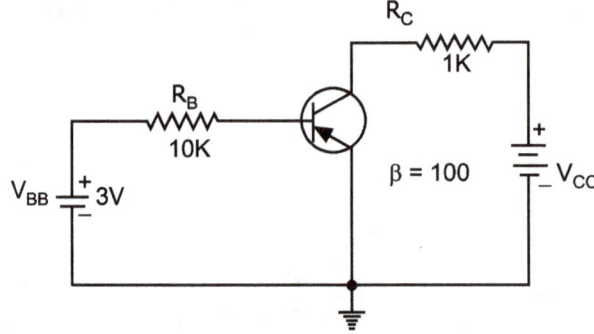

2. $I_C = \beta I_B = 100 \times 80$ μA = **8 mA**

3. $I_E = I_B + I_C = 80$ μA + 12 mA = **8.08 mA**

4. Now, applying KVL to the collector circuit,

We have,

$$V_{CC} - I_C R_C - V_{CE} = 0$$

∴ $$V_{CE} = V_{CC} - I_C R_C$$

$$= 10 - 8 \times 10^{-3} \times 1 \times 10^3$$

$$V_{CE} = \textbf{2 V}$$

2.15 SELECTION OF OPERATING POINT

❖ Important Question Related to this Topic ❖

Explain the criteria for selection of the operating point.

- Q-point is the point on D.C. load line which indicates D.C. voltage (V_{CEQ}) and current (I_{CQ}) through the transistor assuming the input signal $V_i = 0$. To operate the transistor as an amplifier, the Q-point should be located at the centre of the D.C. load line.

  Case 1: If the Q point is set near the saturation region as shown in the Fig. 2.29 at point **S**, even if the base current varies sinusoidally, the collector current gets distorted due to clipping in the positive half cycle. Thus, if the Q-point is set near the saturation region, there is loss of amplification during the positive half cycle.

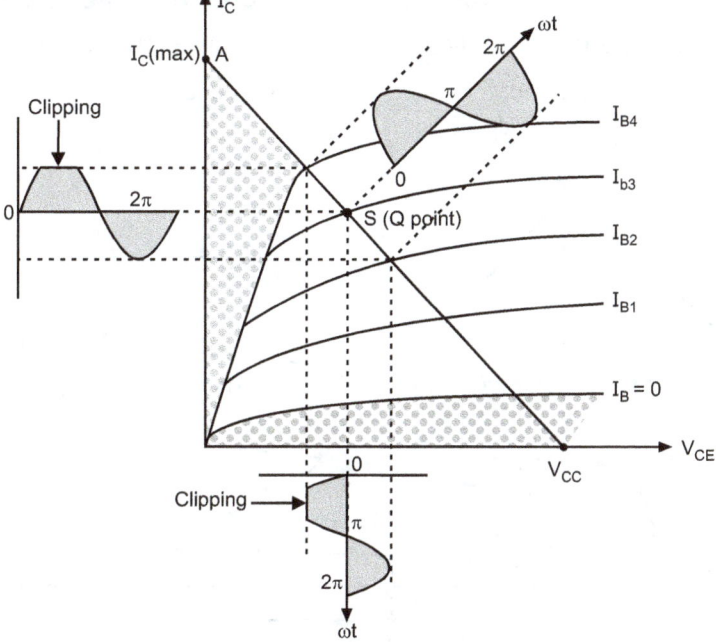

Fig. 2.29: Loss of Amplification at the Positive Peaks if Q Point is Near Saturation

Case 2: If the Q point is set near the cut-off region as shown in Fig. 2.30 at point **C,** even if the base current is sinusoidal, the collector current gets distorted due to the clipping in the negative half cycle. Thus, if the Q-point is set near the cut-off region, then there is a loss of amplification during the negative half cycles.

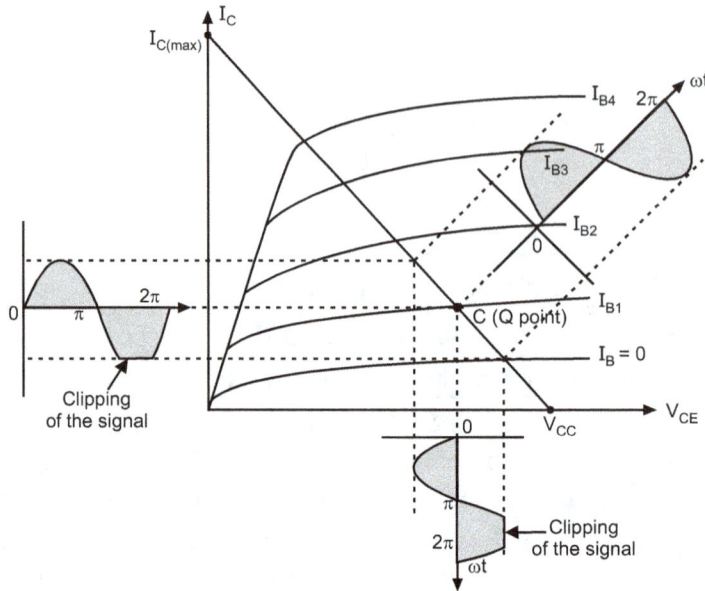

Fig. 2.30: Loss of Amplification at the Negative Peaks if Q Point is near Cut-off

Case 3: If the Q point is set at the centre of the D.C. load line as shown in Fig. 2.31 at point **Q,** the output signal is purely sinusoidal in nature without any distortion. Thus for amplification, the Q-point must be set at the centre of the D.C. load line for faithful amplification without any distortion.

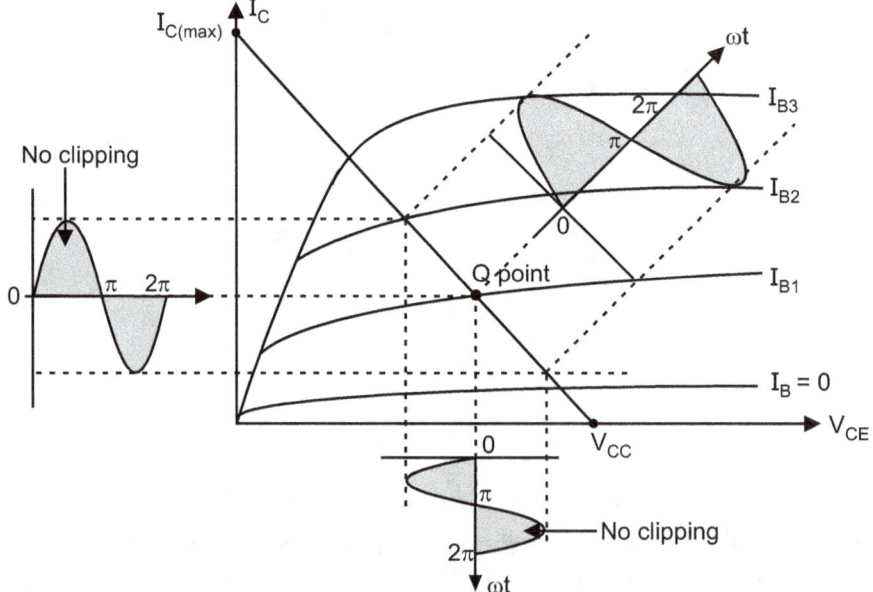

Fig. 2.31: Q Point at the Centre of the D.C. Load Line indicating Faithful Amplification

2.16 IMPORTANT CONDITIONS FOR BIASING

❖ Important Question Related to this Topic ❖
What are the requirements of biasing circuit?

- As discussed earlier, a transistor can be biased to operate in three different regions by making proper selection of the Q point.

- To ensure proper operation of the circuit, the following conditions must be satisfied.

Typical junction voltages for active, cut-off and saturation regions

	V_{CEsat}	V_{BEsat}	$V_{BE\ active}$	$V_{BEcut-in}$	$V_{BEcut-off}$
Si	0.2	0.8	0.7	0.5	0.0
Ge	0.1	0.3	0.2	0.1	-0.1

- **To get maximum amplification in Active region**

$$V_{CE} = \frac{V_{CC}}{2} \quad \text{and} \quad I_{CQ} = \frac{I_{C\ max}}{2}$$

- Also to identify the region of operation of the transistor, we must check for the following conditions:

  ○ For active region: $V_{CE} > V_{CESat}$

  ○ For saturation region: $I_B > I_C / \beta_{dc}$

2.17 BIAS STABILIZATION

- Once the Q point is fixed, it should not get shifted up or down throughout the operation. Practically the Q point is not so stable.

Factors Affecting the Stability of the Operating Point:

- Changes in temperature: The parameters like V_{BE}, I_{CO} and β_{dc} show change with changing temperature.

- Also some parameters like β_{dc} change from transistor to transistor, so in case of replacement the Q point may get shifted.

- **Bias stabilization** is a technique of making the operating point Q, independent of temperature and the transistor parameter variations using resistive networks. The circuits used are known as biasing circuits. There are three types of biasing circuits as follows:

  1. Fixed bias circuit,
  2. Collector to base bias circuit,
  3. Self-bias circuit.

2.17.1 Fixed Bias

❖ **Important Question Related to this Topic** ❖
1. Explain the base bias circuit using N-P-N transistor.
2. What are the advantages and disadvantages of a fixed bias circuit?

- A fixed bias circuit to operate an N-P-N transistor in active region is shown in Fig. 2.32. R_B provides the required base current. R_C limits the collector current. To find the operating point, we derive the equations for I_B, I_C and V_{CE} as below.

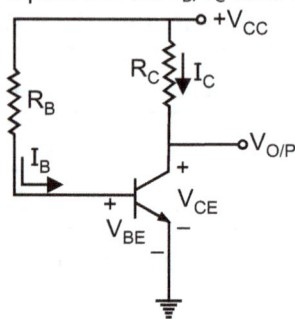

Fig. 2.32: Fixed Bias Circuit

Circuit Analysis:

1. Applying KVL to the base circuit,

   We get, $V_{CC} - I_B R_B - V_{BE} = 0$

   $\therefore \qquad\qquad I_B = \dfrac{V_{CC} - V_{BE}}{R_B}$

   or $\qquad\qquad I_B \approx \dfrac{V_{CC}}{R_B}$ ...... as $V_{CC} >> V_{BE}$

   From the above equation, we see that, the magnitude of I_B is controlled by V_{CC} and R_B. As the values of V_{CC} and R_B are fixed, I_B is also fixed which in turn keeps I_C fixed by the relation,

   $\qquad\qquad I_C = \beta\, I_B$ and hence the name fixed bias.

2. Now, applying KVL to the collector circuit,

   We get, $V_{CC} - I_C R_C - V_{CE} = 0$

   $\therefore \qquad\qquad V_{CE} = V_{CC} - I_C R_C$

Advantage of Fixed Bias:

- The main advantage of fixed bias circuit is that by simply changing the value of R_B, the operating point can be changed to a desired location in active region. Thus the circuit provides flexibility and ease in design, using less number of components.

Disadvantage of Fixed Bias:

- The desired stability of the operating point is not achieved because the magnitude of the collector current depends on β (since $I_C = \beta\, I_B$) which keeps on changing with the temperature.

Example 2.4: *For the circuit shown in Fig. 2.33, calculate the values of* I_B, I_C, V_{CE}, V_{BC}. *Assume* $\beta = 100$ *and* $V_{BE} = 0.7$ V.

Solution:

1. **To find I_B:** Applying KVL to the base circuit,

   We get, $V_{CC} - I_B R_B - V_{BE} = 0$

$$I_B = \frac{V_{CC} - V_{BE}}{R_B} = \frac{(10 - 0.7)\ \text{V}}{1\ \text{M}\Omega}$$

$$= \textbf{9.3 μA}$$

2. $I_C = \beta_{IB} = 100 \times 9.3$ μA

$$= \textbf{0.93 mA}$$

3. **To find V_{CE}:** Applying KVL to the output loop,

   We get, $V_{CC} - I_C R_C - V_{CE} = 0$

$$V_{CE} = V_{CC} - I_C R_C = 10\ \text{V} - (0.93\ \text{mA} \times 2\ \text{k}\Omega)$$

$$= 10\ \text{V} - 1.86\ \text{V} = \textbf{8.14 V}$$

4. **To find $V_{BC} = V_B - V_C$**

   But $V_B = V_{BE} = \textbf{0.7 V}$

   And $V_C = V_{CE} = \textbf{8.14 V}$

   Therefore $V_{BC} = V_B - V_C = 0.7 - 8.14 = \textbf{–7.44 V}$

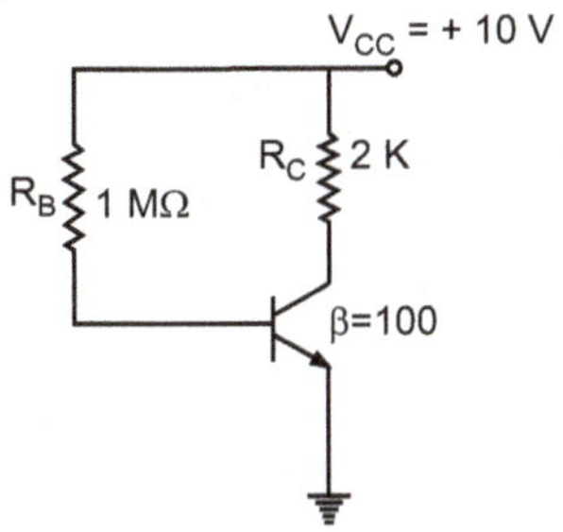

Fig. 2.33

2.17.2 Self Bias or Voltage Divider Bias

❖ Important Question Related to this Topic ❖

Explain the self bias circuit using N-P-N transistor.

- The voltage divider bias, also known as self bias circuit is the most popular biasing circuit.
- It is shown in Fig. 2.34. Here, the resistances R_1 and R_2 form a voltage divider network which provides the necessary fixed base voltage.
- Resistance R_E is used to provide temperature stability and R_C is the load resistance which limits the load current.

- The current **I** through R_1 and R_2 is assumed to be very high as compared to the base current I_B i. e. current through R_1 and R_2 is same.

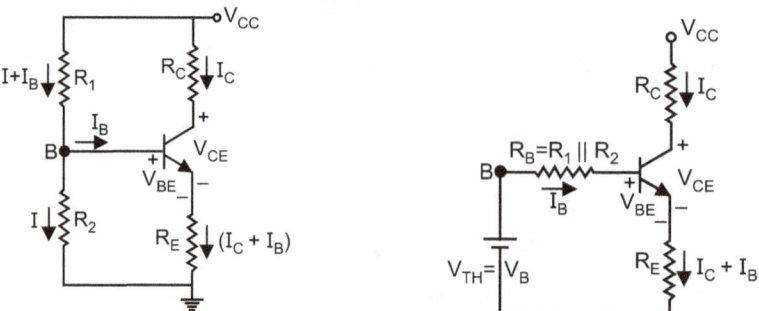

Fig. 2.34: Self-Bias Circuit   **Fig. 2.35: Thevenin's Equivalent**

Circuit analysis: Referring to Fig. 2.35, we can write,

$$R_B = \frac{R_1 R_2}{R_1 + R_2}$$

and

$$V_B = \frac{V_{CC} R_2}{R_1 + R_2} \text{ since } I >> I_B$$

1. Applying KVL to the base circuit,

    We get, $\quad V_B - I_B R_B - V_{BE} - (I_B + I_C) R_E = 0$

    Putting, $\qquad\qquad I_C = \beta I_B$ and solving the equation for I_B,

    We get $\qquad\qquad I_B = \dfrac{V_B - V_{BE}}{R_B + (1 + \beta) R_E}$

2. Applying KVL to the collector circuit,

    We get, $\qquad V_{CC} - I_C R_C - V_{CE} - (I_C + I_B) R_E = 0$

    $$V_{CE} = V_{CC} - I_C R_C - (I_C + I_B) R_E$$

3. The voltage across R_E is $V_E = V_B - V_{BE}$ and $I_E = \dfrac{V_B - V_{BE}}{R_E}$

Advantage:

- The main advantage of the self bias circuit is that, a simple resistor R_E provides stability to the operating point against temperature variations. Consider for example, if the collector current I_C tries to increase, I_E also increases, increasing the drop across the resistor R_E. This in turn reduces the voltage difference between base and emitter. This action reduces I_B and in turn I_C. Thus the increase in I_C is compensated.

2.18 TRANSISTOR AS AN AMPLIFIER   [May 13]

> ❖ **Important Questions Related to this Topic** ❖
> 1. Explain with a circuit diagram a single stage common emitter amplifier. State the function of each component in the circuit.
> 2. Explain how R_i and R_o affect the performance of the voltage amplifier.
> 3. What should be the value of R_i in an ideal voltage amplifier? Justify your answer.

Properties of an Ideal Amplifier:

- **Input resistance R_i:** Ideally the value of input resistance must be infinite. If it is comparable with the source resistance R_s, the actual input to the amplifier is less than the source voltage. So practically it should be as high as possible.

- **Output resistance R_o:** Ideally the value of the output resistance must be zero. If it is comparable with the load resistance R_L, the actual load voltage gets reduced, which in turn reduces the gain of the amplifier. So practically it should be as low as possible.

- **Voltage gain A_v:** Ideally the gain of the amplifier must be infinite i.e. it should be able to amplify the weakest signal to a desired output level. Practically it should be high.

- **Bandwidth:** Ideally the bandwidth of the amplifier must be infinite i.e. it should be able to amplify signals of all the frequencies with equal gain.

2.18.1 Single Stage BJT Amplifier

> ❖ **Important Question Related to this Topic** ❖
> Draw the circuit diagram of a common emitter amplifier. State the function of each component used in it.

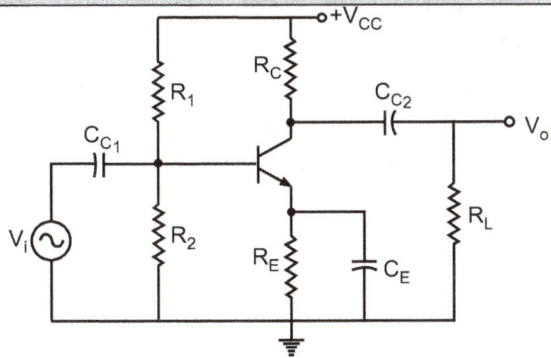

Fig. 2.36: BJT, RC Coupled Amplifier

Fig. 2.36 shows the R-C coupled BJT amplifier.

- The resistances R_1, R_2 and R_E form a voltage divider biasing circuit for the CE amplifier. It sets the operating point for the CE amplifier.

- The input capacitor C_{C1} is used to block the D.C. component present in the signal and pass only the A.C. signal for amplification.

- The capacitor C_E used in parallel with the resistor R_E is called the emitter bypass capacitor. It provides low resistance path to the amplified A.C. signal. If this capacitor is not used, the amplified A.C. signal that passes through the resister R_E will cause a voltage drop across it. This will reduce the output voltage and also the gain of the amplifier.

- The coupling capacitor C_{C2} is used to block the D.C. and couple the A.C. output of the amplifier to the load.

- An important point to be noted here is the input voltage and output voltages are not in phase. The output is 180 degrees out of phase with the input. As we see, during the positive half cycle due to increasing base current, the collector current also increases, which in turn increases the drop across the collector resistor R_C. Since $V_c = V_{cc} - I_c R_c$, the collector voltage decreases as I_c increases. Thus, we see that as V_{input} increases in the positive direction, the V_{out} increases in the negative direction. Therefore we say that there is a phase shift of 180 degrees between the input and output.

2.19 BJT AS A SWITCH   [Dec. 13, Nov. 15, May 13]

❖ **Important Questions Related to this Topic** ❖

1. Explain the operation of BJT as a switch.
2. Why are CC and CB configurations not preferred for BJT as a switch?

- As studied earlier, BJT can be operated as an amplifier as well as a switch. To operate it as an amplifier, it must be biased in active region whereas for switching operation it is biased in cut-off or saturation regions. Most popularly it is used as a switch in Digital Electronics where the input signal is either high (1) or low (0).

- Fig. 2.37 shows an NPN transistor in common emitter configuration, with input voltage V_i = zero. Therefore both junctions of the transistor get reverse biased. Thus the transistor is operated in cut-off region and hence it acts as an open switch. $V_{CE} = V_{CC}$.

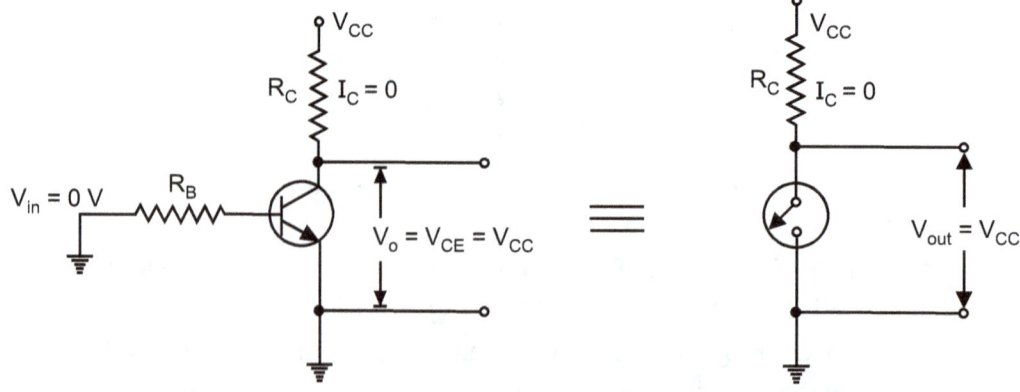

Fig. 2.37: BJT as an Open Switch in the Cut-Off Region

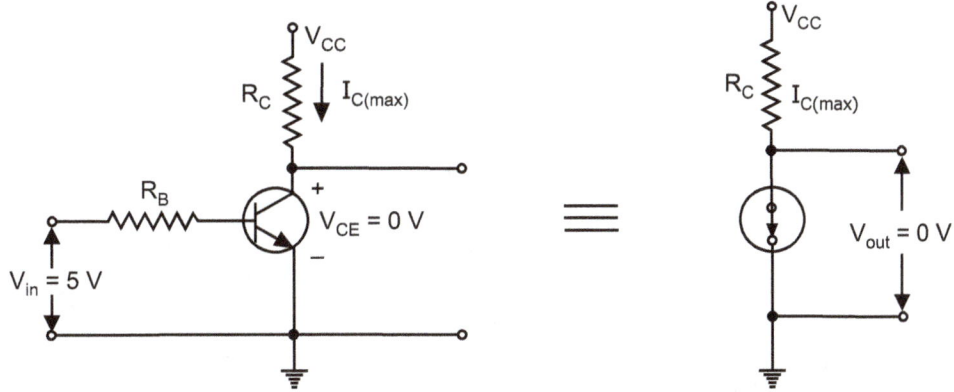

Fig. 2.38: BJT as a Closed Switch in the Saturation Region

- Fig. 2.38 shows an NPN transistor in common emitter configuration, when input voltage V_i is HIGH (+5 V). Therefore both junctions of the transistor get forward biased. Thus the transistor is operated in saturation region and hence it acts as a closed switch.

  $V_{CE} = V_{CE\,(sat)} = 0.2$ or 0.3 V. Hence output voltage is considered to be zero.

Why CC & CB not preferred for BJT as switch applications?

- To use transistor as switch there must be isolation of both voltage and current .

- In common base configuration output current (IC) and input current (IE) are nearly same, Hence, there is no current isolation.

- In common collector configuration output voltage (VE) and input voltage (VC) are nearly same. Hence, there is no voltage isolation.

- Due to this reason CC & CB are not preferred in switching application.

Why CE is preferred ?

- For common emitter configuration the output current (IC) in mA and input current (IB) in µA. hence current isolation is provided.

- In common emitter the output voltage is amplification of input and it is phase shifted version of input, hence voltage isolation is also provided.

- As CE configuration provides both current and voltage isolation it preferred in BJT as switch applications.

Example 2.5 : *Determine whether or not transistor shown in Fig. 2.39 is in saturation. Assume $V_{CE\,(sat)} = 0.2$ V.*

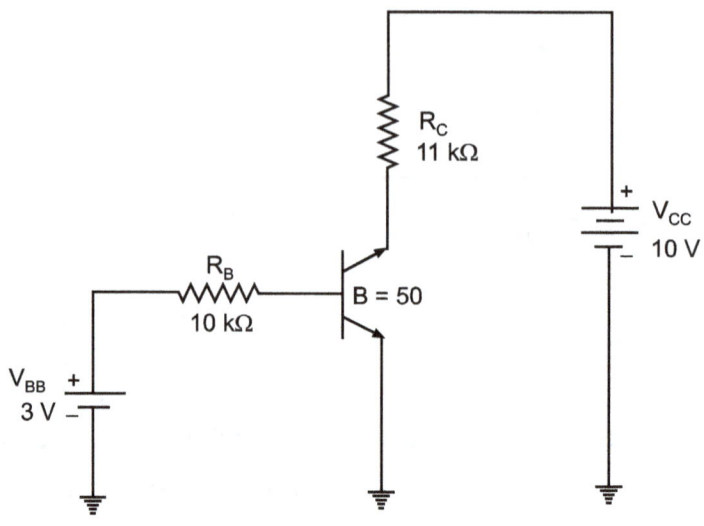

Fig. 2.39

Solution :

(a)
$$I_{CC(sat)} = \frac{V_{CC} - V_{CE(sat)}}{R_C}$$

$$= \frac{10 - 12}{1 \text{ k}\Omega}$$

$$= \frac{9.8}{1 \text{k}\Omega} = \textbf{9.8 mA}$$

(b) Now, see if I_B is large enough to produce $I_{C(sat)}$.

$$I_B = \frac{V_{BB} - V_{BE}}{R_B}$$

$$= \frac{3 - 0.7}{10 \text{ k}\Omega}$$

$$= \frac{2.3}{10 \text{ k}\Omega}$$

$$I_B = \textbf{0.23 mA}$$

$$I_C = B I_B = 50 \times (0.23 \text{ mA})$$

$$I = 11.5 \text{ mA}$$

As $I_C > I_{C(sat)}$ transistor operates in saturation region of operation.

Example 2.6 : *For a transistor circuit shown*

(a) What is V_{CE} when V_{IN} = 0V ?

(b) What minimum value of I_B is required to saturate this transistor if B is 200 ? Neglect $V_{CE(sat)}$.

(c) Calculate maximum value of R_B when V_{IN} = 5V.

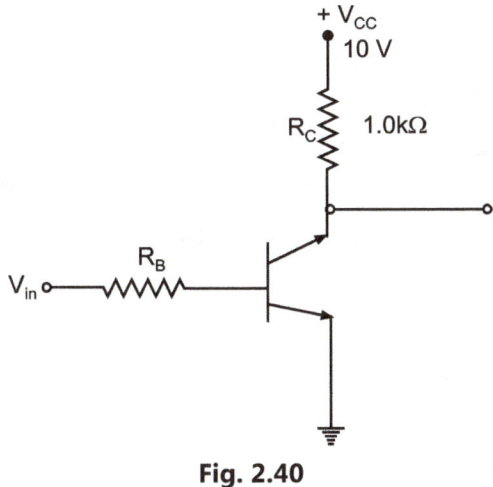

Fig. 2.40

Solution :

(a) When, V_{IN} = 0V, the transistor is in cut-off

V_{CE} = V_{CC} **= 10 V**

(b) ∵ $V_{CE(sat)}$ = 0

$$I_{C(sat)} = \frac{V_{CC}}{R_C} = \frac{10}{1\ k\Omega} = \textbf{10 mA}$$

$$I_{B(min)} = \frac{I_{C(sat)}}{B} = \frac{10\ mA}{200} = \textbf{50 μA}$$

(c) Assume V_{BE} = 0.7 V

V_{RB} = $V_{IN} - V_{BE}$

= 5 − 0.7 **= 4.3 V**

2.20 FET (FIELD EFFECT TRANSISTOR)

❖ Important Questions Related to this Topic ❖

1. Explain why FET is called a unipolar device.

2. Explain why EFT is called a voltage operated device.

3. Give types of FETs and their classification.

Introduction

- As we studied earlier, BJT is a bipolar, current operated semiconductor device. The field effect transistor (FET) is a **unipolar** semiconductor device in which current conduction takes place due to majority charge carriers only. Similar to BJT, the FETs also are used as amplifier or switch. FET is a **voltage operated device** i.e. the input voltage controls the output current (unlike BJT, in which the base current controls the collector current).

- There are two types of FET, the junction field effect transistor (JFET) and metal oxide semiconductor field effect transistor (MOSFET). The MOSFET is also known as an insulated gate field effect transistor (IGFET).

- The three terminals of FET are Drain (D), Source (S) and Gate (G).

- The main **advantages** of FET over BJT are: They do not suffer from thermal runaway, provide high input impedance (typically many mega-ohms), and are less noisy as compared to BJT.

2.20.1 Classification of FET

- The FETs are classified as follows:

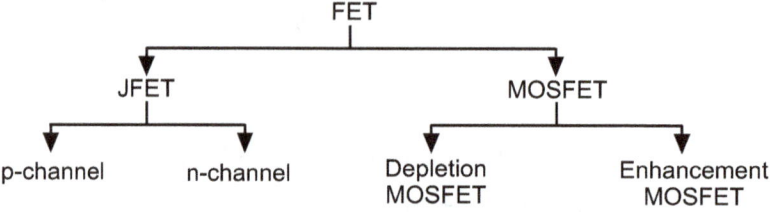

Fig. 2.41: Classification of FET

2.21 MOSFET

- There are two types of MOSFETs:

    1. Depletion type (DMOSFET).

    2. Enhancement type (EMOSFET).

    We are going to study the Enhancement type MOSFET in detail.

2.22 ENHANCEMENT MOSFET (EMOSFET)   [Dec. 12]

❖ **Important Questions Related to this Topic** ❖

1. Explain construction and working of enhancement MOSFET.

2. Draw constructional details and explain operation and characteristics of n-channel MOSFET (enhancement type).

- The EMOSFET does not have a physical channel as in DMOSFET. It operates only in enhancement mode.

2.22.1 Construction of EMOSFET

- Fig. 2.42 shows the construction of N-channel EMOSFET.

- Here, two highly doped N-regions are diffused into a lightly doped P-type substrate. Two terminals drain (D) and source (S) are taken out through metallic contacts. The channel between these two regions is absent. A thin layer of silicon dioxide (SiO_2) isolates the gate is from the substrate.

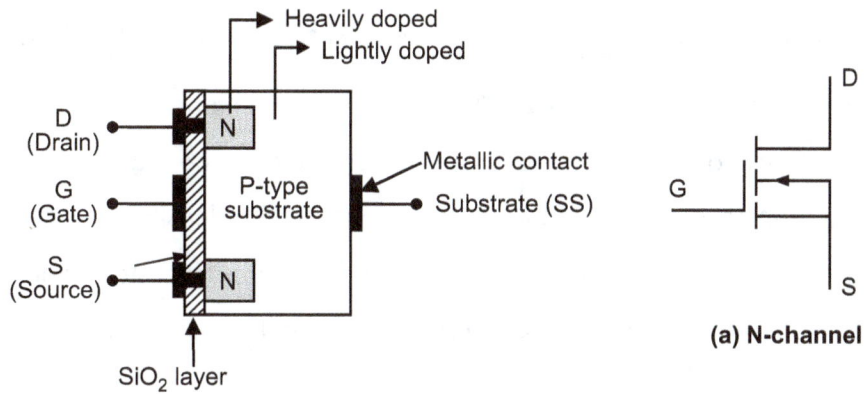

Fig. 2.42: N-Channel EMOSFET (Construction) and Symbol

Operation:

*   When $V_{GS} = 0$, even if (V_{DS}) is applied between the drain and source, no current flows through the device, since there is no physical channel; any voltage does not constitute any current flow. This is quite different from JFET and MOSFET.

*   If V_{GS} is increased in the positive direction, the concentration of electrons, from P-substrate, increases near SiO_2 layer.

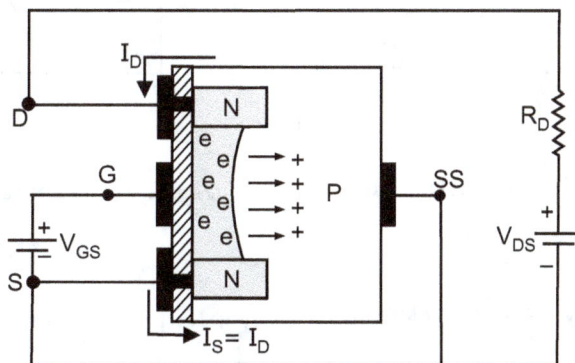

Fig. 2.43: Enhancement Operation when Channel is induced

*   At a particular value of V_{GS}, which is called as threshold voltage (V_T), the gathered electrons near SiO_2 layer connect the two heavily doped N-regions and induce a conducting channel and hence current starts flowing from the source to the drain.

*   If V_{GS} is increased further, the density of electrons getting pulled into the conducting channel increases which enhances the value of the drain current.

*   Therefore, this type of MOSFET is known as Enhancement MOSFET (EMOSFET) in which the conductivity of the channel enhances by increasing the gate to source voltage. For any voltage less than threshold voltage (V_T), conduction does not take place because the channel cannot be formed.

2.22.2 Characteristics of N-channel EMOSFET   [Dec. 14, Nov. 15, May 14]

Drain Characteristics of N-channel EMOSFET: The drain characteristics of an N-channel EMOSFET is shown in Fig. 2.44. From the figure we can see that, the drain current increases as the voltage V_{GS} is increased beyond threshold voltage (as the density of electrons increases in the induced channel). The drain current reaches saturation level at certain value of the input voltage V_{DS}. Note that the pinch-off process, discussed earlier does exist in EMOSFET.

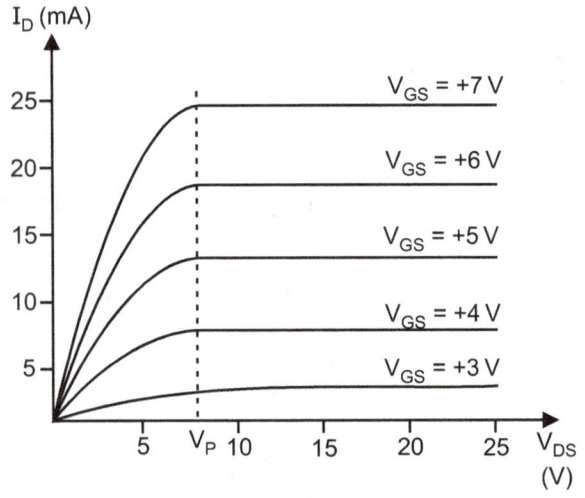

Fig. 2.44: Drain Characteristics of N-Channel EMOSFET

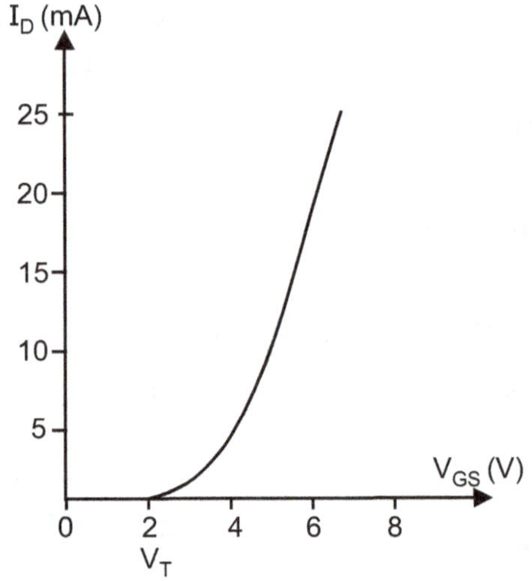

Fig. 2.45: Transfer Characteristics of N-Channel EMOSFET

Transfer Characteristics of EMOSFET: As shown in Fig. 2.45, the drain current is zero till threshold voltage V_T. When V_{GS} becomes greater than V_T, the drain current starts increasing, showing a non-linear relation; given by the following equation: $I_D = K (V_{GS} - V_T)^2$.

2.23 P-CHANNEL EMOSFET

- The construction of P-Channel EMOSFET is exactly opposite to the N-channel EMOSFET as shown in Fig. 2.46 (a). Its symbol is shown in Fig. 2.46 (b). The voltage polarities and current directions are reversed. The drain characteristic is similar except that they are plotted for negative V_{GS} as shown in Fig. 2.46 (c) and the transfer characteristic as shown in Fig. 2.46 (d) is plotted for negative values of the gate voltage (V_{GS}).

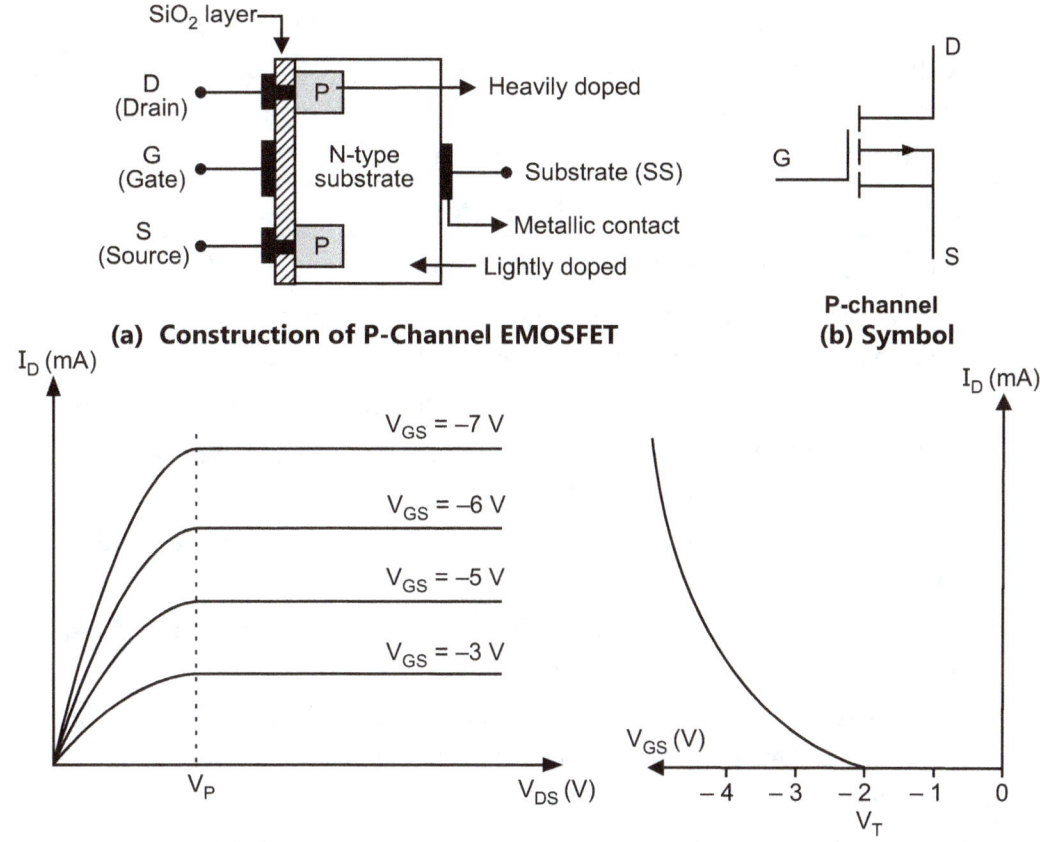

(a) Construction of P-Channel EMOSFET

P-channel
(b) Symbol

(c) Drain Characteristic   **(d) Transfer Characteristic**
Fig. 2.46: Characteristics of P-Channel EMOSFET

2.24 MOSFET AS A SWITCH

- MOSFET can act as a switch just like a transistor. A typical switching circuit using N-channel EMOSFET is shown in Fig. 2.47.

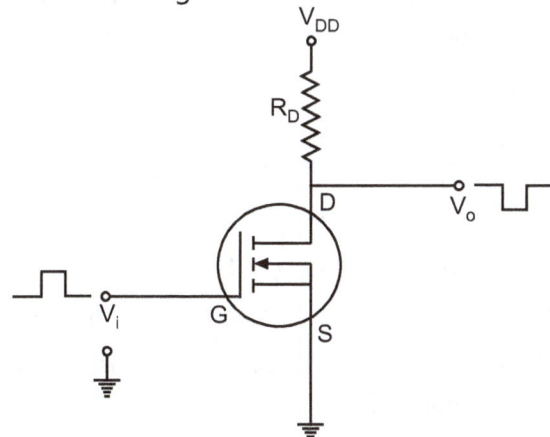

Fig. 2.47: MOSFET Acts as a Switch

- A positive going input pulse (High input) turns on the EMOSFET. Maximum drain current flows and the output voltage drops from $+V_{DD}$ to $R_D I_D$ (ON). So the EMOSFET acts as closed switch. Similarly when the input is low (zero), no drain current and hence the output is equal to $+V_{DD}$. So the EMOSFET acts as an open switch.

QUESTIONS

1. Explain the operation of NPN transistors. Write the equation of Emitter Current.

2. Draw a Sketch to show the various currents component of a BJT. Briefly explain the origin of each current. Write equation relating IE, IB and IC.

3. Draw and explain the input and output characteristics for CE-Configuration.

4. Draw the output characteristics of BJT in CE configuration. Indicate all the three regions of operation on it. Explain the operation of BJT as a switch.

5. Draw the input and output characteristics of BJT in CC configuration. Indicate all the three regions of operation on it.

6. Sketch the typical BJT common base input characteristics and output characteristics. Explain the shape of each set of characteristics.

7. Sketch the family of common base output characteristics for a transistor. Indicate the active, cut-off and saturation regions. Explain the shapes of the curves qualitatively.

8. Explain BJT common collector configuration and draw a circuit for determining common collector characteristics.

9. Sketch BJT CC input and output characteristics. Discuss the shape of characteristics.

10. What are the types of MOSFET? Explain any one in detail.

11. What is DC load line? Derive its equation for a CE amplifier and explain criterion for selection of operating points.

12. Explain how the transistor can be used as an amplifier with the help of DC load line approach.

13. Draw and explain BJT as switch.

14. Draw and explain MOSFET as switch.

15. For a BJT as a switch, Why CB and CC configurations are not preferred?

16. Define alpha Beta D.C. in relation to BJT and derive their inter relation with Gamma.

17. What is dc load line? Derive its equation for CE amplifier and explain the criteria for selection of operating point.

18. Draw the circuit diagram of RC coupled single stage CE AF amplifier and explain its operation with the help of waveform.

19. Draw constructional details and explain operation of p-channel MOSFET.

20. With the help of neat diagram explain operation of n-channel MOSFET. Sketch a typical output characteristics for the same.

21. What is meant by Q-point?

22. What is need of biasing transistor?

23. Describe the construction and operation of a MOSFET in enhancement mode. Draw its characteristics and equivalent circuit of the device.

UNIVERSITY QUESTIONS

Dec. 2012

1. Explain with a circuit diagram a single stage common emitter amplifier. State the function of each component in the circuit. **[6]**

2. Draw constructional details and explain operation and characteristics of n-channel MOSFET (enhancement type). **[6]**

May 2013

1. For a BJT as a switch why CB and cc configurations are not preferred. **[2]**

2. Explain how R_i and R_o affect the performance of the BJT voltage amplifier. **[4]**

Dec. 2013

1. Explain working of transistor as a switch. **[4]**

2. Define current amplification factor for CC, CB, CE configuration. **[2]**

3. Explain drain and transfer chara. of Enhancement type p-channel MOSFET. **[6]**

May. 2014

1. Explain input output characteristics of CE amplifier. **[6]**

2. Explain Drain Characteristics of an n-channel enhancement type MOSFET. **[6]**

Oct. 2014

1. Explain how transistor can be used as an amplifier with the help of D.C. load line approach. **[6]**

2. Explain the operation of n-channel enhancement type MOSFET with its characteristics. **[6]**

May 2015

1. What is de load line? Explain the role of Q-point on de load line.   **[6]**

2. Differentiate between CB, CE and CC configurations.   **[6]**

Nov. 2015

1. Explain operation of n-channel enhancement type MOSFET with its characteristics. **[6]**

2. Draw the output characteristics of BJT in CE configuration. Indicate all the three regions of operation on it. Explain the operation of BJT as a switch.   **[6]**

May 2016

1. Explain CE amplifier with the help of DC loadline.   **[6]**

2. Define α and β in cast of transistor. Derive the relationship between them. If α= 0.98, calculate value of β.   **[6]**

LINEAR INTEGRATED CIRCUITS

3.1 INTRODUCTION

- Operational amplifiers, which are also known as **op-amps** are used in a number of electronic applications. They have become the integral part of electronic systems because of their low cost, less power consumption, small size and high reliability.

- Earlier they were used to perform mathematical operations like add, subtract, multiply etc. and hence the name Operational Amplifier. Now–a–days they are used in amplifiers, filters, oscillators, comparators, regulators and many other applications in fields such as audio and radio communication, medical equipments, instrumentation control systems etc.

3.2 OP-AMP SYMBOL   [Dec. 12]

- Fig. 3.1 shows the symbol of an op-amp.

- An op-amp has two input terminals and one output terminal.

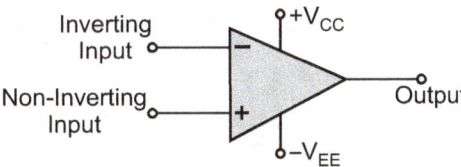

Fig. 3.1: Symbol of op-amp

- The terminal with (–) sign is called the **inverting input**. It gives the output of opposite polarity (out of phase). And the terminal with (+) sign is called the **non-inverting input**. It gives the output of same polarity (in phase).

3.3 OP-AMP IC 741

- Op-amps are available in three basic types:
    1. Flat pack
    2. Metal can pack
    3. Dual in line package (DIP)

- The op-amp packages may contain single, two (dual) or four (quad) op-amps. Typically they have 8, 10 or 14 terminals.

- The most popular µA 741 contains a single op-amp in 8 pin DIP. The pin-out diagram of op-amp IC 741 is as shown in Fig. 3.2. It has two input terminals, one output terminal and two power supply terminals.

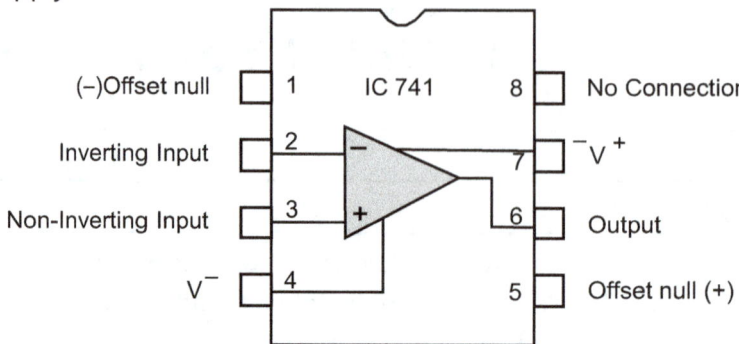

Fig. 3.2: Pin Diagram of IC 741

- The inverting input is given at pin 2, the non-inverting input is given at pin 3 and the output is taken at pin 6. The power supply is given at pins 7 ($+V_{CC}$) and 4 ($-V_{EE}$).

- Pins 1 and 5 are used to nullify the dc offset. Pin 8 is No Connection pin.

3.3.1 Power Supply Connections

- An op-amp works on dual supply. The power supply connections for the op-amp are done as shown in Fig. 3.3.

- The power supply voltages may range from ± 5 V to ± 22 V.

- The $+V_{CC}$ pin is connected to the positive terminal of one source and the $-V_{EE}$ pin is connected to the negative terminal of the other source. The remaining two terminals of the two sources i.e. negative terminal of the first source and positive terminal of the other source are connected together to a reference point or **ground** as shown below.

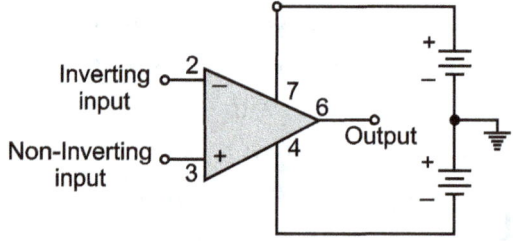

Fig. 3.3: Power Supply Connections

3.4 BLOCK DIAGRAM OF A TYPICAL OP-AMP   [Dec. 12]

❖ **Important Question Related to this Topic** ❖

What is op-amp? Draw and explain the functional block diagram of an op-amp.

- An op-amp basically amplifies the differential voltage present at its two input terminals. As shown in Fig. 3.4, a typical op-amp consists of four cascaded blocks.

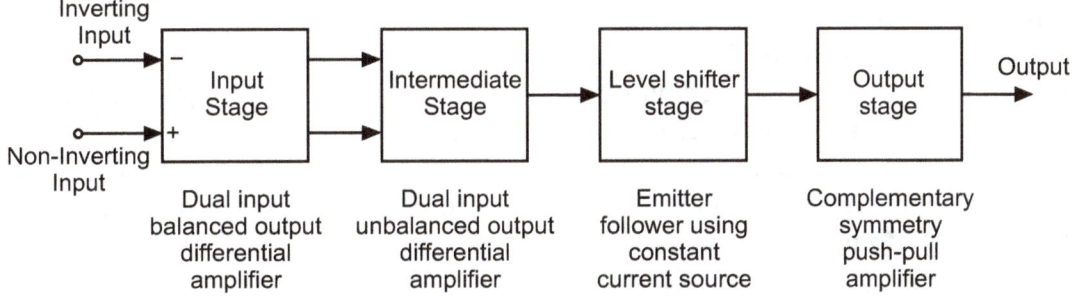

Fig. 3.4: Block Diagram of op-amp

Input Stage: It is a dual-input, balanced-output differential amplifier. This stage provides most of the voltage gain and also provides high input impedance.

Intermediate Stage: This stage is another differential amplifier. The output of first stage drives the Intermediate stage. Usually a dual input unbalanced output differential amplifier is used as an intermediate stage which provides the additional gain and high input impedance with single ended output.

Level Shifting Stage: Due to direct coupling between the amplifier stages, the dc voltage level, at the output of the intermediate stage, gets increased above the ground potential which may drive the internal transistors in saturation. This will give distortion at the output due to clipping. To avoid this situation, level shifter stage is used which adjusts the dc voltage to ground level when no signal is applied at the inputs.

Output Stage: This stage is usually a push-pull complementary amplifier stage which increases the output voltage swing and raises the current supplying capability of the op-amp. It also provides low output resistance.

3.5 OP-AMP INPUT MODES

- To use the op-amp input signal is applied   there are different ways to apply input signals is called input modes of op-amp. Following are the modes of op-amp
    (a) Single ended mode
    (b) Differential mode
    (c) Common mode

(a) Single Ended Mode:

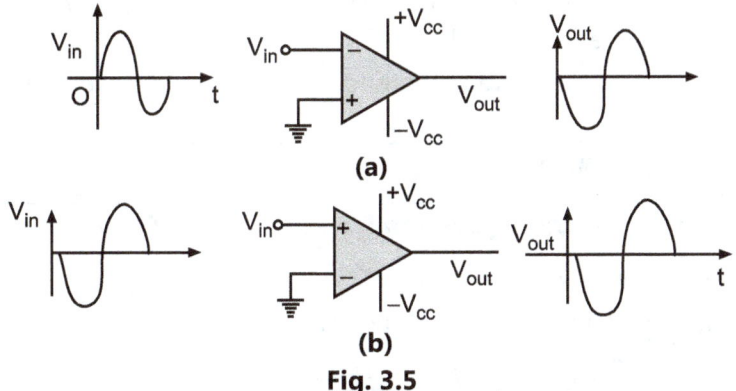

(a)

(b)

Fig. 3.5

- When an op-amp is operated in single ended mode. One of the op-amp terminal is grounded and input signal is applied to the other input.
- When input is applied to inverting input an inverted and amplified signal appears at the output, this mode is called inverting mode as shown in Fig. 3.5 a.
- When input is applied to non-inverting input an non-inverted and amplified signal appears at the output, this mode is called non-inverting mode as shown in Fig. 3.5 b.

(b) Differential Mode:

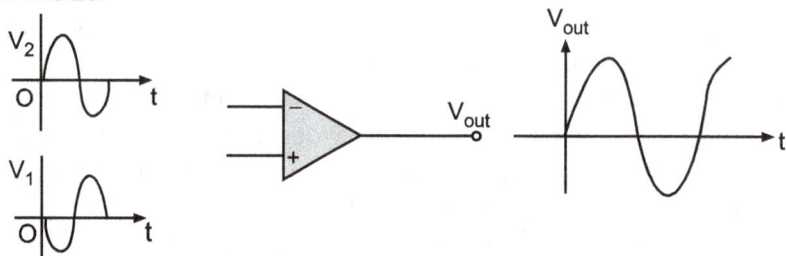

Fig. 3.6

- In differential mode two out of phase signals are applied to the inputs, as shown in Fig. 3.6.
- The amplified difference between the two inputs appears on the output.

(c) Common Mode:

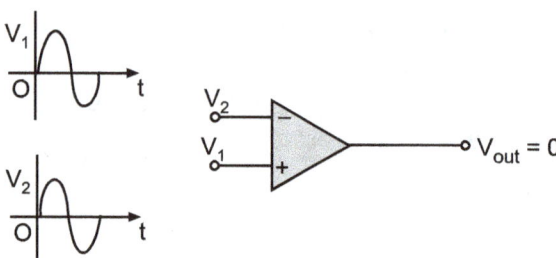

Fig. 3.7

- In common mode two signal voltages having same phase, frequency and amplitude are applied to the two inputs as shown in Fig. 3.7.
- The two equal input voltages cancel each other resulting into zero output voltage.
- This is called common mode rejection in which unwanted signal will not appear on the output and distort the desired signal.
- Noise source may be pick up of radiated energy or adjacent power line interference from 60 Hz signal.

3.6 THE IDEAL OP-AMP   [May 15]

❖ **Important Question Related to this Topic** ❖

1. What are the characteristics of an ideal differential amplifier?
2. Explain the following ideal characteristics of an op-amp:

   (a) CMRR   (b) Slew rate   (c) Bandwidth

An ideal op-amp has the following characteristics:

- **Open-Loop Voltage Gain (A_{OL}):** It is the differential open loop gain and is infinite for ideal op-amp. As the open loop voltage gain (A_{OL}) is infinite, the differential input voltage: $V_d = (V_{NIV} - V_{INV}) = 0$.

- **Input Impedance (R_i):** For an ideal op-amp the input impedance is infinite. So no current can flow into an ideal op-amp. Also it avoids loading on the preceding driver stage.

- **Output Impedance (R_o):** For an ideal op-amp the output impedance is zero. It ensures that there is no voltage drop across it and the output voltage remains the same irrespective of the load resistance. Also it makes possible for the op-amp to drive infinite number of other devices.

- **Bandwidth:** It is infinite for an ideal op-amp. So it can amplify any input signal with frequency range from 0 Hz to ∞ Hz without attenuation.

- **Offset Voltage (V_{ios}):** Ideally V_{ios} is zero i.e. zero output voltage when input voltage is zero.

- **Common Mode Rejection Ratio (CMRR):** The ratio of differential gain to common mode gain is defined as CMRR. Ideally it should be infinite that is zero common mode gain. Therefore the output for common mode noise voltage is zero.

- **Slew Rate:** Ideally it is infinite. Therefore the output voltage follows the change in input voltage simultaneously.

3.6.1 Practical OP-AMP

- The practical op-amp does not possess all the characteristics of an ideal op-amp. But can be made to approximate some of these characteristics using a negative feedback arrangement. The use of an ideal op-amp simplifies the analysis of various op-amp circuits. Typical values of the parameters for practical op-amps are given below:
  - Input impedance is typically more than 1 M Ω. It can be increased further up to several hundred mega-ohms by using FETs in the input stage.
  - Output impedance is typically few hundred ohms. It can be reduced to few ohms by giving negative feedback.
  - Bandwidth of an open loop is very small. It can be increased to a desired level by giving negative feedback.
  - Open loop voltage gain of an op-amp is several thousands. It can be controlled by using negative feedback.

3.7 EQUIVALENT CIRCUIT OF AN OP-AMP

- The equivalent circuit of an op-amp is shown in Fig. 3.8. It helps to understand the basic operating principle of an op-amp.

- We know V_1 and V_2 are the two input voltages. The op-amp amplifies the difference between the two input voltages with gain A_{OL}. i. e. $V_o = A_{OL} \times V_d = A_{OL} \times (V_1 - V_2)$

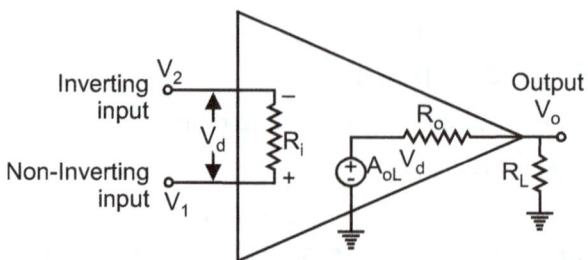

Fig. 3.8: Equivalent circuit of the op-amp

- As the open loop gain (A_{OL}) is very high, the value of the differential voltage required at the input is very small to obtain maximum output voltage.

- As shown in the figure, $A_{OL}V_d$ is an equivalent Thevenin voltage source and R_o is the Thevenin equivalent resistance looking back into the output terminal of the op-amp.

3.8 VOLTAGE TRANSFER CURVES OF AN OP-AMP

- Fig. 3.9 (a) shows the ideal voltage transfer curves of the op-amp. Ideally the open loop gain is infinite.

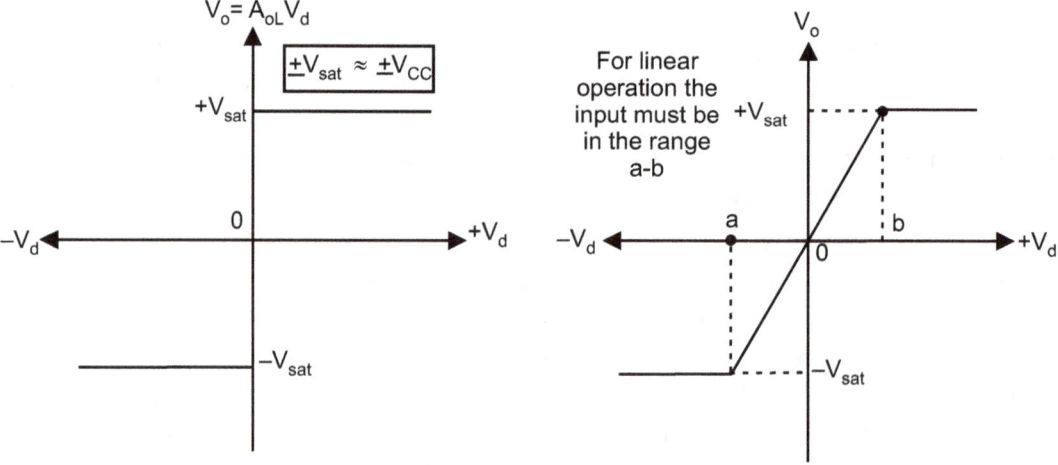

(a) Ideal Voltage Transfer Curve   **(b) Practical Voltage Transfer Curve**

Fig. 3.9

- $A_{OL} = V_o / V_d = \infty$ Therefore $V_d = V_o / \infty = 0$

- Thus ideally, for linear operation of the op-amp, the required differential input voltage is zero. Hence the ideal voltage transfer curve is just a vertical line showing the saturation level of the op-amp with the output voltage $+V_{sat}$ and $-V_{sat}$ at $V_d = 0$ V.

- The practical voltage transfer curve is shown in Fig. 3.9 (b). Practically the open loop gain A_{OL} has some finite high value.

- The curve shows that if the input voltage is more than point 'b', the op-amp gives output $+V_{sat}$ and if it is less than 'a' then the output voltage is $-V_{sat}$.

- Therefore for linear operation, the range of differential input voltage is 'a' to 'b', which is very small.

3.9 PARAMETERS OF PRACTICAL OP-AMP   [May 15]

> ❖ **Important Question Related to this Topic** ❖
>
> Define and give typical values of the following op-amp parameters:
>
> (i)   Voltage gain
>
> (ii) CMRR
>
> (iii) Input offset voltage
>
> (iv) Slew rate

- Various parameters of a practical op-amp are defined as below:

Input Offset Voltage (V_{io}):

- Ideally, if both the input terminals of an op-amp are connected to ground, the output voltage must be zero. But due to internal unbalances, the op-amp produces some output voltage even if $V_{INV} = V_{NIV} = 0$.

- So to make the output voltage zero, some voltage must be applied at the two inputs; it is called the input offset voltage, V_{io}. Normally it ranges in mV. Typically it is 6 mV for 741C.

  Mathematically, $V_{io} = \left| V_{B2} - V_{B1} \right|$

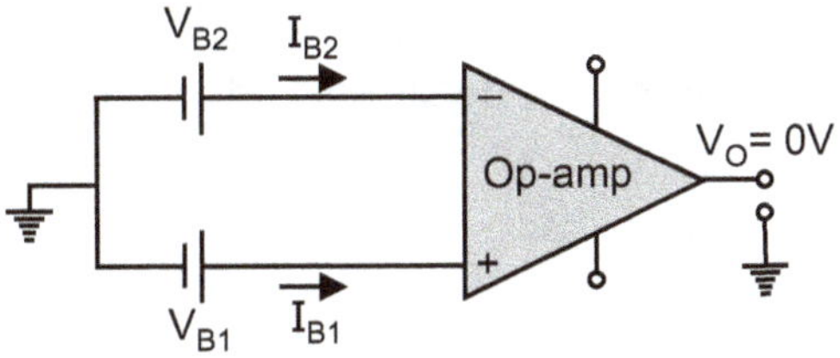

Fig. 3.10: To Calculate Input Offset Current of Practical op-amp

Input Offset Current (I_{io}):

- The input offset current I_{io} is the algebraic difference between the currents flowing into two input terminals of an op-amp. The maximum value of I_{io} for the 741 C is 200 nA.

- Mathematically, $I_{io} = \left| I_{B1} - I_{B2} \right|$

Input Bias Current (I_B):

- The input bias current I_B is the average of the currents that flow into the inverting and non-inverting input terminals of the op-amp. Ideally, it should be zero. Typically it is 500 nA for 741C.

- Mathematically, $I_B = \dfrac{I_{B1} + I_{B2}}{2}$

Input Impedance (R$_i$):

- Input impedance is the differential input resistance measured at either of the input terminals with the other terminal connected to the ground. Ideally it should be infinite. Typically it is 2 MΩ for 741 C.

Output Impedance (R$_o$):

- It is the resistance measured at the output terminal of the op-amp with respect to ground. Ideally it should be zero. Typically it is 75Ω for 741C.

Supply Voltage Rejection Ratio (SVRR also called PSRR):

- The Power Supply Rejection Ratio (SVRR or PSRR) is the change in input offset voltage V$_{io}$ of the op-amp caused by variations in supply voltages. Ideally it should be zero. Typically it is 150 µV/ V.

- Mathematically, SVRR $= \dfrac{\Delta V_{io}}{\Delta V}$ ....   where, ΔV is the change in supply voltage and ΔV$_{io}$ is the corresponding change in input offset voltage.

Common Mode Rejection Ratio (CMRR):

- Common Mode Rejection Ratio is the ratio of differential voltage gain A$_d$ to the common mode voltage gain A$_c$. It is expressed in dB. It shows the ability of the op-amp to reject the common mode signals. Ideally it is infinite. Typically it is 90 dB for 741C.

- Mathematically, CMRR $= \dfrac{A_d}{A_c}$.

Slew Rate (SR):

- The slew rate is defined as the maximum rate of change of output voltage per unit time. It shows how fast the output of an op-amp can change in response to changes in the input. It is expressed in volts/µsecond. Ideally it should be infinite. Typically it is 0.5 V/µs for 741C.

- Mathematically, Slew Rate $= \dfrac{dV_o}{dt}$.

3.10 OPEN-LOOP CONFIGURATION OF AN OP-AMP

❖ **Important Question Related to this Topic** ❖

Why it is necessary to reduce the gain of an op-amp from its open loop value?

- Figure 3.11 shows the open loop configuration of an op-amp. The term 'open loop' means there is no feedback from the output to the input. It is the simplest form of using op-amp.

- V_1 is the signal applied at the non-inverting input terminal and V_2 is the signal applied at the inverting input terminal.

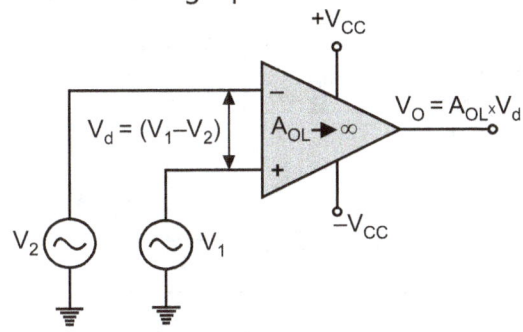

Fig. 3.11: Open Loop Configuration of op-amp

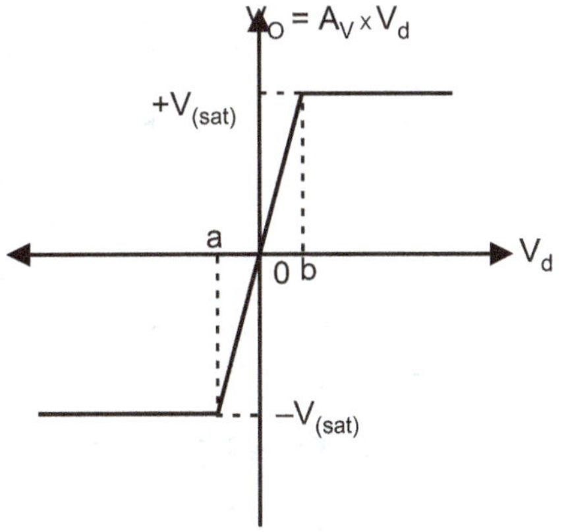

Fig. 3.12: Voltage Transfer Characteristics

- The output voltage V_o is given by,

$$V_o = A_{OL} (V_1 - V_2) = A_{OL} V_d$$

- Thus if the open loop voltage gain A_{OL} is infinite, the output voltage V_o also should be infinite (ideally).
- But practically the output voltage is limited to a value known as 'saturation voltage' (V_{sat}).
- It is given by, $\pm V_{sat} = 0.9$ or 0.95 ($\pm V_{cc}$)
- Thus, the output voltage V_o in open loop configuration is always $+ V_{sat}$ or $-V_{sat}$. Its polarity depends on the polarity of the differential voltage V_d.
- Here linear range between input and output is very small, So to increase this linear range closed loop configuration is used which is possible with the help of feedback which is explained in next section.
- The open loop configuration is used in voltage comparator circuits, zero crossing detectors etc.

3.11 CONCEPT OF FEEDBACK

- In feedback, a part of output is sampled and fed back to input thus forming a closed loop between the input and the output.
- The feedback network can be connected in four different configurations as follows:
  1. Voltage shunt feedback,
  2. Voltage series feedback,
  3. Current shunt feedback,
  4. Current series feedback.
- Fig. 3.13 shows the four types of configurations. Fig. 3.13 (a) and (b) show voltage shunt and voltage series feedback circuits in which the voltage across the load resistor R_L is sampled and fed at the input of the feedback circuit. The output of the feedback circuit is proportional to V_o.

- Fig. 3.13 (c) and (d) show the current series and current shunt feedback circuits in which the load current I_L flows into the feedback circuit. The output of the feedback circuit is proportional to the load current I_L.

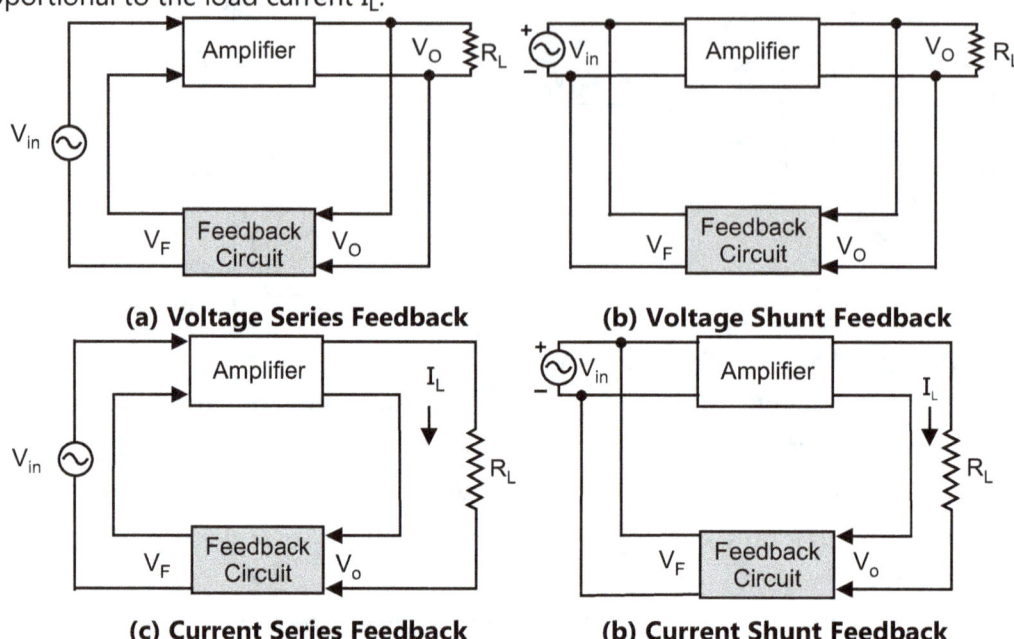

(a) Voltage Series Feedback   **(b) Voltage Shunt Feedback**

(c) Current Series Feedback   **(b) Current Shunt Feedback**

Fig. 3.13: Feedback Configurations

3.11.1 Negative and Positive Feedback

> ❖ **Important Question Related to this Topic** ❖
>
> State the advantages and applications of negative feedback.

- As discussed, in feedback, a part of output is sampled and fed back to the input either directly or via feedback network. There are two types of feedbacks:
  1. **Positive Feedback:** Here, the input signal and the fed back signal are in phase.
  2. **Negative Feedback:** Here, the input signal and the fed back signal are out of phase.

1. Positive Feedback:

- In positive feedback, a part of the output is fed back, **in phase** with the input through the feedback circuit. Due to positive feedback the circuit stops amplifying and starts oscillating. Therefore without any input, the output will continue to oscillate with a frequency that depends upon the feedback network. Such a circuit is called as an **Oscillator**. Thus positive feedback is used in signal generators.
- In an op-amp circuit, if the feedback signal is applied at the non-inverting input terminal then, it becomes a positive feedback.
- Positive feedback is also called as regenerative feedback.

Applications of Positive Feedback:

- Positive feedback is used in oscillators such as R-C phase shift oscillator, Wien bridge oscillator, Schmitt trigger circuits etc.

2. Negative Feedback:

- In negative feedback, the feedback signal is 180° out of phase with respect to the input signal (i.e. of opposite polarity). It is used to control the gain of an amplifier and stabilize the output voltage by self correcting action.
- In an op-amp circuit, if the feedback signal is applied at the inverting input terminal then it becomes a negative feedback.
- Negative feedback is also known as degenerative feedback, it degenerates (reduces) the output voltage and the voltage gain.

Advantages of Negative Feedback:

- It stabilizes the gain and the output voltage.
- It increases the bandwidth and improves the frequency response of the amplifier.
- It reduces distortion at the output.
- It also reduces the effect of input offset voltage at the output.
- It decreases the effect of variations in temperature and supply voltages on the output.

Applications of Negative Feedback:

- It is used in amplifiers such as inverting amplifiers, non-inverting amplifiers, summing amplifiers, difference amplifiers, voltage-to-current amplifiers etc.

3.11.2 Closed Loop Configuration of Op-Amp

- The utility of an op-amp can be significantly increased by providing negative feedback. The negative feedback helps to operate the op-amp linearly (i.e. the output voltage varies linearly with respect to input voltage) thus preventing it from going into saturation.
- The two important basic op-amp circuits with negative feedback are:
  1. Inverting amplifier and
  2. Non-inverting amplifier.

3.12 INVERTING AMPLIFIER

> ❖ **Important Question Related to this Topic** ❖
>
> Prove that for an inverting amplifier, $A_v = - R_f / R_1$

- Fig. 3.14 shows the basic inverting amplifier and the corresponding waveforms are shown in Fig. 3.15. We can observe that, the output voltage is 180 degrees out of phase with respect to the input voltage.
- Here, the input voltage V_{in} is applied at the inverting input terminal through the resistor R_1 and the non-inverting input terminal is grounded. R_F is a feedback resistor through which the output V_o is fed back to the inverting input terminal. The analysis is carried out assuming that the op-amp is ideal.
- First let us study the concept of virtual ground.

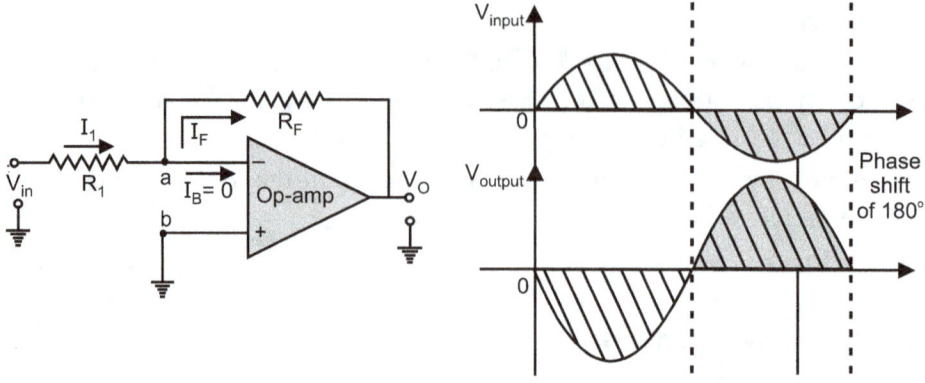

Fig. 3.14: Inverting Amplifier   **Fig. 3.15: Waveforms of Inverting Amplifier**

3.12.1 Virtual Ground

- For an ideal op-amp the input impedance is infinite. Therefore no current into the terminals of an op-amp. That means both the input terminals of an op-amp must be at the same potential, so we can say that the differential input voltage is zero i.e. $V_d = 0$ for an ideal op-amp.
- Now, as seen from Fig. 3.14, the non-inverting input is grounded. Therefore the voltage at this terminal is zero.
- Then for 'V_d' to be zero, the inverting input terminal should be at ground potential.
- Thus the inverting input terminal is not actually connected to the ground but it appears to be at ground potential. So it is called as grounded virtually.
- Thus, according to the virtual ground concept, if any one of the input terminal of op-amp is connected to the ground then the other terminal is also at ground potential.

3.12.2 Analysis of Inverting Amplifier Circuit

- Now, applying Kirchhoff's current law at node 'a' in Fig. 3.14,

  We get, $I_1 = I_B + I_F$
- For ideal op-amp, due to the infinite input impedance, the current I_B flowing into op-amp is zero. (i. e. $I_B = 0$). Hence we can write, $I_1 = I_F$.
- Also, as the non-inverting input terminal is grounded; node 'a' is also at ground potential due to virtual ground.

$$\therefore \qquad I_1 = \frac{V_{in} - V_a}{R_1} = \frac{V_{in} - 0}{R_1} = \frac{V_{in}}{R_1} \qquad \qquad \text{... (1)}$$

$$\text{and} \qquad I_F = \frac{V_a - V_o}{R_F} = \frac{0 - V_o}{R_F} = \frac{-V_o}{R_F} \qquad \qquad \text{... (2)}$$

- Since $I_1 = I_F$, we can equate the above two equations to get,

$$\frac{V_{in}}{R_1} = \frac{-V_o}{R_F}$$

$$\therefore \qquad \frac{V_o}{V_{in}} = \frac{-R_F}{R_1}$$

- $\dfrac{V_o}{V_{in}}$ is the closed loop gain (A_{CL}) of the amplifier.

$$\therefore \qquad A_{CL} = \frac{-R_F}{R_1}$$

- This is known as the gain of an inverting amplifier. The negative sign indicates that there is a phase shift of 180° between V_{in} and V_o.

- From the above equation, we can say that the closed loop gain A_{CL} is a function of two resistors R_F and R_1. By selecting suitable values of R_F and R_1, the gain of the amplifier can be controlled.

SOLVED EXAMPLES

Example 3.1: *For an inverting amplifier, if R_1 = 5 kΩ, R_F = 50 kΩ and V_{in} = 5 V, find the currents I_1 and I_F, closed loop gain A_{CL} and output voltage V_o. Assume the op-amp is ideal.*

Solution:

1. The current flowing through resistor R_1 is $I_1 = \dfrac{V_1 - V_a}{R_1} = \dfrac{5 - 0}{5\ K} =$ **1 mA**

   (Due to virtual ground, $V_a = 0$)

2. In ideal op-amp, the input current of op-amp is zero, therefore $I_1 = I_F =$ **1 mA**

3. The closed loop voltage gain $A_{CL} = \dfrac{-R_F}{R_1} =$ **– 10**

4. The output voltage is $V_o = A_{CL} \times V_{in} = -10 \times 5 =$ **– 50 V**
   The negative sign indicates that, the output is opposite out of phase with respect to input.

Example 3.2 : *For an inverting amplifier, if R_F = 100 kΩ, R_1 = 10 kΩ, V_{CC} = $\pm$ 10 V, V_i = 2V d.c. Calculate: (1) the output Voltage. (2) Is the result in part (1) practically possible? Justify.*

[Nov. 15]

Solution:

1. We know that for an inverting amplifier, $\dfrac{V_0}{V_{in}} = \dfrac{-R_F}{R_1}$

$$\therefore \qquad V_0 = \frac{-R_F}{R_1} \times V_{in} = \frac{-100K}{10K} \times 2 = -\ \textbf{20 V}$$

2. As V_{CC} = + 10 V, the output voltage saturates for $\pm$ 10 V. Hence the output voltage of – 20 V is practically not possible.

3.13 NON-INVERTING AMPLIFIER

❖ **Important Question Related to this Topic** ❖

Derive the expression for the voltage gain of a closed loop non-inverting amplifier using an op-amp.

- Fig. 3.16 shows the circuit of non-inverting amplifier and the corresponding waveforms are shown in Fig. 3.17. As the name suggests, the output of this amplifier does not give the phase shift. The output voltage is in phase with the input voltage.

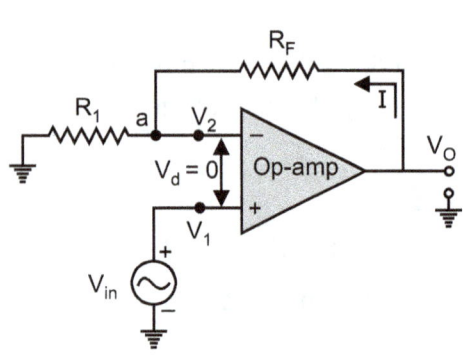

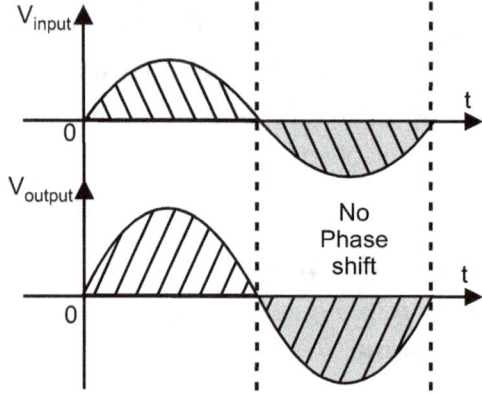

Fig. 3.16: Non-Inverting Amplifier   **Fig. 3.17: Waveforms**

- Here, the input signal V_{in} (ac or dc) is applied at the non-inverting input terminal of the op-amp and the inverting input terminal is grounded through the resistor R_1.

- R_F is a feedback resistor through which the output V_0 is fed back to the inverting input terminal, thus R_F provides negative feedback.

- The analysis is carried out by assuming the op-amp is ideal.

- The voltage at node 'a' $(V_a) = \dfrac{R_1}{R_1 + R_F} \times V_0$ ... (3)

- From Fig. 3.14, we can write,

$$V_1 = V_{in} = V_a$$

- For an ideal op-amp, the differential input voltage $V_d = 0$

$\therefore \qquad\qquad V_d = V_1 - V_2 = 0$

$\therefore \qquad\qquad V_{in} - V_2 = 0$

$\therefore \qquad\qquad V_2 = V_{in}$

But, $\qquad\qquad\qquad V_a = V_{in}$ ... (4)

- Equating the equations (3) and (4) we get,

$$\frac{R_1}{R_1 + R_F} \times V_o = V_{in}$$

$$\therefore \qquad \frac{V_o}{V_{in}} = \frac{R_1 + R_F}{R_1}$$

Therefore the closed loop gain $(A_{CL}) = \dfrac{V_o}{V_{in}} = \dfrac{R_1 + R_F}{R_1}$

$$\therefore \qquad A_{CL} = 1 + \frac{R_F}{R_1}$$

- This is known as the gain of non-inverting amplifier. The gain can be adjusted to unity or more by selecting suitable values of resistors R_F and R_1.

- Also note that, the gain is positive meaning that the output signal is in phase with the input signal.

Example 3.3 : *An op-amp is used in non-inverting mode with $R_1 = 1\ k\Omega$, $R_F = 12\ k\Omega$, $V_{CC} = + 15V$. Calculate output voltage for: (i) $V_{in} = 250\ mV$, (ii) $V_{in} = 3\ V$.*

Solution: We know that for non-inverting mode,

$$A_{CL} = 1 + \frac{R_F}{R_1} = 1 + \frac{12K}{1K} = 13 = \frac{V_o}{V_{in}}$$

(i)   For $V_{in} = 250\ mV$

$V_o = A_{CL} \times V_{in} = 13 \times 250 \times 10^{-3} = $ **3.25 V**

(ii)   For $V_{in} = 3\ V$

$V_o = A_{CL} \times V_{in} = 13 \times 3 = $ **39 V**

As op-amp saturates at $+ V_{CC}$ i.e. 15 V; output voltage of 39 V is not possible practically.

3.14 VOLTAGE FOLLOWER (UNITY GAIN BUFFER)

❖ **Important Question Related to this Topic** ❖

Explain the voltage follower using op-amp with input and output waveforms.

- A voltage follower circuit is a special case of a non-inverting amplifier. If $R_F = 0$ and $R_1 = \infty$, in a non-inverting amplifier, the resulting circuit is called voltage follower circuit as shown in Fig. 3.18. Its waveforms are shown in Fig. 3.19. As the name suggests, the output follows the input i.e. $V_o = V_{in}$. The gain of this amplifier is adjusted to 1.

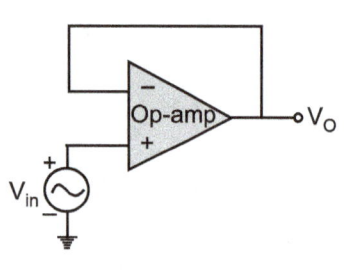

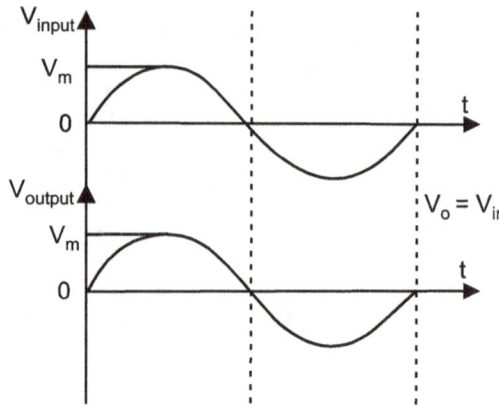

Fig. 3.18: Voltage Follower   **Fig. 3.19: Waveforms**

- The closed loop gain of non-inverting amplifier is given by,

$$A_{CL} = 1 + \frac{R_F}{R_1}$$

Substituting $R_F = 0$ we get, $A_{CL} = 1$

- Thus the closed loop gain of voltage follower circuit is one.

$$\therefore \qquad \frac{V_o}{V_{in}} = A_{CL} = 1$$

Therefore, $V_o = V_{in}$

- Thus for a voltage follower, the output voltage is equal to the input voltage both in magnitude and phase.

Advantages of Voltage Follower:

- The main advantage of this circuit is that, it gives very high input impedance and zero output impedance. Therefore it draws negligible current from the source.
- It has large bandwidth.
- Thus a voltage follower can be used as a buffer for impedance matching i.e. to connect a high impedance source to a low impedance load.

3.15 COMPARATOR

- Comparator is used to compare the amplitude of one voltage with another. In comparator open loop configuration is used as mentioned earlier.

3.15.1 Zero Level Detection

- Fig. 3.20 shows a zero level detector. It is used to indicate greater than or less than relationship of the inputs.

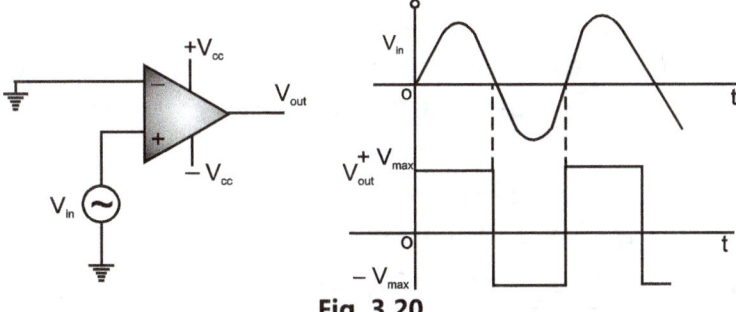

Fig. 3.20

Operation of Circuit:

- When V_{in} greater than zero reference level op-amp enters into positive saturation region, Because gain in open loop is very high. E.g. if gain is 100,000 and the input voltage amplitude is 0.45 mV then, V_o = 45V. So, Op-amp output is limited by power supply voltages i.e. ±20V. Therefore V_o = +V_{sat}.
- When V_{in} less than zero reference level op-amp enters into negative saturation region, Because of same reason that gain in open loop is high. Therefore V_o = −V_{sat}.

3.15.2 Non-zero Level Detection

- The zero level detector shown in Fig. 3.20 can be modified to detect positive and negative voltage by connecting a fix reference voltage source to the inverting input as shown in Fig. 3.21. Reference voltage may be obtained from direct d.c. source shown in Fig. 3.21 a. A standard approach shown in Fig. 3.21 (b) using voltage divider in which V_{REF} = ($R_2/R_1 + R_2$) . (+V). The circuit shown in Fig. 3.21 (c) uses a zener diode to set reference voltage ($V_{REF} = V_Z$)

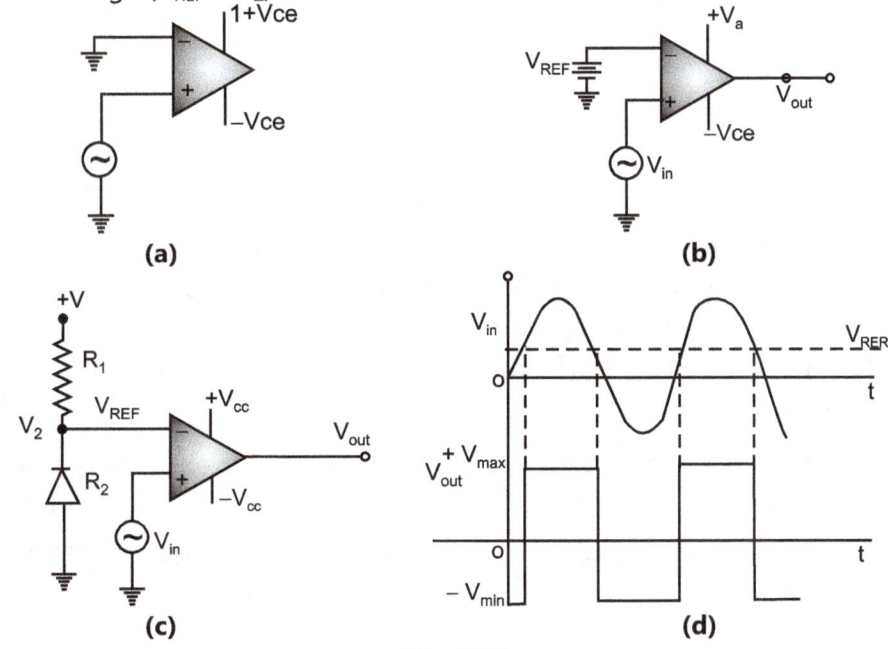

Fig. 3.21

Operation of Circuit:

- When $V_{in} > V_{REF}$ non-inverting potential is greater than inverting potential, Due to this reason op-amp enters into positive saturation region as shown in Fig. 3.21 (d) where $V_o = +V_{sat}$.

- When $V_{in} < V_{REF}$ inverting potential is greater than non inverting potential, Due to this op-amp enters into negative saturation region as shown in Fig. 3.21 (d) where $V_o = -V_{sat}$.

3.15.3 Regenerative Comparator (Schmitt Trigger)

- In a basic comparator, a feedback is not used and the op-amp is used in the open loop mode. As open loop gain of op-amp is very large, very small noise voltages also can cause triggering of the comparator, to change its state. Such a false triggering may cause lot of problems in the applications of comparator as zero crossing detector. This may give a wrong indication of zero crossing due to zero crossing of noise voltage rather than zero crossing of wanted input signal. Such unwanted noise causes the output to jump between high and low states. The comparator circuit used to avoid such unwanted triggering is called regenerative comparator or Schmitt trigger.

Inverting Schmitt Trigger Circuit

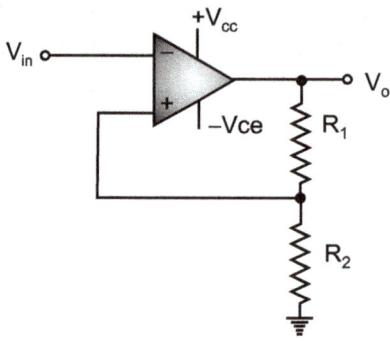

Fig. 3.22

- The Fig. 3.22 shows the basic inverting Schmitt trigger circuit. As the input is applied to the inverting terminal, it is also called inverting Schmitt trigger circuit. The inverting mode produces opposite polarity output. This is feedback to the non-inverting input which is of same polarity as that of output. This ensures positive feedback.

Operation of Circuit:

- When V_{in} is slightly positive than V_{ref}, then the output gets driven into negative saturation region at $-V_{sat}$ level.

- When V_{in} becomes more negative than V_{ref}, then the output gets driven into positive saturation at $+V_{sat}$ level.

- Thus output voltage is always at $+V_{sat}$ or $-V_{sat}$ but the voltage at which it changes its state now can be controlled by resistance R_1 and R_2. Thus V_{ref} can be obtained as per the requirement.

- Now R1 and R2 forms a potential divider and we can write,

$$+ V_{ref} = (V_o/R_1 + R_2).R_2 = (+ V_{sat}/R_1 + R_2).R_2$$
$$- V_{ref} = (V_o/R_1 + R_2).R_2 = (- V_{sat}/R_1 + R_2).R_2$$

- $+V_{ref}$ is related to positive saturation when $V_o = +V_{sat}$ and is called upper threshold voltage denoted as V_{UT}. $-V_{ref}$ is for negative saturation when $V_o = -V_{sat}$ and is called lower threshold voltage denoted as V_{LT}. So V_{UT} and V_{LT} is set by properly selecting the values of R_1 and R_2.

$$V_{UT} = (+ V_{sat}/R_1 + R_2).R_2$$
$$V_{LT} = (- V_{sat}/R_1 + R_2).R_2$$

- The output voltage remains in a given state until the input voltage exceeds the threshold voltage level either positive or negative. The Fig. 3.23 shows the graph of output voltage against input voltage. This is called transfer characteristics of Schmitt trigger.

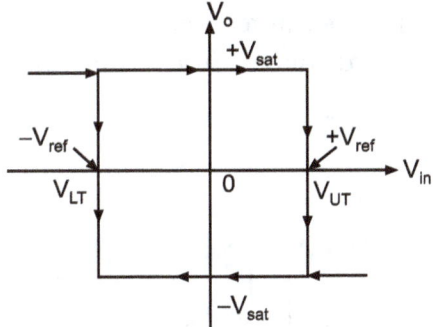

Fig. 3.23

- The graph indicates that once the output changes its state, it remains its state, it remains there indefinitely until the input voltage crosses any of the threshold voltage levels. This is called hysteresis of Schmitt trigger. The hysteresis is also called dead band or dead zone. The difference between V_{UT} and V_{LT} is also called width of hysteresis denoted by H,

$$H = V_{UT} - V_{LT} = 2 [+V_{sat} \cdot R_2/(R_1 + R_2)]$$

- The Schmitt trigger eliminates the effect of noise voltage present the noise voltages less than the hysteresis H, cannot cause triggering. As for positive V_{in} greater than V_{UT}, the output becomes $- V_{sat}$ and for negative V_{in} less that V_{LT}, The output becomes $+V_{sat}$ this is called inverting Schmitt trigger.

- If input applied is purely sinusoidal, the input and output waveforms for inverting Schmitt trigger is shown in Fig. 3.24.

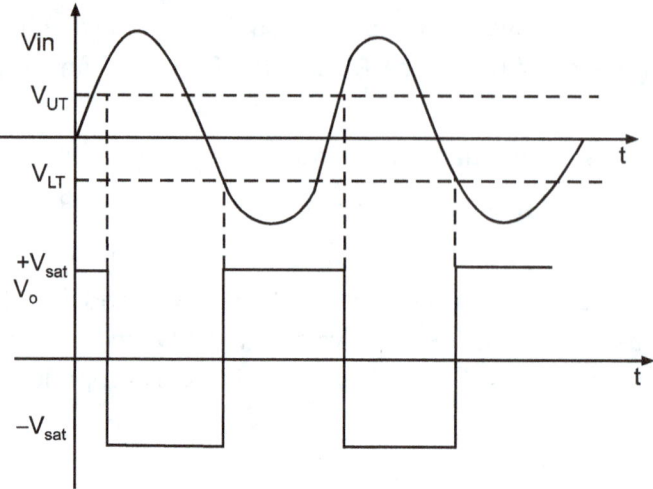

Fig. 3.24

3.15.4 Output Bounding

- In some application there is requirement to limit output voltage levels of comparator to a value less than that provided by the saturated op-amp.
- In Fig. 3.25 Zener diode is inserted in feedback path which limits the output voltage in one direction and to the forward voltage drop in other direction. This process of limiting is called as Bounding.

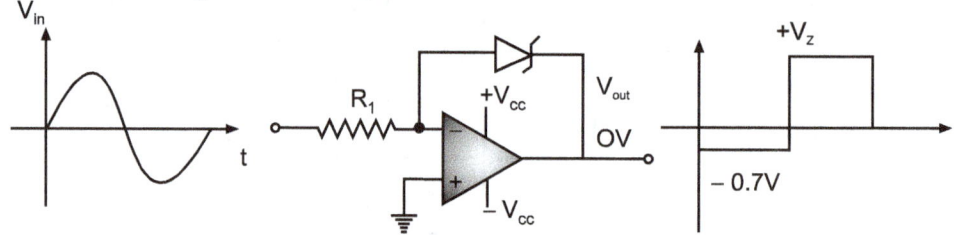

Fig. 3.25

- Here anode of zener diode is connected to input terminal of op-amp which is at virtual ground that is nearly equal to 0V. Therefore, maximum value of positive output voltage is V_z as shown in Fig. 3.25.
- Similarly when output goes negative its maximum value is equal to $-V_z$ as shown in Fig. 3.26.

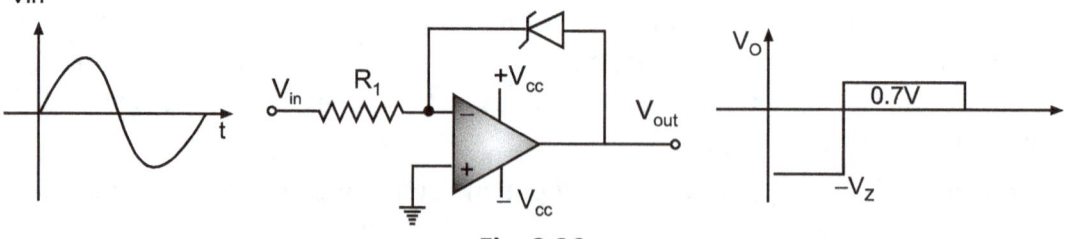

Fig. 3.26

3.16 SUMMING AMPLIFIER

❖ **Important Question Related to this Topic** ❖

1. Describe the use of an op-amp as adder. What type of feedback is used in an op-amp adder? Justify your answer.
2. Draw a neat diagram of three input inverting summing amplifiers using op-amp and obtain the expression for its output voltage.

- As the input impedance of an op-amp is very high, it is possible to apply more than one input to the inverting amplifier. The output can be the sum of several input signals. Such a circuit is called as a **summing amplifier** or a summer or an adder circuit.
- There are two types of summing amplifier:
  1. Inverting summing amplifier,
  2. Non-inverting summing amplifier.

3.16.1 Inverting Summing Amplifier

- As the name indicates, in this type of summing amplifier, the inputs are applied at the inverting input of the op-amp and so the output is an inverting sum of several inputs.
- Fig. 3.27 shows a typical inverting summing amplifier with three input voltages V_1, V_2 and V_3, applied through resistors R_1, R_2 and R_3 respectively at the inverting input terminal.

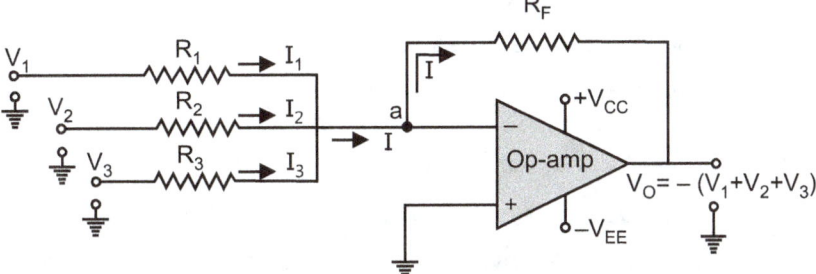

Fig. 3.27: Inverting Summing Amplifier

- R_F is the feedback resistor. Let I_1, I_2 and I_3 be the currents flowing through the resistors R_1, R_2 and R_3 respectively. As the non-inverting input is grounded, node 'a' is also at ground potential due to virtual ground. Hence, $V_a = 0$. We can write equations for:

$$I_1 = \frac{V_1 - V_a}{R_1} = \frac{V_1 - 0}{R_1} = \frac{V_1}{R_1}$$

$$I_2 = \frac{V_2 - V_a}{R_2} = \frac{V_2 - 0}{R_2} = \frac{V_2}{R_2}$$

and $\quad I_3 = \frac{V_3 - V_a}{R_3} = \frac{V_3 - 0}{R_3} = \frac{V_3}{R_3}$

- The total current (I) approaching the node 'a' is the sum of currents I_1, I_2 and I_3.

$\therefore$ $\qquad\qquad\qquad I = I_1 + I_2 + I_3$

$\therefore$ $\qquad\qquad\qquad I = \dfrac{V_1}{R_1} + \dfrac{V_2}{R_2} + \dfrac{V_3}{R_3}$

- Also note that, the current I gets divided at node 'a'. One component flows through the feedback resistor R_F and the other component flows into the op-amp. But since the input impedance of the op-amp is very high, the current flowing into the op-amp is negligible and can be assumed to be zero.

- Therefore the entire current 'I' flows through the feedback resistor R_F. Therefore we can write, $\qquad\qquad I = \dfrac{V_a - V_o}{R_F} = \dfrac{0 - V_o}{R_F} = \dfrac{-V_o}{R_F}$

- Equating the two equations (5) and (6), we get,

$$\dfrac{V_1}{R_1} + \dfrac{V_2}{R_2} + \dfrac{V_3}{R_3} = \dfrac{-V_o}{R_F}$$

$\therefore$ $\qquad\qquad\qquad V_o = -R_F\left(\dfrac{V_1}{R_1} + \dfrac{V_2}{R_2} + \dfrac{V_3}{R_3}\right)$

$\therefore$ $\qquad\qquad\qquad V_o = -\left(\dfrac{R_F}{R_1}V_1 + \dfrac{R_F}{R_2}V_2 + \dfrac{R_F}{R_3}V_3\right)$

- Thus, the output is the inverted weighted sum of inputs.

- Let $R_1 = R_2 = R_3 = R_F = R$

$\therefore$ $\qquad\qquad\qquad V_o = -\left(\dfrac{R}{R}V_1 + \dfrac{R}{R}V_2 + \dfrac{R}{R}V_3\right)$

$\therefore$ $\qquad\qquad\qquad V_o = -(V_1 + V_2 + V_3)$

- Hence, the output voltage is the inverted sum of the three input voltages. This equation can be modified to include any number of input voltages.

Example 3.4: *In Fig. 3.28 let $R_1 = R_2 = 1\ k\Omega$, $R_3 = 5\ k\Omega$, $R_F = 10\ k\Omega$, $V_1 = -1\ V$, $V_2 = 2\ V$ and $V_3 = 4V$. Evaluate V_o.* [May 15, 16]

Solution: To evaluate V_o we have

$$V_o = -\left(\dfrac{R_F}{R_1}V_1 + \dfrac{R_F}{R_2}V_2 + \dfrac{R_F}{R_3}V_3\right)$$

Substituting the given values we get,

$$V_o = -\left(\dfrac{10}{1}(-1) + \dfrac{10}{1}(2) + \dfrac{10}{5}(4)\right)$$

$$= -(-10 + 20 + 8)$$

$$= \mathbf{+18\ V}$$

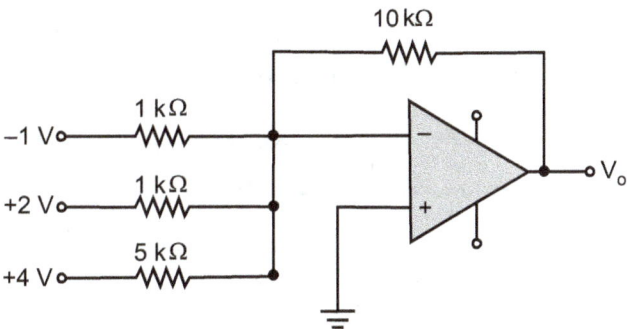

Fig. 3.28

3.16.2 Non-Inverting Summing Amplifier   [Nov. 15]

❖ **Important Question Related to this Topic** ❖

1. Draw a neat diagram of a two input non-inverting summing amplifier using an op-amp and obtain an expression for its output voltage.
2. Draw and explain the circuit diagram for obtaining $V_o = V_1 + V_2$. Derive the equation.

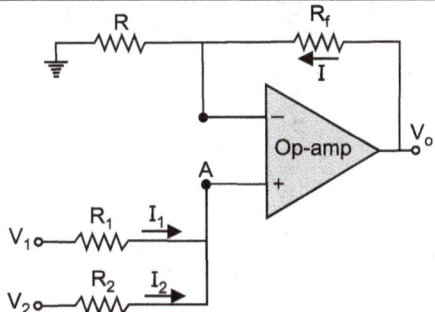

Fig. 3.29: Non-inverting Summing Amplifier

- As shown in Fig. 3.29, in a non-inverting summing amplifier, the input signals are connected to the non-inverting input terminal of the op-amp. Therefore at the output we get, non-inverted sum of several inputs.

- The input voltages V_1 and V_2 are applied through resistors R_1 and R_2 respectively at the non-inverting input terminal of the op-amp.

- First to find the output voltage V_{01} due to V_1 alone, make $V_2 = 0$. The equivalent circuit of this case is shown in Fig. 3.30. This circuit is similar to a non-inverting amplifier with input voltage as V_a; whose gain can be found out by the equation, $\left(1 + \dfrac{R_F}{R}\right)$.

- Now, to find the voltage at node 'a' apply the voltage divider formula,

$$\therefore \qquad V_a = \left(\frac{R_2}{R_1 + R_2}\right) V_1$$

$$V_{01} = \text{Gain} \times V_a$$

$$\therefore \qquad V_{01} = \left(1 + \frac{R_F}{R}\right) \cdot \left(\frac{R_2}{R_1 + R_2}\right) \cdot V_1$$

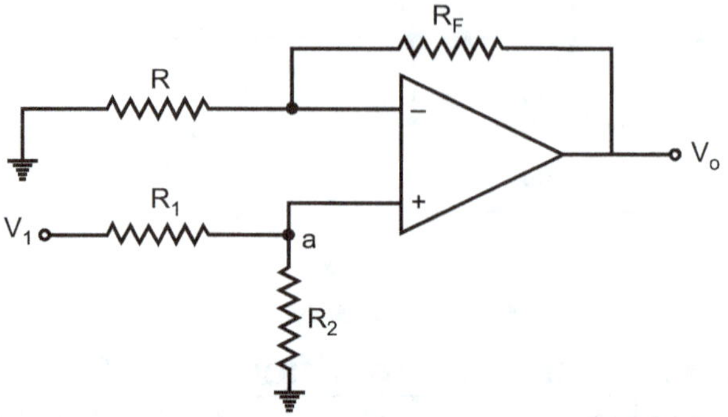

Fig. 3.30: Equivalent Circuit of Fig. 3.29 (For $V_2 = 0$)

- Similarly the output voltage V_{02} due to V_2 alone (with V_1 grounded) can be written as

$$V_{02} = \left(1 + \frac{R_F}{R}\right) \cdot \left(\frac{R_1}{R_1 + R_2}\right) \cdot V_2$$

- By super position theorem, $V_0 = V_{01} + V_{02}$. Now let us put the values of V_{01} and V_{02}.

$$\therefore \qquad V_0 = \left(1 + \frac{R_F}{R}\right)\left(\frac{R_2}{R_1 + R_2}\right) V_1 + \left(1 + \frac{R_F}{R}\right)\left(\frac{R_1}{R_1 + R_2}\right) V_2$$

$$\therefore \qquad V_0 = \left(1 + \frac{R_F}{R}\right)\left[\frac{R_2}{R_1 + R_2} V_1 + \frac{R_1}{R_1 + R_2} V_2\right]$$

If $\qquad R_1 = R_2 = R_F = R$

$$\therefore \qquad V_0 = \left(1 + \frac{R}{R}\right)\left[\frac{R}{R + R} \cdot V_1 + \frac{R}{R + R} \cdot V_2\right]$$

$$\therefore \qquad V_0 = (1 + 1)\left[\frac{R}{2R} V_1 + \frac{R}{2R} V_2\right]$$

$$\therefore \qquad V_0 = 2\left[\frac{1}{2} V_1 + \frac{1}{2} V_2\right]$$

$$\therefore \qquad V_0 = 2 \times \frac{1}{2}\left(V_1 + V_2\right)$$

$$\therefore \qquad V_0 = V_1 + V_2$$

- Thus, the output is the non-inverted sum of the inputs.

Example 3.5: *In a non-inverting summing amplifier $V_1 = 2$ V, $V_2 = -4$ V, $V_3 = 5$ V. The input resistor for all three input signals is the same and is equal to 1 kΩ. The feedback resistor R_f is 2 kΩ. Determine the output voltage. (Assume ideal op-amp).*

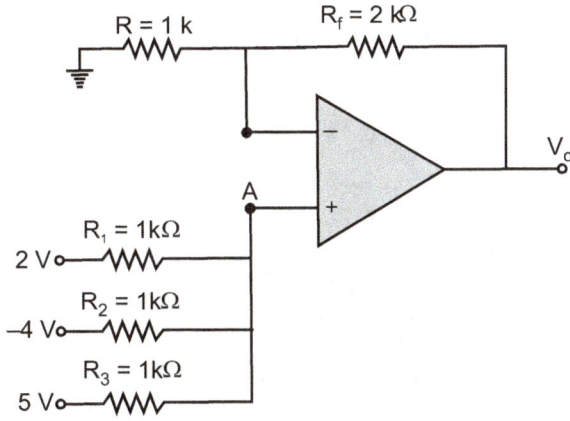

Fig. 3.31

Solution: The circuit is shown in Fig 3.31.

We know, the output V_0 can be found out by the formula given below,

$$V_0 = \left(1 + \frac{R_F}{R}\right)\left(\frac{R_1}{R_1 + R_2 + R_3}V_1 + \frac{R_2}{R_1 + R_2 + R_3}V_2 + \frac{R_3}{R_1 + R_2 + R_3}V_3\right)$$

$$V_0 = \left(1 + \frac{2\,K}{1\,K}\right)\left(\frac{1 \times (2V) + 1 \times (-4V) + 1 \times (5V)}{1+1+1}\right) = \frac{(3)\,(2 - 4 + 5)}{3} = \textbf{3 V}$$

3.16.3 Inverting Averaging Amplifier

❖ **Important Question Related to this Topic** ❖

Show how an op-amp can be used to give output $V_0 = (V_1 + V_2 + V_3) / 3$.

- An averaging amplifier gives the output voltage equal to the average of all the input voltages. That is if there are three input signals, the averaging amplifier should add the input voltages and divide the sum by 3.
- It is a special case of an inverting summing amplifier with all the input resistors made equal to R. i.e. $R_1 = R_2 = ---- = R$ and the feedback resistor R_F equal to R divided by the number of inputs. i.e. $R_F = \dfrac{R}{n}$
- Recall the expression for output voltage of an inverting summing amplifier. It is

$$V_0 = -\left(\frac{R_F}{R_1}V_1 + \frac{R_F}{R_2}V_2 + \frac{R_F}{R_3}V_3\right)$$

- As the number of input signals is three, we have n = 3
- Making all the input resistors equal to R we get,

$$R_1 = R_2 = R_3 = R$$

and the feedback resistor R_F equal to R divided by number of inputs

$$\therefore \qquad R_F = \frac{R}{3}$$

- Substituting these values in the above expression, we get,

$$V_o = -\left(\frac{\frac{R}{3}}{R}V_1 + \frac{\frac{R}{3}}{R}V_2 + \frac{\frac{R}{3}}{R}V_3\right)$$

$$V_o = -\left(\frac{1}{3}V_1 + \frac{1}{3}V_2 + \frac{1}{3}V_3\right)$$

$$V_o = -\left(\frac{V_1 + V_2 + V_3}{3}\right)$$

- Thus, output is the average of the input signals but of opposite phase due to the negative sign (as we have used the inverting amplifier).

3.17 DIFFERENCE AMPLIFIER

❖ Important Question Related to this Topic ❖

Draw a neat circuit diagram of difference amplifier using an op-amp and obtain the expression for its output voltage.

- As the name suggests, the difference amplifier amplifies the difference between the applied input voltages. It is also known as subtractor. The circuit is shown in Fig. 3.32. The expression for the output voltage can be obtained by using the superposition principle.

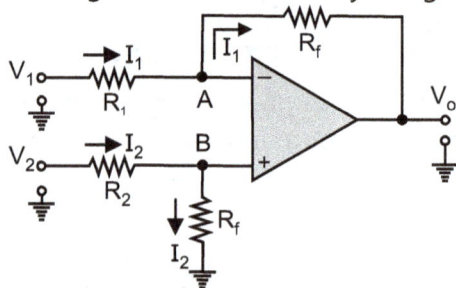

Fig. 3.32: Difference Amplifier

- First to find the output V_{01} due to V_1 alone, we make $V_2 = 0$. The equivalent circuit is as shown in Fig. 3.33. It is similar to an inverting amplifier with input voltage V_1 applied at the inverting input terminal.

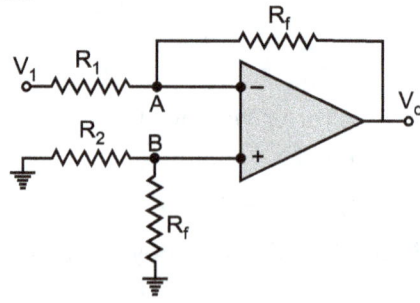

Fig. 3.33: Equivalent Circuit of Fig. 3.22 ($V_2 = 0$ V)

- Now to find the output V_{02} due to V_2 alone, make $V_1 = 0$. The equivalent circuit is as shown in Fig. 3.34. It is similar to a non-inverting amplifier with input voltage V_A, applied at the non-inverting input terminal.

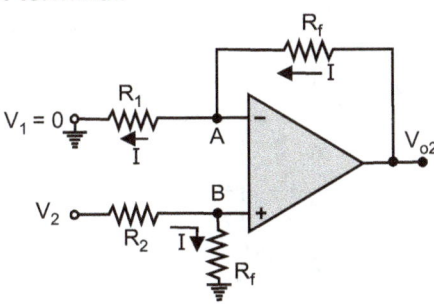

Fig. 3.34: Equivalent Circuit of Fig. 3.23 (V_1 = 0 V)

Therefore V_{01} is given by, $V_{01} = \left(\dfrac{-R_f}{R_1}\right) \times V_1$

If $R_f = R_1$, we get, $V_{01} = -V_1$

- The voltage at node A is equal to voltage at node B. Applying the voltage divider formula, voltage at node B is,

$$V_B = \left(\dfrac{V_2\, R_f}{R_f + R_2}\right)$$

If $R_1 = R_2 = R_f$ then, $V_B = \dfrac{V_2}{2}$

- Recall the equation for the output voltage of a non-inverting amplifier. We get,

$$V_{02} = \left(1 + \dfrac{R_f}{R_2}\right) \cdot \dfrac{V_2}{2}$$

If $R_1 = R_2 = R_f$ then, $V_{02} = (1 + 1) \cdot \dfrac{V_2}{2}$

$\therefore$ $V_{02} = 2 \times \dfrac{V_2}{2}$

$\therefore$ $V_{02} = V_2$

- Applying the superposition theorem, the output voltage V_0 is given by

$$V_0 = V_{01} + V_{02}$$

$\therefore$ $V_0 = -V_1 + V_2$

$\therefore$ $V_0 = V_2 - V_1$

- Thus, output is the difference between the applied input voltages.

Example 3.6: *For the op-amp circuit shown in Fig 3.35, calculate the output voltage V_0.*

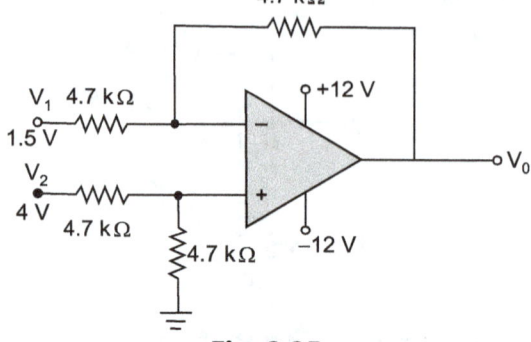

Fig. 3.35

Solution:

Case 1: Let us first calculate V_{01} when only V_1 = 1.5 V is present, assuming the other input V_2 = 0. The circuit acts as an inverting amplifier, with $R_f = R_1 = 4.7\ \Omega$.

$$V_{01} = \frac{-R_f}{R_1} \times V_{in} = -\frac{4.7}{4.7} \times 1.5 = \textbf{-1.5 V}$$

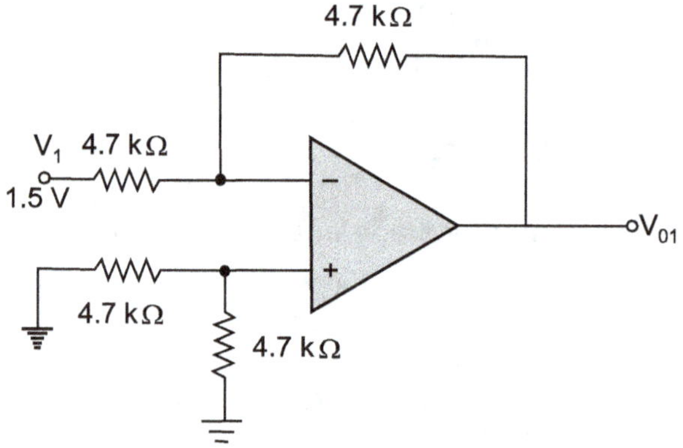

Fig. 3.36

Case 2: Now, to calculate V_{02}, consider only V_2 = 4 V and assume that the other input V_1 = 0.

From voltage divider formula,

$$V_B = \frac{V_2}{2} = \frac{4}{2} = 2\ V$$

$\therefore$

$$V_{02} = \left(1 + \frac{R_F}{R_1}\right) V_B = (1+1)\ 2V = \textbf{4 V}$$

Hence,

$$V_0 = V_{01} + V_{02} = -1.5 + 4 = \textbf{2.5 V}$$

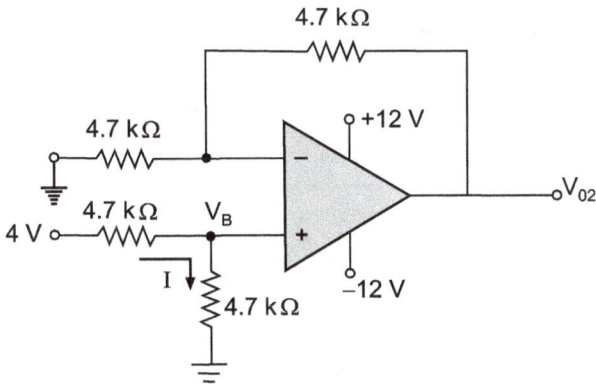

Fig. 3.37

3.18 DIFFERENTIATOR [Nov. 15, May 14]

❖ Important Question Related to this Topic ❖

1. Draw a neat diagram of a basic differentiator. Give its limitations. How they are overcome in practical differentiator.

2. Draw the circuit diagram of an op-amp differentiator and derive the expression for its output voltage.

- A differentiator circuit performs the mathematical operation of differentiation. It gives the output signal which is directly proportional to the derivative of the input signal.

- The resistor R_{comp} provides bias compensation, its value is set equal to R_f.

- Fig. 3.38 shows a differentiator circuit. Here, the input voltage V_{in} is applied at the inverting input terminal of the op-amp through capacitor C_1.

- Let I_1 be the current flowing through C_1. Since the input impedance of the op-amp is very high, the current flowing into the op-amp is negligible and can be assumed to be zero i.e. $I_2 = 0$.

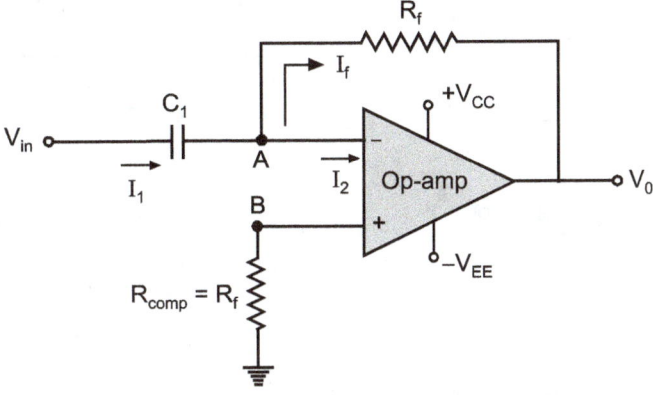

Fig. 3.38: Differentiator

Therefore $I_1 = I_F$ (the current flowing through R_F.)

But
$$I_1 = C_1 \times \frac{d}{dt}(V_{in} - V_A)$$

and
$$I_F = \frac{V_A - V_0}{R_F}$$

Therefore equating the above two equations we get,

$$C_1 \cdot \frac{d}{dt}(V_{in} - V_A) = \frac{V_A - V_0}{R_F}$$

- As the non-inverting input terminal of the op-amp is grounded; due to the virtual ground concept, the inverting terminal is also at ground potential. i.e. $V_A = 0$. Substituting this value in the above equation we get,

$$C_1 \cdot \frac{d}{dt}(V_{in}) = -\frac{V_0}{R_F}$$

∴
$$V_0 = -R_F C_1 \frac{d}{dt}(V_{in})$$

∴
$$V_0 \propto \frac{d}{dt}(V_{in})$$

- Thus, the output signal is directly proportional to the derivative of the input signal. The negative sign in the above equation shows that the output is out of phase with respect to the input

- If the input is a cosine wave, the output is a sine wave. The triangular wave will produce square wave and the square wave will produce a spike at the output. The input and output waveforms of differentiator circuit are as shown below in Fig. 3.39.

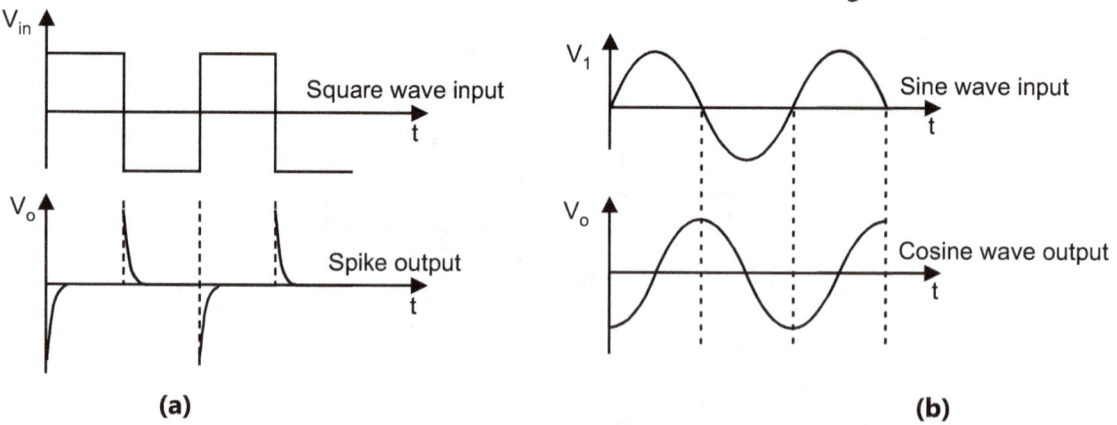

(a)　　　　　　　　　　　　　　　　　　　　　　　　(b)

Fig. 3.39: Input Output Waveforms of Differentiator

Drawbacks of the Ideal Differentiator:

- The basic differentiator circuit faces two problems at high frequency operation.

    1. The gain (R_F / X_{C1}) of the circuit will increase with increasing frequency and due to this the op-amp may go into saturation. Also the circuit may start oscillating.

    2. As the input is applied through capacitor C_1, the input impedance $X_{C1} = \dfrac{1}{2\pi f C_1}$. Therefore the input impedance decreases with the increasing frequency, which makes the circuit sensitive to high frequency noise.

- These problems can be corrected by modifying the basic differentiator circuit. It is known as Practical circuit of differentiator. It is as discussed below.

3.18.1 Practical Differentiator

- The basic differentiator has the problem of high frequency noise and stability. Both the problems can be corrected by adding two components R_1 and C_F. This circuit, shown in Fig. 3.40 is called as a practical differentiator.

- In this circuit, resistor R_1 is connected in series with the capacitor C_1. And the capacitor C_F is connected in parallel with the resistor R_F. This will control the amount of increase in gain at high frequencies thus providing gain stability and also R_1 increases the input impedance considerably to decrease the noise susceptibility.

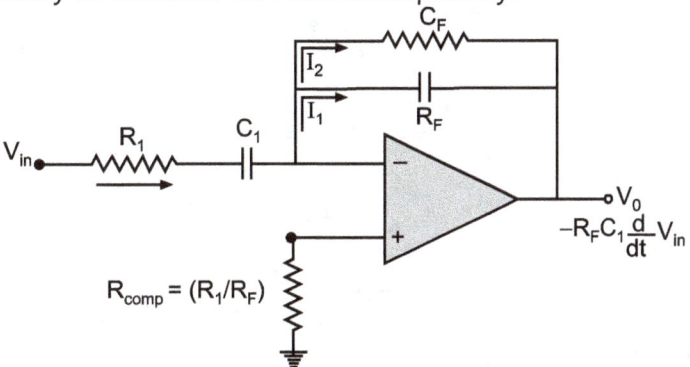

Fig. 3.40: Practical Differentiator

Applications of Practical Differentiator:
- In FM demodulators,
- In wave shaping circuits.

3.19 INTEGRATOR

❖ Important Question Related to this Topic ❖

1. Draw a circuit diagram of an op-amp integrator and derive the expression for its output voltage.
2. Draw a neat circuit diagram of an ideal integrator and explain its operation. Draw the input and output waveforms. Give drawbacks of this circuit. How are they overcome in a practical integrator?

- An integrator circuit performs mathematical operation of integration and gives the output which is directly proportional to the integration of the input signal. Fig. 3.41 shows the basic integrator circuit in which the input signal V_{in} is applied at the inverting input terminal of the op-amp through resistor R_1. Note that a basic integrator circuit can be obtained by interchanging the resistor and capacitor of the basic differentiator circuit.

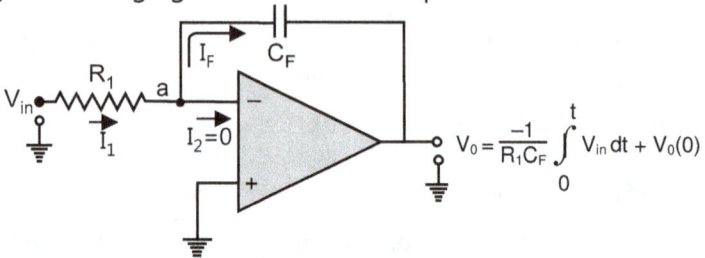

Fig. 3.41: Integrator

- Let the current flowing through R_1 be I_1. As discussed earlier, the current flowing into the terminals of the op-amp is almost zero due to the high input impedance of the amplifier. Therefore $I_2 \doteq 0$ and hence I_1 = I_F = the current through the feedback capacitor.

- Also due to virtual ground, the voltage at node 'a' (V_a) = 0

But
$$I_1 = \frac{V_{in} - V_a}{R_1}$$

$$= \frac{V_{in} - 0}{R_1} = \frac{V_{in}}{R_1} \qquad \text{... (7)}$$

and
$$I_F = C_F \cdot \frac{d}{dt}(V_a - V_o)$$

$$= C_F \cdot \frac{d}{dt}(0 - V_o) = - C_F \frac{d}{dt}(V_o) \qquad \text{... (8)}$$

- Equating the equations (7) and (8) we get,

$$\frac{V_{in}}{R_1} = - C_F \frac{d}{dt}(V_o)$$

$$\therefore \qquad \frac{d V_o}{dt} = \frac{-1}{R_1 C_F} \cdot V_{in}$$

$$\therefore \qquad d V_o = \frac{-1}{R_1 C_F} \cdot V_{in}\, dt$$

- Integrating both sides we get,

$$\int_0^t dV_0 = \frac{-1}{R_1 C_F} \int_0^t V_{in} \cdot dt$$

$$\therefore \qquad V_O(t) \;=\; -\,\frac{1}{R_1 C_F}\int_0^t V_{in}\,dt \;+\; V_O(0)$$

where $V_0(0)$ is the initial output voltage.

- Thus, the output voltage is proportional to the time integral of the input and $R_1 C_F$ is the time constant of the integrator. The negative sign indicates that there is a phase shift of 180 degrees between input and output.

Drawbacks of Basic Integrator:

- In the circuit of basic integrator, the capacitor C_f is connected in the feedback path. Therefore the gain $(-X_F / R_1)$ of the circuit depends on the capacitive reactance X_F.

- At zero frequency, the reactance $(\frac{1}{2\pi f C_f})$ is infinite and hence the gain is infinite. C_f behaves as an open circuit and hence does not provide any feedback. The op-amp thus operates in an open loop resulting in a saturated output voltage. Therefore the amplifier will amplify any input offset voltage present and produce error voltage at the output.

- These problems can be corrected by modifying the basic integrator circuit. It is known as Practical circuit of integrator. It is as discussed below.

3.19.1 Practical Integrator

- To overcome the problems associated with the basic integrator, resistor R_F is connected in parallel with the capacitor C_f. The circuit, as shown in Fig. 3.42, is known as the practical integrator.

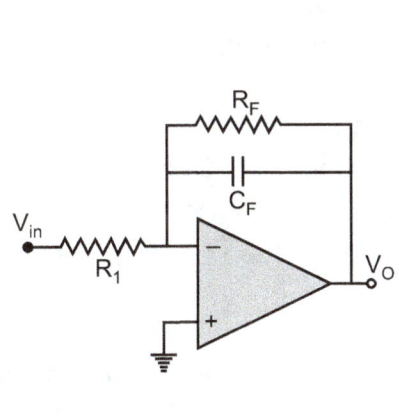

Fig. 3.42: Practical Integrator

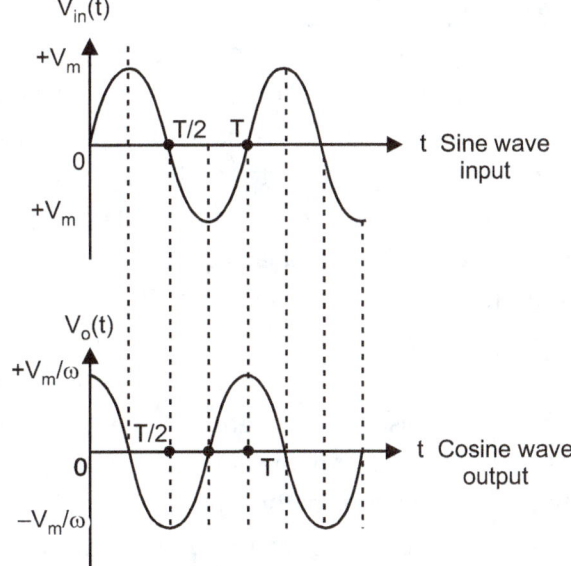

Fig. 3.43: Waveforms

- The problem of saturation at low frequencies is overcome by the feedback resistor R_F.

- Fig. 3.43 and Fig. 3.44 show the input and output waveforms of the integrator. A square wave at the input produces a triangular wave at the output. A step input gives a ramp output and a sign wave produces a cosine wave at the output.

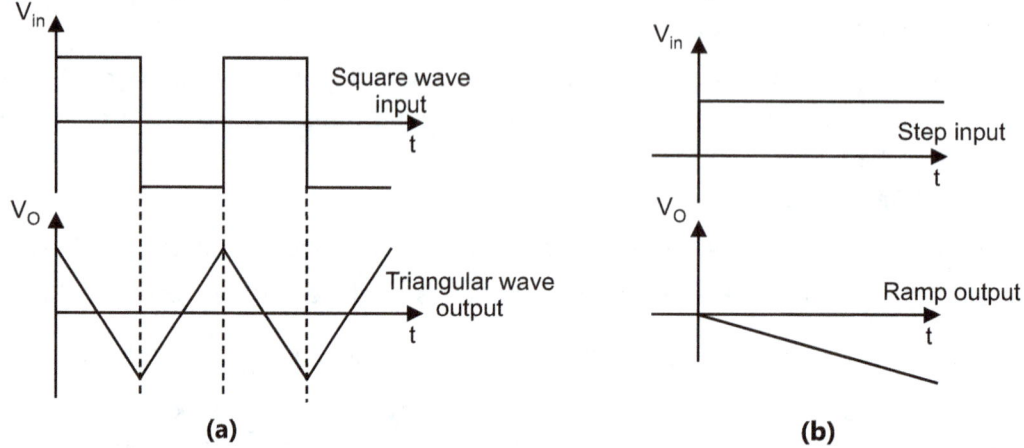

(a)   (b)

Fig. 3.44: Input Output Waveforms of Integrator

Applications of Practical Integrator:

- In wave shaping circuit,
- In analog to digital convertors,
- In analog computers,
- In ramp generators.

3.20 IC 555 TIMER

- The 555 timer is a versatile integrated circuit with many applications. The basic use of this IC is it is used to generate square waveform with variable duty cycle.
- Fig. 3.45 shows internal schematic of IC555 which basically consist of two comparators, a flip flop, a discharge transistor and resistive voltage divider.
- The flip flop which has two states (Explained chapter 4) either logic 0 or logic 1. The flip flop output can be either a high voltage level by giving input Set(S) = logic 1 or low voltage level by giving input Reset(R) = logic 1. The state output can be changed with proper input signals.
- The resistive voltage divider is used to set the reference voltage at input of comparator.
- All the three resistors are of equal values. Therefore, the upper comparator has reference voltage of $2/3V_{CC}$, and the lower comparator has reference $1/3V_{CC}$. The comparators output is used to control the state of flip-flop.
- When trigger voltage goes below $1/3V_{cc}$ the lower comparator sets the flip flop, since non inverting potential is greater than inverting potential. The value of output for this case is equal to maximum level ($+V_{CC}$).

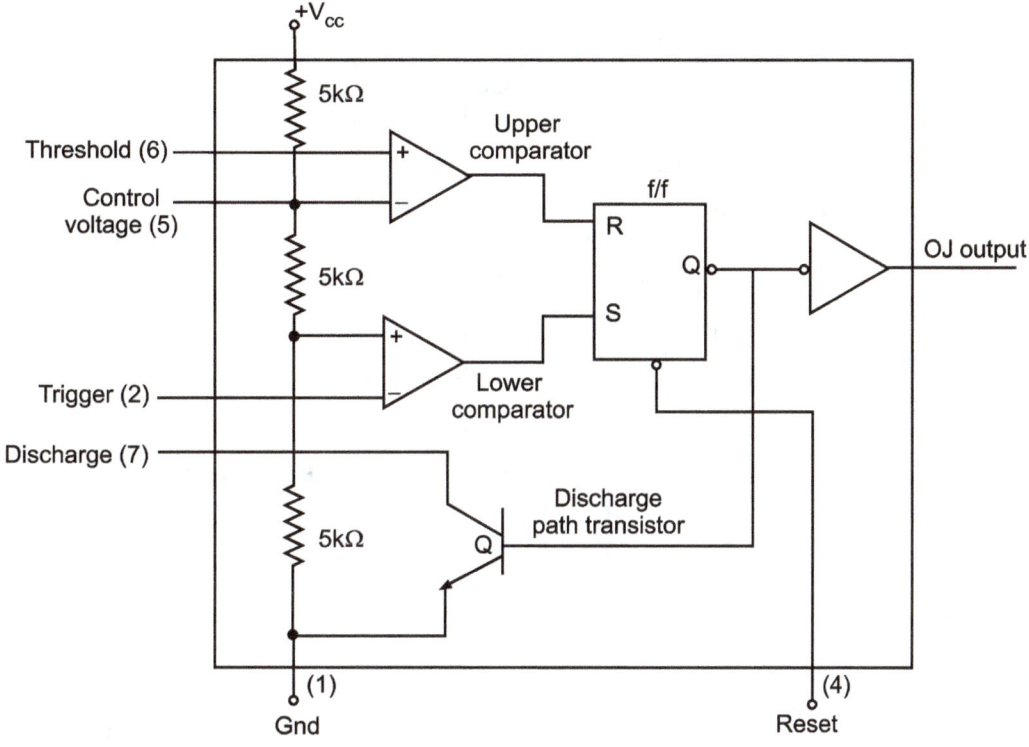

Fig. 3.45

- The threshold input is normally connected to an external RC timing circuit.

- When external capacitor voltage exceeds $2/3V_{CC}$ the upper comparator resets the flip flop, since non inverting potential is greater than inverting potential. The value of output for this case is equal to minimum level (0).

- Transistor Q turns ON when output is low and provides path for rapid discharge of external capacitor.

- By connecting external capacitor IC can be used as oscillator or time delay element.

3.20.1 Astable Multivibrator

- A 555 timer connected to operate in astable mode as a free running relaxation oscillator is shown in Fig. 3.46.

- For this mode threshold and trigger points are connected together. The external components R_1, R_2 and C form the timing circuit that sets the frequency of oscillation.

- The 0.01 µF capacitor connected to the control (CONT) input is strictly for decoupling and has no effect on the operation.

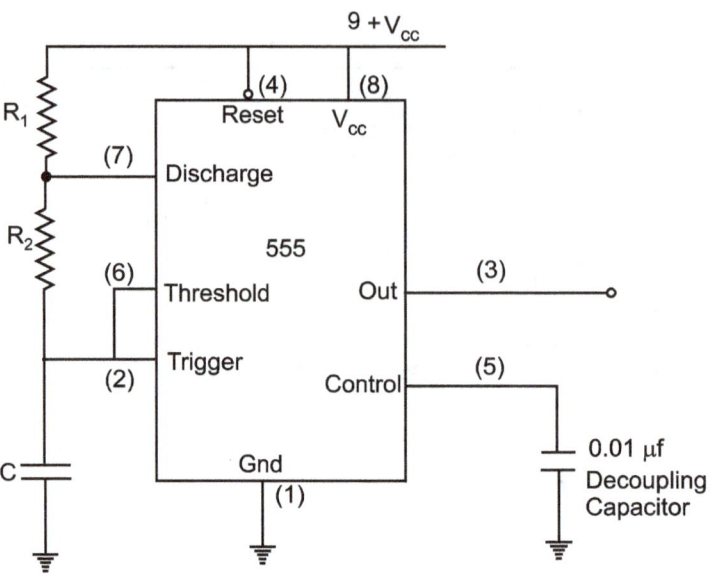

Fig. 3.46

Operation of Circuit

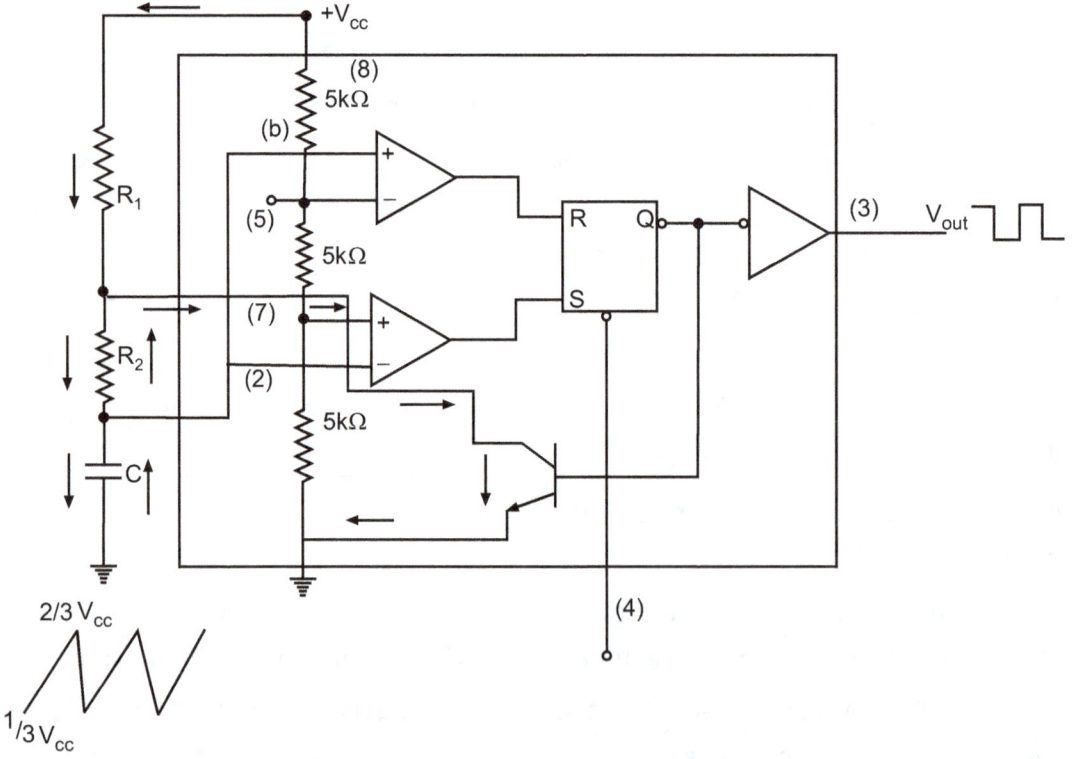

Fig. 3.47

- Initially when the power is turned on, the capacitor C is uncharged and thus the trigger voltage is at 0V. This causes the output of the lower comparator to be high and the output of upper comparator low. Forcing the output of the flip-flop and thus the base of Q low and keeping transistor OFF. Now, C begins charging through R_1 and R_2 as indicated in Fig. 3.47. When the capacitor voltage reaches 1/3Vcc, the lower comparator switches to its low output state, and when the capacitor voltage reaches 2/3 V_{CC}, the upper comparator switches to high output state. This resets the flip-flop, causes base of transistor Q go high, and turns on the transistor. This sequence creates a discharge path for the capacitor through R_2 and the transistor, as indicated. The capacitor now begins to discharge, causing the upper comparator to go low. At the point the point capacitor discharges down to 1/3 V_{CC}, the lower comparator switches high, setting the flip flop, which makes the base of Q low and it turns off the transistor. Another charging cycle begins, and the entire process repeats. The result is a square wave output whose duty cycle depends on the values of R_1 and R_2. The frequency of oscillation is given by $f_o = 1.44/(R_1 + 2R_2).C$.

- By selecting R_1 and R_2, the duty cycle of the output can be adjusted. Since C charges through $R_1 + R_2$ and discharges only through R_2, duty cycles approaching a minimum of 50% can be achieved if $R_2 >> R_1$ so that the charging and discharging times are approximately equal.

- A equation to calculate the duty cycle is developed as follows. The time that the output is high (T_{ON}) is how long it takes C to charge from 1/3V_{CC} to 2/3V_{CC}. It is expressed as

$$T_{ON} = 0.694 \cdot (R_1 + R_2) \cdot C$$

- The time that the output is low (T_{OFF}) is how long it takes C to discharge from 2/3V_{CC} to 1/3V_{CC}. It is expressed as,

$$T_{OFF} = 0.694 \cdot R_2 \cdot C$$

- The period T, of the output waveform is the sum of T_{ON} and T_{OFF}. The following formula for T is reciprocal of frequency given by f_o.

$$T = T_{ON} + T_{OFF} = 0.694 \cdot (R_1 + 2R_2) \cdot C$$

- Finally, the %duty cycle is

$$\%D = (T_{ON}/T) \times 100$$

$$\%D = (R_1 + R_2/R_1 + 2R_2) \times 100$$

- To achieve duty cycles of less than 50%, the circuit in Fig. 3.46 can be modified so that C charges through only R_1 and discharges through R_2. This is achieved with a diode. D_1, placed as shown in Fig. 3.48. The duty cycle can be made less than 50% by making R_1 less than R_2. Under this condition, the formula for % duty cycle is

$$\%D = (R_1/R_1 + R_2) \times 100$$

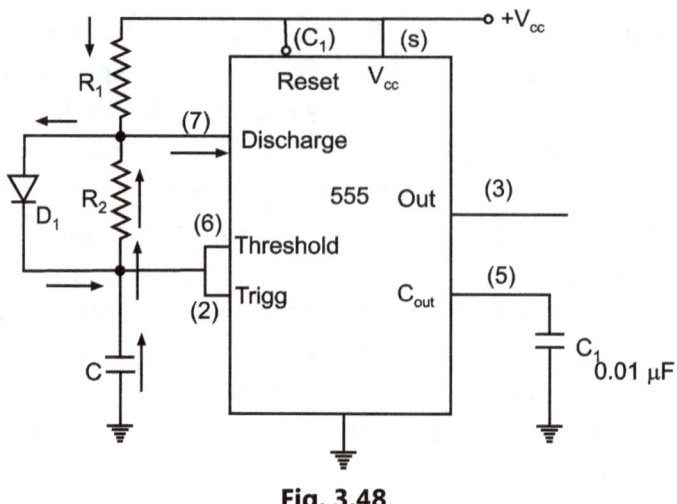

Fig. 3.48

3.20.2 Voltage Controlled Oscillator

- A 555 timer can be set-up to operate as V_{CO} by using the same external connections as for astable operation, with the exception that a variable control voltage is applied to the control input as indicated in Fig. 3.49.

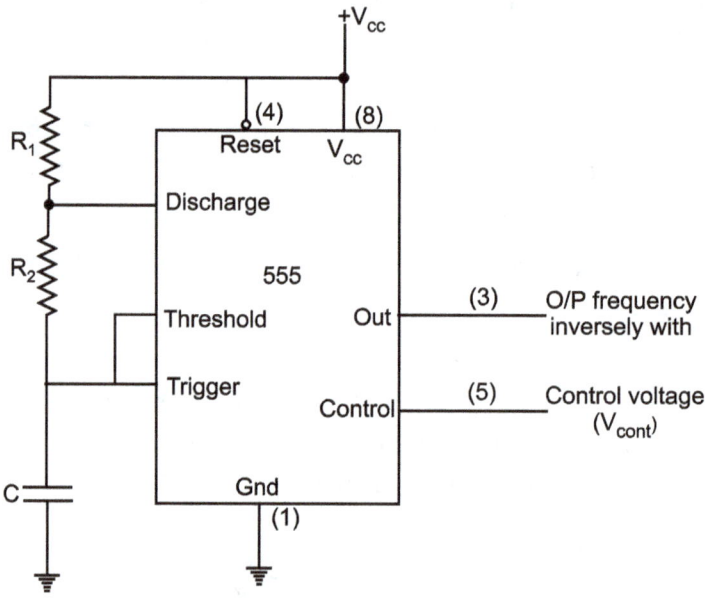

Fig. 3.49

- As shown in Fig. 3.50 the control voltage (V_{cont}) changes the threshold values of $1/3V_{CC}$ and $2/3V_{CC}$ for the internal comparators. With control voltage, the upper values is V_{cont} and lower values is $\frac{1}{2} V_{cont}$, as you can see by examining the internal diagram of the 555 timer. When the control voltage is varied. The output frequency also varies. An increase in V_{cont} increases the charging and discharging time of the external capacitor and causes the frequency to decrease. A decrease in V_{cont} decreases the charging and discharging time of the capacitor and causes the frequency to increase.

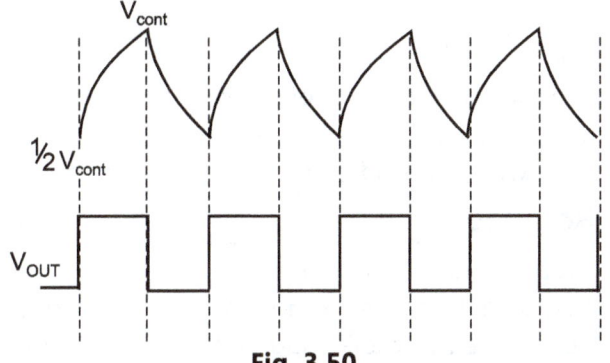

Fig. 3.50

3.21 VOLTAGE REGULATION   [May 14]

3.21.1 Line Regulation

- When the dc input voltage changes, an electronic circuit called a regulator maintains nearly constant output voltage as shown in Fig. 3.51.

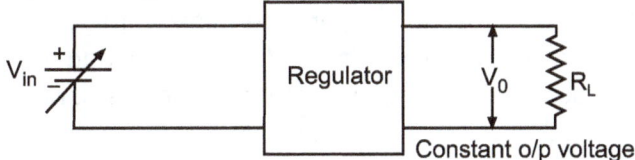

Fig. 3.51

- Line regulation can be defined as the percentage change in the output voltage for a given change in the input voltage. When taken over a range of input voltage values, line regulation is expressed as a percentage by the following formula

$$\text{Line regulation} = (\Delta V_{out} / \Delta V_{in}) \times 100\%$$

- Line regulation can be expressed in units of %/V. For example, a line regulation of 0.05%/V means that output voltage changes 0.05% when the input voltage increases or decreases by one volt. Line regulation can be calculated using the following formula

$$\text{Line regulation} = [(\Delta V_{out} / V_{out}) / \Delta V_{in}] \cdot 100\%$$

3.21.2 Load Regulation

- When the amount of current through a load changes due to a varying load resistance, the voltage regulator must maintain a nearly constant output voltage across the load as shown in Fig. 3.52.

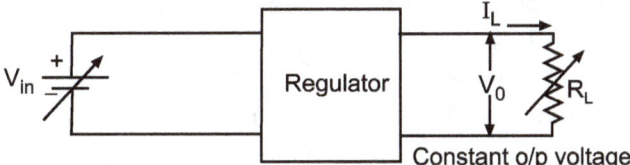

Fig. 3.52

- Load regulation can be defined as the percentage change in output voltage for a given change in load current. One way to express load regulation is as a percentage change in output voltage from no load(NL) to full load(FL).

$$\text{Load regulation} = (V_{NL}\text{-}V_{FL}/V_{FL}) \cdot 100\%$$

- Alternately, the load regulation can be expressed as a percentage change in output voltage for each mA change in load current. E.g. 0.01%/mA means that the output voltage changes 0.01 % when the load current increases or decreases 1mA.

3.21.3 IC Voltage Regulator

- Generally, the linear regulators are three terminal devices that provide either positive or negative output voltages that can be fixed or adjustable. A power supply can be built using a transformer connected to the ac supply line to step the ac voltage to a desired amplitude, then rectifying that ac voltage, filtering with a capacitor and RC filter, if desired, and finally regulating the dc voltage using an IC regulator. The regulator can be selected for operation with load currents from hundreds of mA to 10A, corresponding to power ratings from mW to tens of Watts.

- **Three Terminal Voltage Regulators**

  Fig. 3.53 shows the basic connection of three terminal voltage regulator IC to load. The fixed voltage regulator has an unregulated dc input voltage Vi applied to one input terminal, a regulated output dc voltage Vo from a second terminal, and the third terminal connected to ground. IC device specifications list a voltage range over which the input voltage can vary to maintain regulated output voltage over a range of load current. The specifications also list the amount of output voltage change resulting from change in load current or in input voltage line regulation.

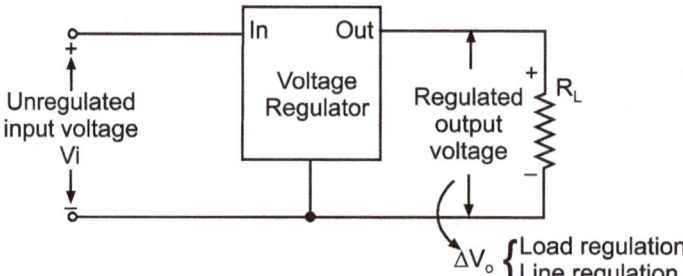

Fig. 3.53

- **Fixed Positive Voltage Regulators**

  The series 78 regulators provide fixed regulated voltages from 5V to 24V. Fig. 3.54 shows how one such IC, a 7810, is connected to provide voltage regulation with output from this unit of +12V dc. An unregulated input voltage Vi is filtered by capacitor C_1 and connected to IC's IN terminal. The IC's OUT terminal provides regulated +12V, which is filtered by capacitor C_2. The third IC terminal now connected to ground(GND). Whereas input voltage may vary over some permissible voltage range and the output load may vary over some acceptable range, the output voltage remains constant within specified voltage variation limits. These limitations are provided by manufacturer's data sheet.

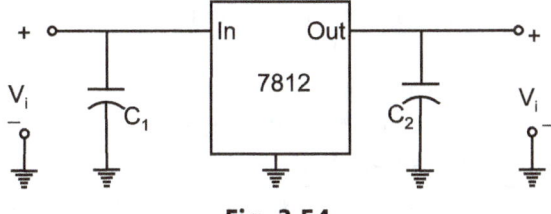

Fig. 3.54

- A table of positive voltage regulator ICs is provided in Table 5.1

IC	Output Voltage(V)	Minimum Vi(V)
7805	+5	7.3
7806	+6	8.3
7808	+8	10.5
7810	+10	12.5
7812	+12	14.6
7815	+15	17.7
7818	+18	21.0
7824	+24	27.1

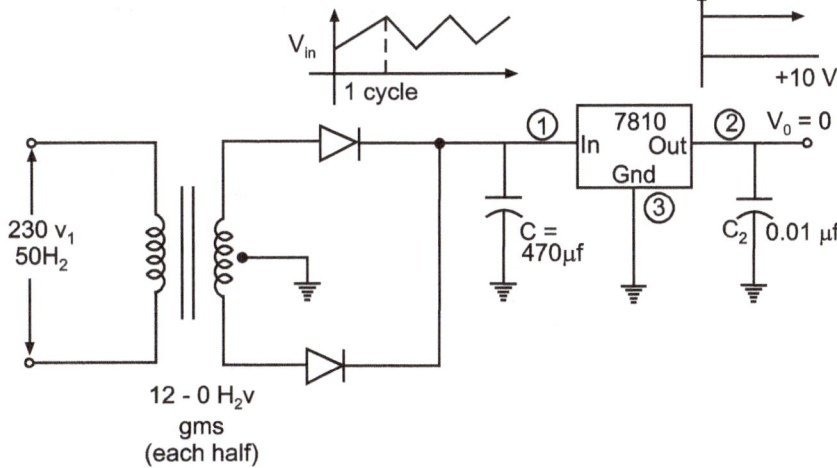

Fig. 3.55

- The connection of IC7810 in a complete voltage supply is shown in connection of Fig. 3.55. The ac line voltage 230V is stepped down to 12Vrms across each half of the center tapped transformer. IC7810 then provides an output that is a regulated +10V dc.

- **Fixed Negative Voltage Regulators**

  The series 7900 provide negative voltage regulators, similar to those providing positive voltages. A list of negative voltage regulator ICs is provided in Table 5.2. As shown IC regulators are available for a range of fixed negative voltages, the selected IC providing the rated output voltage as long as the input voltage is maintained greater than the minimum input value. For example, the 7909 provides an output of -9V as long as the input to the regulator IC is more negative than -11.5V.

IC	Output Voltage(V)	Minimum Vi(V)
7905	− 5	− 7.3
7906	− 6	− 8.4
7908	− 8	− 10.5
7909	− 9	− 11.5
7812	− 12	− 14.6
7815	− 15	− 17.7
7818	− 18	− 20.8
7824	− 24	− 27.1

- **Adjustable Voltage Regulators**

  Voltage regulators are also available in circuit configurations that allow the user to set the output voltage to a desired regulated value. The LM 317, for example can operate with output voltage regulated at any setting over the range of voltage from 1.2V to 37V. Fig. 3.56 shows how the regulated output voltage of an LM317 can be set.

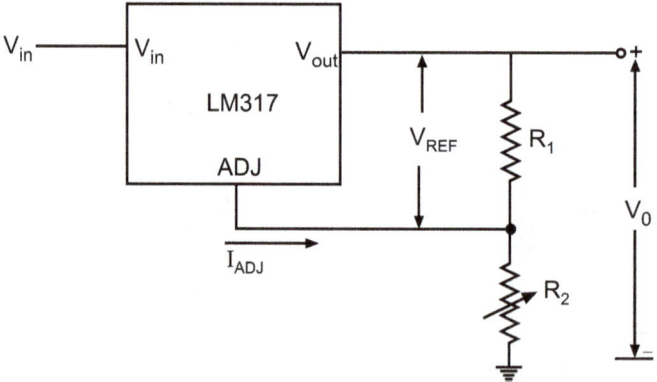

Fig. 3.56

Resistor R_1 and R_2 set the output to any desired voltage over the adjustment range 1.2 V to 37 V. The output voltage desired can be calculated using

$$V_0 = V_{ref} (1 + R_2/R_1) + I_{adj} \cdot R_2$$

With typical IC values of V_{ref} = 1.25 V and I_{adj} = 100 μA.

For example, if we take R_1 = 240 Ω and R_2 = 1.8 KΩ

$$V_o = 1.25 \text{ V} (1 + 1.8 \text{ KΩ} / 240 \text{ Ω}) + (100 \text{ µA}) (1.8 \text{ KΩ})$$
$$= 10.625 \text{ V} + 0.18 \text{ V} = 10.805 \text{ V}$$

Example 3.7 : *A 555 timer is configured to run in astable mode with R_1 = 4 kΩ, R_2 = 4 kΩ and C = 0.01 µF. Determine the frequency of the output and duty cycle.*

Solution : Frequency output is given by :

$$df = \frac{1.44}{(R_1 + 2R_2) \cdot C} = \frac{1.44}{(4 + 2 \times 4) \times 10^3 \times 0.01 \times 10^{-6}}$$

$$f = 12 \text{ kHz}$$

$$D = \frac{R_1 + R_2}{R_1 + 2R_2}$$

$$= \frac{4 + 4}{4 + (2 \times 4)} = 0.6667$$

$$D = 66.7\%$$

Example 3.8 : *Calculate the output voltage of the adjustable regulator shown in Fig. 3.57.*

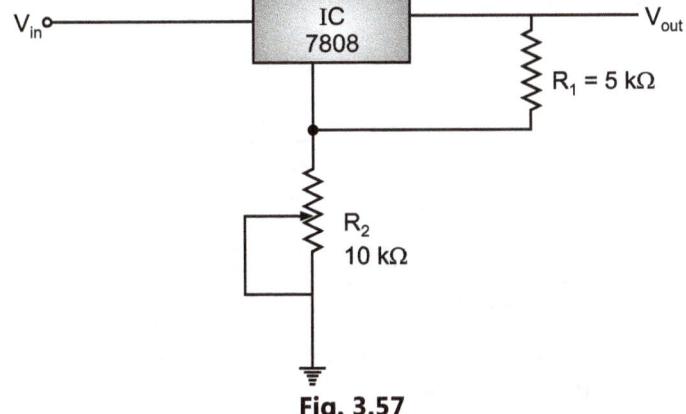

Fig. 3.57

If R_2 is varied from 1 kΩ to 10 kΩ find the range of output voltage.

Solution : R_1 = 5 kΩ, R_2 = 10 kΩ.

The IC 7808

So

$$V_{regulated} = + 8V$$

$$V_{out} = V_{reg} \cdot \left[1 + \frac{R_2}{R_1}\right]$$

$$= 8 \cdot \left[1 + \frac{10}{5}\right] = 8 \times 3 = 24 \text{ V}$$

Now,

$$R_Z = 1 \text{ kΩ then}$$

$$V_{out} = 8\left[1 + \frac{1}{5}\right] = 9.6 \text{ V}$$

V_{out} can be varied from 9-6 V to 24 V, by varying R_Z from like 1 kΩ to 10 kΩ.

Example 3.9 : *Determine the minimum and maximum output voltages for the voltage regulator shown in Fig. 3.58. Assume I_{adj} is 50 μA.*

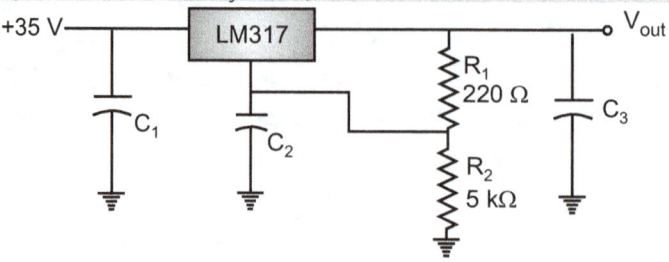

Fig. 3.58

Solution : $\qquad\qquad\qquad V_{R1} = V_{REF} = 1.25 \text{ V}$

When R_2 is set at its minimum of 0 Ω.

$$V_{out\,(min)} = V_{ref} \times \left(1 + \frac{R_2}{R_1}\right) + I_{adj} \times R_2$$

$$V_{out\,(min)} = 1.25 \times (1) = \textbf{1.25 V}$$

When R_2 is set maximum of 5 $k\Omega$.

$$V_{out\,(max)} = V_{ref} \cdot \left(1 + \frac{R_2}{R_1}\right) + I_{adj} \times R_2$$

$$= 1.25 \cdot \left(1 + \frac{5 \text{ k}\Omega}{220 \text{ }\Omega}\right) + 50 \text{ }\mu A \cdot 5 \text{ k}\Omega$$

$$V_{out\,(max)} = 29.66 \text{ V} + 0.25 \text{ V} = \textbf{29.9 V}$$

QUESTIONS

1. Draw and explain functional block diagram of Op-amp.

2. Draw a neat circuit diagram of Inverting amplifier using Op-amp and obtain the expression for its output voltage.

3. Draw a neat circuit diagram of Non-inverting amplifier using Op-amp and obtain the expression for its output voltage.

4. Draw Op-amp equivalent circuit for ideal condition. List six characteristics of the ideal op-amp. Also give their typical values for IC741.

5. Write a short note on practical Op-amp characteristics.

6. Draw and explain the circuit of Integrator using output equation and waveforms.

7. Draw and explain the circuit of Differentiator using output equation and waveforms.

8. Explain the following terms. Also give its practical values for IC741 :
   (a) CMRR
   (b) PSRR
   (c) Input Offset Voltage
   (d) Input offset current

    (e) Input Bias Current

    (f)   Slew Rate.

9. State the advantages and applications of negative feedback.

10. List advantages of negative and positive feedback.

11. Compare positive and negative feedback.

12. Define comparator. Explain non-inverting comparator using neat circuit diagram and input output waveform.

13. State the applications of comparator.

14. Draw a neat circuit diagram for the application in which an Op-amp is used to compare any given input voltage with a standard, fixed reference voltage, Explain its working. Draw input output waveforms assuming input is a sinusoidal signal.

15. What is application of Op-amp in open loop configuration?

16. What is Schmitt trigger? What are threshold levels and hysteresis? Explain with neat circuit diagram.

17. Explain Schmitt trigger circuit.

18. Explain unit gain buffer using Op-amp.

19. Describe use of an Op-amp adder. What type of feedback is used in an Op-amp adder? Justify your answer.

20. Draw a neat diagram of three input inverting summing amplifier using Op-amp
And obtain the expression of output voltage.

21. Draw a neat diagram of three input non inverting summing amplifier using Op-amp and obtain the expression of output voltage.

22. Draw a neat circuit diagram of difference amplifier using op-amp and obtain the expression for its output voltage.

23. Draw neat circuit diagram of an ideal differentiator and explain its operation. Draw output waveforms for sinusoidal and square wave inputs. Also give any two applications of the same.

24. Draw the circuit diagram of integrator and explain its working. Draw the output waveform for square wave input.

25. Draw a neat diagram of basic differentiator. Give its limitations. How they are overcome in practical differentiator.

26. What is regulation? Define line regulation and load regulation.

27. Write a short note on IC voltage regulators.

28. Draw and explain the functional block diagram of basic three terminal IC regulator.

29. Explain with a circuit diagram the operation of 3-pin voltage regulator IC.

30. Write two applications of IC78XX.

31. Draw and explain typical circuit connection of IC78XX regulator.

32. What are the advantages of IC voltage regulators?

33. Draw the functional block diagram of IC555 and explain it.

34. Explain the working of IC555 as timer. State its applications.

35. Explain with neat sketch, the working of IC555 as an Oscillator.

36. How astable mode of IC 555 can be modified to get square wave generator?

37. Draw and explain astable multivibrator using IC555. Draw the output and capacitor voltage waveforms; State the expressions for on-time and off-time in astable mode.

UNIVERSITY QUESTIONS

Dec. 2012

1. What is op-amp? Draw and explain the functional block diagram of an op-amp. **[6]**
2. With the help of block diagram of IC 555 explain its operation in astable mode. **[6]**

May 2013

1. In Fig. C if V_a = +2V V_b = + 4 V **[4]**

   $R_a = R_b = R_1 = 1k\ \Omega$ and $R_f = 3\ k\ \Omega$

   determine the voltage V_1 at non-inverting terminal of OP-AMP and output voltage V_o

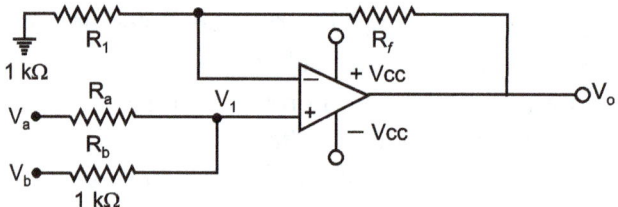

Fig. 1

Dec. 2013

1. Draw and explain Internal block diagram of IC 555. **[6]**
2. Find output voltage V_o of op-amp circuit shown in Fig. (b) below: **[6]**

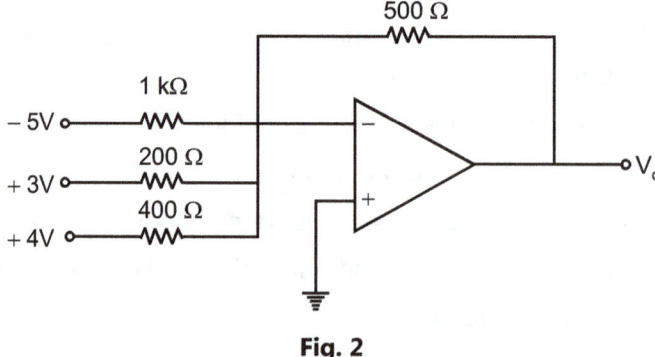

Fig. 2

May 2014

1. Explain Daw the circuit diagram and write the output equation for   **[6]**

   (i) Inverting summer with three inputs

   (ii) Ideal differentiator

2. Draw three pin IC voltage regulator. Define load and Line regulation.   **[6]**

Oct. 2014

1. Explain the working of inverting summing amplifier with two inputs along with its waveforms.   **[6]**

2. With the help of block diagram of IC555 explain its operation in Astable mode.   **[6]**

May 2015

1. In shown in the following Fig. 3 let $R_1 = R_2 = 1$ kΩ. $R_3 = 5$ kΩ, $R_f = 10$ kΩ, $V_1 = -1$ V, $V_2 = 2$ V and $V_3 = 4$ V. Calculate Vo.   **[6]**

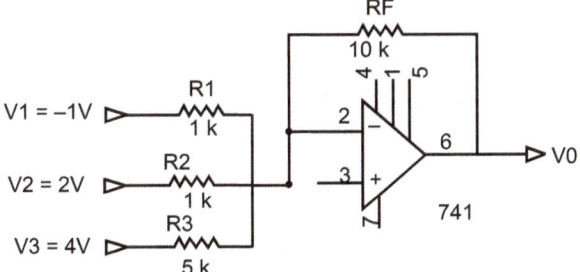

Fig. 3

2. Define the following parameters of op-amp :   **[6]**

   (i) BW   (ii) PSRR   (iii) CMRR.

Nov. 2015

1. Draw the circuit diagram and write output equation for: **[6]**

   (i) Non-inverting summer with three inputs

   (ii) Ideal differentiator.

2. For inverting amplifier using op-amp if $R_f = 100$ kΩ, $R_1 = 10$ kΩ, $V_{CC} = \pm 10$ V, $V_i = 2$ V d.c. :   **[6]**

   (i) Calculate output voltage

   (ii) Is the result in part (i) is practically possible? Justify.

May 2016

1. Draw a neat diagram of 3-input inverting summing amplifier and obtain expression for its o/p voltage. **[6]**

2. For the given circuit. Find V_o. **[6]**

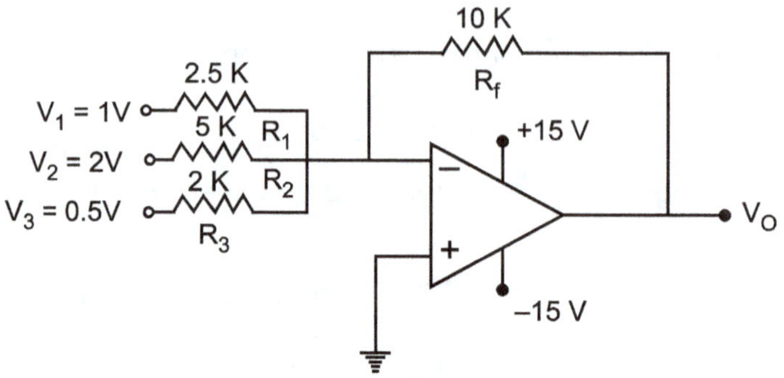

Fig. 4

◇ ◇ ◇

DIGITAL ELECTRONICS

4.1 INTRODUCTION

- An analog signal is a continuous signal varying with time. Any electronic system which processes an analog signal is referred to as an analog system in which the output can be controlled continuously by input.

- Digital signal is discrete with respect to time and has only two distinct voltage levels denoted by logic '1' (high) and logic '0' (low). Digital systems process digital signals and store information in the binary form. Modern computers and electronic systems operate on digital data. So the analog signals are first converted into digital form and then processed using digital techniques.

Advantages of using Digital Technique

- The devices used in digital circuits operate in one of two states, known as ON and OFF, results into very simple operation.

- Digital circuits are easy to understand.

- A large number of ICs are available for performing various operations. These are highly reliable, accurate small in size and the speed of operation is high. A large number of programmable ICs are also available.

- The fluctuations in characteristics of the components, ageing of components, temperature and noise etc. is very small in digital circuits.

- Digital circuits have memory capability which makes these circuits highly suitable for computers, calculators, watches, telephones etc.

- The display of data and other information is very convenient, accurate using digital technique.

4.2 CONCEPT OF POSITIVE AND NEGATIVE LOGIC

❖ **Important Question Related to this Topic** ❖

Explain the concept of positive and negative logic.

- Digital signal has two discrete levels or values. These levels can be represented by using the term *Low* or *High* as shown in Fig. 4.1. These two discrete levels, high and low, are also represented by the binary digits '1' and '0' or in case of logic operations they are represented by TRUE or FALSE.

- In the positive logic system, the higher of the two voltages represents a 1 and the lower voltage represents a 0.

- In the negative logic system, the lower voltage represents a 1 and the higher voltage represents a 0.

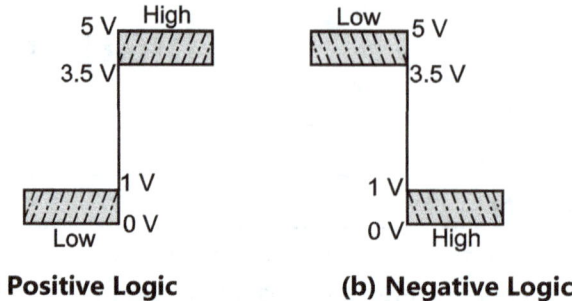

(a) Positive Logic   **(b) Negative Logic**

Fig. 4.1

4.3 BASIC DIGITAL CIRCUITS   [May 15]

❖ Important Question Related to this Topic ❖

Explain NAND, NOR and EX-OR gates with the help of Boolean expression and truth table.

- An electronic logic gate is a digital circuit that can operate on one or more number of binary inputs (voltages) and give only one output after performing a logical operation like ANDing, ORing, or complementing (NOT) the inputs.

- The operation of a logic gate can be easily understood with the help of the **"truth table"**. A truth table shows the output condition for all different combinations of inputs.

- Classification of logic gates is as shown below:

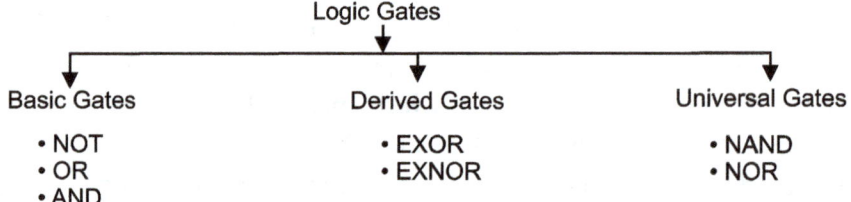

Table 4.1 : Logic Gates

Symbol	Truth Table		Pin Diagram
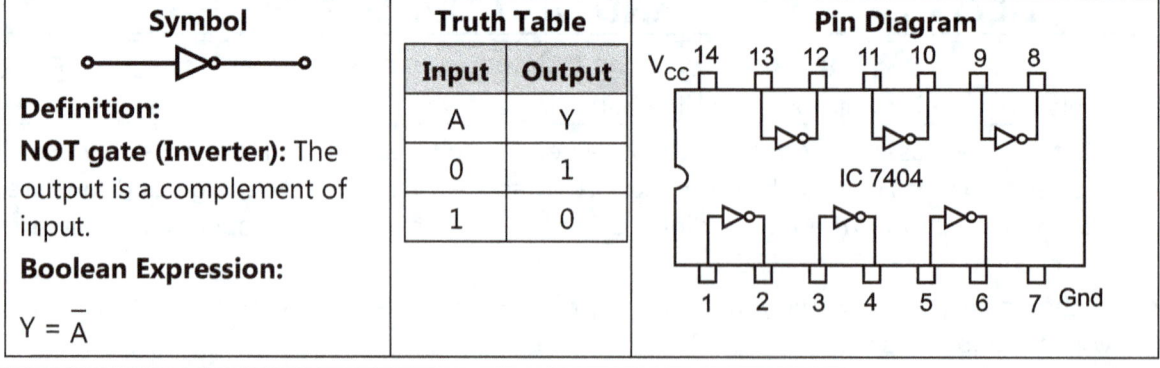			

Symbol	Input	Output	Pin Diagram

Definition:

NOT gate (Inverter): The output is a complement of input.

Boolean Expression:

$Y = \bar{A}$

Input	Output
A	Y
0	1
1	0

Symbol	Truth Table		Pin Diagram

Symbol

A ⊸⊐ Y
B ⊸

Definition:

AND gate: The output is high only when all inputs are high.

Boolean Expression:

$Y = A \cdot B$

Truth Table

Input		Output
A	B	Y
0	0	0
0	1	0
1	0	0
1	1	1

Pin Diagram

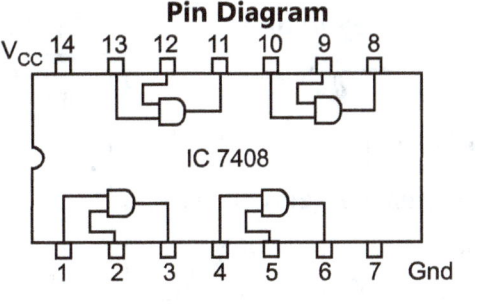

IC 7408

Symbol

A ⊸⊐ Y
B ⊸

Definition:

OR gate: The output is high when any of the inputs is high

Boolean Expression:

$Y = A + B$

Truth Table

Input		Output
A	B	Y
0	0	0
0	1	1
1	0	1
1	1	1

Pin Diagram

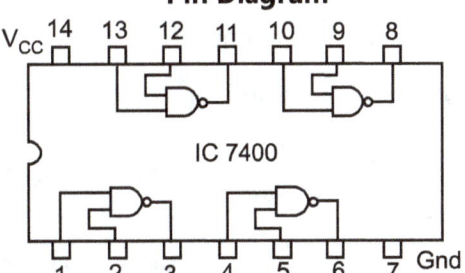

IC 7432

Symbol

A ⊸⊐∘ Y
B ⊸

Definition:

NAND gate: The output is high only when one of the inputs is Low.

Boolean Expression:

$Y = \overline{A \cdot B}$

Truth Table

Input		Output
A	B	Y
0	0	1
0	1	1
1	0	1
1	1	0

Pin Diagram

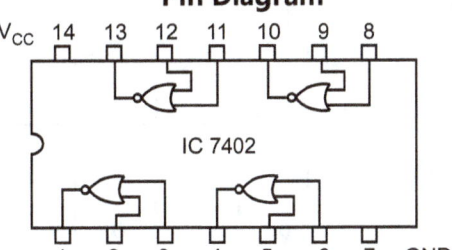

IC 7400

Symbol

A ⊸⊐∘ Y
B ⊸

Definition:

NOR gate: The output is high when all the inputs are low.

Boolean Expression:

$Y = \overline{A + B}$

Truth Table

Input		Output
A	B	Y
0	0	1
0	1	0
1	0	0
1	1	0

Pin Diagram

IC 7402

Symbol	Truth Table	Pin Diagram
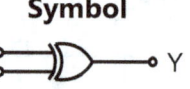 **Definition:** **Exclusive OR (Ex-OR) gate:** The output is high only when odd number of inputs are high. **Boolean Expression:** $Y = A \oplus B$	<table><tr><td colspan="2">Input</td><td>Output</td></tr><tr><td>A</td><td>B</td><td>Y</td></tr><tr><td>0</td><td>0</td><td>0</td></tr><tr><td>0</td><td>1</td><td>1</td></tr><tr><td>1</td><td>0</td><td>1</td></tr><tr><td>1</td><td>1</td><td>0</td></tr></table>	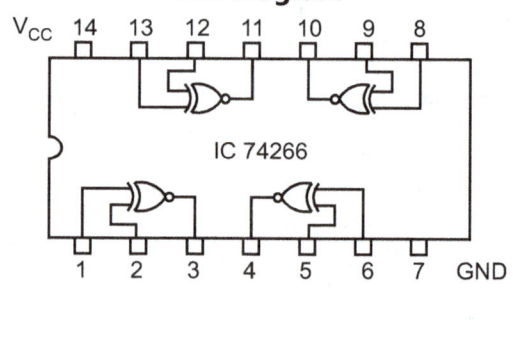 IC 7486

Symbol	Truth Table	Pin Diagram
 **Definition:** **Exclusive NOR (Ex-NOR) gate**: The output is high if both the inputs are equal. **Boolean Expression:** $Y = \overline{A \oplus B}$	<table><tr><td colspan="2">Input</td><td>Output</td></tr><tr><td>A</td><td>B</td><td>Y</td></tr><tr><td>0</td><td>0</td><td>1</td></tr><tr><td>0</td><td>1</td><td>0</td></tr><tr><td>1</td><td>0</td><td>0</td></tr><tr><td>1</td><td>1</td><td>1</td></tr></table>	IC 74266

Table 4.2: Timing Diagram Of Logic Gates

Gate	Timing Diagram
NOT	

NAND

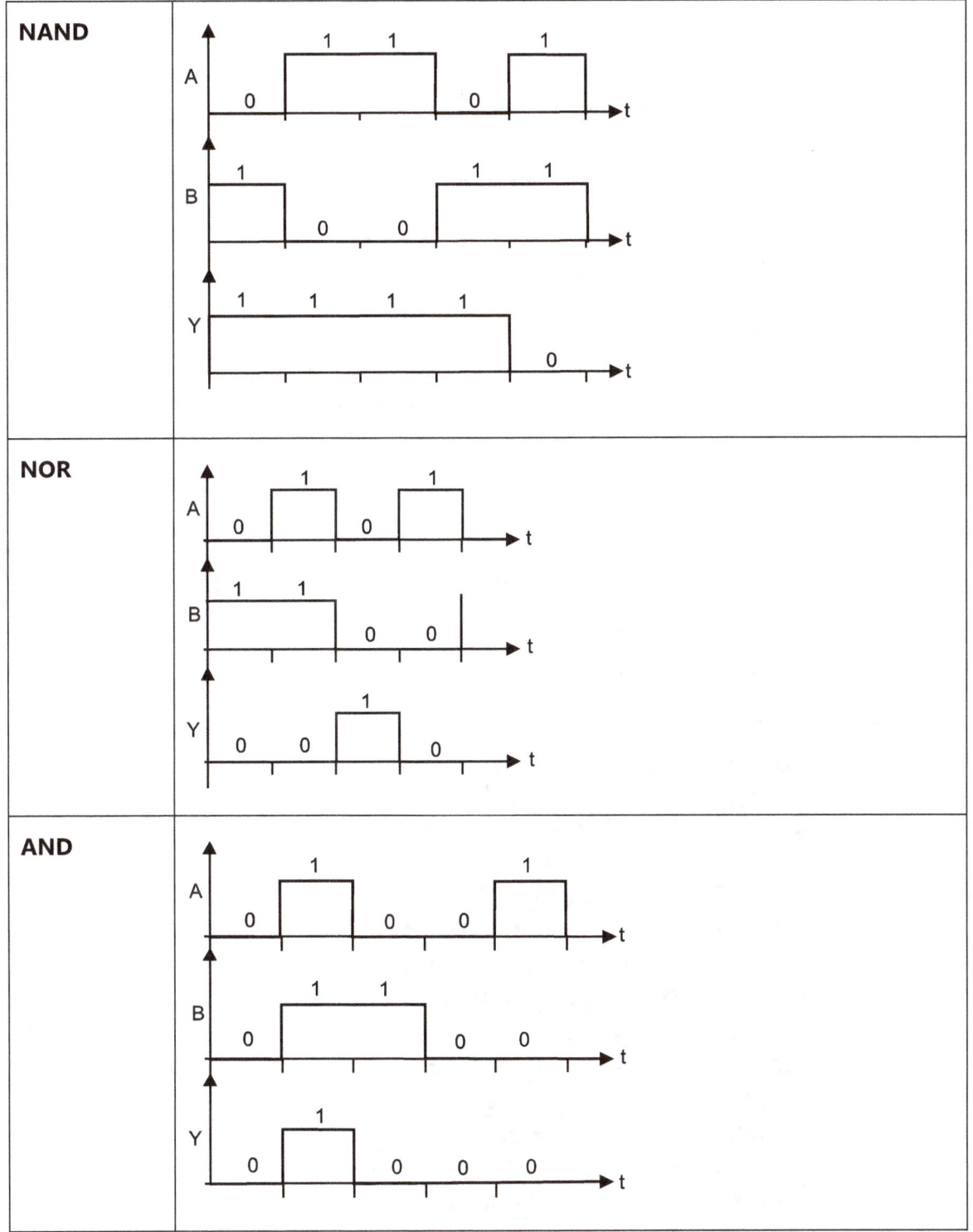

NOR

AND

OR	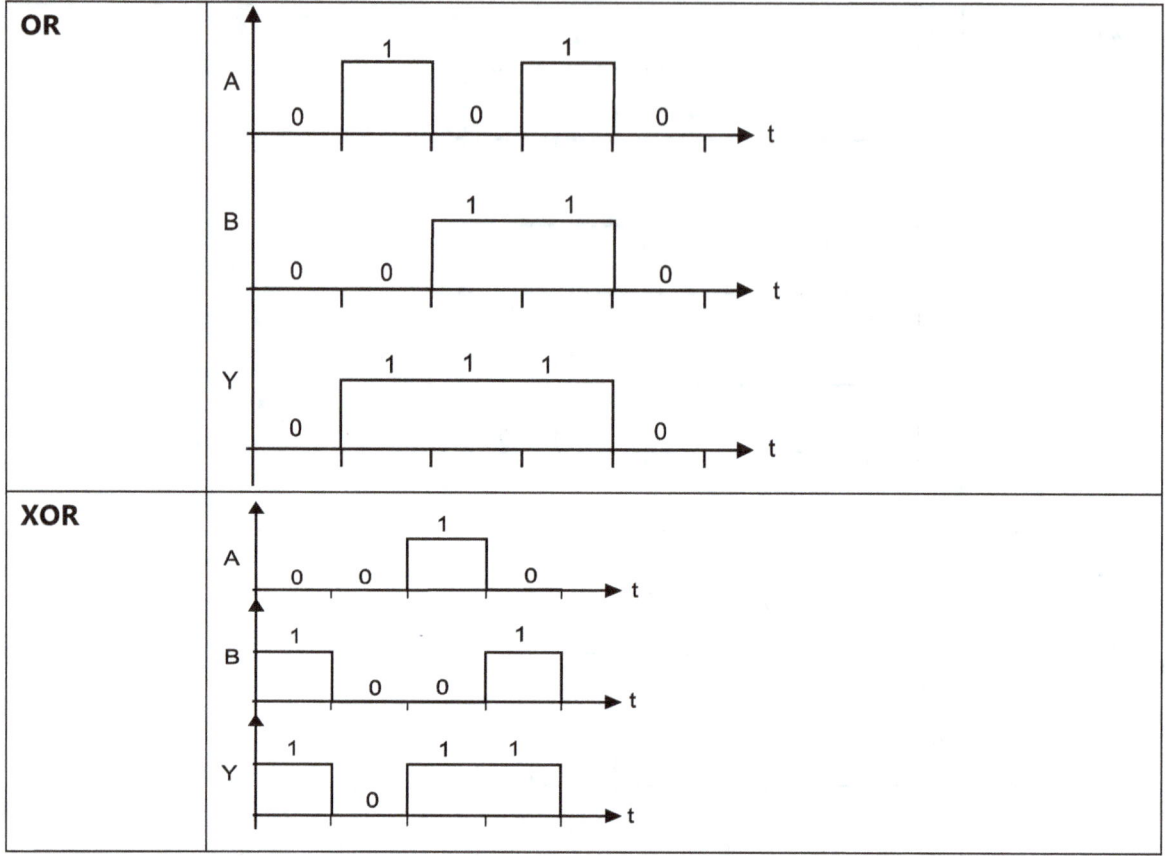
XOR	

Examples of IC Gates:

IC No.	Description
IC7400	**Quad 2-input NAND gates**
IC7402	**Quad 2-input NOR gates**
IC7404	**Hex inverters**
IC7408	**Quad 2-input AND gates**
IC7410	**Triple 3-input NAND gates**
IC7411	**Triple 3-input AND gates**
IC7420	**Dual 4-input NAND gates**
IC7421	**Dual 4-input AND gates**
IC7427	**Triple 3-input NOR gates**
IC7430	**8-input NAND gates**
IC7432	**Quad 2-input OR gates**
IC7486	**Quad EXOR gates**
IC74135	**Quad EX-OR/NOR gates**
IC74260	**Dual 5-input NOR gate**

4.4 BOOLEAN ALGEBRA

- The rules of manipulation for binary numbers developed by George Boole are known as Boolean Algebra.
- Symbols used in Boolean Algebra do not represents numerical values.
- Arithmetic operations are not performed in Boolean algebra.
- Boolean algebra allows only two possible values '0' or '1'.

Laws of Boolean Algebra:

Sr. No.	Type of Law	Laws
1.	AND Laws	$A \cdot 0 = 0$ $A \cdot 1 = A$ $A \cdot A = A$ $A \cdot \overline{A} = 0$
2.	OR Laws	$A + 0 = A$ $A + 1 = 1$ $A + A = A$ $A + \overline{A} = 1$
3.	NOT or Inversion Laws	$\overline{\overline{A}} = A$
4.	Commutative Law (Allows change of position of variables)	$A + B = B + A$ $A \cdot B = B \cdot A$
5.	Associative laws (allows grouping of variables)	$A + (B + C) = (A + B) + C$ $A \cdot (B \cdot C) = (A \cdot B) \cdot C$
6.	Distributive laws (allows distribution of terms)	$A \cdot (B + C) = A \cdot B + A \cdot C$ $A + B \cdot C = (A + B) \cdot (A + C)$ $A + \overline{A}B = (A + \overline{A})(A + B)$ $\quad = A + B$

SOLVED EXAMPLES

Examples on Reducing the Boolean Expression

Example 4.1: $Y = (A + B) \cdot (A + C)$

Solution :
$$= A \cdot A + A \cdot C + B \cdot A + B \cdot C \qquad \text{Distributive law}$$
$$= A + AC + B \cdot A + B \cdot C \qquad \because \quad A \cdot A = A$$
$$= A(1 + C) + B \cdot A + B \cdot C$$

$$= A + AB + B \cdot C$$ $$\because 1 + C = 1$$

$$= A \cdot (1 + B) + B \cdot C$$ $$\because 1 + B = 1$$

$$Y = A + B \cdot C$$

Example 4.2: $$Y = ABCD + A\bar{B}CD$$

Solution : $$= ACD (B + \bar{B})$$ Distributive law

$$Y = ACD$$ $$(B + \bar{B} = 1)$$

Example 4.3: $$Y = AB + ABC + AB \cdot (D + E)$$

Solution : $$= AB(1 + C + D + E)$$

$$= AB$$ $$(\because 1 + C + D + E = 1)$$

Example 4.4: $$Y = XY + XYZ + XY\bar{Z} + \bar{X}YZ$$

Solution : $$= XY(1 + Z) + XY\bar{Z} + \bar{X} \cdot YZ$$

$$= XY + XY\bar{Z} + \bar{X} \cdot Y \cdot Z$$

$$= XY(1 + \bar{Z}) + \bar{X} \cdot YZ$$

$$= XY + \bar{X}YZ$$

$$= Y(X + \bar{X}Z)$$

$$= Y(X + Z)$$ $$\because A + \bar{A}B = A + B$$

Example 4.5: $$Y = (A + B) \cdot (A + \bar{B}) \cdot (\bar{A} + B)$$

Solution : $$Y = (A + B) \cdot (A + \bar{B}) \cdot (\bar{A} + B)$$

$$= (AA + A\bar{B} + BA + B\bar{B}) \cdot (\bar{A} + B)$$

$$\because A \cdot A = A$$

$$B \cdot \bar{B} = 0$$

$$= (A + A (B + \bar{B})) \cdot (\bar{A} + B)$$

$$\because B + \bar{B} = 1$$

$$= (A + A) \cdot (\bar{A} + B)$$

$$Y = A \cdot (\bar{A} + B)$$ $$\because A + A = A$$

$$Y = A \cdot \bar{A} + A \cdot B$$

$$Y = A \cdot B$$ $$\because A \cdot \bar{A} = 0$$

4.4.1 De-Morgan's Theorems   [Dec. 12, 14, May 16]

❖ **Important Question Related to this Topic** ❖

State and prove the De-Morgan's Theorems. De-Morgan discovered two important theorems which are known as De-Morgan's theorems. The two theorems are,

1. $\overline{A + B} = \bar{A} \cdot \bar{B}$ i.e. NOR gate equals bubbled AND gate.

2. $\overline{A \cdot B} = \bar{A} + \bar{B}$ i.e. NAND gate equals bubbled OR gate.

1. De-Morgan's First Theorem

• The statement of De-Morgan's first theorem goes like this, *"The complement of the sum of variables is equal to the product of their individual complements"*.

Table 4.3: Truth Table

A	B	$\bar{A}$	$\bar{B}$	A + B	$\overline{A + B}$	$\bar{A} \cdot \bar{B}$
0	0	1	1	0	1	1
0	1	1	0	1	0	0
1	0	0	1	1	0	0
1	1	0	0	1	0	0

• From the above table we see $\overline{A + B} = \bar{A} \cdot \bar{B}$

Thus, a NOR gate is equivalent to a bubbled AND gate.

Logic diagram:

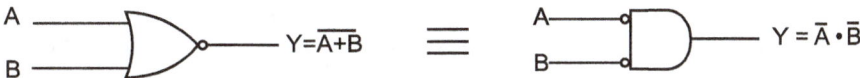

Fig. 4.2

2. De-Morgan's Second Theorem

• The statement of De-Morgan's second theorem goes like this, *"The complement of a product of variables is equal to the sum of their individual complements"*.

Table 4.4: Truth Table

A	B	$\bar{A}$	$\bar{B}$	A · B	$\overline{A \cdot B}$	$\bar{A} + \bar{B}$
0	0	1	1	0	1	1
0	1	1	0	0	1	1
1	0	0	1	0	1	1
1	1	0	0	1	0	0

- From the above table we see $\overline{A \cdot B} = \overline{A} + \overline{B}$

Thus, a NAND gate is equivalent to a bubbled OR gate.

Logic diagram:

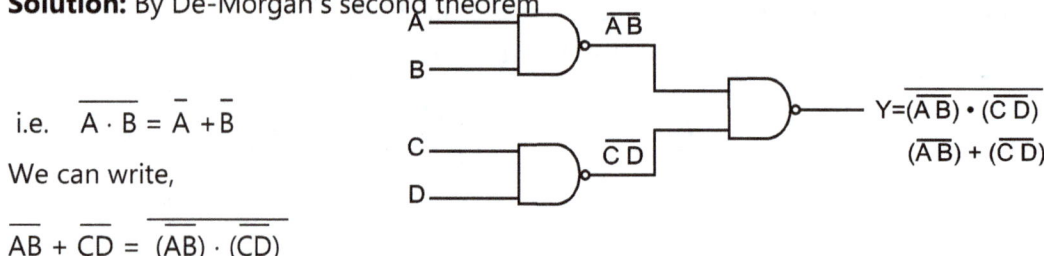

Fig. 4.3

Example 4.6: *Implement the logic equation $Y = \overline{AB} + \overline{CD}$ using NAND gates.*

Solution: By De-Morgan's second theorem

i.e. $\overline{A \cdot B} = \overline{A} + \overline{B}$

We can write,

$\overline{AB} + \overline{CD} = \overline{(AB) \cdot (CD)}$

Hence the circuit is as shown in Fig. 4.4.   **Fig. 4.4**

Example 4.7: *Use De-Morgan's theorem to simplify the following Boolean expression*

$\overline{\overline{AB} + A\overline{B}}$.

Solution:

$$\overline{\overline{AB} + A\overline{B}} = (\overline{\overline{AB}}) \cdot (\overline{A\overline{B}}) \qquad \text{(by De-Morgan's 1}^{st}\text{ theorem)}$$

$$= (\overline{\overline{A}} + \overline{B}) \cdot (\overline{A} + \overline{\overline{B}}) \qquad \text{(by De-Morgan's 2}^{nd}\text{ theorem)}$$

$$= (A + \overline{B}) \cdot (\overline{A} + B) \qquad (\because \overline{\overline{A}} = A, \overline{\overline{B}} = B)$$

$$= A\overline{A} + AB + \overline{B}\overline{A} + \overline{B}B$$

$$= AB + \overline{A}\overline{B} \qquad (\because A\overline{A} = B\overline{B} = 0)$$

Example 4.8: *The Boolean expressions of the two variables X and Y in terms of the three inputs A, B and C are given by:*

$$X = ABC + A\overline{B}\overline{C} + \overline{A}B\overline{C}$$

$$Y = (\overline{A} + \overline{B} + \overline{C}) \cdot (\overline{A} + B + C) \cdot (A + \overline{B} + C)$$

Write the relationship between X and Y.

Solution:

$$X = ABC + A\bar{B}\bar{C} + \bar{A}B\bar{C}$$

$$\therefore \quad X = \overline{\overline{ABC + A\bar{B}\bar{C} + \bar{A}B\bar{C}}}$$

$$= \overline{(\overline{ABC}) \cdot (\overline{A\bar{B}\bar{C}}) \cdot (\overline{\bar{A}B\bar{C}})} \qquad \text{... DeMorgan's Theorem}$$

$$= \overline{(\bar{A}+\bar{B}+\bar{C}) \cdot (\bar{A}+\bar{\bar{B}}+\bar{\bar{C}}) \cdot (\bar{\bar{A}}+\bar{B}+\bar{\bar{C}})}$$

$$= \overline{(\bar{A}+\bar{B}+\bar{C}) \cdot (\bar{A}+B+C) \cdot (A+\bar{B}+C)} \; ...... \; (\because \bar{\bar{A}} = A)$$

$$= Y$$

$$\therefore \quad X = Y$$

Example 4.9: *Prove the following using De- Morgan's theorem:*

1. $AB + CD = \overline{\overline{AB} \cdot \overline{CD}}$
2. $\overline{(A+B)\cdot(C+D)} = (\bar{A} \cdot \bar{B}) + (\bar{C} \cdot \bar{D})$

Solution:

1.
$$AB + CD = \overline{\overline{AB + CD}}$$

$$= \overline{\overline{AB} \cdot \overline{CD}} \qquad \text{... De-Morgan's theorem}$$

2.
$$\overline{(A+B)\cdot(C+D)} = \overline{(A+B)} + \overline{(C+D)} \qquad \text{... De-Morgan's theorem}$$

$$= (\bar{A} \cdot \bar{B}) + (\bar{C} \cdot \bar{D}) \qquad \text{... De-Morgan's theorem}$$

4.5 UNIVERSAL GATES

❖ **Important Question Related to this Topic** ❖

1. List the universal gates and derive the basic gates using any universal gate.
2. Explain OR gate by using NAND gate and NOR gate.
3. What is meant by Universal Gate? By using any universal gate draw all the basic gates.

- NAND and NOR gates are called universal gates because any logic function can be implemented using NAND or NOR gates. All basic gates can be implemented using NAND and NOR gates.

4.5.1 NAND as a Universal Gate

Table 4.5 : NAND as a Universal Gate

Sr. No.	Gate	NAND Gate Implementation
1.	NOT gate A —▷o— $\bar{A}$	A —[NAND]— $Y = \bar{A}$
2.	OR gate A B —[ ]— Y	A, B —[NAND gates]— $Y = A + B$

...Conti.

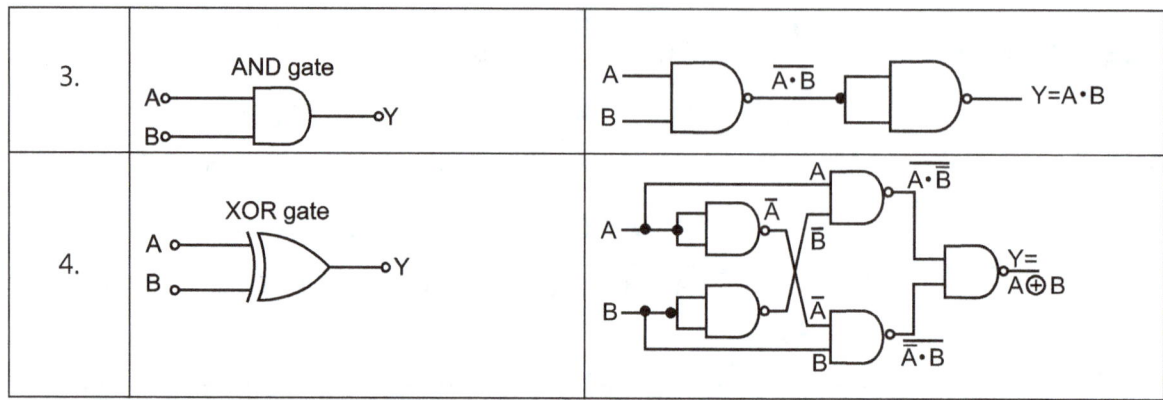

| 3. | AND gate | $\overline{A \cdot B}$ ... $Y = A \cdot B$ |
| 4. | XOR gate | ... $Y = A \oplus B$ |

- NOR can be implemented by cascading the NOT gate using NAND to the output of OR and XOR can be implemented by cascading the NOT gate using NAND to the output of XNOR.

4.5.2 NOR as a Universal Gate

Table 4.6 : NOR as a Universal Gate

Sr. No.	Gate	NOR Implementation
1.	NOT gate $A \rightarrow \overline{A}$	$A \rightarrow Y = A$
2.	OR gate	$\overline{A+B}$ ... $Y = A + B$
3.	AND gate	$\overline{A}$ ... $\overline{B}$ ... $Y = A \cdot B$
4.	XOR gate	$Y = A \oplus B$

- NAND and XNOR gates can be implemented by cascading the NOT gate using NOR to the output of AND and XOR gates respectively.

4.6 STANDARD REPRESENTATION OF LOGIC FUNCTION

- Logic functions are expressed in terms of logical variables. The values of logic functions as well as logical variables are in the binary form. Logic functions can be expressed in the following forms:

  (a) SOP (Sum of Products)

  (b) POS (Product of Sums)

(a) SOP (Sum of Products)

A sum of product expression consist of product term logically added. Product term is logical product of many variables. The variables used may or may not be complemented.

Example: $A \cdot B + \overline{A} \cdot B + A \cdot \overline{B}$

       $A + A \cdot \overline{B} + \overline{B} \cdot C$

(b) POS (Product of Sums)

A product of sum expression consist of sum terms logically multiplied. A sum term is the logical addition of several variables.

Example: $(A + B) \cdot (\overline{A} + \overline{B})$

       $(A + \overline{B}) \cdot (B + C) \cdot (A + B + C)$

4.6.1 Minterm and Maxterm

Minterm: Minterm is used to represent SOP form in which unbarred letters represent 1's and barred letters represents 0's.

Example: $Y = \overline{A} \cdot B \cdot C + A \cdot B \cdot C + \overline{A} \cdot B \cdot \overline{C}$

		Binary		**Decimal**	
$\overline{A} \cdot B \cdot C$	$\Rightarrow$	011	=	3	Resultant binary is expressed
$A \cdot B \cdot C$	$\Rightarrow$	111	=	7	as decimal number
$\overline{A} \cdot B \cdot \overline{C}$	$\Rightarrow$	010	=	2	

Y is expressed as:

$$Y = \sum m \ (2, \ 3, \ 7)$$

$\sum$ represents sum and m as minterm.

Example 4.10: *Find expression for* $Y = \sum m \ (1, \ 3, \ 5, \ 7)$. *Maximum value is 7 and to represent it in binary 3-bits required i.e. three input variables. For example, A. B, C.*

Solution:

Decimal	Binary	Expression
7	111	$A \cdot BC$
1	001	$\bar{A} \cdot \bar{B} \cdot C$
3	011	$\bar{A} \cdot B \cdot C$
5	101	$A \cdot \bar{B} \cdot C$

$$Y = A \cdot B \cdot C + \bar{A} \cdot \bar{B} \cdot C + \bar{A} \cdot B \cdot C + A \cdot \bar{B} \cdot C$$

Maxterm: Maxterm is used to represent POS form in which unbarred letters represent 0's and barred letters represents 1's.

Example: $Y = (A + B + C) \cdot (A + \bar{B} + C)(A + \bar{B} + \bar{C})$

                             Binary   **Decimal**

$A + B + C \Rightarrow$ 000 $=$ 0

$A + \bar{B} + C \Rightarrow$ 010 $=$ 2

$A + \bar{B} + \bar{C} \Rightarrow$ 011 $=$ 3

Y is expressed as:

$$Y = \Pi M (0, 2, 3)$$

    Π represent product

    m stands for maxterm.

Example 4.11: *Find expression for Y = πm (0, 2, 3, 5).*

Solution:

Decimal	Binary	Expression
0	000	$(A + B + C)$
2	010	$(A + \bar{B} + C)$
3	011	$(A + \bar{B} + \bar{C})$
5	101	$(\bar{A} + B + \bar{C})$

$$Y = A \cdot B \cdot C + \bar{A} \cdot \bar{B} \cdot C + \bar{A} \cdot B \cdot C + A \cdot \bar{B} \cdot C$$

4.7 ADDERS

❖ Important Question Related to this Topic ❖

What is the difference between a Half adder and Full adder?

- A digital circuit can be used for arithmetic operations. The basic rules of binary addition are:

$$0 + 0 = 0$$
$$0 + 1 = 1$$
$$1 + 0 = 1$$
$$1 + 1 = 10$$

The last rule 1+1=10 shows that a carry (1) is generated after the addition and the sum is zero.

There are Two Types of Binary Adders:

1. Half Adder
2. Full Adder

4.7.1 Half- Adder

* The half-adder has two inputs (A, B) and two outputs (sum, carry).
* The block diagram of half-adder is shown in Fig. 4.5.

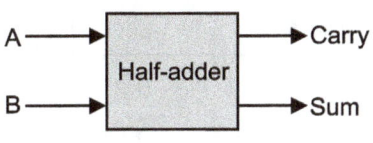

Fig. 4.5

Table 4.7: Truth Table

A	B	Sum	Carry
0	0	0	0
0	1	1	0
1	0	1	0
1	1	0	1

* Sum and C_{out} is expressed by finding its equivalent sum of product expression, where output is 1.

∴   Carry output $= AB$

∴   Sum $= \overline{A}B + A\overline{B}$

                         $= A \oplus B$

                           ↑

                     XOR

Half-Adder Circuit

* Fig. 4.6 shows the half-adder circuit

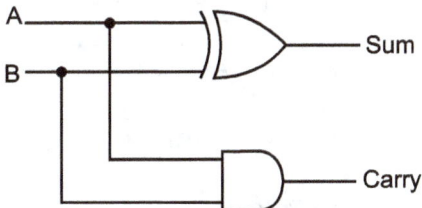

Fig. 4.6: Half Adder

Note: The half-adder circuit cannot add two bits along with a previous carry input. Hence they have limited applications. To overcome this drawback a full-adder is used.

4.7.2 Full-Adder   [May 13, 15]

- Full-adder is a combinational circuit that can perform the arithmetic sum of three input bits i.e. A, B, C_{in} and gives two outputs Sum, and C_{out}. It has an additional input of previous carry in. Fig. 4.7 shows the logic block diagram of full-adder.

Table 4.8 : The truth table of full-adder

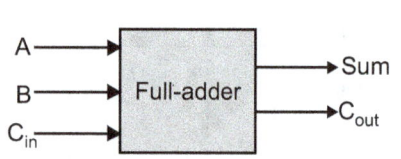

Fig. 4.7: Block Diagram of Full-Adder

Inputs			Outputs	
A	**B**	**C_{in}**	**C_{out}**	**Sum**
0	0	0	0	0
0	0	1	0	1
0	1	0	0	1
0	1	1	1	0
1	0	0	0	1
1	0	1	1	0
1	1	0	1	0
1	1	1	1	1

- Sum and Cout is expressed by finding its equivalent sum of product expression, where output is 1.

$$\text{Sum} = \bar{A}\bar{B}C_{in} + \bar{A}B\bar{C}_{in} + AB C_{in} + A\bar{B}\bar{C}_{in}$$

$$\text{Sum} = \bar{A}\bar{B}C_{in} + \bar{A}B\bar{C}_{in} + A\bar{B}\bar{C}_{in} + ABC_{in}$$

$$= C_{in} (\bar{A}\bar{B} + AB) + \bar{C}_{in} (\bar{A}B + A\bar{B})$$

$$= C_{in} \oplus (A \oplus B)$$

- From the solved expression for sum we say that, the sum is the XORed output of A, B and C_{in} inputs.

Full-Adder Circuit

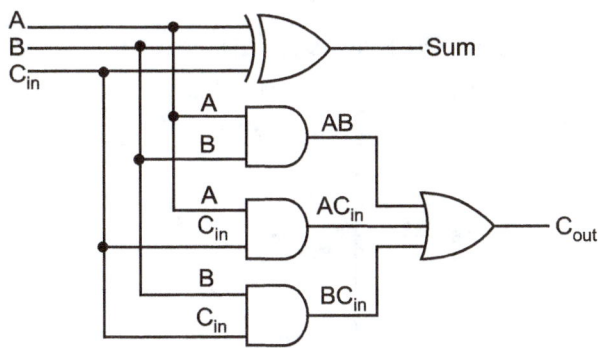

Fig. 4.8

4.7.3 Full-Adder Circuit using Half-Adder   [Nov. 15]

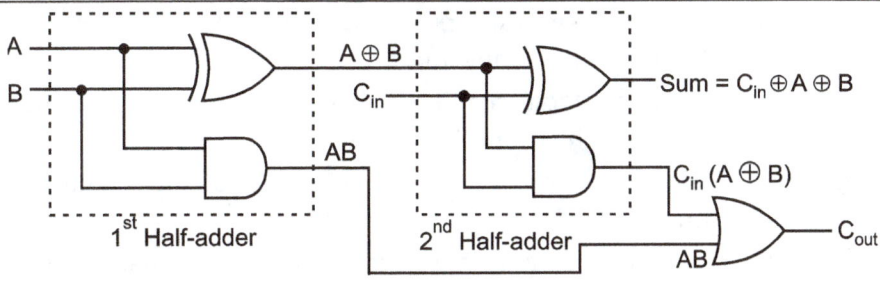

Fig. 4.9

$$C_{out} = AB + C_{in}(A\bar{B} + \bar{A}B)$$

$\therefore$
$$C_{out} = AB(C_{in} + 1) + C_{in}(A\bar{B} + \bar{A}B)$$

$$= AB\,C_{in} + AB + A\bar{B}\,C_{in} + \bar{A}B\,C_{in}$$

$$= AB + AC_{in}(B + \bar{B}) + \bar{A}B\,C_{in}$$

$$= AB + AC_{in} + \bar{A}B\,C_{in}$$

$$= AB(C_{in} + 1) + A\,C_{in} + \bar{A}B\,C_{in}$$

$$= AB\,C_{in} + AB + A\,C_{in} + \bar{A}B\,C_{in}$$

$$= AB + A\,C_{in} + B\,C_{in}(A + \bar{A})$$

$$= AB + C_{in}(A + B)$$

$$= AB + A\,C_{in} + B\,C_{in}$$

- This equation for C_{out} is exactly the same, as the expression derived earlier; hence it is proved that the circuit formed cascading two Half-adder circuit works exactly the same as the circuit shown in Fig. 4.8.

4.8 MULTIPLEXER [MUX]   [May 14]

❖ **Important Questions Related to this Topic** ❖

What is multiplexer? Draw the circuit of 8:1 Mux. What is the relation between the number of select lines and inputs? Give applications of Multiplexers.

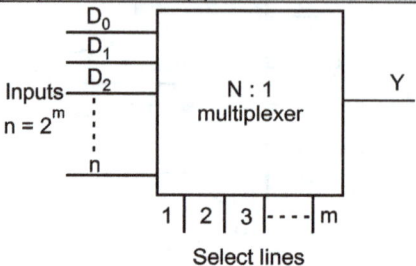

Fig. 4.10: n : 1 Multiplexer

- A multiplexer circuit can have several inputs and only one output. It works as digital switch. The word 'multiplex' means 'many into one'.

- Multiplexer is a combinational logic circuit which accepts many inputs and allows only one of them to get through to the output, at an instance of time.

- The control signal "**select**" is used to select one particular input line whose data is transferred to the output.

- Usually there are 2^n input lines and n select lines. So, for 8 input lines we need 3 select lines.

- Multiplexers are essential block of many important digital circuits such as microprocessors and microcontrollers. The symbolic representation of a multiplexer is shown in Fig. 4.10.

4.8.1 2 : 1 Multiplexer   [Dec. 13]

- A 2 : 1 multiplexer has two data input lines D_0 and D_1 and only one output; with one select line (m).

- 'Enable or Strobe', is an active low input signal; which is always kept at logic 0 to activate the IC.

- Fig. 4.11 (a) and (b) show the truth table, Block schematic of 2: 1 multiplexer.

Enable ($\bar{E}$)	S_0	Y
1	X	0
0	0	D_0
0	1	D_1

$$Y = \bar{S_0}D_0 + S_0D_1$$

(a) Truth Table of 2 : 1 Multiplexer

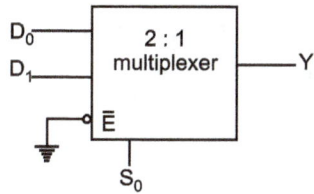

(b) Block schematic of 2 : 1 Multiplexer

Fig. 4.11

4.8.2 4 : 1 Multiplexer

- 4 : 1 multiplexer circuit has four data input lines D_0 to D_3 and one output line Y, with two select lines S_0 and S_1. The Enable or Strobe input (E) is connected to ground since it is active low.
- Fig. 4.12 (a), (b) shows the truth table and block schematic of a 4 : 1 multiplexer.
- The Boolean expression for Y output is,

$$Y = \overline{S_1}\,\overline{S_0}D_0 + \overline{S_1}S_0D_1 + S_1\overline{S_0}D_2 + S_1S_0D_3$$

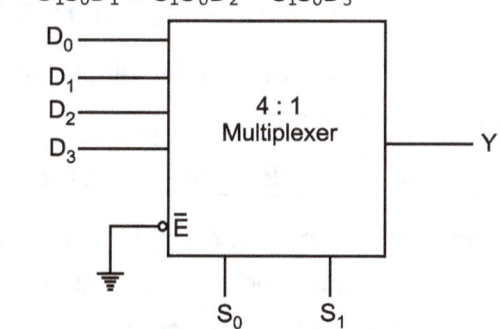

$\overline{E}$	Inputs		Output
	S_1	S_0	Y
1	X	X	0
0	0	0	D_0
0	0	1	D_1
0	1	0	D_2
0	1	1	D_3

Fig. 4.12 (a): Truth table of 4 : 1 Multiplexer

Fig. 4.12 (b): Block Schematic of 4 : 1 Multiplexer

4.8.3 8 : 1 Multiplexer

- The truth table and block schematic of 8 : 1 MUX are shown in Fig. 4.13 (a), (b) below.

S_2	S_1	S_0	Y
0	0	0	D_0
0	0	1	D_1
0	1	0	D_2
0	1	1	D_3
1	0	0	D_4
1	0	1	D_5
1	1	0	D_6
1	1	1	D_7

(a) Truth Table

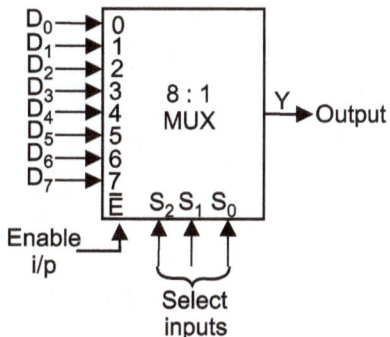

(b) Block Schematic of 8:1 MUX

Fig. 4.13

Applications of Multiplexers:

Multiplexers are,

- Used in A/D and D/A converter.

- Used in Data acquisition systems.

- Used in time multiplexing systems.

- Used as a channel selector.

- Used in implementing logic circuits.

4.9 DEMULTIPLEXER [DEMUX]   [Dec. 13, May 14]

- Demultiplexer is a combinational logic circuit that has one input and several outputs. It accepts a single input and sends it to one of the output lines. The output line is selected by control signal or select line input.

- The number of select lines is m, for an n-output demultiplexer, where $n = 2^m$.

- Symbolic representation of 1 : n demultiplexer is shown in Fig. 4.14.

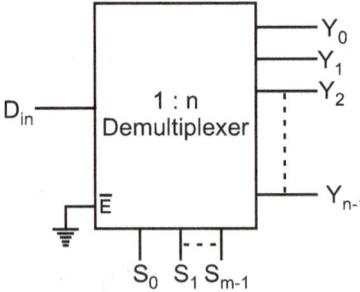

Fig. 4.14: 1 : n Demultiplexer

- This 1 : n demultiplexer is also known as a binary-to-decimal decoder with binary inputs applied at the select lines, and the decoded output will be obtained on the output line.

- A 1 : 4 demultiplexer requires two select lines. It's truth table, logic circuit is as shown below:

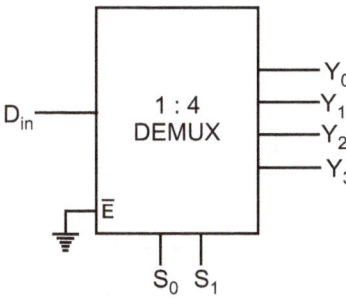

Fig: 4.15: 1 : 4 Demultiplexer

Select Inputs		Outputs			
S_0	S_1	Y_0	Y_1	Y_2	Y_3
0	0	1	0	0	0
0	1	0	1	0	0
1	0	0	0	1	0
1	1	0	0	0	1

4.9.1 1 : 8 Demultiplexer

- The truth table and block schematic of 1: 8 DEMUX are shown in Fig. 4.16 below

Enable	S_2	S_1	S_0	Y_0	Y_1	Y_2	Y_3	Y_4	Y_5	Y_6	Y_7
1	X	X	X	0	0	0	0	0	0	0	0
0	0	0	0	1	0	0	0	0	0	0	0
0	0	0	1	0	1	0	0	0	0	0	0
0	0	1	0	0	0	1	0	0	0	0	0
0	0	1	1	0	0	0	1	0	0	0	0
0	1	0	0	0	0	0	0	1	0	0	0
0	1	0	1	0	0	0	0	0	1	0	0
0	1	1	0	0	0	0	0	0	0	1	0
0	1	1	1	0	0	0	0	0	0	0	1

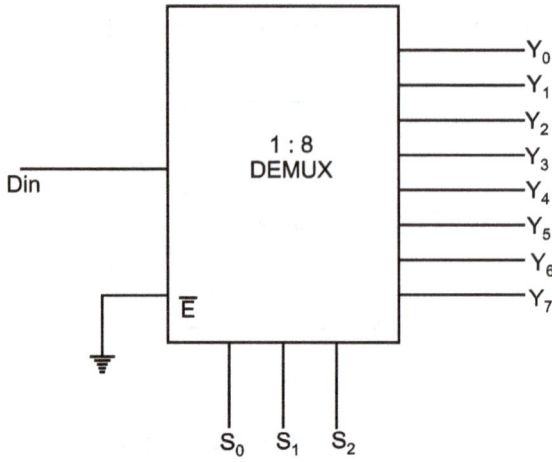

Fig. 4.16: 1 : 8 Demultiplexer

4.10 FLIP-FLOP

❖ Important Question Related to this Topic ❖

1. Draw and explain the operation of D flip-flop.

2. Give applications of flip-flops.

- Flip-Flops are the basic building blocks of the most sequential circuits. A flip-flop is capable of storing 1-bit binary information. There are many types of flip-flops such as SR Flip-Flop, JK Flip-Flop, T Flip-Flop etc.

- Flip-flop is nothing but memory element which holds its value until a new value is placed into its input terminal. Current state of flip-flop is called present state denoted by Q_n and when new input is applied stored data is modified depending on internal circuit of flip-flop is called next state (Q_{n+1}) of flip-flop.

Triggering

- Triggering is process of applying stimulus. In addition with normal input terminal flip-flop has one additional terminal called clock which acts as stimulus.

- Clock is square waveform with 50% duty cycle. i.e. clock with equal ON and OFF time.

- Flip-flop uses edge triggering method shown in Fig. 4.17. As a Clock has two transition one from low to high level and another from high to low level. There are two triggering method positive edge triggering and negative edge triggering respectively.

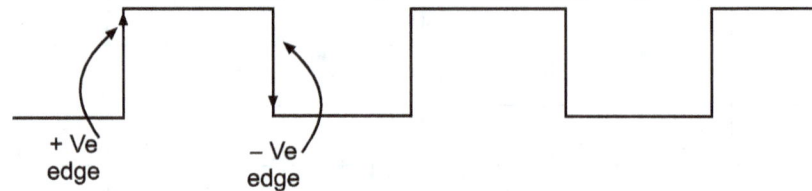

Fig. 4.17

D Flip-Flop

- D flip-flop is also called as 'Delay' flip-flop, which has input D, Clock and output Q and Q
- (Complement of Q) as shown in Fig. 4.18.

Operation of D Flip-Flop:

- As there is no bubble at the clock input terminal of flip-flop triggering method is positive edge triggering method.
- That means flip-flop changes its state from present state to next state only when clock edge is positive So if Clock=0, D may be zero or one (X-Don't care) but present state retained as it is.
- When Clock=1, D=0 present state (Q_n) of flip-flop may be 0 or 1 but the next state (Q_{n+1}) is 0.
- When Clock=1, D=1 present state (Q_n) of flip-flop may be 0 or 1 but the next state (Q_{n+1}) is 1.
- This operation is shown in Fig. 4.18 with the help of truth table and waveform.

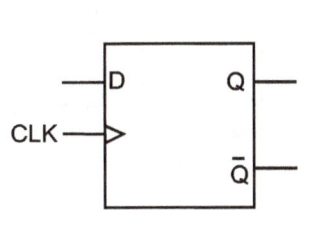

Clock	D_{in}	Q_n (Present State)	Q_{n+1} (Next State)
0	X	Qn	Qn
↑	0	0	0
↑	0	1	0
↑	1	0	1
↑	1	1	1

(a) Block Schematic   (b) Truth Table of D flip-flop

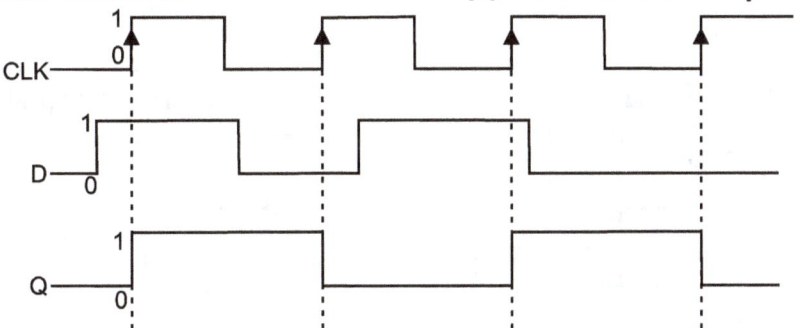

(c) Input and Output Waveforms of Clocked D Flip-Flop

Fig.4.18

Applications of D Flip-Flops:

- Used as basic building block in sequential circuits like counters and registers.
- Used as a memory element.
- Used to eliminate key bounce
- Used as a delay element.

4.10.1 T Flip-Flop

- T flip-flop is also called as 'Toggle' flip-flop, which has input T, Clock and output Q and $\bar{Q}$ (Complement of Q) as shown in Fig. 4.19.

Operation of T Flip-Flop:

- As there is no bubble at the clock input terminal of flip-flop triggering method is positive edge triggering method.
- That means flip-flop changes its state from present state to next state only when clock edge is positive So if Clock=0, T input may be zero or one (X-Don't care) but present state retained as it is.
- When Clock=1, T=0 present state (Q_n) of flip-flop may be 0 or 1 but the next state (Q_{n+1}) is equal to present state.
- When Clock=1, T=1 present state (Q_n) of flip-flop may be 0 or 1 but the next state (Q_{n+1}) is toggle of present state (Invert of present state).
- This operation is shown in Fig. 4.19 with the help of truth table and waveform.

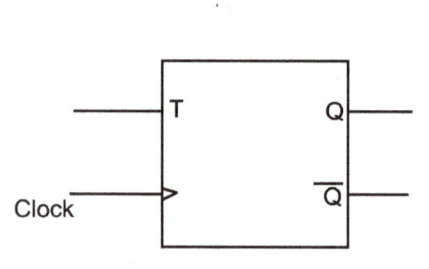

Clock	T	Q_n (Present State)	Q_{n+1} (Next State)
0	X	Q_n	Q_n
↑	0	0	0
↑	0	1	1
↑	1	0	1
↑	1	1	0

(a) Block Schematic   **(b) Truth Table of T Flip-Flop**

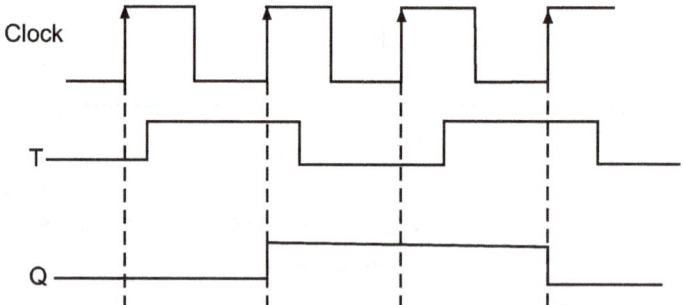

(c) Input and Output Waveforms of Clocked T Flip-Flop

Fig. 4.19

Application of T flip-flop

- It is used to construct counters.

4.11 REGISTERS

- Registers are used to store one or more bit data. 'n' flip-flops can store n bits of data. Register is composed of a group of flip-flops. Thus a register is a group of cascaded flip-flops used to store binary information. Fig. 4.20 shows a four-bit buffer register using D flip-flop.

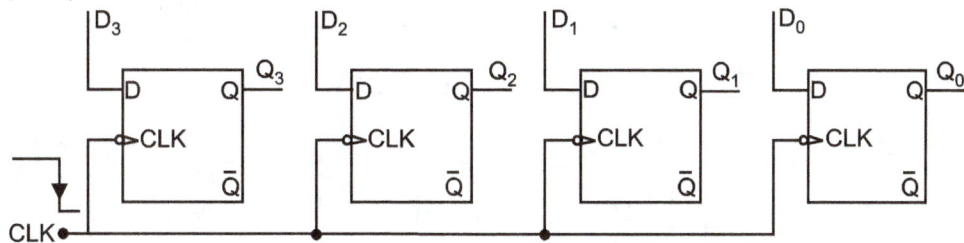

Fig. 4.20: 4-Bit Buffer Register

- To store 4-bit information, four flip-flops are required. As shown in the Fig. 4.20, four negative edge triggered D flip-flops are used. The information (4-bit binary data) to be stored is applied at $D_3 D_2 D_1 D_0$ inputs.

- On application of the negative edge of the clock input, the 4-bits get stored in the flip-flops and $Q_3 Q_2 Q_1 Q_0 = D_3 D_2 D_1 D_0$.

4.12 SHIFT REGISTER

❖ Important Question Related to this Topic ❖

1. What is a Shift Register? Explain the operation of a 4-bit shift register with serial-in, serial-out data.

2. Explain the basic types of shift registers in terms of data movement.

3. Draw and explain 4-bit parallel-in parallel-out (PIPO) shift register.

- Shift registers are the arrays of flip-flops in which the stored binary information can be shifted bit by bit to right or left; by applying appropriate clock pulse at the CLK input of the flip-flops.

- This bit shifting is necessary for certain arithmetic and logic operations used in microprocessors. For example, division and multiplication.

- Shift registers are very important in systems that are used for data storage and data transfer.

There are Four Types of Shift Registers:

1. Serial-In, Serial-Out (SISO) shift register.
2. Serial-In, Parallel-Out (SIPO) shift register.
3. Parallel In Serial-Out (PISO) shift register.
4. Parallel-In Parallel-Out (PIPO) shift register.

4.12.1 Serial-In, Serial-Out (SISO) Shift Register

- Fig. 4.21 (a), (b) show the block diagram and logic diagram using D flip-flop of SISO shift register. It accepts the data input serially and outputs it serially bit by bit for each negative edge of the clock pulse.

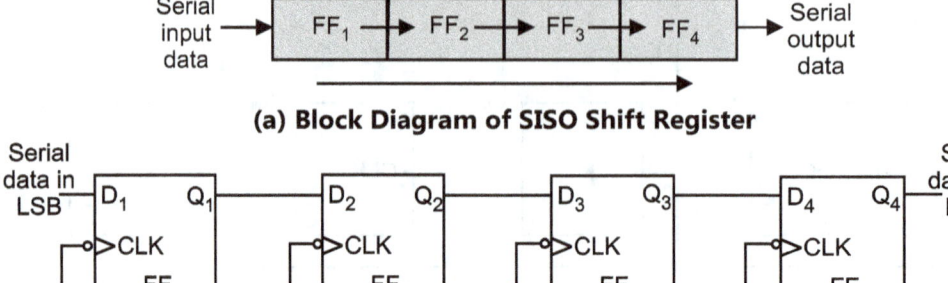

(a) Block Diagram of SISO Shift Register

(b) SISO Shift Register Using D Flip-Flop

Fig. 4.21

- Initially all the flip-flops are cleared to make $Q_1Q_2Q_3Q_4 = 0000$. FF_1 is a LSB flip-flop and FF_4 is a MSB flip-flop. It requires four clock cycles to store four bits of data.

- Consider for example, the input data bits are 0011. The following table illustrates the serial shifting of data.

After clock pulse	Serial input D_{in}	Output Q_1	Q_2	Q_3	Q_4
0	1	0	0	0	0
1	1	1	0	0	0
2	0	1	1	0	0
3	0	0	1	1	0
4		0	0	1	1

Final output is 0011 after 4 clock cycles

Fig. 4.22: Data Shifting in SISO

- At the falling edge of the first clock pulse input $D_{in} = 1$ will enter into FF_1, so the content of the register will be, $Q_1Q_2Q_3Q_4 = 1000$.

- At the falling edge of the second clock pulse, the input of $D_{in} = '1'$, so the content of the register will be, $Q_1Q_2Q_3Q_4 = 1100$.

- Similarly, at the third falling edge of the clock pulse, the input of $D_{in} = '0'$, so the content of the register will be, $Q_1Q_2Q_3Q_4 = 0110$.

- At the fourth falling edge of the clock pulse, the content of the register will be, $Q_1Q_2Q_3Q_4 = 0011$.

Disadvantages of SISO Register:

- It requires n-clock pulses to store n-bit data.
- The data gets lost, once it has been read.

4.12.2 Serial-In, Parallel-Out (SIPO) Shift Register

- Fig. 4.23 and Fig. 4.24 show the block diagram and logic diagram using D flip-flop of SIPO shift register. In this type of shift register the data is entered serially, and taken out in parallel form for each negative edge of the clock pulse.

- As shown in Fig. 4.24, the output of first flip-flop drives the input of the second and so on.

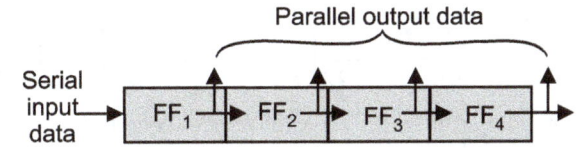

Fig. 4.23: Block Diagram of SIPO Shift Register

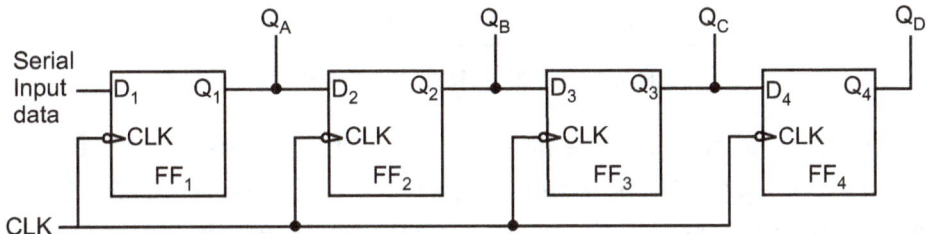

Fig. 4.24: Logic Circuit of SIPO Shift Register

- The serial data is applied at the input D_1 of the first flip-flop FF_1. The output is taken from the output terminal of each flip-flop simultaneously. The remaining operation of SIPO is similar to that of SISO shift register.

- The advantage of SIPO is that it does not require clock pulses to read and the data does not get lost after the read operation.

4.12.3 Parallel-In, Serial-Out (PISO) Shift Register

- Fig. 4.25 (a), (b) show the block diagram and logic diagram using D flip-flop of PISO shift register. The data input is entered in parallel form and output is taken serially bit by bit for each negative edge of the clock pulse.

- The shift/load is the control input used for read or load operation.

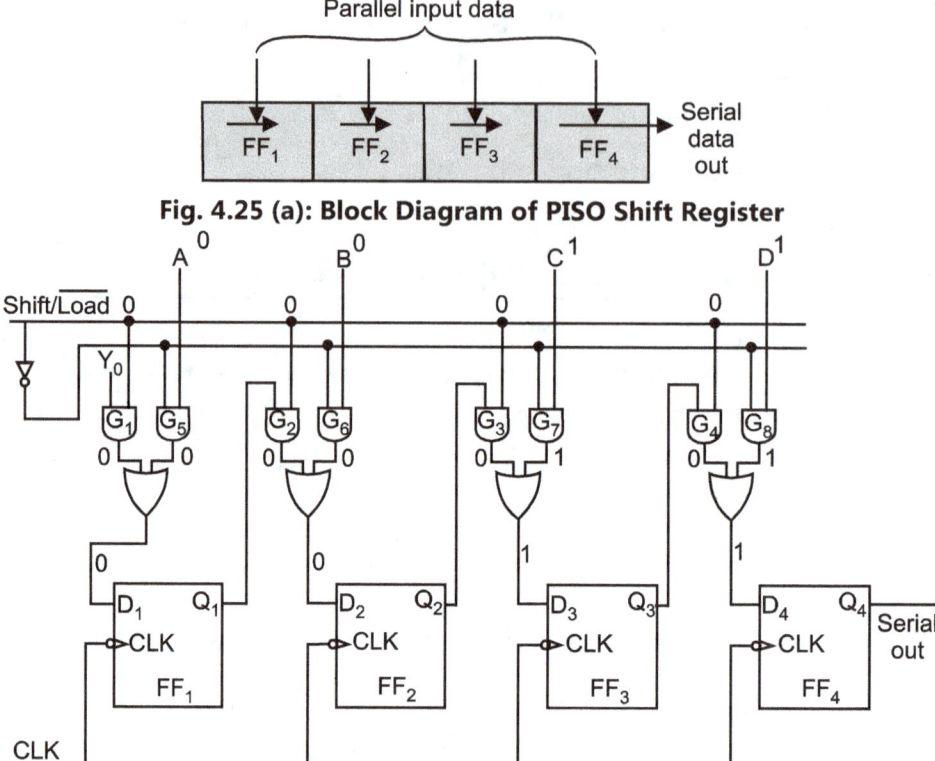

Fig. 4.25 (a): Block Diagram of PISO Shift Register

Fig. 4.25 (b): Logic Circuit of PISO Shift Register

- To load the data input into the flip-flops, the shift/load line is kept at logic '0'. Then, the output of G_1, G_2, G_3, G_4 is zero whereas the output of G_5, G_6, G_7, G_8 is A, B, C, D. Thus the data inputs A, B, C and D are fed simultaneously at the D input of each flip-flop. This is known as synchronous loading. The output is taken serially from Q_4 (flip-flop FF_4)

- When shift/load is high, the gates G_5, G_6, G_7, G_8 are disabled, whereas G_1, G_2, G_3, G_4 are enabled. This allows the shifting of the data bits to left at the arrival of each tailing edge of the clock cycle. The data is read from Y_0 bit-by-bit at every clock pulse.

4.12.4 Parallel-In, Parallel-Out (PIPO) Shift Register

- Fig. 4.26 (a), (b) show the block diagram and logic diagram of PIPO shift register using D flip-flop. The data input is entered in parallel form and output also is taken in parallel form (simultaneously) at negative edge of the clock pulse.

- The input from the four data lines A, B, C, D is loaded simultaneously at each input of the D flip-flop and the output is taken simultaneously from Q_1, Q_2, Q_3, Q_4 data lines.

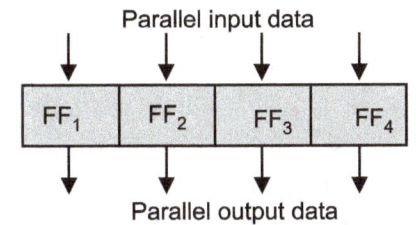

Fig. 4.26 (a): Block Diagram of PIPO

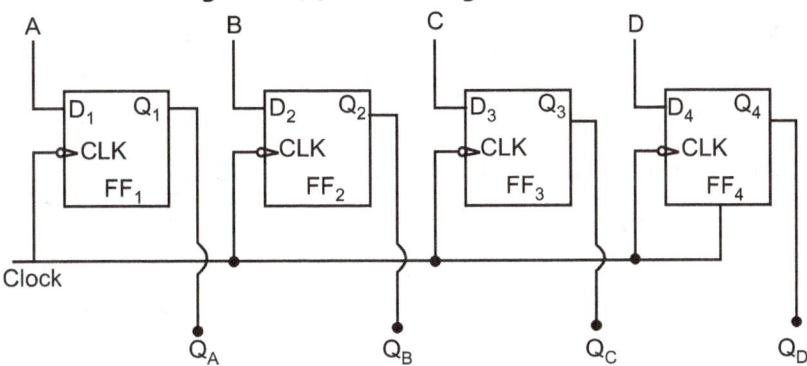

Fig. 4.26 (b): Logic Circuit Diagram of PIPO

Applications of Shift Register:

- Used in digital multiplication (data is left shifted and added).
- Used for parallel to serial data conversion and serial to parallel data conversion.
- Used as a delay line.
- Used in digital counters like ring and twisted ring counter.
- Sequence generator and detector.

4.13 COUNTERS [Dec. 13]

❖ **Important Questions Related to this Topic** ❖

1. Synchronous counters are more advantageous than Asynchronous counters. Explain. Describe in brief some important applications of Counters.
2. What do you mean by counters?
3. State different types of counters.

- Digital counter is a sequential circuit which counts the electric pulses. It is made up of registers. It counts number of clock pulses arriving at the input or number of occurrence of events; like counting number of objects passing on a conveyor or number of persons entering/leaving a room.
- Counters are used in Analog-to-Digital Converters (ADCs), frequency division and synthesis circuits.
- Counters are classified into two groups: Asynchronous and Synchronous.

- In Asynchronous counters, the external clock signal is applied to one flip-flop and then the output of preceding flip-flop is given to the clock signal of the successive flip-flop. The output does not change in synchronization with the clock. Therefore, propagation delay is more. They are also called as ripple counters.

- In synchronous counters, the flip-flops are clocked simultaneously. The output of synchronous counter changes in synchronization with the clock. They are faster than the Asynchronous counters.

- Number of states of a counter is given by 2^n where n is number of flip-flops.

- Relation between number of flip-flop and state $2^n = m$. m means number of states.

- N bit counter count the number from 0 to $2^n - 1$.

4.13.1 Asynchronous Counters/Ripple Counters

❖ **Important Question Related to this Topic** ❖

Explain the 2-bit asynchronous counter using flip-flops.

- As we know, in asynchronous counters the flip-flops are not clocked simultaneously. The first flip-flop is clocked by the external clock pulse and then each successive flip-flop is clocked by the output of the previous flip-flop.

- To design and implement 2-bit asynchronous up counter using flip-flops, two flip-flops are required. It is also called as a mod-4 counter since it has $2^2 = 4$ distinct states from 0 to 3.

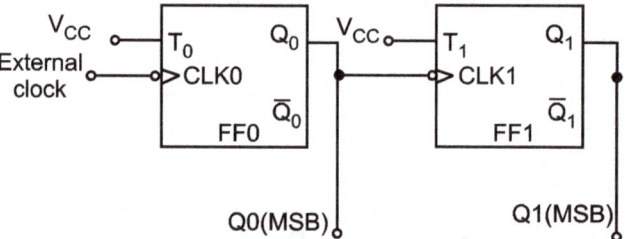

Fig. 4.27: 2-Bit Ripple Up Counter

- Fig. 4.27 shows the logic diagram of 2-bit ripple up counter using toggle flip-flop. The number of flip-flops used is 2. The input 'T' of each flip-flop is connected to logic 1. External clock is applied to the clock input of first flip-flop (FF_0) and output Q_0 drives the clock input of the next flip-flop FF_1.

  - Initially all the flip-flops are reset. $\therefore Q_1 Q_0 = 00$.

  - The moment when the falling edge of the clock signal arrives at the clock input, it will toggle making $T_0 = 1$. Hence $Q_0 = 1$.

  - As Q_0 is connected to clock input of FF_1, and Q_0 has made transition from 0 to 1, it is treated as the positive edge of the clock. Therefore Q_1 does not change. $\therefore$ After 1st clock pulse the counter output is $Q_1 Q_0 = 01$.

- At the second falling edge of clock, FF_0 toggles again and makes $Q_0 = 0$ i.e. it changes from 1 to 0. This is a negative signal at the clock input of FF_1. Therefore Q_1 becomes 1.

  $\therefore$ After 2nd clock pulse the counter output is $Q_1 Q_0 = 010$

- At third falling edge of clock, FF_0 toggles to make $Q_0 = 1$. This does not change the output of FF_1. $\therefore$ Q_1 remains 1.

  $\therefore$ After the 3rd clock pulse the counter output is $Q_1 Q_0 = 11$.

- In the similar manner the output of the counter takes values as shown in the table. It can also be understood by Fig. 4.28.

Table 4.9: Count Sequence of 2-Bit Up Counter

Q_1	Q_0	State of the counter
0	0	0
0	1	1
1	0	2
1	1	3

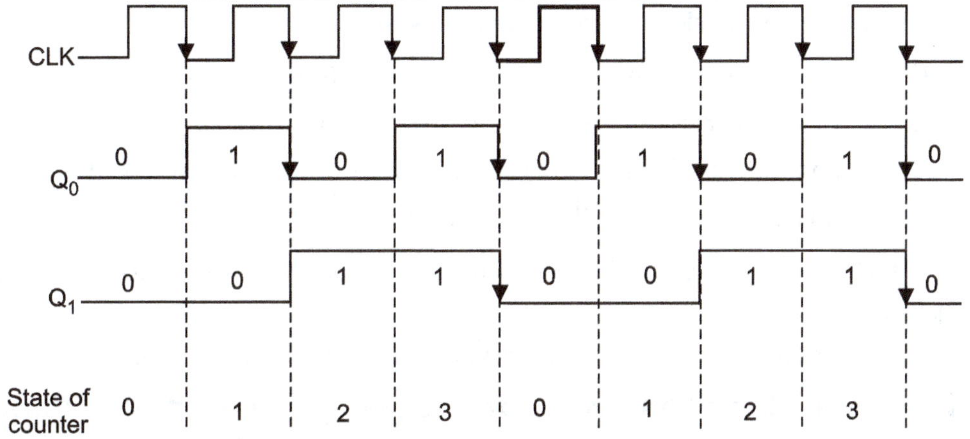

Fig. 4.28: Waveforms/Timing Diagram of 2-Bit Ripple Up Counter

4.13.2 Synchronous Counters

- In synchronous counters all the flip-flops are clocked simultaneously. Therefore it is faster in operation. It can be designed for any count sequence which need not be always straight binary.

2-bit Synchronous Up Counter

- Fig. 4.29 shows a 2-bit synchronous counter. It is also known as mod – 4 counter.

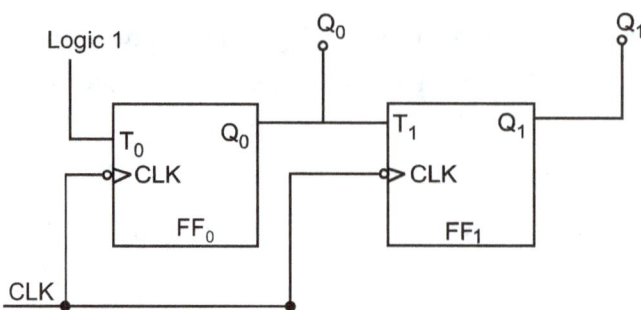

Fig. 4.29: 2-Bit Synchronous Up Counter

- The toggle input (T_0) of the first flip-flop (FF_0) is connected to logic 1. The output of FF_0 is connected to T_1 i.e. toggle input of first flip-flop.
- Initially all the flip-flops are cleared.

$$\therefore \qquad Q_1 Q_0 = 00$$

- At 1st negative clock pulse, Q_0 toggles from 0 to 1. But at the instant when clock is applied, $Q_0 = 0$, therefore $T_1 = 0$ and hence $Q_1 = 0$. Thus at 1st negative edge of the clock pulse, Q_1 remains unchanged and the output of counter will be $Q_1 Q_0 = 01$.
- At 2nd negative clock edge, FF_0 again toggles changing state of Q_0 from 1 to 0. But at the instant when the clock pulse arrives the state of Q_0 is 1. So $T_1 = 1$, hence $Q_1 = 1$. Thus after 2nd negative edge of clock signal the output will be $Q_1 Q_0 = 10$.
- At the 3rd negative clock edge, FF_0 toggles to change Q_0 from 0 to 1. But at the instant when it arrives, Q_0 is 0. So $Q_0 = 0$. This keeps Q_1 unchanged. Therefore at the 3rd negative edge of the clock, the state of output $Q_1 Q_0 = 11$.
- At the 4th negative clock edge FF_0 toggles changes Q_0 from 1 to 0 and the cycle repeats.
- Timing diagram of synchronous and asynchronous counter is same.

4.13.3 Difference Between Synchronous and Asynchronous Counters

[May 16]

❖ **Important Question Related to this Topic** ❖
Give the comparison between synchronous and asynchronous counters.

- All the flip-flops are clocked simultaneously in case of synchronous counters. In case of the asynchronous counters, an external clock is applied to one of the flip-flops and for the remaining flip-flops the output of the previous stage is connected as the clock input of the next stage.
- Synchronous counters are faster than the asynchronous counters.

- Synchronous counters can be designed for any count sequence while asynchronous counters can be designed to generate straight binary sequences in the up or down directions.

- Design of the asynchronous counters is simpler as compared to that of the synchronous counters.

- Asynchronous counters can be implemented with only MSJK & T type of flip-flop, while synchronous counters can be implemented with any type of flip-flop.

4.14 MICROPROCESSOR

❖ Important Question Related to this Topic ❖
Draw and explain the block diagram of a microprocessor.

- A microprocessor, as the term has come to be known, is general purpose digital computer central processing unit (CPU) also known as computer on a chip, microprocessor is in no sense a complete digital computer. Fig. 4.30 shows a block diagram of microprocessor CPU, which contains arithmetic and logic unit (ALU), a program counter (PC), a stack pointer (SP), some working registers, a clock timing circuit, and interrupts circuits.

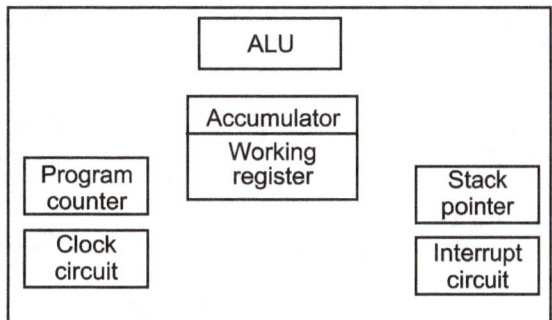

Fig. 4.30: Block diagram of Microprocessor

- To make a complete microcomputer, one must add memory, usually read only program memory (ROM) and random access data memory (RAM), memory decoders, an oscillator, and a number of input/output devices such as interrupt handlers and counters, may be added to relieve the CPU from time consuming counting or timing operations. Equipping the microcomputer with mass storage devices, commonly floppy and hard disk drives and I/O peripherals, such as keyboard and CRT display, yields a small computer that can be applied to a range of general purpose software applications.

- The key term to describe the design of microprocessor is general purpose. The hardware design of a microprocessor CPU is arranged so that a small or very large system can be configured around the CPU as the application demands.

- The basic use of a microprocessor is to read data, perform extensive calculations on that data, and store those calculations in a mass storage device or display the results for human use. The programs used by the microprocessor are stored in the mass storage device and loaded into RAM as the user directs. A few microprocessor programs are stored in ROM. The ROM based programs are primarily small fixed programs that operate peripherals and other fixed devices that are connected to the system. The design of the microprocessor is driven by the desire to make it as expandable and flexible as possible.

4.15 MICROCONTROLLER

❖ Important Questions Related to this Topic ❖

1. Give a comparison between the microprocessor and microcontroller.
2. State the advantages of a microprocessor and microcontroller.
3. Explain the importance of microprocessors.

- The prime use of microcontroller is to control the operation of a machine using fixed program that is stored in ROM and that does not change over lifetime of the system.

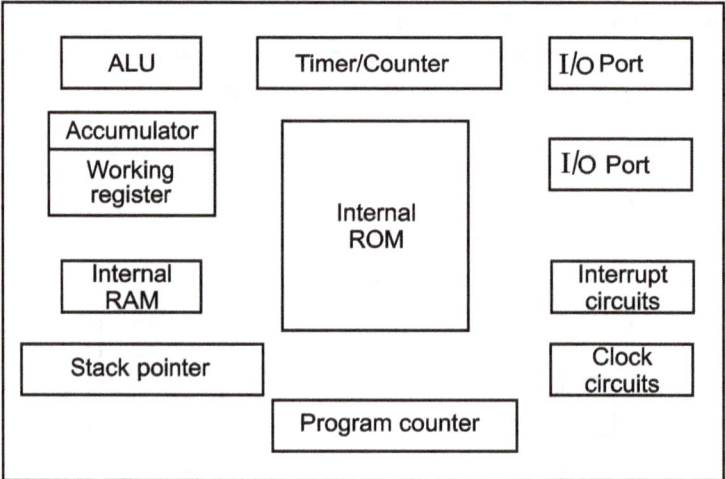

Fig. 4.31: Block Diagram of Microcontroller

- A microprocessor is necessary, but just not enough to create a complete microcomputer system. It needs memories such as RAM, ROM etc., number of I/O devices, timers, interrupt controllers, DMA controllers and many other supporting devices to improve its flexibility and performance.
- Fig. 4.31 shows block diagram of microcontroller which has built-in microprocessor, memory (RAM and ROM), I/O interfacing circuits and peripheral devices such as A to D converters, interrupt circuits, serial I/O etc.
- Because of the built-in memory and I/O the operating speed is high.
- A microcontroller based design requires less hardware.

Advantages of Using Microprocessors and Microcontrollers:

- The systems based on Microprocessors and Microcontrollers are very compact and cost effective.

- They are versatile; the programs can be changed easily to accept changes in the system.
- They can be programmed to execute a number of tasks simultaneously.
- Can be used for manipulating numerical data.
- Microcontroller systems are speedy in operation due to built-in peripherals. They also require less hardware which in turn increases their reliability.
- Intelligence can be brought in the systems.
- They reduce development cost, time and size of the system.

Applications of Microprocessors and Microcontrollers

Microprocessors and Microcontrollers have a wide range of applications. Some of them are listed below:

- Embedded systems
- Data acquisition systems
- Military applications
- Calculators
- Personal computers
- Laptops
- Processes controllers
- Game machines
- Communication systems

4.16 COMPARISON BETWEEN MICROPROCESSOR AND MICROCONTROLLER

Sr. No.	Microcontroller	Microprocessor
1.	Microcontroller contains microprocessor, memory (ROM and RAM), I/O interfacing circuit and peripheral devices such as, serial I/O, A/D converter, timer etc.	Microprocessor contains ALU, control unit (clock and timing circuit), different register and interrupt circuit.
2.	It has few instructions to move data between memory and CPU.	It has many instructions to move data between memory and CPU.
3.	It has many bit handing instructions.	It has few bit handing instructions.
4.	Has separate memory for data and program.	Does not have separate memory for data and program.

...Conti.

5.	Less access time for built-in memory and I/O devices.	More access time for memory and I/O devices.
6.	Microcontroller based system requires less hardware.	Microprocessor based system requires more hardware.
7.	Offers less flexibility in design.	Offers more flexibility in design.

QUESTIONS

1. Explain Positive Logic and Negative Logic.
2. State and Prove Demorgans theorem.
3. Draw and explain the operation of following gates using CMOS
   (a) NOT   (b) AND   (c) OR   (d) NAND   (e) NOR   (f) EX-OR.
4. Write a short note on various classifications of IC technologies
5. What is multiplexer? What is the relation between number of select lines and inputs? Draw the diagram of 2:1, 4:1, 8:1 MUX & Explain the significance of STROBE pin? Give application of multiplexers.
6. What is demultiplexer? Draw the diagram of 1:2, 1:4, 1:8 DEMUX & Explain the Significance of ENABLE pin? Give application of Demultiplexers.
7. What do you mean by flip-flop? Explain the operation of D-flip-flop with PRESET and CLEAR.
8. Explain the following terms in relation with the counter
   (a) Size   (b) Clocking   (c) UP/DOWN control   (d) Load   (e) Clear
9. Explain the term modulo-n.
10. What are the types of Counter? Which counter is called as ripple counter? Why?
11. What do you mean by counter? Compare Synchronous and Asynchronous counter in terms of Clocking, Advantages, Disadvantages?
12. What is shift register? Give its application? What are the modes in shift register? Which flip-flop is used to construct shift register?
13. Draw the basic diagram of shift register? Explain each control?
14. Write the difference between Microcontroller and Microprocessor.
15. Draw and explain the block diagram of Microcontroller.
16. Draw and explain the block diagram of Microprocessor.
17. Sketch the block diagram of Microcontroller and Microprocessor. Explain each block.
18. Compare combinational logic and sequential logic.
19. Write Rules of Boolean Algebra.
20. Design and implement full adder (3-bit adder) using basic gates. Use K-map technique, Give its application.

21. Design and implement half adder (2-bit adder) using basic gates. Use K-map technique, Give its application.

22. Explain the operation of CMOS Ex-or.

23. Implement OR gate using Universal NAND gate.

24. What do you mean by flip-flop? Explain the operation of clocked D flip-flop with the help of neat circuit diagram.

25. What is multiplexer? Explain its working with the help of block diagram.

26. A burglar alarm should activate when two conditions given below are simultaneously satisfied.

    (a) the main entrance door of the building is open, and

    (b) the bedroom door and /or the kitchen door is open.

    Write truth table and construct logic circuit to operate alarm using one AND gate and one OR gate.

27. Draw the 1 : 16 DEMUX logic circuit and explain its working with the help of truth table.

28. What is universal gate? By using any universal gate draw all basic gates.

UNIVERSITY QUESTIONS

Dec. 2012

1. State and prove the De-Morgan's theorems. Use De-morgan's theorem to simplify the following Boolean expression. $Y = \overline{\overline{A}B + A\overline{B}}$.   **[6]**

2. Give a comparison between the microprocessor and microcontroller.   **[6]**

May 2013

1. Draw the block diagram of full adder using two half adder, explain its working with proper expression for sum and carry.   **[6]**

2. Implement the following logic expression with minimum number of NAND gate.   **[6]**

    (i) $y_1 = B(\overline{D} + \overline{C}D)$

    (ii) $y_2 = AB + CD + B\overline{C}$

Dec. 2013

1. Draw the schematic diagram and explain working of 4:1 mux and 1:4 demux.   **[6]**

2. State different types of counter and design 3-bit negative edge triggered asynchronous down counter.   **[6]**

May 2014

1. Explain the operation of multiplexer and Demultiplexer.   [6]
2. Implement the following with minimum number of NAND gates.   [6]
   (i) $y = AD + CB$

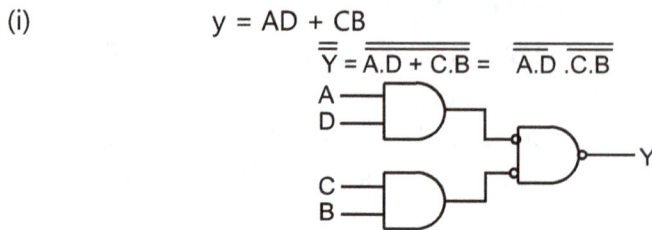

$\overline{\overline{Y}} = \overline{\overline{A.D + C.B}} = \overline{\overline{A.D} \cdot \overline{C.B}}$

$z = A(\overline{B} + CD)$

$\overline{\overline{Z}} = \overline{\overline{A(B + C.D)}} = \overline{(\overline{A.\overline{B}}) \cdot (\overline{A.C.D})}$

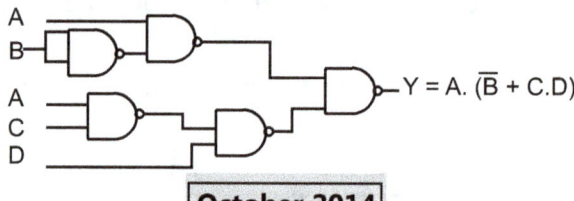

October 2014

1. State and prove the De-Morgan's theorem. Simplify the following Boolean

   expression: $\overline{\overline{AB} + \overline{AB}}$ [6]
2. Compare Microprocessor and microcontroller.   [6]

May 2015

1. State the IC number for the following two input logic gate: [6]
   (i) AND (ii) NAND (iii) OR (iv) NOR (v) EX-OR (vi) NOT
2. Draw the explain full adder using two half adder with its truth table.   [6]

Nov. 2015

1. Compare microprocessor and microcontroller.   [4]
2. Prove the following using De Morgan's theorem.   [2]

   $\overline{(A + B) \cdot (C + D)} = (\overline{A} \cdot \overline{B}) + (\overline{C} \cdot \overline{D}).$

3. How to implement full adder using 2 half adders and logic gates? Explain. [6]

May 2016

1. Compare synchronous and asynchronous counter.   [4]
2. State Demorgan's theorem.   [2]
3. Compare microprocessor and microcontroller.   [4]

INDUSTRIAL ELECTRONICS

POWER CONTROL DEVICES

5.1 SCR (SILICON CONTROLLED RECTIFIER OR THYRISTOR)

[Dec. 12, 13, May 14, 15, 16]

- As discussed in chapter one, a simple diode is used as a rectifier. But the output power of such type of rectifier cannot be controlled.
- SCR is a unidirectional device. It allows the current flow only in one direction like diodes, but their switching action can be controlled by an additional input called gate of SCR. The output power of the device can be controlled and hence is called as Silicon Controlled Rectifier (SCR). It can be used as a rectifier element like a diode, to convert AC to DC.

> ❖ **Important Questions Related to this Topic** ❖
> 1. Explain the construction of SCR.
> 2. Draw construction diagram and explain the working with the help of transistor equivalent circuit of SCR. Also draw the V-I characteristics.

- Construction of SCR device is as shown in Fig. 5.1.
- SCR is a four layer semiconductor device with three P-N junctions called J_1, J_2, and J_3. As shown in the figure above. The three terminals of SCR are Anode, Cathode and Gate.

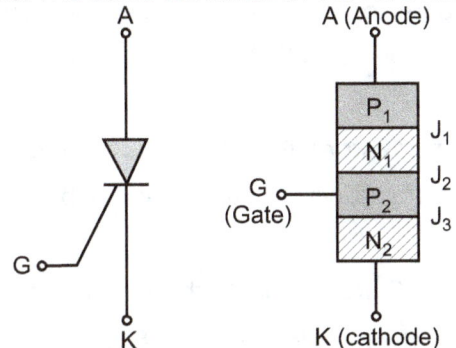

Fig. 5.1: Symbol and Construction Representation of SCR

5.1.1 Operation of SCR

- **With Open Gate:** As shown in Fig. 5.2, when a forward anode to cathode voltage is applied keeping the gate terminal open, junctions J_1 and J_3 are forward biased and J_2 is reverse biased. Therefore only the leakage current flows which is negligible and SCR is said to be OFF. This state is called the Forward blocking state.

If the forward voltage is gradually increased, at a particular value J_2 breaks down and the SCR starts conducting heavily. This voltage is called forward breakover voltage V_{BO}.

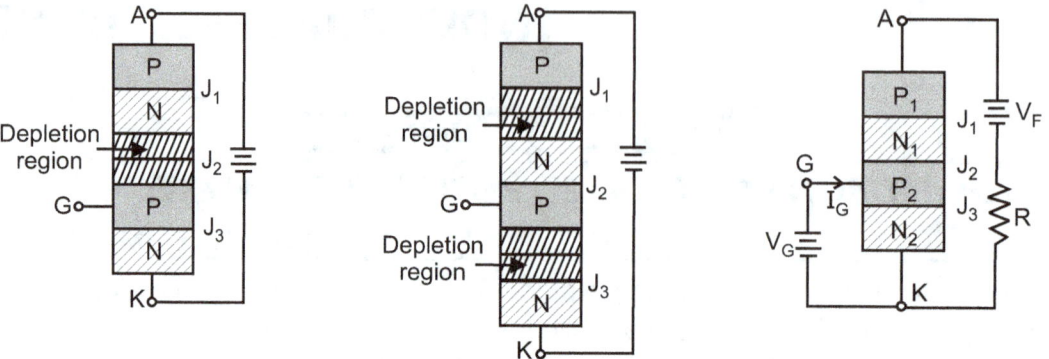

Fig. 5.2: With Gate Open   Fig. 5.3: With Reverse Bias   Fig. 5.4: With Gate Signal

- **With Reverse Bias:** As shown in Fig. 5.3 if a reverse voltage is applied between the anode and cathode, J_1 and J_3 are reverse biased and J_2 is forward biased. Therefore, negligible leakage current flows through the SCR and the SCR is said to be in a reverse blocking state.

- **With Gate Signal:** As shown in Fig. 5.4 consider the case when the SCR is in forward blocking state and a small voltage is applied between the gate terminal and cathode i.e. junctions J_1 and J_3 are forward biased. Junction J_2 breaks down in a short time due to regenerative action and the SCR starts conducting heavily. Once the SCR starts conducting heavily; the gate loses its control over the device. Latching current, is the forward current, through the SCR in ON state where the device remains ON even if the gate supply is removed.

  ○ SCR is like a junction transistor with a fourth layer and three P-N junctions called J_1, J_2, and J_3. The two outer junctions are forward biased and the inner junction is reverse biased.

  ○ The three terminals of SCR are Anode, Cathode and Gate.

  ○ There are two modes of operation of SCR, forward and reverse mode. But SCR is always operated in the forward mode.

5.1.2 Characteristics of SCR   [Dec. 12, 14]

❖ Important Question Related to this Topic ❖
1. Draw and explain the characteristics of SCR.

- The characteristic curve of SCR is as shown in Fig. 5.5.

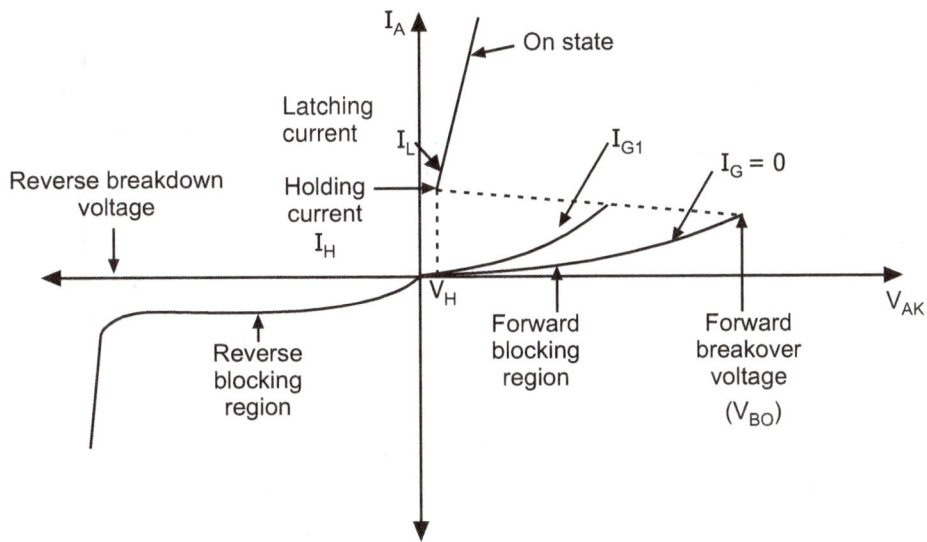

Fig. 5.5: SCR Characteristics for Different Values of Gate Current

5.1.3 Forward Characteristics

- When gate current is zero, the SCR is said to be in forward blocking state. As the forward voltage between the cathode and anode is increased, at a particular voltage V_{BO}, SCR starts conducting heavily and the drop across the SCR becomes very low. The current must be limited by the limiting resistor connected in series with the SCR.

- By giving a small positive gate voltage, an SCR can be turned ON at lower value of V_{AK} because the centre junction J_2 breaks down earlier.

- If the forward current is made less than the holding current, the SCR goes into forward blocking state. Note that $I_{Latching} > I_{Holding}$.

5.1.4 Reverse Characteristics

- If a reverse voltage is applied between the anode and cathode, the device enters into reverse blocking state and negligible leakage current flows through it.

- If the reverse voltage is gradually increased, at a particular voltage V_{BR}, due to reverse breakdown, large current flows through the device.

- Note that the forward breakover voltage is greater than the reverse breakdown voltage because the width of J_2 is greater.

5.1.5 Two Transistor Analogy

❖ Important Question Related to this Topic ❖
Explain the working of SCR using the two transistor analogy.

- The operation of SCR can be easily understood by the two transistor analogy circuit shown below in Fig. 5.6.

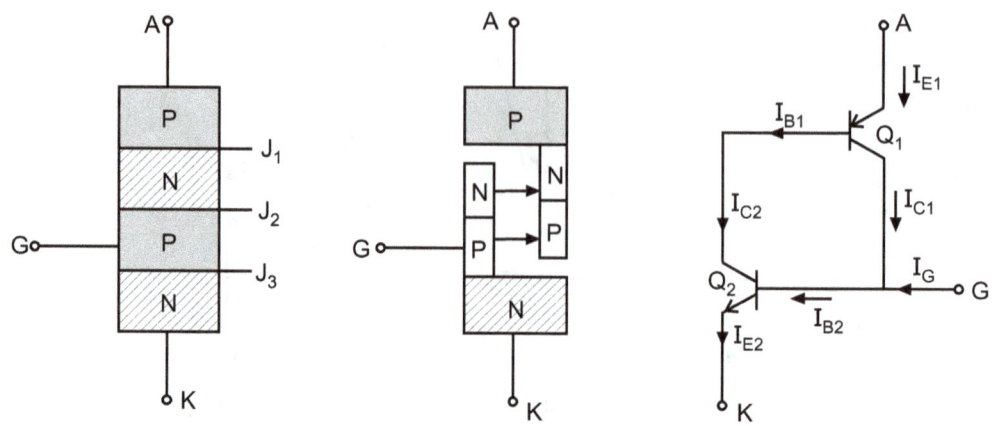

Fig. 5.6: Transistor Analogy for SCR

- When a forward voltage is applied between anode and cathode terminals of the SCR, no current flows because transistors are not conducting.

- Now, if a small voltage is applied at the base of transistor Q_2 and the cathode terminal, transistor Q_2 will turn and I_{C2} starts increasing ON therefore its collector voltage falls down. This action turns on transistor Q_1 since it is a PNP transistor. And current I_{B1} starts flowing through it.

- Again this will try to increase I_{B2}; increasing I_{C2} further. This regenerative process continues and both the transistors are driven into saturation region and large anode current flows through the device.

- Thus a small positive voltage at the gate is sufficient to turn the SCR ON. Once it goes into ON state, the device can only be turned OFF by removing the supply voltage. Also, note that the current flow is unidirectional through the SCR.

- If a reverse voltage is applied between anode and cathode, the conduction is not possible, even with the gate current.

5.1.6 Specifications of SCR   [Nov. 15]

❖ Important Question Related to this Topic ❖
Define :   1. Holding current   2. Latching current   3. Forward breakover voltage   4. Reverse breakdown voltage   5. Turn ON time for SCR.

- **Holding Current (I_H):** It is the minimum current required to keep the SCR in ON state. If the forward anode current is reduced below I_H, SCR will be turned-off.

- **Latching Current (I_L):** It is the minimum anode current required to latch the SCR in the ON state. It is a little greater than I_H.

- **Forward Breakover Voltage (V_{BO}):** It is the voltage above which the SCR enters into the conduction state. This factor depends on the gate bias.

- **Reverse Breakdown Voltage (V_{BR}):** It is the reverse voltage above which reverse breakdown occurs. That is when the anode is negative w.r.t. the cathode and current starts flowing through SCR at V_{BR}.

- **Turn on Time (t_{ON}):** It is the time required by SCR to reach full conduction after triggering. Typically t_{ON} is 2 to 4 micro seconds.

Advantages of SCR:
- SCRs can withstand high voltages and currents.
- Can handle large power.
- A small gate signal can trigger it, and is thus easy to turn ON.
- Can control the power delivered to the load.
- Simple fuse can be used to protect SCR and hence it is easy to handle.

Disadvantages of SCR:
- Low operating frequency.
- Gate loses its control once the device is turned on.
- Additional protection circuitry is required.
- Conducts only in one direction.

Applications of SCR:
- Controlled rectifiers.
- Static switch.
- Battery chargers.
- A.C. voltage stabilizers.
- In dimmerstats to control light intensity.
- Heat control.
- Speed control of motors.

5.2 DIAC   [Dec. 13, 14, Nov. 15, May 13, 14, 15]

> **❖ Important Question Related to this Topic ❖**
> 1. What is DIAC? Explain the construction of DIAC.
> 2. Draw and explain the characteristics of a DIAC.
> 3. What are the applications of DIAC?

- DIAC is a power device having two terminals and four layers. It is a bidirectional device mainly used to trigger the TRIACs.
- The construction, symbol and V-I characteristics of the DIAC is as shown in Fig. 5.7. The operation of a DIAC can be analysed by an equivalent circuit as two parallel Shockley

diodes connected in opposite directions. It is considered as two SCRs connected in opposite directions with $I_G = 0$. MT_1 and MT_2 are the two terminals of the DIAC between which the external voltage is applied.

- If MT_1 is positive with respect to MT_2, and if this applied voltage is gradually increased; at a particular voltage, which is the breakover voltage of one of the SCRs, the current starts flowing through it.

- Similarly when MT_2 is positive with respect to MT_1, the other SCR conducts after the breakover voltage is reached. Thus current flows in both the directions and the device acts as closed switch.

- As shown in the Fig. 5.7 (c), the V-I characteristics is similar to SCR with no gate signal in the first and third quadrant showing opposite polarities of voltage and current.

- DIAC shows a **negative resistance characteristic** in both directions, when it begins to conduct. That is, the voltage across it decreases and the current through it increases, once the device starts conducting.

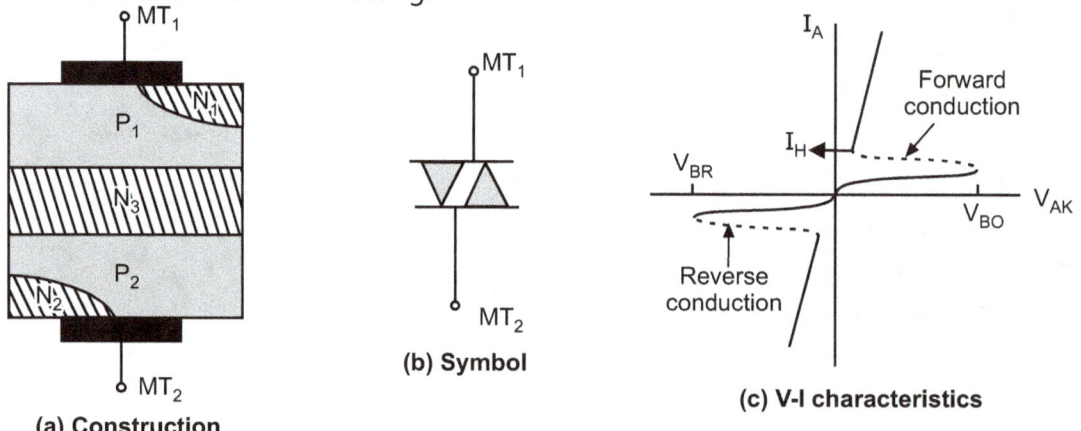

(a) Construction   (b) Symbol   (c) V-I characteristics

Fig. 5.7: DIAC Construction, Symbol and V-I Characteristics

Applications of DIAC:

- Diac is basically a triggering device. It is used in
- Triggering of TRIAC,
- Light dimmers,
- Temperature controllers,
- Speed controllers

5.3 TRIAC

> ❖ **Important Questions Related to this Topic** ❖
> 1. Draw and explain the V-I characteristics of a TRIAC.
> 2. What are the applications of a Triac?

- TRIAC is a bilateral power device which operates in both the forward and reverse mode. Its operation is similar to two parallel SCRs connected in opposite direction with a common gate terminal as shown below.

- The construction, symbol shown in Fig. 5.8 and equivalent circuit and characteristics are as shown in 5.9.

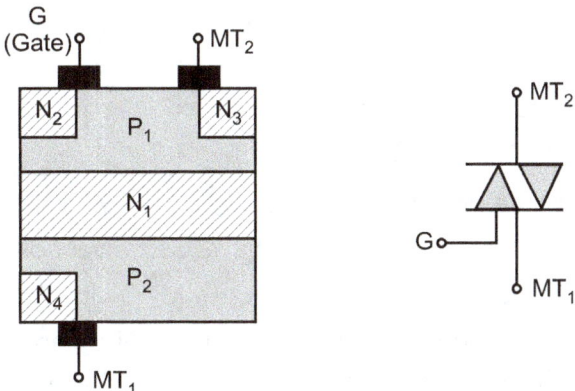

Fig. 5.8: Construction, Symbol of TRIAC

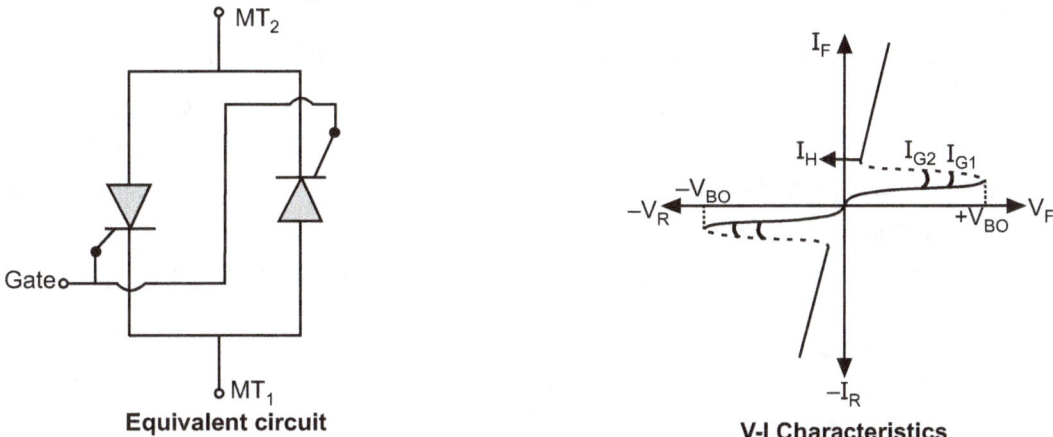

Equivalent circuit   V-I Characteristics

Fig. 5.9: Equivalent Circuit and V-I Characteristics of TRIAC

Operation:

- As the TRIAC is equivalent to two SCRs connected in parallel its characteristic is similar to that of an SCR. If the gate is open and MT_2 is made positive with respect to MT_1, the device remains OFF until the forward breakover voltage (VBO) is reached. This is the forward blocking region of the TRIAC. Beyond VBO the TRIAC conducts heavily.

- Now, if the gate is open and MT_1 is made positive with respect to MT_2, the device remains off until the reverse breakover voltage (V_{BR}) is reached. This is the reverse blocking region of the TRIAC. Beyond V_{BR} the TRIAC conducts heavily in opposite direction.

- The Gate terminal can be supplied with voltage of appropriate magnitude and polarity to trigger the TRIAC at lower magnitude of forward or reverse voltages between MT_1 and MT_2.

- Thus a TRIAC can be used as a switch and phase control device.
- The main difference between TRIAC and SCR is that a TRIAC is a bidirectional device whereas SCR is Unidirectional. Also a TRIAC can be triggered into conduction by applying either a positive or negative voltage to the gate with respect to MT_1 whereas the SCR can be triggered by applying positive gate trigger only.

5.3.1 Triggering Modes of TRIACs   [Dec. 12]

- Terminal MT_2 is made positive with respect to MT_1, with a positive voltage between gate and MT_1: In this mode the TRIAC behaves as conventional SCR.
- Terminal MT_2 is made positive with respect to MT_1, with a negative voltage between gate and MT_1: In this mode the TRIAC switches ON by an operation called junction gate operation. Even if the gate current is negative, the TRIAC operates in first quadrant. This form of gate drive is not normally used because it involves high switching therefore.
- Terminal MT_2 is made negative with respect to MT_1, with a positive voltage between gate and MT_1: In this mode, the TRIAC operates in the third quadrant. And the characteristic is exact replica of that of the conventional SCR in third quadrant.
- Terminal MT_2 is made negative with respect to MT_1, with a negative voltage between gate and MT_1: In this mode, the TRIAC operates in the third quadrant. The gate current is negative. This mode is recommended for application of a negative gate pulse.

Advantages of TRIACs:
- Gives power control in both directions due to the ability to conduct in both directions.
- Can withstand high voltage and currents.
- No external commutation circuitry is required.
- Less expensive.

Disadvantages of TRIACs:
- Not suitable for D.C. power control.
- Similar to SCRs, in TRIACs also, the gate loses its control once the device is ON.
- Very small switching frequencies.

Applications of TRIACs:
- Light dimmers.
- Static switches.
- Temperature controllers.
- Heat controllers.
- A.C. Power flashers.
- Power controllers for loads .
- Proximity detector circuits.

5.4 INTRODUCTION TO TRANSDUCER

- In many industrial processes physical factors like temperature, pressure, displacement, velocity, level, pH etc. are required to be controlled and measured correctly.
- Electronics has made this task easy and reliable with its sophisticated monitoring systems. In this chapter we will study measurement of the physical quantities like temperature, pressure, level, and displacement using various methods.

5.5 MEASUREMENT SYSTEM (INSTRUMENTATION SYSTEM)

[Dec. 13]

❖ **Important Question Related to this Topic** ❖

1. Draw the block diagram of instrumentation system and state the function of each block.
2. What is a transducer?

- Fig. 5.10 shows the block diagram of a typical measurement system. It will help to study any instrumentation system in general.

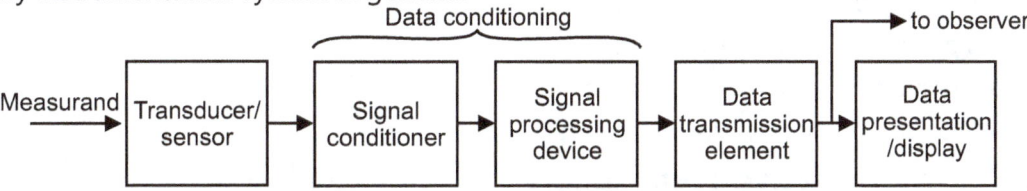

Fig. 5.10: Block Diagram of Measurement System

- As shown in Fig. 5.10, a typical measurement system mainly consists of three stages: a transducer, a data conditioning device and a data presentation element.
- The quantity to be measured is called a 'measurand'. It is fed as input to the system. Measurand could be temperature, pressure, displacement, velocity or acceleration etc.
- The detector stage detects or senses the input physical quantity and generates proportional signal at the output to drive the next stage.
- The intermediate stage, which is the data (or signal) processing stage, modifies the output signal suitable to drive the indicator or recorder or the display device. It performs required amplification, filtration, modulation, integration or differentiation etc.
- The next stage is the data transmission element that provides the transmission path to transmit the control signals to the rest of the system. For example, electric cables, optical fiber links etc.
- The final stage is the data presentation and display unit that is used to present the results of the measurement. For example, seven segment displays, printers etc.

5.6 TRANSDUCER

- Transducer is a device which when actuated, converts energy from one form to another.
- A transducer can be defined as 'a device which can convert physical quantity to be measured into an equivalent electrical signal'.

- Thus a transducer can be used to measure and control, non-electrical (or physical) input like temperature, pressure, flow etc. by converting it into equivalent electrical signal.

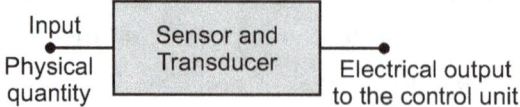

Fig. 5.11: Transducer

5.7 CLASSIFICATION OF TRANSDUCERS

❖ Important Questions Related to this Topic ❖

1. Compare active and passive transducers.
2. Give classification of transducers.
3. With a neat diagram explain primary and secondary transducers.

Transducers can be classified according to various criteria as stated below:

- According to the transduction principle used,
- As analog or digital transducers.
- As passive or active transducers.
- As primary or secondary transducers.
- According to the application area.

5.7.1 Passive or Active Transducers   [May 16]

- Passive transducers are those which do not produce any electrical signal on their own. They need an external power source to obtain the electrical equivalent of the input. Thus they are "not self generating type" transducers.
- They produce output signal in the form of variation in resistance, inductance or capacitance in response to the input physical quantity.
- For example, a potentiometer can be used for the measurement of displacement as shown in Fig. 5.12. An external dc source is used drive the POT, which shows linear change in the value of resistance for change in the displacement applied as input to the wiper.

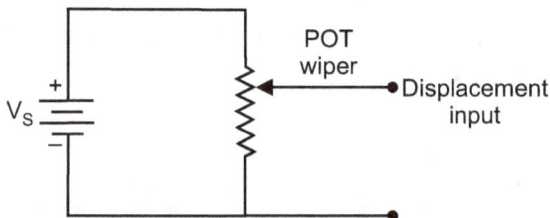

Fig. 5.12: Potentiometer as a Passive Transducer

- Active transducers are also known as "self generating type transducers" as they do not require any external power source to produce the output in electrical form (current/ voltage).

- They can be further classified as thermo electric, piezoelectric, photo voltaic, electromagnetic etc.

- For example, a thermocouple which produces equivalent thermoelectric e.m.f. can be used to measure the changes in the temperature. As shown in Fig. 5.13, wires of two different metals are joined together at a point and their junction is used to sense the temperature.

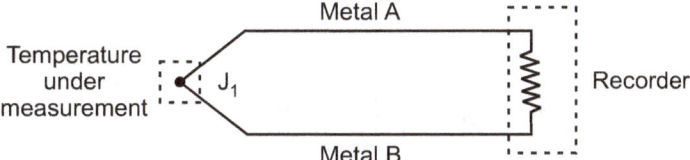

Fig. 5.13: Thermocouple as an Active Transducer

5.7.2 Comparison between Passive and Active Transducers

Sr. No.	Passive Transducers	Active Transducers
1.	These are not self generating type transducers as they require an external power source for their operation.	These are self generating type transducers as they do not require any external power source for their operation.
2.	They generate change in the electrical parameter such as resistance or capacitance proportional to the physical quantity under measurement.	They generate electrical parameter such as voltage or current proportional to the physical parameter under measurement.
3.	For example, Thermistor, LDR, RTD, LVDT, phototransistor.	For example, Thermocouple, photocell, piezoelectric and electromagnetic transducers.

5.7.3 Primary or Secondary Transducers

- A transducer which converts a physical quantity into a mechanical signal is called primary transducer. They do not require any electrical power for operation. For example, bourdon's tube that converts pressure into displacement.

- A transducer which converts mechanical signal into an electrical signal is called secondary transducer. They require electrical power for their operation. For example, LVDT (linear variable differential transformer) which converts displacement into electrical signal.

- As shown in Fig. 5.14, a 'C' shaped bourdon tube acts as primary transducer and LVDT acts as secondary transducer for pressure measurement.

- Here, first the applied pressure is converted into displacement by the bourdon tube and causes movement of the soft iron core of the LVDT which further converts this displacement into proportional voltage at the output.

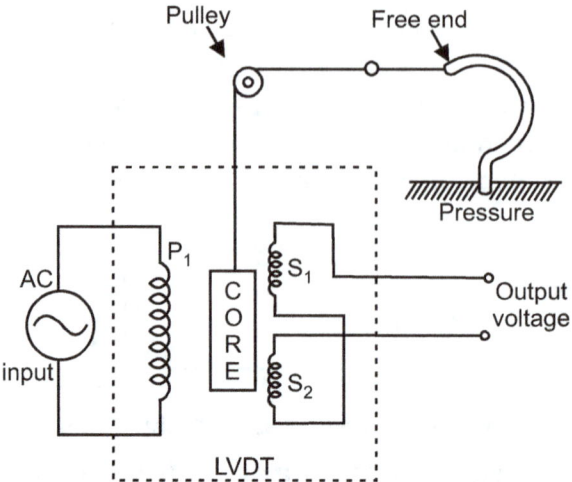

Fig. 5.14: Pressure Measurement Using Bourdon Tube and LVDT

5.7.4 Analog or Digital Transducers

- Transducers are classified according to the output obtained from them as analog and digital.
- **Analog transducers** convert the physical quantity applied at the input, into proportional analog signal at the output varying continuously with time For example, LVDT, thermocouple etc.
- **Digital transducers** convert the physical quantity applied at the input, into proportional digital signal at the output. The digital output is in the form of pulses; having values either 0 or 1.

5.8 SELECTION CRITERIA FOR TRANSDUCER   [Dec. 14, May 13, 14, 15]

❖ **Important Questions Related to this Topic** ❖
1. Write a short note on selection criteria for transducers.
2. Mention the factors to be considered while selecting a transducer for an application.

- It is very important to choose the best suited type of transducer from a wide variety of transducers available in the market, for a particular application. Depending upon the various conditions discussed below, the selection of a transducer is made.

(i) Characteristics of Measurand:
- A transducer must be selected depending upon the type of quantity to be measured (i. e. measurand) like, temperature, displacement, pressure, flow etc.
- The selected transducer should respond only to the measurand and it should be insensitive to every other possible input.

(ii) Electrical Parameters:
Transducer must be selected depending upon the electrical parameters like:
- The type of excitation available: ac or dc.
- The type of converter required: I to V (current to voltage) or R to V (resistance to voltage) etc.

- The type of output required: analog or digital.
- The type of signal conditioner required: amplifier or filter etc.
- The input and output impedance, dynamic response and linearity of the transducer.
- Operating range: The range of the input for which the transducer gives best results.

(iii) The Environmental Conditions:

- The output of the transducer should not get affected with the environmental changes like temperature, moisture and humidity etc.
- Also the output should remain stable for all working conditions (except for the parameter under measurement), like changes in pressure or viscosity of fluid etc.

(iv) Mechanical Characteristics:

- Transducer's shape, size, ruggedness, weight, dimensions must be taken into consideration while selecting it for any application.

(v) Cost and Availability:

- Also, the transducer's cost; maintenance and availability are the general factors which are involved while selecting a transducer.

5.9 RESISTIVE TRANSDUCER

- Resistive transducer are those in which the resistance changes due to change in some physical phenomenon. The change in the value of the resistance with the change in length of conductor can be used to measure displacement.
- The resistivity of materials changes with changes in temperature. This property can be used for the measurement of temperature.

5.9.1 Potentiometer

- A resistive potentiometer consists of a resistance element provided with a sliding contact, called a wiper. The motion of the sliding contact may be translatory or rotational. Translatory resistive elements, as shown in Fig. 5.15 (a) are linear devices. Rotational resistive devices are circular and are used for the measurement of angular displacement, as shown in Fig. 5.15 (b). Some have combination of both, with resistive elements in the form of a helix as shown in Fig. 5.15 (c).

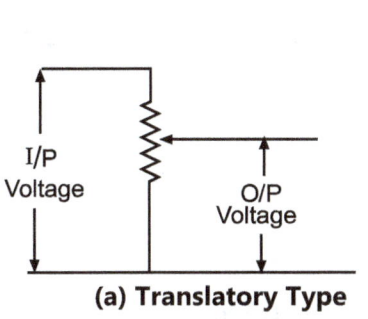

(a) Translatory Type

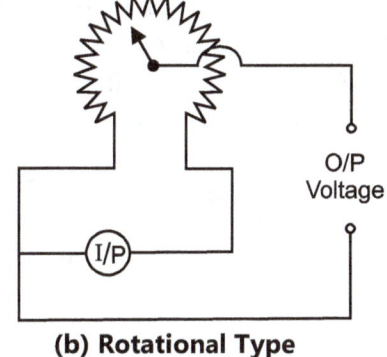

(b) Rotational Type

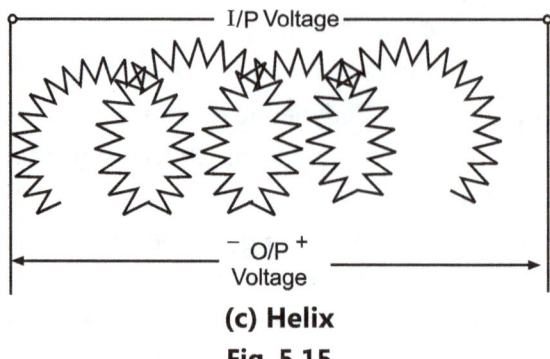

(c) Helix

Fig. 5.15

Advantages of Potentiometers:
- They are inexpensive.
- Simple to operate and are useful for applications where the requirement are not particularly severe.
- They are useful for measurement of large amplitudes of displacement.
- Electrical efficiency is very high.

Disadvantages:
- When using a linear potentiometer, a large force is required to move the sliding contacts.
- The sliding contacts can wear out and generate noise.

5.9.2 Strain Gauge

❖ **Important Questions Related to this Topic** ❖
1. Explain the principal of operation of strain gauge.
2. Explain briefly the different types of strain gauges.

- Strain gauge is a resistive type transducer which converts change in mechanical displacement into a proportional change in resistance. It is the most commonly used method of displacement measurement. Their working principle is based on piezo-resistive effect.
- The piezo-resistive effect states that if a metal conductor is stretched or compressed, its length and diameter changes. Therefore its resistance also gets changed. Similarly the resistance of a metal conductor changes when it is strained.
- Fig. 5.16 shows an unstrained wire of elastic material with length = L, Diameter= D and Area of cross-section = A.

$$R = \rho \frac{L}{A} = \rho \frac{L}{(\pi/4)\, D^2}$$

$$R = \rho \frac{L}{A} = \rho \frac{L}{\left(\dfrac{\pi}{4}\right) D^2}$$

Where, ρ = Resistivity of the wire in $\Omega - m$

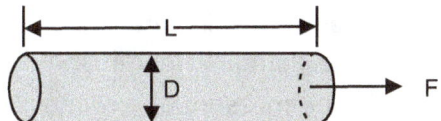

Fig. 5.16: Unstrained

- If this wire of elastic material is subjected to tension, its length increases and diameter reduces. These changes in the dimensions due to applied force are shown in Fig. 5.17.

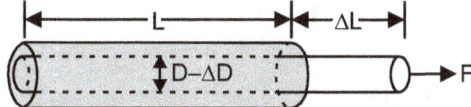

Fig. 5.17: Elastic Wire (Strain Gauge)

- Let the change in length = ΔL and change in diameter = ΔD. To find the change in resistance (ΔR) due to applied force we use Poisson's ratio.

$$\text{Using Poisson's ratio } (\mu) = \frac{(\Delta D/D)}{(\Delta L/L)}$$

But

$$\frac{\Delta L}{L} = \sigma = \text{Strain}$$

Therefore,

$$\Delta D = \mu \cdot \sigma \cdot D$$

Thus the change in resistance is given by $\Delta R = R\sigma(1 + 2\mu)$

- From the above equation, we can conclude that the resistance of the wire increases due the applied force.

- The gauge factor (G) of a strain gauge is defined as the unit change in resistance per unit change in length. Therefore $G = \dfrac{(\Delta R/R)}{(\Delta L/L)}$ (Ranges from 1.5 to 1.7)

- Let us discuss some types of strain gauges.

5.9.3 Bonded Strain Gauge

❖ Important Question Related to this Topic ❖
Explain briefly unbonded and bonded resistance wire strain gauge.

- A bonded strain gauge consists of a grid of fine wire which is fixed on a base of a thin paper sheet as shown in Fig. 5.18. The paper sheet is bonded with an adhesive to the spot under measurement.

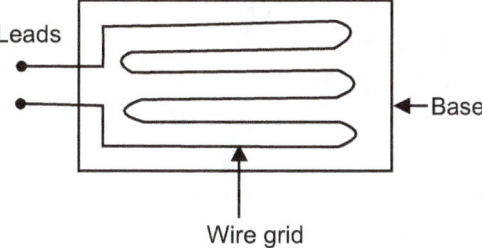

Fig. 5.18: Bonded Type Strain Gauge

- When force is applied to the surface, to which the strain gauge is bonded, the resistance of the grid wire changes due to the change in length and diameter of the wire.
- This change in the resistance can be measured by connecting the strain gauge in one of the arms of the Wheatstone bridge that generates equivalent voltage.
- The bonded strain gauge is useful only for measuring very small displacements.
- To measure large displacements, the strain gauge is bonded to a flexible element like cantilever beam. The displacement can then be measured at the end of the cantilever beam.

5.9.4 Unbonded Strain Gauge

- As shown in Fig. 5.19, an unbonded strain gauge is constructed by fitting the gauge wire on a stationary frame having a movable armature fixed at the centre. The armature can be moved only in one direction and its travel is limited by four strain gauge wires.
- If an external force is applied to the strain gauge or the armature is moved, the gauge wire gets stretched showing a proportional change in its resistance value which can be measured with the Wheatstone bridge. The output voltage of the Wheatstone bridge can be calibrated according to displacement of the armature.

Fig. 5.19: Unbonded Type Strain Gauge

Advantages of Strain Gauge:
- High accuracy and reliability.
- Small size and easy to use.

Disadvantages of Strain Gauge:
- High cost.
- The changes in temperature may affect the output.

5.10 TEMPERATURE MEASUREMENT

> **❖ Important Question Related to this Topic ❖**
>
> Draw and explain different temperature transducers with their advantages and disadvantages.

- Temperature is one of the most fundamental parameter which is required to be measured and controlled in industry.

- Fahrenheit ($^\circ$F), Centigrade or Celsius ($^\circ$C) and Kelvin ($^\circ$K) are the commonly used scales for temperature measurement.
- When a substance is heated, it undergoes various changes like change in volume, resistance, e.m.f., radiation and colour which can be used for measurement of temperature.
- The methods of temperature measurement based on change in volume, electric resistance and thermoelectric e.m.f. are discussed below.

5.10.1 Resistance Temperature Detector (RTD)

> ❖ **Important Question Related to this Topic** ❖
> What is RTD? Draw its constructional diagram and explain its operation?

- The resistance of conductors changes with change in temperature. This behaviour is used for temperature measurement in RTDs.
- RTDs show **Positive Temperature Coefficient** (PTC) of resistance as their resistance increases with the increase in temperature. Metals like platinum, nickel and copper are commonly used as RTDs in industry.
- Platinum is used widely because its resistance characteristic remains stable over a wide range of temperature. Also its resistivity is very high, so less material is required for the construction of RTD. RTDs are useful for temperature range: -200°C to $+650^\circ$C.
- The relation between the resistance of RTD and the temperature is given by,

$$R_T = R_0 (1 + \alpha T + \beta T^2).$$

where, R_T = Resistance of RTD at temperature T$^\circ$C.

              R_0 = Resistance of RTD at 0°C.

            α, β = Temperature coefficient of resistance of the material used for RTD.

              T = change in temperature.

5.10.2 Construction of RTD

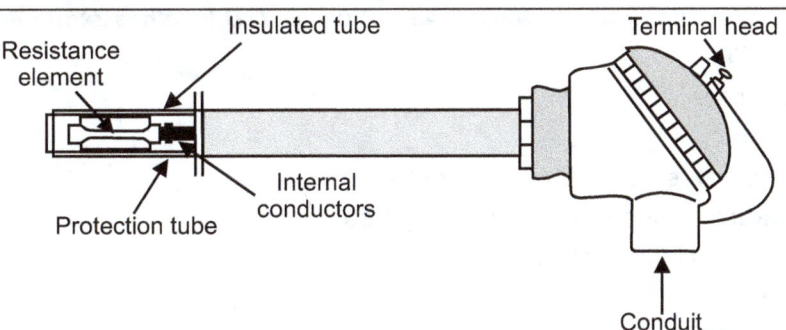

Fig. 5.20: Construction of RTD

- Fig. 5.20 shows the construction of RTD. It consists of a resistance element, internal conductors, insulated tube, protection tube, reinforcing tube and a terminal head.

- **Resistance Element:** As discussed above, an RTD uses platinum, nickel or copper as the resistance element. Usually, the resistance element is constructed by winding a platinum wire on a glass bobbin as a bifilar with a stainless steel fin. It is placed in a protection tube to provide excellent resistance against vibration.
- **Internal Lead Wire:** It is used to connect the resistance element to the terminal. A standard nickel lead wire is generally used for this purpose.
- **Insulated Tube:** It is used for insulating the internal lead wire. It also gives protection against a short circuit. For high temperature, a ceramic insulator is used and for medium temperatures a fiber glass is used.
- **Protection Tube:** It protects the resistance element, internal lead wires etc. when operated in extreme ambient conditions. So the material used for it must be selected properly.
- **Terminal Head:** It is used to connect the RTD to the external lead wire.

5.10.3 Measurement using RTD

- The temperature measurement can be carried out by using a Wheatstone bridge. As shown in Fig. 5.21 the bridge is formed by resistors R_1, R_2, R_3 and the RTD (R_4) whose resistance varies with change in temperature.
- As the temperature changes, resistance of the RTD changes, therefore the bridge gets unbalanced and produces change in the output voltage. Thus we get a change in output voltage for corresponding change in the input temperature.

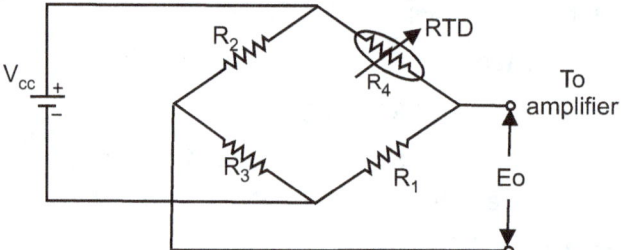

Fig. 5.21: Temperature Measurement using RTD in Wheatstone Bridge

Advantages of RTD:

- Fast response.
- High accuracy.
- Wide range of temperature measurement.
- Temperature compensation is not required.
- Good reproducibility and stability.
- Small in size.

Disadvantages of RTD:

- The resistance of RTD may change due to self heating.
- Require a bridge circuit and external power supply for measurement.
- High cost.

5.10.4 Thermistor

❖ **Important Questions Related to this Topic** ❖
1. State the materials used in a thermistor.
2. Explain the principle of operation of a thermistor.

- Another type of temperature dependent resistor is Thermistor (thermal resistor). They are constructed using semiconductor materials. So they have NTC (Negative Temperature Coefficient) of resistivity.

- Thermistors are composed of a sintered mixture of metallic oxides such as manganese, cobalt, nickel, copper, uranium and iron.

- They have **negative temperature coefficient** (NTC) of resistance, that is, their resistance decreases with increase in temperature. Fig. 5.22 gives the graphical representation of variation in resistance of a thermistor with respect to temperature.

- The curve shows that, thermistors offer a large change in resistance for small changes in temperature. Thus, they have high resolution. Also they have high sensitivity to detect very small changes in temperature.

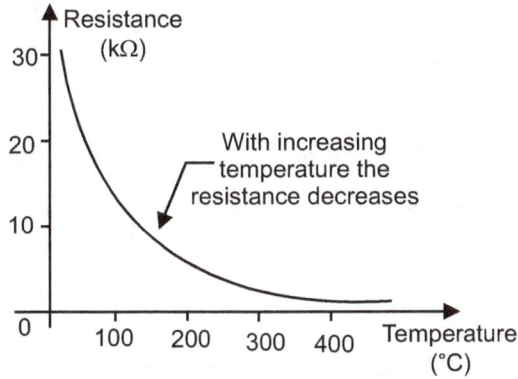

Fig. 5.22: Resistance Vs Temperature Curve for Thermistor

- Thermistors are available in a variety of sizes and shapes such as beads, discs and rods. They are as shown in Fig. 5.23.

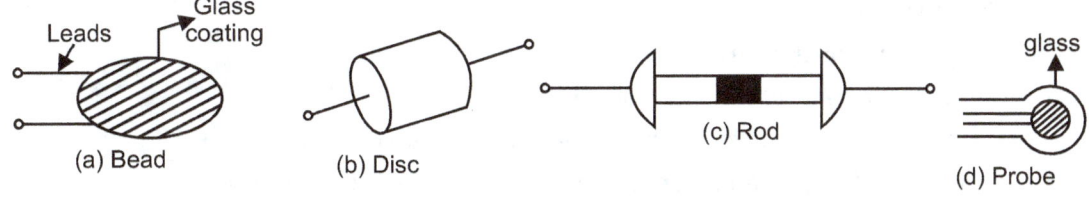

Fig. 5.23: Various Shapes of Thermistors

- The relationship between the resistance of a thermistor and temperature is given by,

$$R_T = R_0 \exp\left[\beta\left(\frac{1}{T_1} - \frac{1}{T_2}\right)\right]$$

where, R_T = Resistance of thermistor at temperature T.

          R_0 = Resistance of thermistor at temperature T_0.

and   β = Constant. It depends on the type of material used for the construction of a thermistor.

Thermistors are used for the measuring temperature in the range: −100°C to +300°C.

5.10.5 Temperature Measurement using Thermistor

- The temperature measurement can be carried out by using a Wheatstone bridge by connecting the thermistor in the Wheatstone bridge. As shown in Fig. 5.24, the bridge is formed by R_1, R_2, R_3, and the thermistor acting as R_4.

- Under balanced condition, the output voltage is zero.

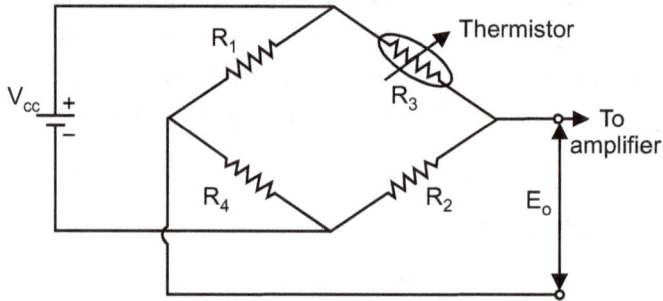

Fig. 5.24: Thermistor in a Wheatstone Bridge for Temperature Measurement

- If the temperature changes, the resistance of the thermistor (R_4) changes. So the bridge gets unbalanced and thus produces the output voltage proportional to the change in temperature.

Advantages of Thermistor:
- High sensitivity, hence used for precision measurement.
- Temperature compensation is not required.
- High resolution.
- Small in size.
- Give fast response.

Disadvantages of Thermistor:
- Cannot be operated for wide range of temperatures.
- They have non-linear temperature resistance characteristic.
- A bridge circuit and an external power supply is required for measurement.

Applications of Thermistor:
- It is used in biomedical instruments.
- Mainly used as temperature transducer.
- Used in remote measurement and control systems.

5.10.6 Thermocouple

> ### ❖ Important Questions Related to this Topic ❖
>
> 1. Explain thermocouple on the basis of following points:
>   (i) Principal of operation, (ii) Materials used, (iii) Advantages, (iv) Applications,
>   (v) Comparison with RTD.
> 2. Explain the principle of operation and construction of a thermocouple. Mention the different materials used for it.

- Thermocouple is an active type of transducer used to measure temperature. It does not require any external power supply to produce output.

- A thermocouple works on the principle of thermo-electric effect which is also called as **Seebeck effect**. It states that, if two dissimilar metals are connected together so as to form a closed circuit of two junctions and if the junctions are kept at two different temperatures, then current flows in that closed circuit. This current is proportional to the temperature difference of the two junctions. Due to this current, an e.m.f., called as thermoelectric e.m.f. , is produced which is proportional to the temperature difference of the two junctions.

- Fig. 5.25 shows the construction of a thermocouple using two different metals A and B, joined at two points forming two junctions J_1 and J_2 to make a closed loop circuit.

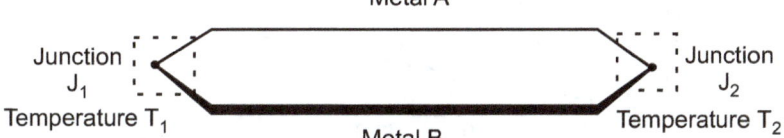

Fig. 5.25: A Thermocouple

- One junction is kept at a known temperature. It is called as **'reference'** or **'cold'** junction. Usually, the 'cold' junction is kept at 0°C. The other junction is called as the **'hot'** junction. It is used to sense the changes in temperature at the measuring end.

- An e.m.f. is generated proportional to the temperature difference of the two junctions. Thus the output voltage is a direct measure of changes in temperature of the hot junction.

- The thermoelectric e.m.f. that is generated by the thermocouple is given by,

$$E = C(T_1 - T_2) + K\left(T_1^2 - T_2^2\right)$$

where, T_1 = Temperature hot junction.

                T_2 = Temperature of cold junction.

                C, K = Constants. They depend upon the type of metals used.

5.10.7 Types of Materials used for Thermocouples

- As shown in the table below, there are various types of thermocouples depending upon the metals or alloys used for construction. For example, Type J thermocouple, type K thermocouple etc.

Table 5.1

Type	Material	Temperature range
J	Iron – Constantan	– 190°C to + 760°C
K	Chromel – Alumel	– 190°C to + 1260°C
T	Copper – Constantan	– 250°C to + 400°C
S	Platinum – Platinum/Rhodium	0°C to + 1400°C
E	Chromel – Constantan	– 190°C to + 800°C

- Fig. 5.26 shows different voltage versus temperature curves for various types of thermocouples, with the cold junction at 0°C.

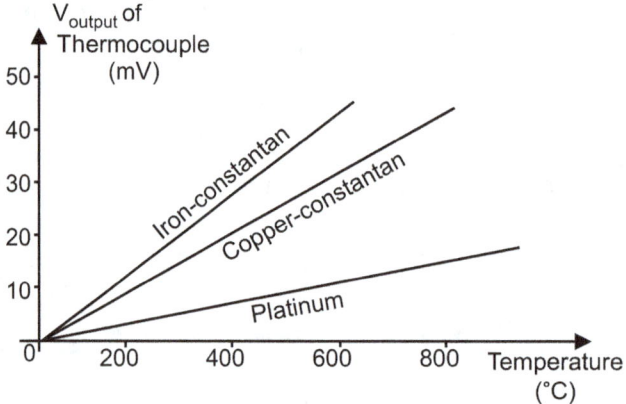

Fig. 5.26: Voltage Vs Temperature Curve for Various Types of Thermocouples

5.10.8 Laws of Thermoelectric Circuit

- The operation of Thermocouples follows the Seebeck effect as well as thermoelectric laws. These laws are as stated below:

1. **Law of Homogeneous Metal:** The thermoelectric e.m.f. cannot be generated if two junctions are formed using a 'single' homogeneous metal and those two junctions are maintained at different temperatures. This operation is shown in Fig. 5.27. So a thermocouple must be constructed using two different metals or alloys.

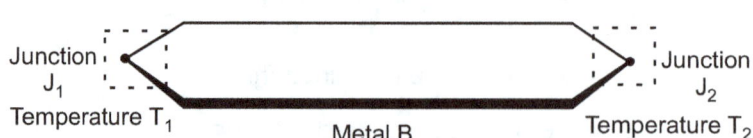

Fig. 5.27: Law of Homogeneous Metal

2. **Law of Intermediate Metal:** If a third homogeneous metal is introduced within a thermocouple, maintaining its two newly formed junctions at same temperature; the e.m.f. produced by the thermocouple does not get affected.

- As shown in Fig. 5.28, let the third metal C is inserted in a thermocouple formed by two dissimilar metals A and B.

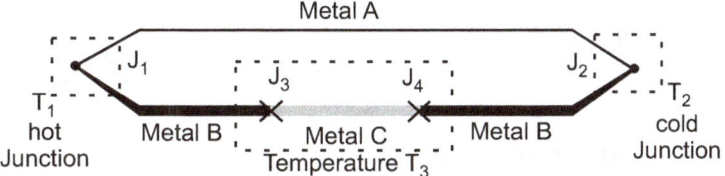

Fig. 5.28: Law of Intermediate Metal

- Due to the insertion of the homogeneous metal C, two new junctions J_3 and J_4 are formed. If both these junctions are kept at same temperature say T_3, the e.m.f. produced by this thermoelectric circuit remains unchanged.

3. **Law of Intermediate Temperature:** If a thermocouple produces e.m.f. E_1 for the junction temperatures T_1 and T_2 and the same thermocouple produces e.m.f. E_2 for the junction temperatures T_2 and T_3 then the thermocouple produces e.m.f. $E_3 = (E_1 + E_2)$ for the junction temperatures T_1 and T_3. Fig. 5.29 shows this operation.

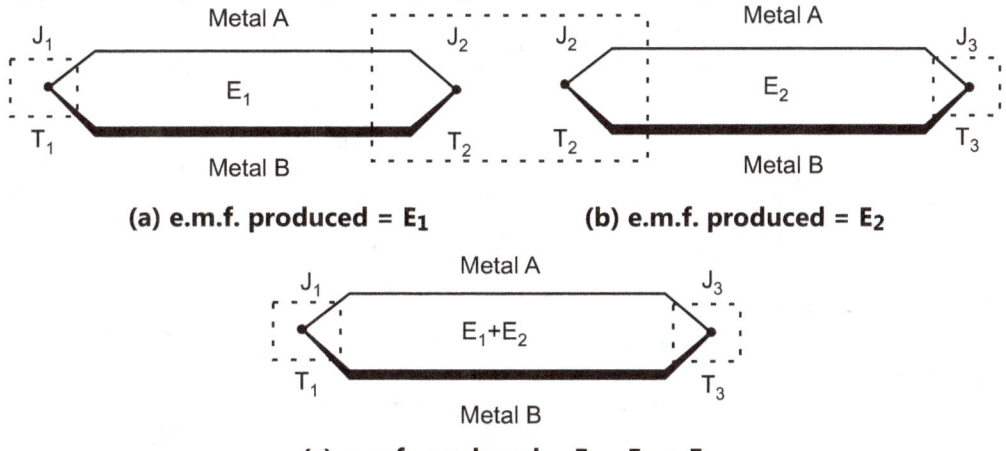

Fig. 5.29: Law of Intermediate Temperature

Advantages of Thermocouples:

- Do not require a bridge circuit or an external power supply.
- High accuracy and reproducibility.
- Rugged construction.
- Low cost.
- Simple to use.

Disadvantages of Thermocouples:

- Their resolution is less because the voltage verses temperature curve is not exactly linear.
- It is required to maintain the cold junction temperature of $0^{\circ}C$ constant.
- The output of the thermocouple needs to be amplified.

Applications of Thermocouples:

- Used in remote temperature measurement applications. They are widely used in industries.
- Used for wide temperature range.
- Used for continuous measurement and recording of temperature.

5.10.9 Comparison of Temperature Transducers

❖ **Important Question Related to this Topic** ❖

Compare the three types of temperature transducers.

Table 5.2

Parameter	RTD	Thermocouple	Thermistor
Principle of operation	If the temperature increases, the resistance also increases.	The voltage is generated corresponding to the temperature difference between cold junction and hot junction.	If the temperature increases the Resistance decreases.
Material Used	Nickel, Copper, Platinum etc.	Copper-constantan Iron-constantan Chromel-Alumel etc.	Manganese, Nickel, Cobalt, Copper, Iron, and Uranium
Operating temperature range	$-200\ ^{\circ}C$ to $+650\ ^{\circ}C$	$-270\ ^{\circ}C$ to $2700\ ^{\circ}C$	$-100\ ^{\circ}C$ to $+200\ ^{\circ}C$
Characteristic	Linear	Non-linear	Non-linear
Speed of response	High	High	High over a narrow temperature range
Accuracy	High	Moderate	Moderate
Type of transducer	Passive	Active	Passive
Cost	High	Low	Low
Size	Large	Small	Small

...Conti.

Applications	Suitable for applications where speed of response and accuracy are more important.	Suitable for applications which require wide temperature range.	Suitable for applications where required temperature range is small and sensitivity requirement is high.
Compensation	Not required	Cold junction compensation is required.	Not required

5.11 INDUCTIVE TRANSDUCER

- This type of transducer may be either of self generating or the passive type.
- Self generating type uses electrical generator principle i.e. motion between conductor and magnetic field induces a voltage in the conductor.
- An inductive electromechanical transducer is a device that converts physical motion into a change in inductance.
- Transducer of variable inductance type work upon principle of self inductance and mutual inductance.
- Its main use is for measurement of displacement. The displacement to be measured is arranged to cause variation of three variables.
    1. Number of turns
    2. Geometric configuration
    3. Permeability of the magnetic material or magnetic circuits.

5.11.1 Inductive Transducer Based on Change Number of Turns

- Fig. 5.30 shows inductive transducer whose operation is based on change in number of turns for measurement of linear displacement and having air core. Here as the number of turns are changed, the self inductance and the output also changes.

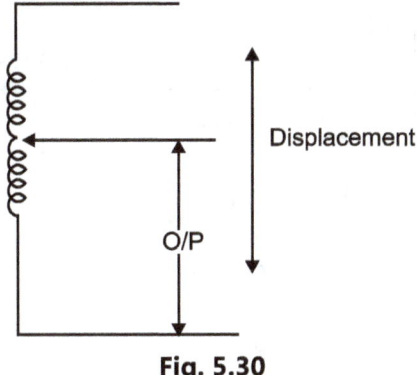

Fig. 5.30

5.11.2 Transducer based on Change in Self Inductance with Change in Permeability

- Fig. 5.31 shows transducer based on change in self inductance with change in permeability causing change in inductance. The iron core is surrounded by winding. If the iron core is inside the winding, its permeability is increased and so is inductance. When the iron core is moved out of the winding, the permeability is decreased and inductance also decreases.

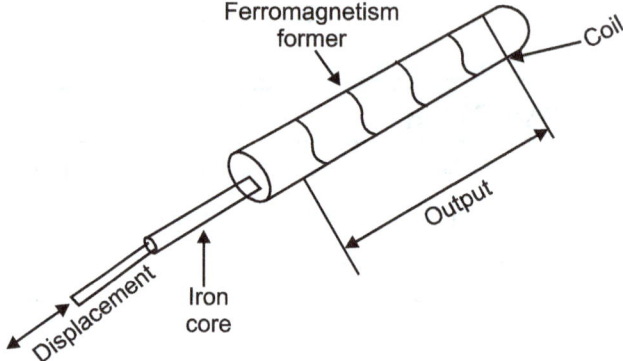

Fig. 5.31

5.11.3 Variable Reluctance Type Transducer

- Here coil is wounded on a ferromagnetic core. The displacement to be measured is applied to a ferromagnetic target. The target does not have any physical contact with the core on which it is mounted. The core and target is separated by an air gap, as shown in Fig. 5.32.
- The reluctance of magnetic path is determined by the size of the air gap. The inductance of the coil depends upon the reluctance of the magnetic circuits.

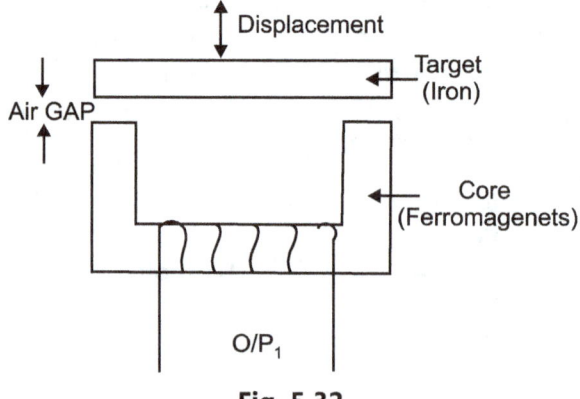

Fig. 5.32

- The inductance is given by,

$$L = N^2/R_i + R_g$$

where,   N = Number of turns,

R_i = Reluctance of iron parts,

R_g = Reluctance of air gap.

The reluctance of the iron part is negligible compared to that of the air gap. Therefore $L = N^2/R_g$

- But reluctance of the air gap is given by

$$R_g = l_g/\mu_o \times A_g$$

where, l_g = Length of the air gap,

A_g = Area of the flux path through air,

μ_o = Permeability.

Rg is proportional to lg, as μo and Ag are constants.

Hence L is proportional to 1/lg i.e. the self inductance of the coil is inversely proportional to length of airgap.

- When target is near the core, the length is small and therefore the self inductance is large. But when target is away from the core the reluctance is large, resulting in a smaller self inductance value. Hence the inductance of the coil is function of distance of the target from the core, i.e. the length of the air gap.

5.12 LINEAR VARIABLE DIFFERENTIAL TRANSFORMER (LVDT) (INDUCTIVE TYPE)   [Dec. 12, 13, May 15, 16]

❖ **Important Questions Related to this Topic** ❖

1. Draw the construction details of LVDT. Explain its working. State its applications
2. With a neat diagram explain the construction and working of LVDT. Give its advantages and disadvantages.
3. Explain the principle of operation and working of displacement transducer.
4. Draw and explain weight measurement using LVDT.

- LVDT is the most commonly used inductive type transducer which is used to convert linear motion (displacement) into an electrical signal.

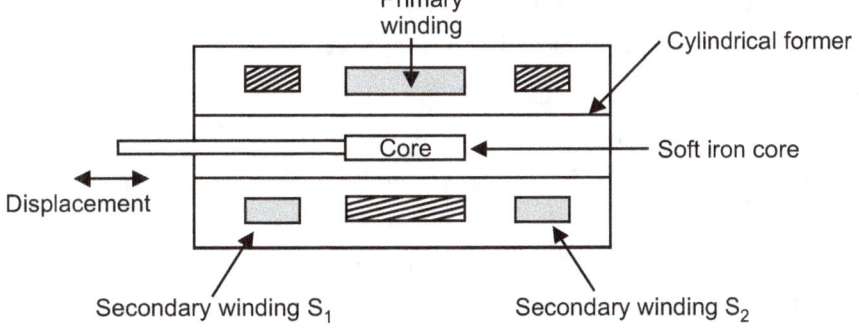

Fig. 5.33: Construction of LVDT

- As shown in Fig. 5.33, LVDT consists of a single primary winding P_1 and two identical secondary windings S_1 and S_2 wound on a cylindrical coil former.
- The two secondary windings are constructed with equal number of turns and are placed on either side of the primary winding in identical fashion.
- Inside the coil assembly, a rod shaped magnetic core is placed at the center, to provide low reluctance path for the magnetic flux linking the windings.
- The AC source is connected to the primary winding and the two secondary windings are connected in series opposition so the voltage induced in them is of opposite polarities.
- The displacement to be measured is applied to the arm attached to the soft iron core which is placed inside the former.

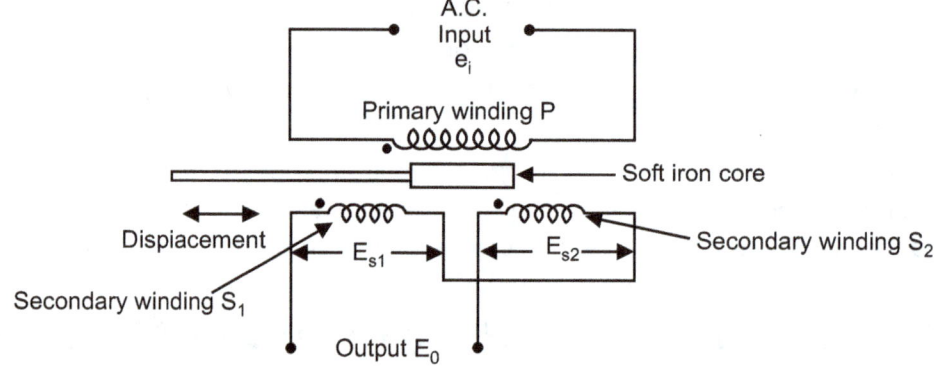

Fig. 5.34: Schematic Diagram of LVDT

Operation:
- An AC source is applied to the primary winding so it produces an alternating magnetic field. This in turn induces AC voltages in the two secondary windings which are connected in series opposition.
- If
$$E_{S1} = \text{The output voltage of secondary } S_1, \text{ and}$$
$$E_{S2} = \text{The output voltage of secondary } S_2,$$

Then the output voltage (E_0) of the transducer is given by,
$$E_0 = E_{S1} - E_{S2}$$

- When the core is at the exact centre position or the 'Null' position, the flux linking with both the secondary windings is equal and hence, $E_{S1} = E_{S2}$.

Therefore, at null position the output voltage $E_0 = 0$.

- Now, if the core is moved to the right of the null position, the flux linking with the winding S_2 is greater than S_1. Therefore, the voltage $E_{S2} > E_{S1}$. Thus, output voltage E_0 is a negative non-zero voltage.
- Similarly, if the core is moved to the left of the null position, more flux links with the winding S_1 than S_2. Hence the voltage $E_{S1} > E_{S2}$. Therefore the output voltage E_o is a positive non-zero voltage.

- Thus, the magnitude of the output voltage is proportional to the amount of displacement applied to the core. The sign of the output voltage indicates the direction of the displacement.
- It must be noted that, ideally, the output voltage must be zero at null position. But practically there exists a small voltage called "residual voltage" at the null position due to, the harmonics present in the supply voltage, or electrical unbalance of the secondary windings or due to properties of iron core.
- Fig. 5.35 shows the practical transfer characteristic of LVDT showing the residual voltage. The curve is plotted for output voltage of LVDT versus displacement.

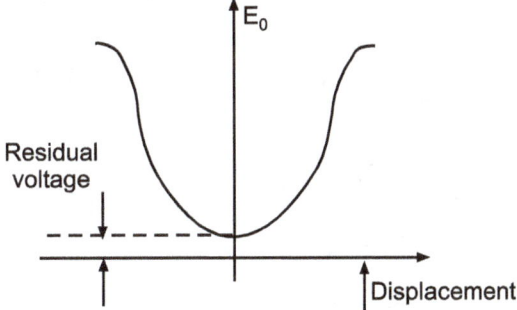

Fig. 5.35: Practical Transfer Characteristic of LVDT

Advantages of LVDT:
- It is a frictionless device as there is no physical contact between the movable core and the coil structure.
- High reliability, sensitivity, stability and accuracy.
- Wide operating range.
- Provide sufficiently high output voltage so amplification is not required.
- Small in size and easy to install.
- Consume less power.

Disadvantages of LVDT:
- They are sensitive to external magnetic fields, so shielding is required.
- Their performance gets affected by the changes in temperature.
- Not suitable for fast displacements due to the mass of the core.
- Larger displacements are needed to get considerable output.

Applications of LVDT:
- LVDTs can also used in the measurement of pressure, force, load, weight etc.
- They are useful for wide range of displacement measurements.

5.13 LOAD CELL (PRESSURE CELL)

- A load cell is used to weigh extremely heavy loads. A length of bar, usually steel, is used as active element. The weight of the load applies a particular stress to the bar. The amount of stain which results in the bar for different values of applied stress is determined, so that the strain may be used as a direct measure of the stress causing it.

- The load cell shown in Fig. 5.36 is a good example of the use of strain gauges in weighing operations.

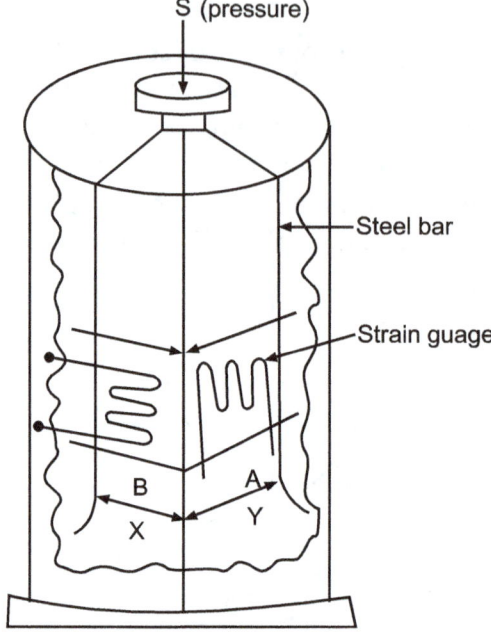

Fig. 5.36

- As the stress is applied along the direction of S shown the steel bar experiences a compression along that axis and an expansion along the X and Y axes. As a result, gauge A experiences decrease in resistance while gauge B undergoes increase in resistance. When these two gauges and the gauges on the two remaining sides of the steel are connected to form a bridge circuit, four times the sensitivity of a simple gauge bridge is obtained. This makes load cell very sensitive to very small values of applied stress as well as to extremely heavy loads.

5.14 PHOTOTRANSISTOR   [Dec. 14]

- The sensitivity of a photo diode can be increased by as much as 100 times by adding a junction, resulting in an NPN device. A simple representation of the construction is shown in Fig. 5.36.

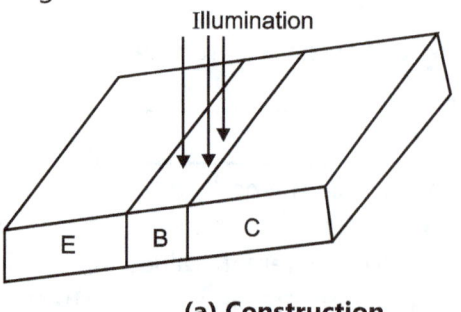

(a) Construction

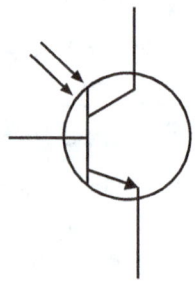

(b) Symbol

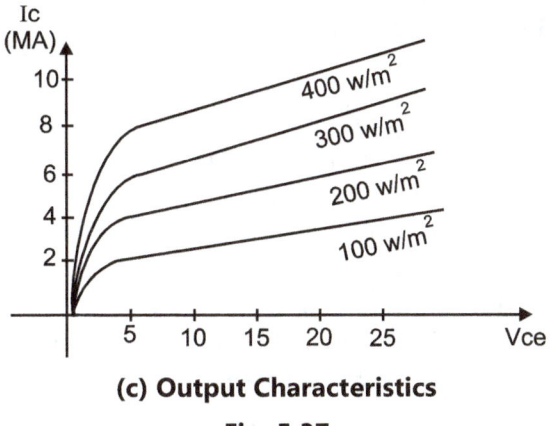

(c) Output Characteristics

Fig. 5.37

- Illumination of the central region causes the release of electron hole pairs. This lowers the barrier potential across both junctions, causing an increase in the flow of electrons from the left region into centre region and on to the right region.

- For a given amount of illumination on a very small area, the photo-transistor provides a much larger output current than that available from photo diode, i.e. a photo-transistor is more sensitive.

- Array of transistors and low current photo diodes are widely used as photo detectors for such applications as punched card and tape readouts. But in comparison photo-diode have a faster switching time.

- One application of photo-transistor is shown in Fig. 5.38 where controlling of relay is achieved with the help of photo-transistor. The light incident on the photo-transistor causes its current to increase and therefore increases both the voltage drop across 50 KΩ and the input to the transistor which drives the relay. This increases current to the operational level.

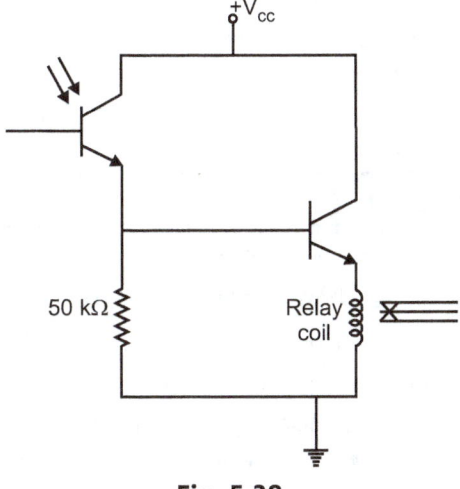

Fig. 5.38

5.15 FLOW MEASUREMENT

- The measurement of flow rate and quantity is the oldest of all measurements of process variables in the field of instrumentation.
- It is used to determine the amount of materials flowing in or out of a process.
- Without flow measurements, plant material balancing, quality control and the operation of any continuous process would be impossible.
- Flow velocities are also measured by inductive transducers.
- The measurement of liquids containing suspended solids, such as sewage or feed to paper mills, present considerable problems. This is overcome by the use of a flow meter.
- It is also used to measure the flow of any flowing material that is electrically conductive.
- Two saddle coils are arranged opposite each other and electrodes diametrically opposite are arranged flush with the inside of the lining. If the coils energized, the moving liquid, cuts the lines of force, resulting in the generation of an electromotive force that is picked-up by the electrodes. By suitable circuitry and amplification, an electrical signal proportional to the flow can be obtained.
- Many accurate and reliable methods are available for the measuring flow, some of which are applicable only to liquids, some only to gases and some others to both. Temperature may range from cryogenic to hundreds of $^\circ$C.
- Flow rate may vary from a few drops per hour to thousands of gallons per minute.

Mechanical Flow Meter

- In mechanical flow meters, there is a mechanism in the path of the flow which moves continuously at a speed which is proportional to the flow rate. These are generally used for metering liquids however with certain modifications, they can be designed to meter gases also. They can be divided into two main categories, with further subgroups.
  1. Displacement type
  2. Inferential type
- The displacement type are volumetric in operation, the cyclic displacement of the detecting element, For example, Piston, being directly proportional to the volume of the fluid passing through the meter during each cycle.
- Inferential type flow meters are current type flow meters and measure the velocity of flow, from which the volume of flow is inferred.

5.16 DIGITAL THERMOMETER   [Nov. 15, May 14, 15]

❖ Important Question Related to this Topic ❖
Draw a neat diagram of a digital thermometer and explain its operation.

- The block diagram of a digital thermometer is as shown in Fig. 5.39.
- Usually the temperature measurement is carried out by using thermocouples and RTDs. The conventional method of recording the measured temperature is very time consuming due to the non-linear characteristics of the sensors and may introduce human errors.

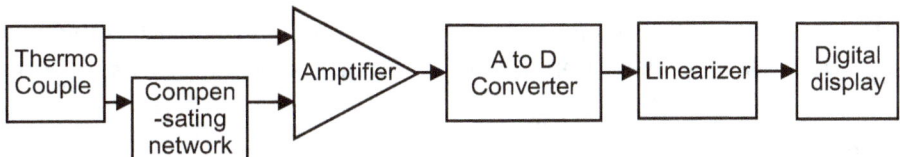

Fig. 5.39: Block Diagram of Digital Thermometer

- Hence digital thermometers are developed to obtain the direct display of the temperature. The linearizer used in digital thermometers is very important block. Using microprocessor based linearization technique, same unit can be used for different types of thermocouples.

Fig. 5.39 shows the block diagram a digital thermometer. It consists of:

- Temperature sensor like thermocouple.
- Compensating network to provide the reference temperature to the thermocouple.
- Signal conditioner like amplifier.
- Analog to digital converter (ADC), and
- Electronic display unit for direct display of the temperature.

- The thermocouple senses the temperature and produces proportional thermoelectric e.m.f. (voltage) in response to the changes in temperature.

- The compensating network provides the reference point for the thermocouple by producing a compensating voltage proportional to the reference temperature.

- The output of the thermocouple is further amplified by the amplifier. This amplified analog signal is fed as input to the ADC (Analog to digital Converter) which converts it into an equivalent digital form.

- The digital voltage from A to D Converter is linearized by the linearizing system and then used to drive the electronic display unit to give the digital display corresponding to the measured temperature.

Advantages of Digital Thermometer:

- Temperature readout is simple.
- High accuracy.
- Small in size.

5.17 ELECTRONIC WEIGHING MACHINE   [Dec. 12, Nov. 15, May 13, 15]

❖ **Important Questions Related to this Topic** ❖

1. Write a short note on electronic weighing machine.
2. Explain with a block diagram an electronic weighing machine.

- An electronic weighing machine has become very popular instrument for weight measurement in various industrial and commercial applications due to its high accuracy, fast response, stability, ruggedness and ease in operation.

- Fig. 5.40 shows the block diagram of an electronic weighing machine which mainly consists of load cell, amplifier, filter, analog to digital converter, processor and the display unit.

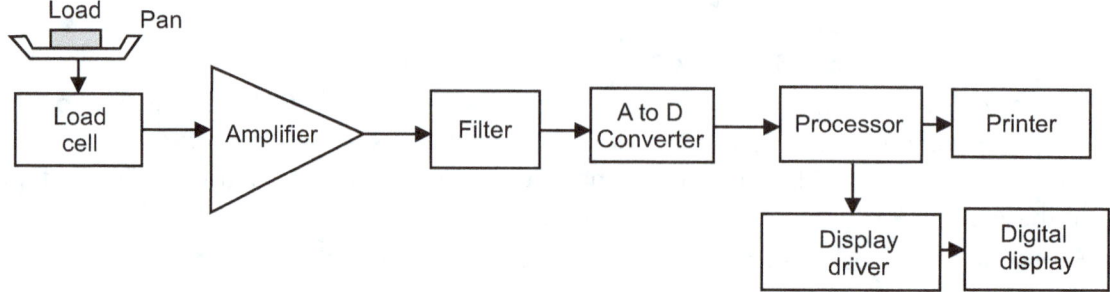

Fig. 5.40: Block Diagram of a Weighing Machine

- The load is placed on the load cell pan. The load cell contains bounded strain gauge transducers which convert the applied weight into equivalent electrical output using Wheatstone bridge. Zero setting arrangement is provided for the load cell.

- The output voltage from the Wheatstone bridge is then amplified by the amplifier and further filtered to remove the unwanted noise.

- This amplified and filtered analog signal is then fed to the Analog to Digital Converter (ADC) to convert it into equivalent digital form.

- The processor processes this input data stores it in the memory and calculates the cost of the item. The display driver generates the control signals for the printer and displays the data on the digital display unit. The processor also supports various functions. This type of weighing machine is used in super markets.

Advantages of Electronic Weighing Machine:

- High accuracy.
- Fast response.
- Small in size.
- High resolution.

Applications of Electronic Weighing Machine:

- These machines are utilized in almost all industries and commercial applications.
  - In grocery shops and super markets.
  - For precision weight measurements like weighing gold, silver, diamond and other precious stones.
- In platform weighers, animal and human weighing, truck weighing, crane weighing and textile industries etc.

QUESTIONS

1. Explain construction diagram and explain working with the help of Transistor Equivalent circuit of SCR. Also draw V-I characteristics.

2. Explain construction working and V-I characteristics of TRIAC.

3. Draw and explain two transistor analogy of SCR.

4. Explain construction, working and characteristics of DIAC.

5. Compare SCR, DIAC and TRIAC.

6. Show structure and circuit representation of a silicon controlled rectifier. Explain its principle of operation. Draw V-I characteristics. Define holding and latching current.

7. Name the different pressure sensors. Explain working of any two pressure sensors briefly.

8. Explain operation of thermistor with suitable diagram. State material used and application of thermocouple.

9. Compare RTD, Thermistor and thermocouple.

     Or

   Compare the three types of temperature transducer.

10. Compare active and passive transducer.

11. What are the desirable characteristics of resistance wire stain gauge.

12. Explain principal and working of :

   (a) Piezoelectric transducer.

   (b) Displacement transducer.

13. Mention the factors to be considered while selecting a transducer for an application.

14. Explain the following characteristics of transducer:

   (a) Accuracy

   (b) Ruggedness

   (c) Linearity

   (d) Repeatability

   (e) Stability

   (f) Reliable

15. What is RTD? Draw its constructional diagram and explain its operation.

16. What is piezoresistivity? Explain the operation of transducer working on Principle. State its advantages and disadvantage.

17. What is pressure transducer? Explain any one.

18. Explain principle of operation and construction of thermocouple. Mention Different materials used for it.

19. Explain principal of operation of strain gauge and its different types in brief.

20. Explain principal of operation of LVDT. Draw and Explain the construction of a LVDT. State its advantages and disadvantage.

21. What do you mean by active transducer? Explain any two type of active transducer.

22. What do you mean by passive transducer? Explain any two type of passive transducer.

23. Draw the block diagram of Instrumentation system and state the function of each block.

24. Explain in brief different types of strain gauges.

25. Explain two types of displacement transducer.

26. What is load cell? What is it used?

27. Draw a neat diagram of Digital thermometer and explain its operation.

28. Write a short note of Electronics Weighing Machine.

29. List different pressure transducer. Explain the working of any one in detail.

30. Explain construction, working and characteristics of phototransistor.

31. Write short note on Flow meter.

UNIVERSITY QUESTIONS

Dec. 2012

1. Draw construction diagram and explain the working with the help of transistor equivalent circuit of SCR. Also draw its V-I characteristics. **[7]**

2. Draw construction diagram and explain the V-I characteristics of a TRIAC. What are the applications of a TRIAC? **[7]**

3. With a neat diagram explain the construction and working of LVDT. Give its advantages and disadvantages. **[6]**

4. Explain with a block diagram an electronic weighing machine. **[6]**

May 2013

1. Explain in detail, the selection criteria for transducer. **[6]**

2. Explain in detail. **[7]**
   (i) Construction of TRIAC
   (ii) Characteristics of TRIAC
   (iii) Modes of operation

3. Explain with block diagram an electronic weighing machine. **[6]**

4. Explain the construction of DIAC w.r.t **[7]**
   (i) Characteristics
   (ii) Application

Dec. 2013

1. Draw and explain operation of SCR using two transistor equivalent circuit. **[6]**
2. Draw and explain block diagram of instrumentation system. **[7]**
3. Draw constructional diagram and explain working of V-I characteristic of Diac. **[6]**
4. Draw and explain the construction and operation of LVDT. **[7]**

May 2014

1. Explain with block diagram Digital Thermometer. **[7]**
2. Explain construction of SCR. **[6]**
3. Explain various criteria used to select a transducer. **[7]**
4. Explain Characteristics of DIAC.   [06]

$$z = A(\overline{B} + CD)$$

$$\overline{\overline{Z}} = \overline{\overline{A(B + C.D)}} = \overline{(A.\overline{B})} \cdot \overline{(A.C.D)}$$

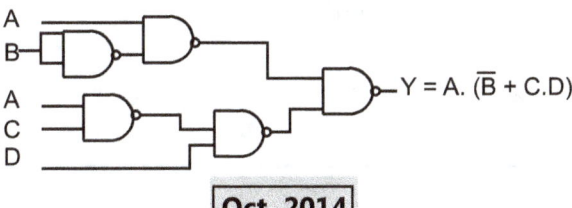

$$Y = A. (\overline{B} + C.D)$$

Oct. 2014

1. Explain the operation of SCR with the help of V-I characteristics. **[7]**
2. Explain the selection criteria of a Transducer. **[6]**
3. Define 'Dark current'. Draw and explain the characteristics of photo transistor. **[6]**
4. Explain the construction of DIAC and draw its characteristics. **[7]**

May 2015

1. With a neat diagram explain the construction and working of LVDT. Give its advantages, disadvantages and applications. **[7]**
2. Draw a neat block diagram of a digital thermometer and explain its operation. **[6]**
3. Write a short note on selection criterion for transducers. **[7]**
4. Compare : (i) SCR and TRIAC (ii) DIAC and TRIAC **[6]**

Nov. 2015

1. Draw block diagram of electronic weighing machine and explain its operation. **[6]**
2. Explain the construction of DIAC. Draw and explain its characteristics. **[7]**
3. Explain digital thermometer with block diagram. **[6]**

4. Define the following terms for SCR :   **[5]**
   (i) Holding Current
   (ii) Latching Current
   (iii) Forward Breakover Voltage
   (iv) Reverse Breakover Voltage
   (v) Turn ON time for SCR.

1. Draw a constructional diagram of SCR and Explain its working with the help of two transistor analogy.   **[6]**
2. With a neat diagram explain construction and working of LVDT. Give its advantages and applications.   **[6]**
3. Compare :   **[6]**
   (i) SCR and TRIAC
   (ii) DLAC and TRIAC
4. Draw and explain electronic weighting machine.   **[5]**
5. Define :
   (i) Active Transducer
   (ii) Passive Transducer.   **[6]**

◈ ◈ ◈

ELECTRONICS COMMUNICATION

6.1 INTRODUCTION

- In general, the field of electronics may be classified into three main areas: Computers, Communication and Control. The latest of the three is the computer field, whereas the communication field is the oldest. The main function of communication system is to transfer the information signal like sound, video, digital data, etc. from one point to another. The information signal is transmitted from one location which is called the transmitting end and is received at another location called receiving end.

6.1.1 Block Diagram of Communication System   [Dec. 13]

❖ **Important Question Related to this Topic** ❖

Draw and explain the block diagram of an electronic communication system.

- Fig. 6.1 shows the block diagram of an electronic communication system which mainly consists of a transmitter, a communication channel or medium and a receiver.

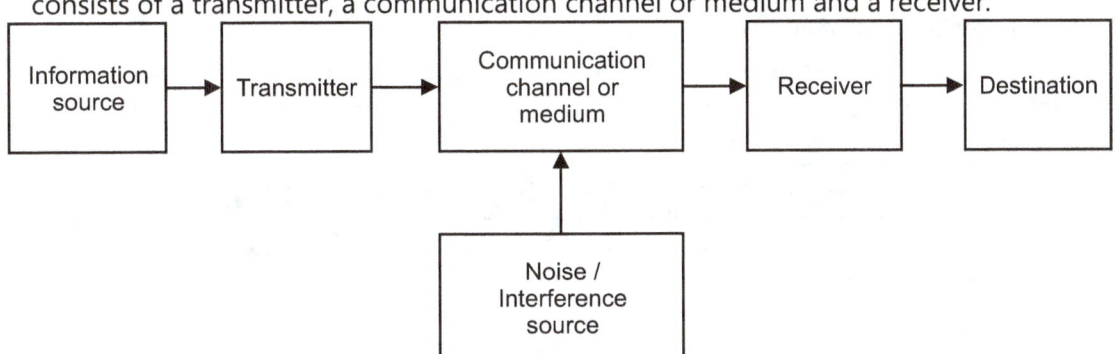

Fig. 6.1: Block Diagram of Electronic Communication System

The fundamental blocks of a communication system are:

- Information source (includes input transducer),
- Transmitter,
- Medium or Communication Channel,
- Noise (unwanted noise is inherently present in the channel),
- Receiver (includes output transducer).

- **Information or Input signal:** The communication systems are developed for exchanging desired information between two locations. The information signal or the message could be a digital signal, human voice, a video signal or the combination of all. Many times the information signal must be converted into suitable electrical form by using suitable transducer.

- **Transmitter (T_X):** The message coming from the information source may not be suitable for immediate transmission. The transmitter block converts the information into a suitable code and also gives its electrical equivalent. It consists of power amplifiers that increase the power level of the incoming signal so as to cover a large range. In addition, it consists of amplifier, mixer, oscillator etc. The amplifiers amplify the incoming signal so that it can be faithfully received at the receiving end. The encoders are used for coding the information before transmission. Suitable transducers convert the coded message into electrical signals.

- **Communication Channel or Medium:** A communication channel is the medium by which the signal is transmitted from one end to the other. It can be a pair of conducting wires, coaxial cables, optical fibre cables or free space.

- **Noise:** Noise is a random, unwanted electrical signal energy that gets added with the information signal while passing through the communication medium. Separating the noise from the original information signal is very difficult. Noise cannot be eliminated completely, but must be minimized by the reduction techniques as it degrades the overall performance of the communication system.

  Noise can be external or internal. The external noise can be caused due to thunderstorms in atmosphere or extraterritorial noise, whereas the internal noise is caused due to thermal agitation of the electronic components or shot noise that is caused by the random movement of electrons.

- **Receiver:** A receiver consists of amplifier, mixer, oscillator, detector, demodulator, driver amplifier and power amplifier etc. through which it processes the received signal and converts it back to its original form.

6.2 CLASSIFICATION OF COMMUNICATION SYSTEM

Based on Direction of Communication, they are classified as follows:
1. Simplex systems,
2. Half duplex systems,
3. Full duplex systems.

1. **Simplex Systems:** In these systems, the information is communicated only in one direction. For example, radio and TV broadcasting systems.
2. **Half Duplex Systems:** These systems are bidirectional. They can transmit and receive but not simultaneously. For example, walkie-talkie.
3. **Full Duplex Systems:** These systems allow communication in both directions simultaneously. These systems can transmit and receive simultaneously. For example, Telephone systems.

Based on the communication medium used, the communication systems are classified as follows:
1. Wired communication,
2. Wireless communication.

1. **Wired Communication:** In this type, simple wires, coaxial cables or optical fibre links are used for communication. It requires actual physical communication between the transmitter and the receiver therefore wired communication is not recommended for long distance communication. The telephone system, cable T.V. system or the leased lines of internet are some of the examples of wired communication system.

2. **Wireless Communication:** In this type, the communication takes place by using electromagnetic waves without establishing any physical connection between the transmitter and receiver. It is also called as Radio communication. The information signal is transmitted in the air, in the form of electromagnetic waves through the transmitter and is received by the receiving antenna at the destination. It is used for long distance communication like satellite communication.

Based on the Nature of Transmission, Communication Systems are Classified as follows:

   1. Analog communication system,

   2. Digital communication system.

1. **Analog Communication:** In analog communication systems, the signal to be transmitted is analog in nature i.e. it varies continuously with time.

2. **Digital Communication:** In these systems, the signal to be transmitted is digital in nature i.e. the signal has two distinct levels High (1) and Low (0).

- Analog and digital communication systems can be further classified as shown below:

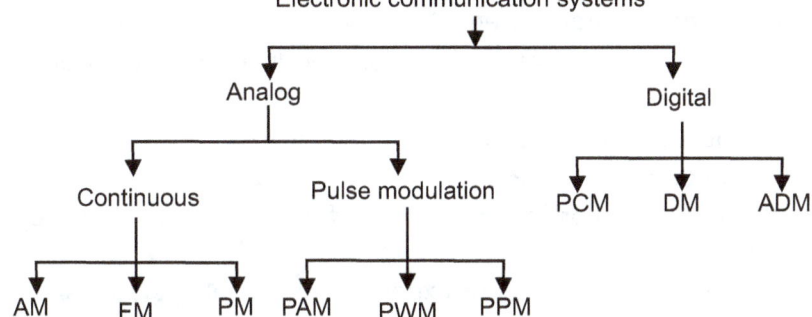

Fig. 6.2: Classification of analog and digital communication systems

6.2.1 Analog Communication

- An analog communication system uses a technique called Analog Modulation for transmission of analog information signal.

- Analog modulation can be defined as the modulation system in which one of the characteristics of the carrier is changed in proportion with the instantaneous value of the modulating signal is called as analog modulation system.

- If the carrier is sinusoidal, then its amplitude, frequency or phase is changed in accordance with the modulating signal to obtain AM, FM, PM respectively. They come under the continuous modulation technique.

- Whereas in pulse modulation, the carrier is in the form of rectangular pulses. The amplitude, width or position of the carrier pulses are varied in accordance with the modulating signal to obtain the PAM, PWM or PPM outputs.

Advantages of Analog Communication:
- Transmitters and receivers are simple to design.
- Require less bandwidth.

Disadvantages of Analog Communication:
- Susceptible to noise.
- Noise cannot be separated from the signal.
- Coding is not possible.
- Privacy and security of the data is not possible.

Applications of Analog Communication:
- Telephones,
- TV broadcasting,
- Radio broadcasting.

6.2.2 Digital Communication

- Digital communication system uses a technique called digital modulation to transmit the digital data.
- Digital modulation is defined as the modulation system in which the transmitted signal is in the form of digital pulses of constant amplitude, constant frequency and phase is called as the digital modulation system.
- PCM (Pulse Code Modulation) and delta modulation are examples of digital communication.
- This technique requires more bandwidth.

Advantages of Digital Communication:
- The analog signals can be converted to digital form, before transmission, as they have the following advantages:
- Digital communication systems are less expensive than analog systems.
- Excellent noise immunity.
- Multiplexing can be easily implemented in digital systems.
- In digital systems, the received signals can be corrected by error detecting codes.
- Greater dynamic range, small size as well as considerable reduction in power due to VLSI technology.
- In general, more efficient and reliable way of communication.

Applications of Analog Communication:
- Long distance communication between earth and space ships.
- Satellite communication.
- Telephone systems.
- Data and computer communications.
- Military applications.

6.3 BASEBAND TRANSMISSION SYSTEMS   [Dec. 13]

- The information signal in a communication system can be analog i.e. sound, video (picture) or it can be digital in nature e.g. in form of 0 and 1. This original information signal called as baseband signal.

- In baseband transmission systems, the baseband signal is directly transmitted. For example, in local telephone systems, the voice is converted into equivalent electrical signal which is directly transmitted through the telephone. Sometimes the analog signals can be converted into digital form and then transmitted through the coaxial cables.

- The main drawback of baseband transmission system is that, it requires large bandwidth. Also, sometimes the voice signal radiated by an antenna gets attenuated or suppressed and hence cannot travel a long distance in air. Therefore, the baseband signals are transmitted using modulation techniques.

6.4 IEEE FREQUENCY SPECTRUM / ELECTROMAGNETIC SPECTRUM   [Dec. 14, May 15, 16]

❖ **Important Question Related to this Topic** ❖

Draw and explain the electromagnetic spectrum.

- As discussed earlier, the electromagnetic waves (or Radio Frequency waves) act as the media of transfer in wireless communication system; because they are capable of carrying the information signal over a long distance through air. Electromagnetic waves consist of both electric and magnetic fields.

- The electromagnetic waves are sinusoidal in nature and are used in satellite communication systems, cellular telephones, radio, TV etc. The entire range of frequency of the electromagnetic waves varies from very low value to extremely high values and is referred to as RF spectrum. It is as shown in Fig. 6.3 along with both frequency and wavelengths.

- Frequency is defined as the number of cycles per second; its unit is Hertz (Hz) and wavelength (λ/m) is the distance travelled by the electromagnetic wave during one cycle. The relationship between frequency (F) and wavelength (λ) can be given as

$$\text{Wavelength } (\lambda) = \frac{\text{Speed of light}}{\text{Frequency}} = \frac{3 \times 10^8}{f}$$

- The frequency spectrum is divided into various segments. Beyond the RF spectrum, electromagnetic energy takes the form of infrared (IR), visible light, ultraviolet (UV), X-rays, and gamma rays. Some wireless devices such as remote control boxes and cordless microphones operate at IR or visible light frequencies.

- The International Telecommunication Union (ITU) has divided the RF spectrum into number of bands and allocated the bands to various services and applications.

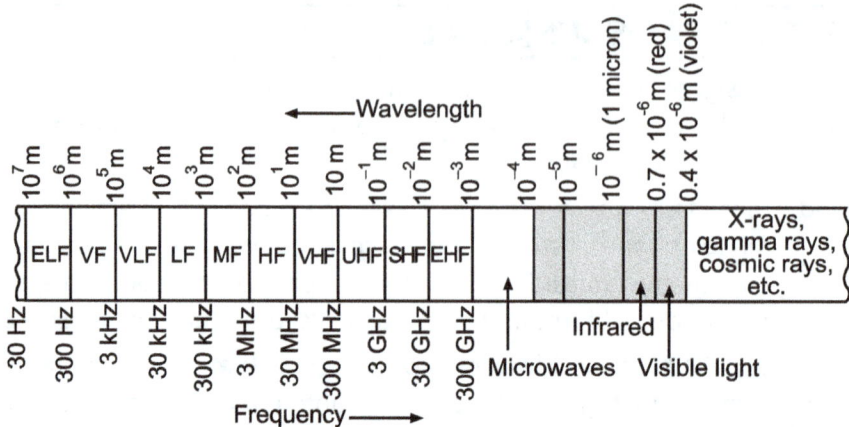

Fig. 6.3: Entire RF spectrum (Electromagnetic spectrum)

Table 6.1: Symbols used to denote radio frequencies

Frequency	Powers	In Hertz
1 kHz (kilohertz)	10^3 Hz	1000 Hz
1MHz (megahertz)	10^6 Hz	1,00,000 Hz
1 GHz (gigahertz)	10^9 Hz	1,00,00,000 Hz
1 THz (terahertz)	10^{12} Hz	1,000,000,000,000 Hz
1 PHz (petahertz)	10^{15} Hz	1,000,000,000,000,000 Hz
1 EHz (exahertz)	10^{18} Hz	1,000,000,000,000,000,000 Hz

6.4.1 Radio Frequency Spectrum and its Applications

- The table 6.2 shows the radio frequency spectrum and its applications according to various frequency bands.

Table 6.2

Band Name	ITU band	Frequency	Wavelength	Applications
Extremely low frequency (ELF)	1	3 - 30 Hz	100,000 km – 10,000 km	Communication with submarines
Super low frequency (SLF)	2	30 - 300 Hz	10,000 km – 1000 km	Communication with submarines
Ultra low frequency (ULF)	3	300 - 3000 Hz	1000 km – 100 km	Communication within mines
Very low frequency (VLF)	4	3 - 30 kHz	100 km – 10 km	Submarine communication, avalanche beacons, wireless heart rate monitors, geophysics

...Conti.

Low frequency (LF)	5	30 - 300 kHz	10 km – 1 km	Navigation, time signals, AM longwave broadcasting
Medium frequency (MF)	6	300 - 3000 kHz	1 km – 100 m	AM (Medium-wave) broadcasts
High frequency (HF)	7	3 - 30 MHz	100 m – 10 m	Shortwave broadcasts, amateur radio and over-the-horizon aviation communications
Very High frequency (VHF)	8	30 - 300 MHz	10 m – 1 m	FM, television broadcasts and line-of-sight ground-to-aircraft and aircraft-to-aircraft communications
Ultra high frequency (UHF)	9	300 - 3000 MHz	1 m – 100 mm	Television broadcasts, mobile phones, wireless LAN, Bluetooth and two-way radios such as FRS and GMRS radios
Super high frequency (SHF)	10	3 - 30 GHz	100 mm – 10 mm	Microwave, devices, wireless LAN, most modern radars
Extremely high frequency (EHF)	11	30 - 300 GHz	10 mm – 1 mm	Radio astronomy, high-speed, Microwave radio relay

- **Visible Spectrum:** Light is a particular type of electromagnetic radiation which is used in various electronic communication applications. In optical fibre communication system, sound, video and computer data etc. are converted into equivalent light signals and then transmitted after modulation.

6.5 MODULATION TECHNIQUES　　　　　　　　　[Dec. 13]

- Modulation is a process in which a high frequency "carrier signal" carries the low frequency "modulating signal (information signal)" from one point to another.
- It is analogous to a person travelling in a vehicle from one location to another. The person is analogous to the modulating signal and the vehicle is analogous to the carrier signal which carries him from one point to another.
- Mathematical equation of a carrier wave (sinusoidal wave) is

$$X = A \sin(\omega t + \phi)$$

where,
A = Maximum amplitude,

ω = Angular velocity = $2\pi f$ (f is the frequency)

ϕ = Phase angle

X = Instantaneous value of voltage or current

- Modulation is a process in which any one of the three parameters (amplitude, frequency or phase) of the carrier wave is varied in accordance with the modulating signal. Thus, there are three types of modulation techniques as given below:
  1. **Amplitude Modulation (AM):** Here, the amplitude (A) of the carrier signal is varied in accordance with the modulating signal, keeping its frequency (F) and phase (ϕ) constant.
  2. **Frequency Modulation (FM):** Here, the frequency (F) of the carrier signal is varied in accordance with the modulating signal, keeping its amplitude (A) and phase (ϕ) constant.
  3. **Phase Modulation (PM):** Here, the phase (ϕ) of the carrier signal is varied in accordance with the modulating signal, keeping its frequency (F) and amplitude (A) constant.

6.5.1 Necessity of Modulation (Need for Modulation)   [Nov. 15]

> ❖ **Important Questions Related to this Topic** ❖
> 1. What is the need of modulation?
> 2. Explain the advantages of using modulation technique.

- As discussed earlier, the baseband signals cannot be transmitted directly over long distance.

The Advantages of using Modulation Technique are:

- It reduces the required antenna height.
- Avoids mixing of signals.
- Increases the range of communication.
- Allows Multiplexing of signals.
- Allows adjustment in the bandwidth.
- Improves the quality of reception.

1. **Required Antenna Height Reduces:** According to the antenna theory, the required height of the antenna, for radiating the radio waves; is a function of the wavelength of the input signal frequency. The minimum antenna height must be ($\lambda/4$), where λ is the wavelength.

We know, $$\lambda = \frac{\text{Speed of light}}{\text{Frequency of signal}} = \frac{3 \times 10^8}{f}$$

Therefore, required antenna height $= \dfrac{3 \times 10^8}{4 \times f}$

Example: For an analog baseband signal with f = 10 kHz

$\therefore$ $$\lambda = \frac{3 \times 10^8}{4 \times 10 \times 10^3} = 7500 \text{ metres.}$$

Practically, it is impossible to build an antenna with height = 7500 m.

Now, consider, if a carrier signal of 1 MHz frequency modulates the 10 kHz frequency signal, then $f = 1 \times 10^6$ Hz

∴   Required antenna height $= \dfrac{3 \times 10^8}{4 \times 1 \times 10^6} = 75$ metre

From the above example, we can observe that the required antenna height for radio communication reduces from 7500 m to 75 metres due to modulation.

2. **Avoids Mixing of Signals:** We know, the audio frequency range is 20 Hz to 20 kHz. If audio signals are transmitted without modulation by various transmitters, all the signals will get mixed up together at the receiver. Separating those signals at the receiver is a very difficult task. For example, as shown in Fig. 6.4, three different sound signals are transmitted in the same range 20 Hz to 20 kHz. Then at the receiving end we will hear the mixture of all the three sound signals.

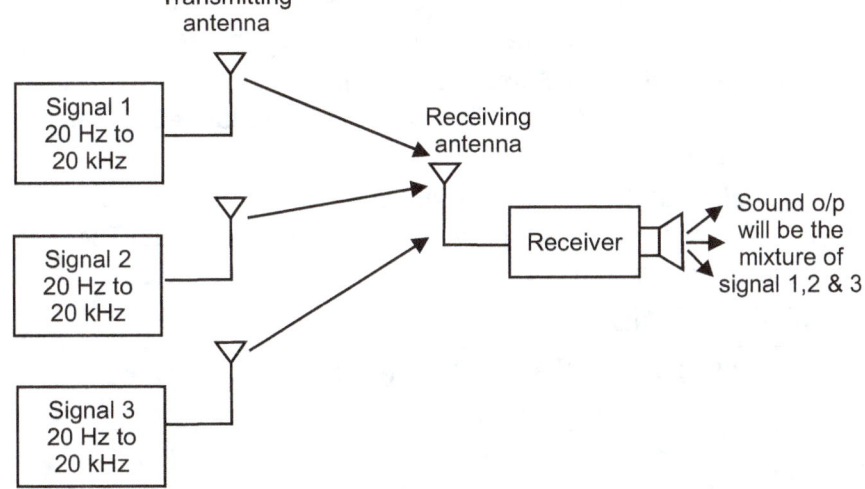

Fig. 6.4: Baseband communication for three sound signals

To avoid such mixing, modulation technique is used. As shown in Fig. 6.5, three different carrier signals are used to modulate the three different sound signals. And at the receiver, particular channel can be tuned to recover the signal.

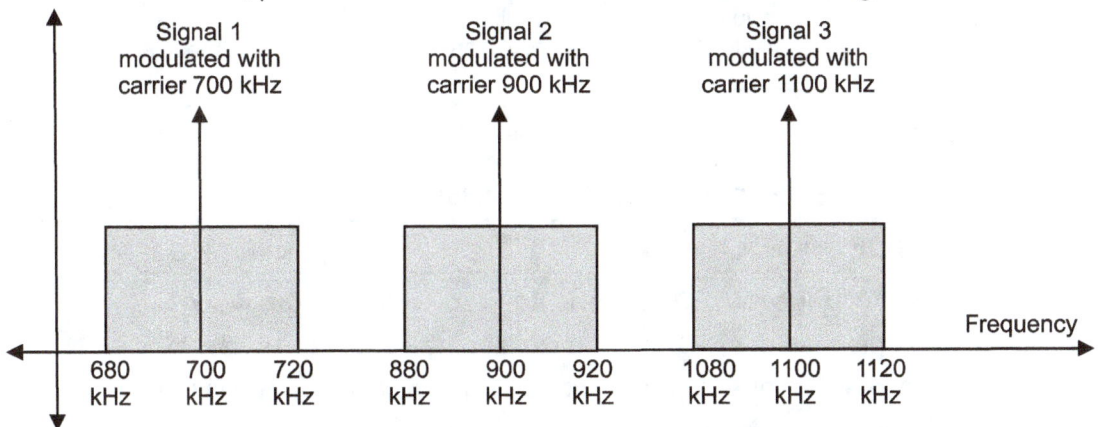

Fig. 6.5: Modulation avoids mixing of signals

3. **Increases the Range of Communication:** The baseband signal is a low frequency signal which, when transmitted, cannot travel long distance due to attenuation. In the modulation process, the frequency of the signal, to be radiated, is increased; so the attenuation gets reduced and the signal can travel over longer distances. Thus, modulation process increases the range of communication.

4. **Multiplexing of Signals is Possible:** Modulation allows multiplexing of different signals. Multiplexing means transmission of two or more signals simultaneously over the same channel. Common examples of multiplexing are simultaneously operating TV channels or the number of radio channels operating simultaneously in radio broadcast.

   Modulation allows multiplexing technique therefore different signals can be sent simultaneously over the same channel without disturbing each other.

5. **Allows Adjustment in the Bandwidth:** Signal to noise ratio in the receiver is a function of the signal bandwidth. Bandwidth of a modulated signal can be changed to improve the signal to noise ratio.

6. **Improves Quality of Reception of the Signal:** Frequency modulation and pulse code modulation techniques are proven to have high S/N ratio. They reduce effect of noise to a great extent. Thus, reduction in noise improves the quality of reception.

6.5.2 Types of Modulation

> ❖ **Important Question Related to this Topic** ❖
> What are the different types of modulation?

- The different types of modulation are as follows:

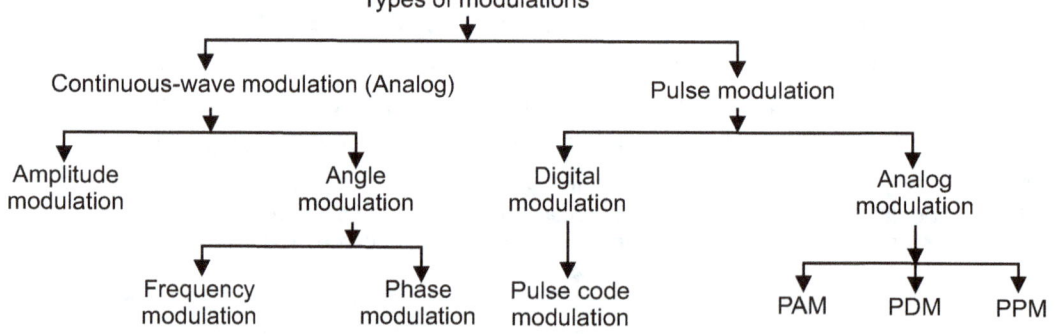

Fig. 6.6: Classification of modulation techniques

6.6 AMPLITUDE MODULATION   [Dec. 12, 13, May 15, 16]

> ❖ **Important Questions Related to this Topic** ❖
> 1. Write the expression of AM. Draw and explain the frequency spectrum of AM.
> 2. Write the expression of AM. Define modulation index and draw waveforms of AM.
> 3. What is modulation? Explain Amplitude Modulation technique in detail.

- Fig. 6.7 shows time domain representation of the amplitude modulated signal.
- In Amplitude Modulation, the instantaneous amplitude of the high frequency carrier signal is varied according to the amplitude of the modulating signal; keeping its frequency and phase constant.

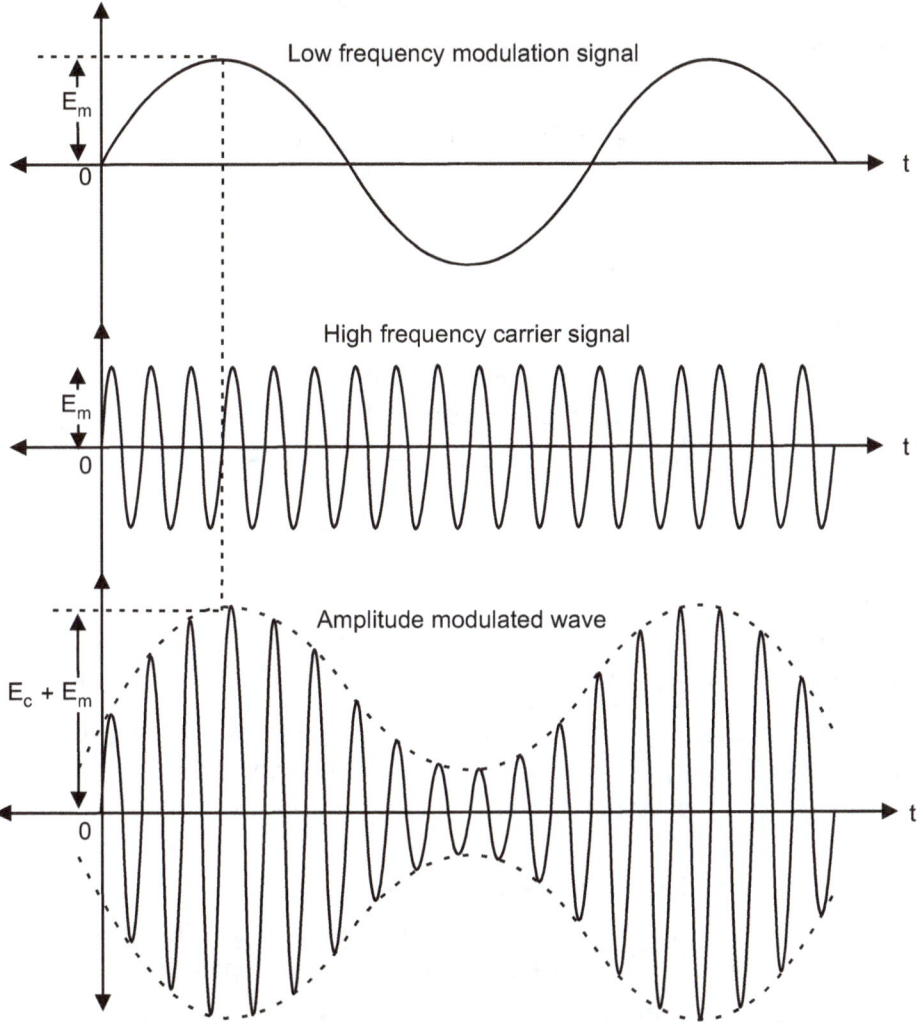

Fig. 6.7: Amplitude modulated wave

6.6.1 Mathematical Representation of AM Wave   [Dec. 12]

- Here we have assumed that the modulating signal and the carrier signal are sinusoidal in nature. In practice you can have any shape of the waveform only the frequency of the modulating signal should be low compared to the carrier signal frequency.

Instantaneous Value of the Modulating Signal:

$$e_m = E_m \sin \omega_m t$$

where,
e_m = Instantaneous amplitude

E_m = Maximum amplitude

ω_m = $2\pi f_m$ = angular frequency

f_m = Modulating signal frequency

Instantaneous value of the Carrier Signal:

$$e_c = E_C \sin \omega_c t$$

where,
e_c = Instantaneous amplitude

E_c = Maximum amplitude

ω_c = $2\pi f_c$ = angular frequency

f_c = Carrier signal frequency

Instantaneous Value of the AM Signal:

The mathematical expression for the complete modulated AM wave can be written as,

$$E_{AM} = E_c + E_m \sin \omega_m t$$

Thus, the instantaneous amplitude of the amplitude modulated wave is given by,

$$e_{AM} = E_{AM} \sin \omega_c t$$

Therefore,
$$e_{AM} = (E_c + E_m \sin \omega_m t) \sin \omega_c t$$

This is the complete expression for an amplitude modulated signal.

6.6.2 Modulation Index (M) [Dec. 12, May 13]

- The relationship between amplitude of the modulating signal (E_m) and the amplitude of the carrier signal (E_c) is expressed in the terms of their ratio, known as **modulation index (m).** It is also known as Modulation factor or Coefficient of modulation or Degree of modulation.

- Mathematically, the modulation index (m) is given by,

$$m = \frac{\text{Modulating signal voltage (amplitude)}}{\text{Carrier signal voltage (amplitude)}} = \frac{E_m}{E_c}$$

- Practically, the value of modulation index (m) should lie between 0 and 1; that is E_m must be less than E_c for distortionless output. If the value of m exceeds 1, the output gets distorted due to **over modulation**.

SOLVED EXAMPLES

Example 6.1: *Draw the amplitude modulated wave for the modulation index m = 0.75, m = 1 and m = 1.25.* **[Nov. 15]**

Solution:

1. For m = 0.75, the amplitude modulated wave is as shown in Fig. 6.8 (a).

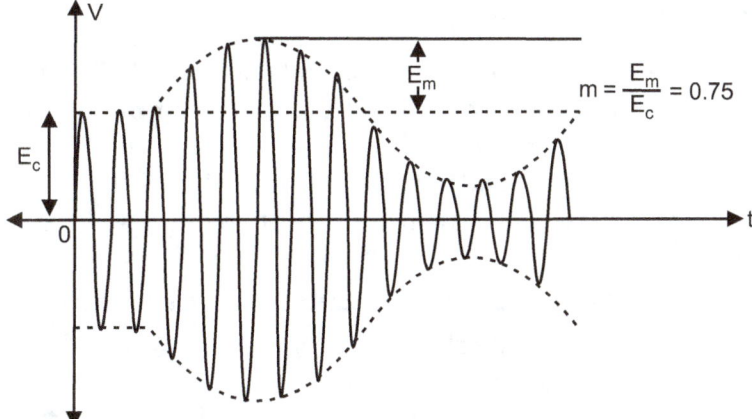

Fig. 6.8 (a): Amplitude Modulated Wave for m = 0.75

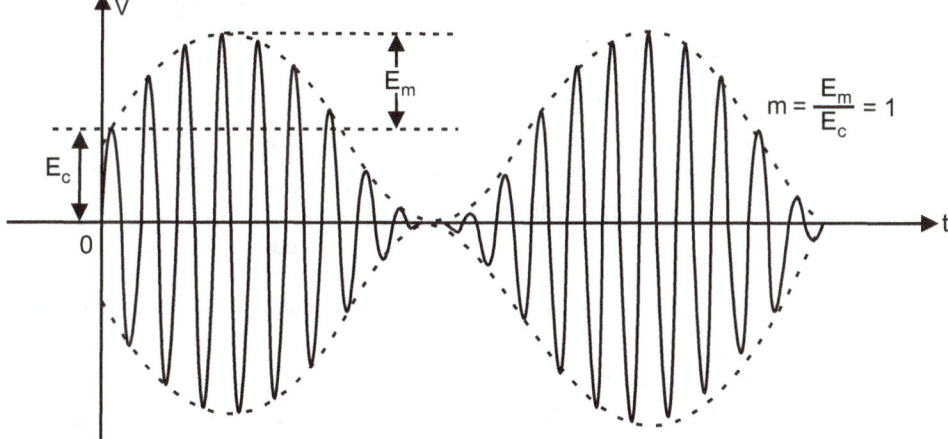

Fig. 6.8 (b): Amplitude Modulated Wave for m = 1

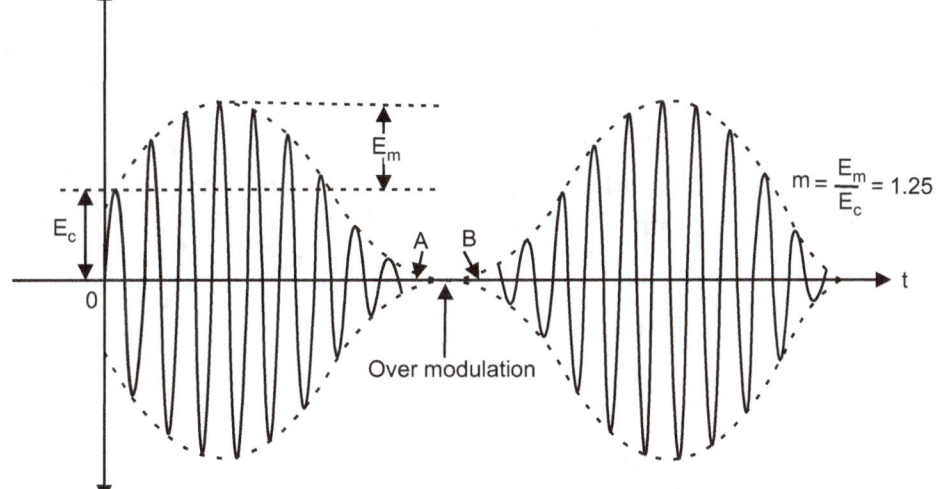

Fig. 6.8 (c): Amplitude Modulated Wave for m = 1.25

6.6.3 Concept of Over Modulation

- Carefully observe the waveform drawn in Fig. 6.8 (c) for m = 1.25. The AM wave goes to zero for some time duration. This condition is known as **over modulation**. i.e. from point A to B the amplitude of the carrier signal is not proportional to the amplitude of the modulating signal. Due to this condition, there is loss of information or distortion in the waveform. For distortionless transmission and reception of the AM wave over modulation must be avoided.

6.6.4 Trapezoidal Display Method to Calculate Modulation Index

- Fig. 6.9 shows the arrangement to calculate the modulation index using Trapezoidal display method. Using this method the modulation index can be calculated directly on the oscilloscope.

- Here, the modulated wave is applied to the vertical deflection plates and the modulating signal is applied to the horizontal deflection plates of the oscilloscope. The electron beam spot is deflected vertically by the carrier voltage.

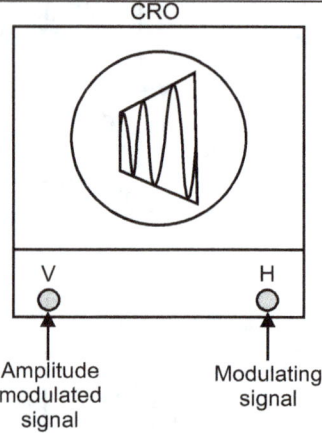

Fig. 6.9: Arrangement of Trapezoidal Display Method

- Depending upon the amplitude of the modulating signal, the electron beam spot changes its direction of deflection on the oscilloscope towards left or right forming a trapezoidal pattern on the screen as shown in Fig. 6.10.

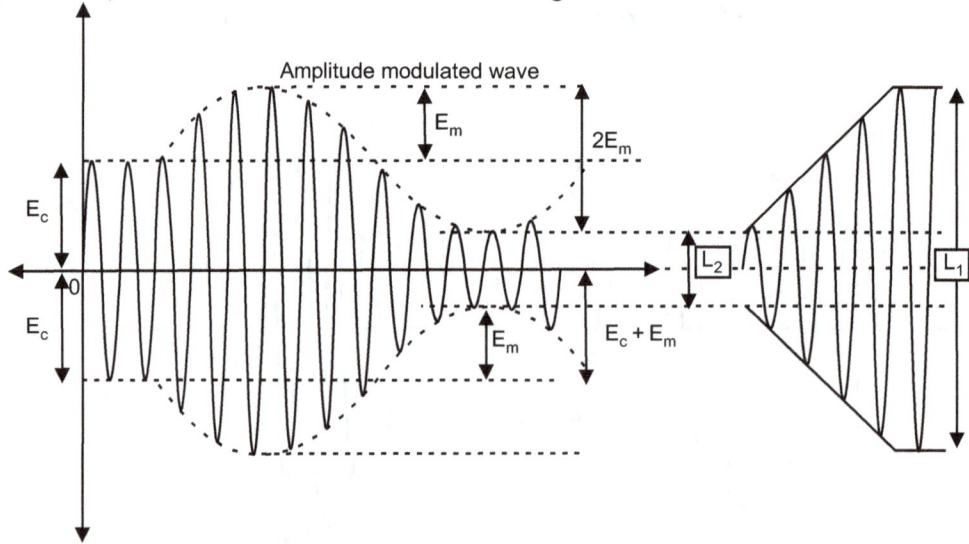

Fig. 6.10: Trapezoidal Display of AM Wave

From Fig. 6.10 we can write,

$$L_1 = 2 (E_c + E_m)$$

$$L_2 = 2 (E_c - E_m)$$

Solve the above equations to get E_m and E_c in terms of L_1 and L_2:

$$L_1 - L_2 = [2 (E_c + E_m)] - [2 (E_c - E_m)]$$

$$= 2E_c + 2E_m - 2E_c + 2E_m = 4E_m$$

$$\therefore \quad E_m = \frac{L_1 - L_2}{4}$$

Again,

$$L_1 + L_2 = [2(E_c + E_m)] + [2(E_c - E_m)]$$

$$= 2E_c + 2E_m + 2E_c - 2E_m = 4E_c$$

$$\therefore \quad E_c = \frac{L_1 + L_2}{4}$$

We know, modulating index $m = \dfrac{E_m}{E_c}$

Putting the values of E_m and E_c we get,

$$m = \frac{E_m}{E_c} = \frac{\dfrac{L_1 - L_2}{4}}{\dfrac{L_1 + L_2}{4}} = \frac{L_1 - L_2}{L_1 + L_2}$$

Thus, the modulation index can be calculated simply by measuring the values of L_1 and L_2.

Example 6.2: *Calculate the modulation factor and peak-to-peak voltage of the unmodulated carrier signal for the Fig. 6.11.*

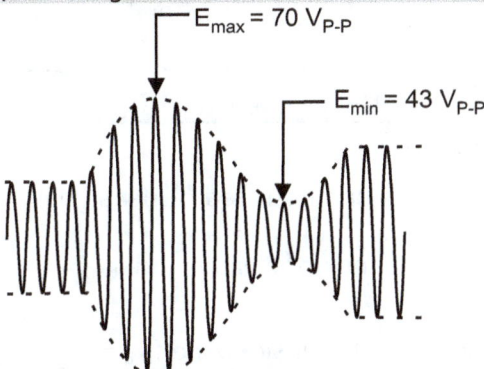

$E_{max} = 70\ V_{P-P}$

$E_{min} = 43\ V_{P-P}$

Fig. 6.11: AM Wave

Solution:

We know,
$$m = \frac{E_{max} - E_{min}}{E_{max} + E_{min}} = \frac{70 - 43}{70 + 43} = 0.23$$

$\therefore$ % modulation $= 0.23 \times 100 = 23\%$

The peak-to-peak voltage of the unmodulated carrier wave is given by,

$$E_c = \frac{L_1 + L_2}{4} = \frac{70 + 43}{4} = 28.25 \, V_{p\text{-}p}$$

6.6.5 Frequency Spectrum of the AM Wave

- The plot of amplitude verses frequency is called the frequency spectrum of the AM wave. It contains two side band frequencies (f_{usb} and f_{lsb}) which occur above and below the carrier frequency.

$$f_{USB} = f_c + f_m$$

$$f_{LSB} = f_c - f_m$$

- Recall the equation for AM wave,

$$e_{AM} = (E_c + E_m \sin \omega_m t) \sin \omega_c t$$

We know, $m = \dfrac{E_m}{E_c}$; Therefore, $E_m = m \, E_c$.

Substituting this value in the above equation we get,

$$e_{AM} = E_c [1 + m \sin \omega_m t] \sin \omega_c t$$

After simplification we get,

$$e_{AM} = E_c \sin \omega_c t + m \, E_c \sin \omega_m t \, \sin \omega_c t$$

Solving this equation further trigonometrically we get,

$$e_{AM} = \underbrace{E_c \cos \omega_c t}_{\text{Carrier signal}} + \underbrace{\frac{mE_c}{2} \cos (\omega_c + \omega_m) t}_{\text{Upper sideband}} + \underbrace{\frac{mE_c}{2} \cos (\omega_c - \omega_m) t}_{\text{Lower sideband}}$$

- This equation has three terms:

  1. The first term represents the unmodulated carrier signal with frequency f_c.

  2. The second term represents the upper sideband $f_{USB} = f_c + f_m$ and amplitude $= \dfrac{mE_c}{2}$

  3. The third term represents the lower sideband $f_{LSB} = f_c - f_m$ and amplitude $= \dfrac{mE_c}{2}$

  4. Thus, frequency spectrum of the AM can be plotted as shown below in Fig. 6.12.

Bandwidth of AM wave:

$$BW = F_{USB} - F_{LSB}$$
$$= (f_c + f_m) - (f_c - f_m)$$
$$= f_c + f_m - f_c + f_m$$
$$= 2 f_m$$

∴ $BW = 2 \times$ Modulating signal frequency

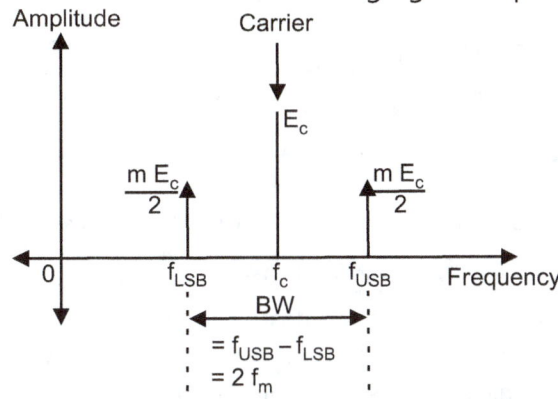

Fig. 6.12: Frequency Spectrum of AM Wave

Example 6.3: *A modulating signal 20 sin ($2\pi \times 10^3 t$) is used to modulate a carrier signal 40 sin ($2\pi \times 10^4$ t). Find: (1) Modulating index, (2) Percentage modulation, (3) Sideband frequencies and their amplitude, (4) Bandwidth of AM wave, (5) Draw the frequency spectrum.*

Solution:

1. We know that Modulating signal is given by,

$$e_m = E_m \sin (2\pi f_m t) = 20 \sin (2\pi \times 10^3 t)$$

Comparing the above two equations, we get, $E_m = 20$ V, $f_m = 1$ kHz

2. Similarly, carrier signal,

$$e_c = 40 \sin (2\pi \times 10^4 t) = E_c \sin (2\pi f_c t)$$

Comparing these equations we get, $E_c = 40$ V, $f_c = 10$ kHz

(1) Modulating index (m) $= \dfrac{E_m}{E_c} = \dfrac{20}{40} = 0.5$

(2) % modulation $= m \times 100 = 0.5 \times 100 = 50\%$

(3) Sideband frequencies and their amplitude:

- Lower sideband frequency (F_{LSB}) $= f_c - f_m = 10$ kHz $- 1$ kHz $= 9$ kHz

- Upper sideband frequency (F_{USB}) $= f_c + f_m = 10$ kHz $+ 1$ kHz $= 11$ kHz

- Amplitudes of both the sidebands $= \dfrac{mE_c}{2} = 0.5 \times \dfrac{40}{2} = 10$ volt

(4) Bandwidth of AM Wave (B.W.) = $2 \times f_m = 2 \times 1$ kHz = 2 kHz

(5) Frequency spectrum:

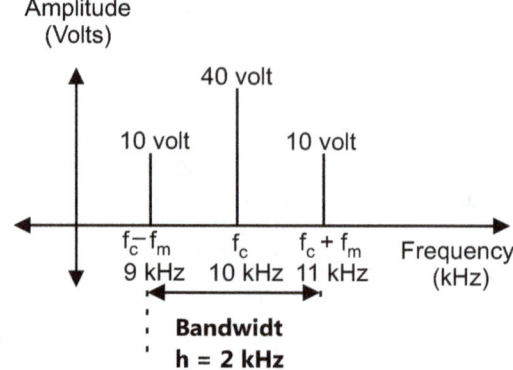

Fig. 6.13: Frequency Spectrum for given Example

6.6.6 Average Power for Sinusoidal AM

- As seen above, an AM wave consists of three components viz. the unmodulated carrier, lower side band and upper side band. Therefore, the total power of AM wave is given by the sum of the power of all the three components.

$$P_{Total} = P_C + P_{LSB} + P_{USB} = \frac{V_C^2}{R} + \frac{V_{LSB}^2}{R} + \frac{V_{USB}^2}{R}$$

where,   R = the characteristic impedance of the antenna.

Note that the voltages represent the r.m.s. values.

1. **Carrier Power:** $P_C = \dfrac{V_C^2}{R}$

    ∴ The average carrier power= $\dfrac{(V_C/\sqrt{2})^2}{R} = \dfrac{V_C^2}{2R}$

2. **Power in Sidebands:**

    Similarly, the average power for two sidebands can be given as,

$$P_{LSB} = P_{USB} = \frac{1}{R} \times \left[\frac{\frac{mV_C}{2}}{\sqrt{2}}\right]^2 = \frac{m^2 V_C^2}{8R}$$

- We can see from the above equation that, the transmission efficiency increases with increase in the modulation index, as it increases the sideband power.

- Therefore, it is desirable to have higher modulation index. But at the same time it should be less than 1 to avoid over modulation.

$$\therefore \qquad P_{LSB} = P_{USB} = \frac{m^2 V_C^2}{8R} = \frac{m^2}{4} \times \frac{V_C^2}{2R}$$

But,
$$\frac{V_C^2}{2R} = P_C$$

$\therefore \qquad P_{LSB} = P_{USB} = \frac{m^2}{4} P_C$

3. The Average Total Power:

$$P_{Total} = \frac{V_C^2}{2R} + \frac{m^2 V_C^2}{8R} + \frac{m^2 V_C^2}{8R}$$

$$= \frac{V_C^2}{2R}\left[1 + \frac{m^2}{4} + \frac{m^2}{4}\right] = \frac{V_C^2}{2R}\left[1 + \frac{m^2}{2}\right]$$

$\therefore \qquad P_{Total} = P_C\left[1 + \frac{m^2}{2}\right]$

As m can be 1 (maximum), maximum total power of amplitude modulated wave is 1.5 P_C.

4. Modulation Index in Terms of P_{Total} and P_C:

We know, $\qquad P_{Total} = P_C\left[1 + \frac{m^2}{2}\right]$

$\therefore \qquad \frac{P_{Total}}{P_C} = 1 + \frac{m^2}{2}$

$\therefore \qquad \frac{m^2}{2} = \frac{P_{Total}}{P_C} - 1$

$\therefore \qquad m = \sqrt{2\left[\frac{P_{Total}}{P_C} - 1\right]}$

5. Transmission Efficiency:

The ratio of the transmitted power containing the information (i.e. sideband power) to the total transmitted power (P_{Total}) is known as the transmission efficiency.

$\therefore$ Transmission efficiency $= \eta = \dfrac{P_{LSB} + P_{USB}}{P_{Total}}$

$\therefore \qquad \eta = \dfrac{\left[\dfrac{m^2}{4} P_C + \dfrac{m^2}{4} P_C\right]}{\left[1 + \dfrac{m^2}{2}\right] P_C} = \dfrac{\dfrac{m^2}{2}}{1 + \dfrac{m^2}{2}}$

$\therefore \qquad \eta = \dfrac{m^2}{2 + m^2}$

$\therefore$ The percentage transmission efficiency is given as, % $\eta = \dfrac{m^2}{2 + m^2} \times 100\%$.

Example 6.4: *An audio frequency signal 10 sin 2π x 500t is used to amplitude modulate a carrier of 50 sin 2π x 10^5. Calculate: (1) Modulation index, (2) Sideband frequencies, (3) Amplitude of each sideband frequency, (4) Bandwidth required, (5) Total power delivered to the load of 600 Ω (6) Transmission efficiency.*

Solution: Given: V_m = 10 sin 2π × 500 t, V_C = 50 sin 2π × 10^5 t

∴ V_m = 10, f_m = 500 Hz and V_C = 50, f_C = 100 kHz

1. Modulation index m $= \dfrac{V_m}{V_C} = \dfrac{10}{50}$ = 0.2

    ∴ % modulation = 0.2 × 100 = 20%

2. Sideband frequencies:

    f_{USB} = f_C + f_m = 100 kHz + 500 = 100.5 kHz

    f_{LSB} = f_C − f_m = 100 kHz − 500 = 99.5 kHz

3. Amplitude of both the sideband frequencies

    Amplitude of upper and lower sidebands $= \dfrac{mV_C}{2} = \dfrac{0.2 \times 50}{2}$ = 5 V

4. Required bandwidth

    BW = f_{USB} − f_{LSB} = 100500 − 99500 = 1000 Hz

5. Total power delivered into a load of 600 Ω

    We know, $P_{Total} = \dfrac{V_C^2}{2R}\left[1 + \dfrac{m^2}{2}\right] = \dfrac{(50)^2}{2 \times 600}\left[1 + \dfrac{(0.2)^2}{2}\right]$ = 2.125 watts

6. Transmission efficiency, $\eta = \dfrac{m^2}{2 + m^2} = \dfrac{(0.2)^2}{2 + (0.2)^2}$ = 0.0196

    ∴   % η = 0.0196 × 100 = 1.96%

6.7 FREQUENCY MODULATION   [Nov. 15, May 13, 14, 16]

> ❖ **Important Question Related to this Topic** ❖
>
> Explain the following things about FM:
>
> (a) Deviation ratio,
>
> (b) Mathematical representation of FM,
>
> (c) Advantages and disadvantages of FM,
>
> (d) Effect of modulation index in FM.

● In the process of frequency modulation, the frequency of a carrier signal is varied in accordance with the modulating signal while, the amplitude and phase of the carrier signal are held constant. Fig. 6.14 shows the time domain representation of the FM signal.

- From 0 to 90° the modulating signal voltage increases from zero to its maximum positive value, so the carrier frequency increases from its center value to maximum.
- For 90° to 180°, the modulating signal voltage decreases from maximum to zero; hence the carrier frequency decreases and attains its center value.
- Again from 180° to 270°, the modulating signal goes from zero to negative peak, so the carrier frequency changes to its lowest value.
- And finally from 270° to 360° the modulating voltage increases towards zero hence the carrier frequency varies and attains its center value.

  Thus, the carrier frequency varies above and below its center value, with the changing amplitude of the modulating signal.

  The main advantage of Frequency Modulation is that, as its amplitude is held constant; noise signals cannot interfere the FM signal i.e. the noise cannot affect the fidelity of the FM signal.

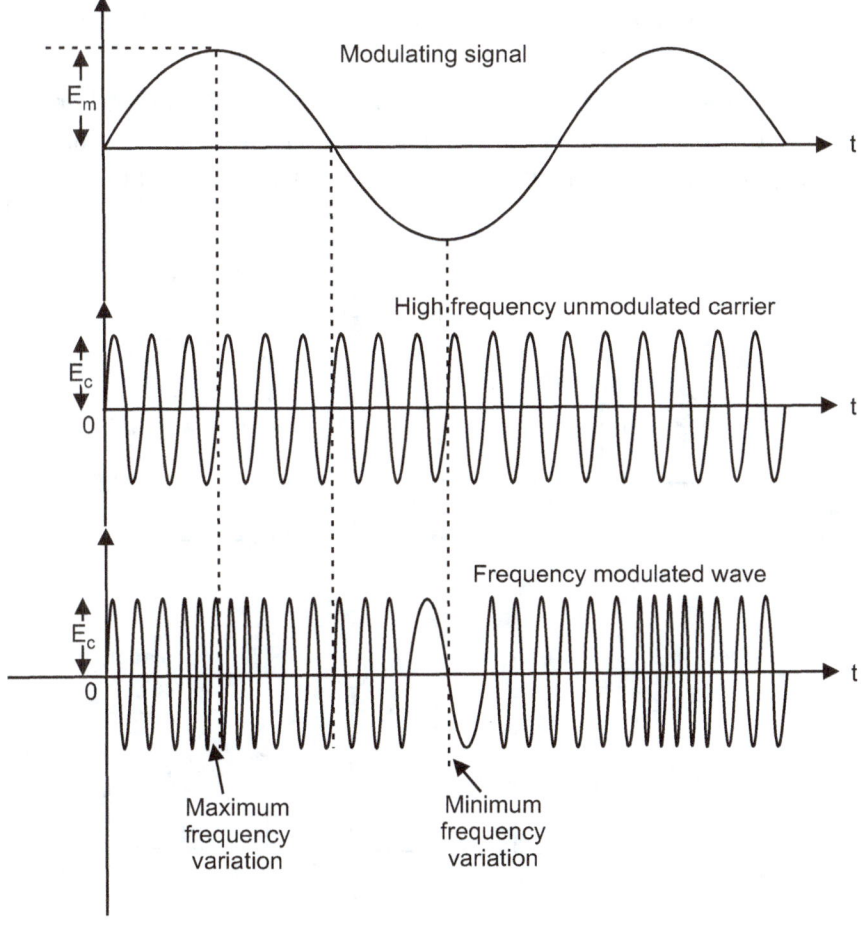

Fig. 6.14: Frequency modulated signal

6.7.1 Modulation Index in FM [May 16]

- First let us discuss the parameter called Frequency deviation in FM. The amount by which the carrier frequency varies from its unmodulated value is called frequency deviation (δ) which is proportional to instantaneous value of the modulating signal.

  The maximum frequency of the FM wave is $f_{max.} = f_c + \delta$

  The minimum frequency of the FM wave is $f_{min.} = f_c - \delta$

- The Modulation Index is defined as the ratio of frequency deviation (δ) to the modulating frequency (f_m).

$$\text{Modulation Index } m_f = \frac{\text{Frequency deviation}}{\text{Modulating frequency}} = \frac{\delta}{f_m}$$

6.7.2 Number of Sidebands

- In FM, unlimited sidebands are produced which are placed on either sides of the carrier frequency. The amplitudes of the sideband components can take various values indicating that most of the power of the FM signal is in sidebands.

- The number of sidebands depends upon both the amplitude and frequency of the modulating signal. The number of sidebands increases as the amplitude of the modulating signal increases and it also increases as the frequency of the modulating signal decreases.

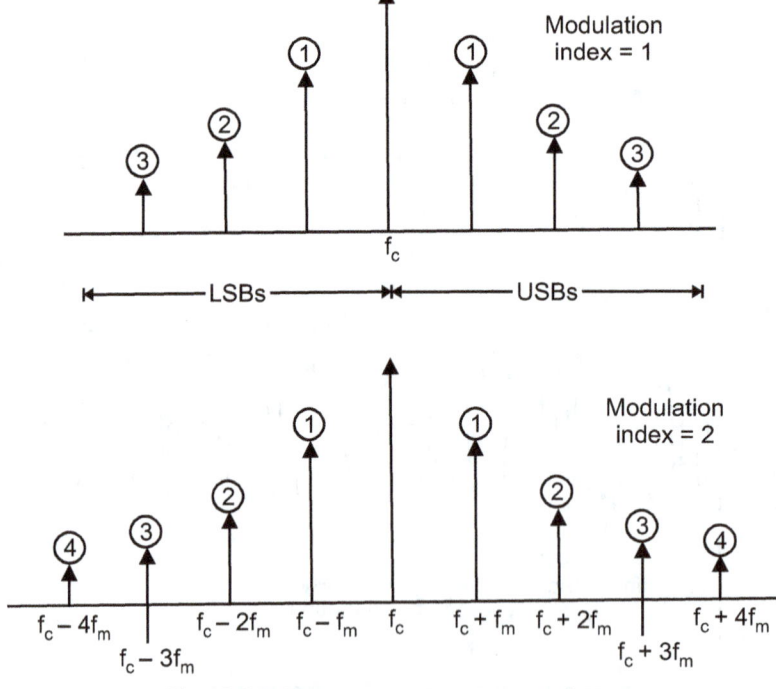

Fig. 6.15: Frequency spectrum of FM

- The frequency deviation (δ) changes with change in the amplitude of modulating signal, and hence will change the modulation index (m_f). The modulation index decides the bandwidth and the number of sidebands in FM wave.
- Fig. 6.15 shows the frequency spectrum of the FM wave. The number of sidebands with significant amplitude increases as the modulation index increases. It is also known as the frequency domain response of the FM wave.

6.7.3 Deviation Ratio   [May 16]

- As seen earlier, in FM, the carrier frequency shifts above or below its center frequency as the amplitude of the modulating signal changes. Deviation ratio is defined as the ratio of maximum frequency deviation to maximum modulating frequency.

$$\text{Deviation Ratio} = \frac{\text{Maximum frequency deviation}}{\text{Maximum modulating frequency}} = \frac{\delta_{max}}{f_{m\,max}}$$

- According to the rules of the Federal Communications Commission (FCC), the maximum value of frequency deviation is limited to 75 kHz and the maximum modulating frequency is limited to 15 kHz, in FM broadcasting.

6.7.4 Percentage Modulation of FM

- The percentage modulation is defined as the ratio of the actual frequency deviation produced by the modulating signal to the maximum allowable frequency deviation.

$$\therefore \qquad \text{\% Modulation} = \frac{\text{Actual frequency deviation}}{\text{Maximum allowed deviation}}$$

6.7.5 Mathematical Representation of FM

1. **Modulating Signal:** Let the modulating signal be sinusoidal in nature.

$$\therefore \quad e_m = E_m \cos \omega_m t$$

where,
$$e_m = \text{Instantaneous amplitude of modulating signal}$$
$$\omega_m = \text{Angular velocity} = 2\pi f_m$$
$$f_m = \text{Modulating frequency}$$

2. **Carrier Signal:** The carrier wave also is sinusoidal in nature.

$$\therefore \qquad e_c = E_c \sin (\omega_c t + \phi)$$

where,
$$e_c = \text{Instantaneous amplitude of the carrier signal}$$
$$\omega_c = \text{Angular velocity} = 2\pi f_c$$
$$f_c = \text{Carrier frequency}$$
$$\phi = \text{Phase angle}$$

3. **FM Wave:** The FM signal is nothing but the deviation of frequency.

$$\therefore \qquad f = f_c (1 + K E_m \cos \omega_m t)$$

where, f_c = Unmodulated carrier frequency

K = Constant of proportionality

$E_m \cos \omega_m t$ = Instantaneous amplitude of modulating signal

- The maximum deviation will occur, when $\cos \omega_m t = \pm 1$. Substitute this value in the above equation, $\therefore$ $f = f_c + (1 \pm K E_m)$

  $\therefore$ $f = f_c \pm K E_m f_c$ ... (1)

  Compare this equation with the that of frequency of FM wave

  i.e. $f = f_c \pm \delta$

  $\therefore$ The maximum deviation δ will be given by,

  $$\delta = K E_m f_c$$

- The instantaneous amplitude of FM signal is given by,

  $$e_{FM} = E_c \sin [f(\omega_c, \omega_m)]$$

  $$= E_c \sin \theta \qquad \qquad ... (2)$$

  where, $f(\omega_c, \omega_m)$ is some function of the carrier and modulating frequencies.

  Writing the equation (1) in terms of ω we get,

  $$\omega = \omega_c (1 + K E_m \cos \omega_m t)$$

- Integrate this equation with respect to time to find θ.

  $\therefore$

  $$\theta = \int \omega \, dt$$

  $$= \int \omega_c (1 + K E_m \cos \omega_m t) \, dt$$

  $$= \omega_c t + \frac{K E_m \omega_c \sin \omega_m t}{\omega_m}$$

  $$= \omega_c t + \frac{K E_m f_c \sin \omega_m t}{f_m} \qquad \begin{bmatrix} \because & \omega_c = 2\pi f_c \\ \because & \omega_m = 2\pi f_m \end{bmatrix}$$

  $$= \omega_c t + \frac{\delta \sin \omega_m t}{f_m} \qquad [\because \quad \delta = K E_m f_c]$$

  $\therefore$

  $$\theta = \omega_c t + \frac{\delta}{f_m} \sin \omega_m t$$

- Substitute value of θ in equation (2).

  $\therefore$

  $$e_{FM} = E_c \sin \left(\omega_c t + \frac{\delta}{f_m} \sin \omega_m t \right)$$

  $\therefore$

  $$e_{FM} = E_c \sin (\omega_c t + m_f \sin \omega_m t) \qquad \left(\because \quad m_f = \frac{\delta}{f_m} \right)$$

  This is the equation of FM wave where m_f represents the modulation index.

Advantages of FM:

- Since, the amplitude of FM wave remains constant, the transmitted power remains constant independent of the modulation depth. Therefore, low level modulation is possible in FM transmitters. Also, in FM all the transmitted power is useful, whereas in AM most of the transmitted power is in the carrier; which is totally wasted as the carrier does not carry any intelligence.
- FM receivers are more immune to noise as they use amplitude limiter circuits.
- Covers large area with low power transmission also.
- The Signal-to-Noise ratio can be increased by increasing the frequency deviation, whereas in AM the modulation depth cannot be increased beyond 100%.

Disadvantages of FM:

- FM broadcasting requires large bandwidth as compared to AM.
- Designing, repairing and servicing of FM transmitters and receivers is complex.
- The area of reception of the FM signal is limited upto the line of sight, due to space wave propagation of FM wave.

6.7.6 Comparison of AM and FM   [Dec. 14, Nov. 15, May 15]

❖ Important Question Related to this Topic ❖			
Differentiate between AM and FM.			

Sr. No.	Parameter	AM	FM
1.	Definition	Amplitude of the carrier is varied in accordance with the amplitude of the modulating signal keeping frequency and phase constant.	Frequency of the carrier is varied in accordance with the amplitude of the modulating signal keeping amplitude and phase constant.
2.	Noise immunity	AM receivers are not immune to noise.	FM receivers are immune to noise.
3.	Transmitted power	Depends on the modulation index. Carrier power is useless.	All the transmitted power remains constant and is useful. It is independent of m_f.
4.	Modulated signal	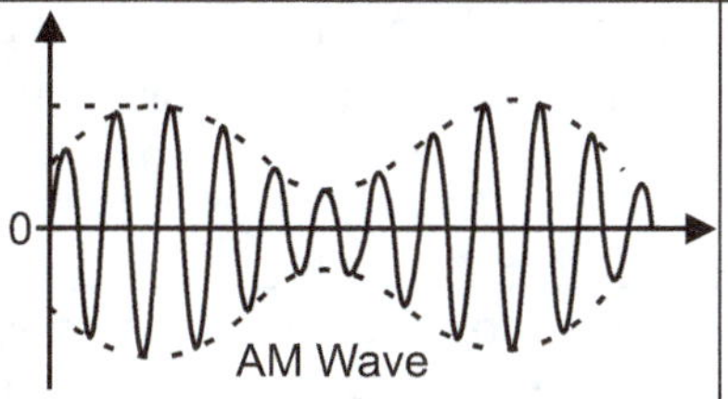 AM Wave **Fig. 6.16**	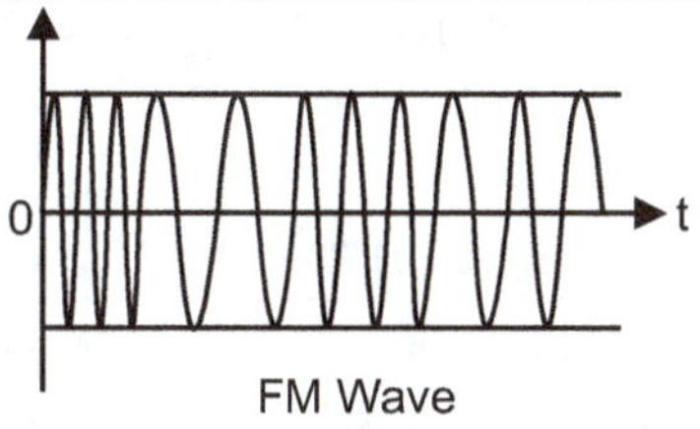 FM Wave **Fig. 6.17**

...Conti.

5.	Area covered	Larger area is covered than FM because ground wave and sky wave propagation is used.	The radius of transmission is limited to line of sight because space wave propagation is used.
6.	Complexity	AM equipments are less complex.	FM transmission and reception equipments are more complex.
7.	Actual information	The information is contained in the amplitude variation of the carrier.	The information is contained in the frequency variation of the carrier.
8.	Modulation Index	$m = \dfrac{E_c}{E_m}$	$m = \dfrac{\delta}{f_m}$
9.	Number of sidebands	Only two.	Infinite and depends on m_f.
10.	Bandwidth	$BW = 2f_m$ BW is much less than FM.	$BW = 2\,(\delta + f_{m\,(max)})$. BW is large. Hence, wide channel required.
11.	Application	Radio and TV broadcasting.	Broadcasting FM, audio transmission in TV, Point to point communication.

6.8 COMMUNICATION CHANNEL OR MEDIUM

❖ **Important Question Related to this Topic** ❖

Name the different types of wired links used in a communication system. Give the advantages of an optical fibre link over other links.

- Communication channel is required to provide a connection between the transmitter and receiver to exchange information. It is broadly classified into two categories as:
  1. Guided (Wired) and
  2. Unguided (Wireless). (As discussed in section 6.1.2)
- Now, we will discuss some types of wired communication channels which include transmission lines, parallel wire, coaxial cable, waveguides, and optical fibre.
- Depending upon the factors like applied frequency, power-handling capacity, type of installation, characteristic impedance, etc. a particular medium is selected for an application.

6.8.1 Transmission Lines

- The transmission lines are used to carry the RF energy from one end to the other end of a communication system. A typical example of a transmission line is shown in Fig. 6.18. Any transmission line has its own characteristic impedance due to which losses occur during transmission process.

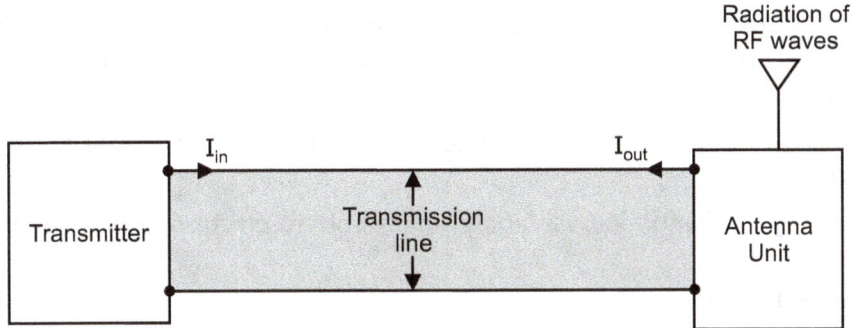

Fig. 6.18: Basic transmission line

- A two-wire transmission line has two ends. One end which is connected to the source is called the input end, transmitting end, sending end or the source end. The other end of the line is called the output end or the receiving end.

6.8.2 Parallel Wires Transmission Line

- There are two sub-types of parallel wire transmission line:
    - Two-wire line type.
    - Two-wire ribbon type.

1. Two-Wire Line Type

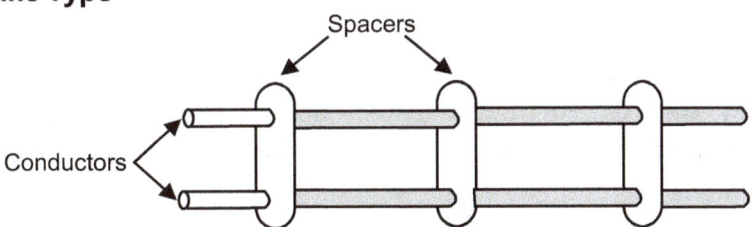

Fig. 6.19: Two-wire line type cable

- This type of transmission line consists of two conducting wires that are separated by insulating spacers. This type of parallel line is shown in Fig. 6.19. They are widely used for power line communication, telegraph lines and telephone lines etc.

Advantage: Simple in construction, easy installation and maintenance, cheap.

Disadvantage: High radiation losses, highly susceptible to electromagnetic interference.

2. Two-Wire Ribbon Type

- This type of line is also known as twin lead type of transmission line as shown in Fig. 6.20.

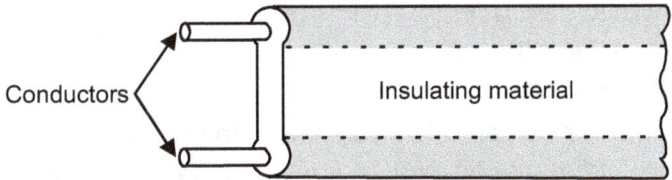

Fig. 6.20: Two-wire ribbon type line

- This type of transmission line is used to connect Yagi-Uda TV antenna output to home television set. The two conductors are separated by low loss dielectric, usually polyethylene.

Advantage: This can work at high frequencies, simple in construction, easy to install and for maintenance, cheap.

Disadvantage: High radiation losses, highly susceptible to electromagnetic interference, low power handling capacity.

6.8.3 Twisted Pair Cables   [Nov. 13]

❖ **Important Questions Related to this Topic** ❖

1. Write a short note on twisted wire cables.
2. Explain the problems associated with twisted pair cables. Write different types of twisted pair cables.

- A twisted wire cable consists of two insulated conductors, twisted together. The rubber insulation is used as a dielectric between the two wires as shown in Fig. 6.21.

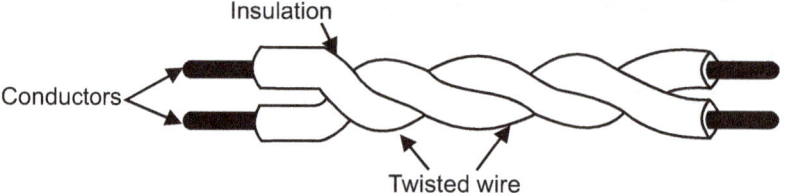

Fig. 6.21: Twisted pair transmission line

- Generally, they are used for low frequency application because the dielectric losses increase at high frequency operation. Used in digital data communication like LAN (Local Area Network).

Advantages:
- Cross-talk is minimized.
- Simple in construction.
- Cancellation of EMI pickup from the neighbour wire.

Disadvantages:
- Costlier than the twin feeder wire.
- High dielectric losses at high frequency operation.
- Cannot be operated beyond 100 Mbps in digital communication.

The Two Types of Twisted Pair Cables are:
- Unshielded Twisted Pair (UTP).
- Shielded Twisted Pair (STP).

Unshielded Twisted Pair (UTP):
- A typical unshielded twisted pair cable is as shown in Fig. 6.22. It is not shielded. It is used in telephone signal transmission and in computer communication like LAN. It is less expensive but is susceptible to the external noise and electromagnetic interference.

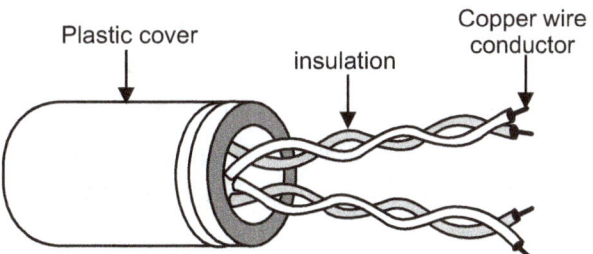

Fig. 6.22: Four pair UTP cable used in LAN (Local Area Network)

Shielded Twisted Pair (STP):

- A typical STP cable is as shown in Fig. 6.23.

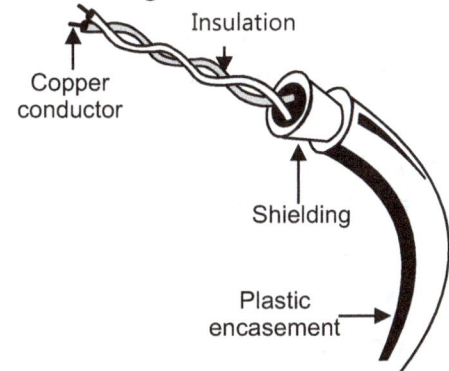

Fig. 6.23: Typical two pair shielded twisted pair cable (STP cable)

- STP has a protective shielding around the copper wire which reduces the EMI pickup. This type of cable can be used in noisy environments where EMI is more. STP gives better performance at lower data rates but can go up to 500 mbps for 100 metre distance.

Advantages: Noise pickup is less as compared to UTP cables. It can be used for both analog and digital communication.

Disadvantages: Costlier than UTP cables, in digital communications repeaters are required after 100 metres.

6.8.4 Coaxial Cable   [May 13, 14, 16]

❖ **Important Question Related to this Topic** ❖

Write a short note on a co-axial cable.

- A typical coaxial cable is as shown in Fig. 6.24. It can be used to transmit both digital and analog signals. The cost of coaxial cable is less than STP cable. Installation of a coaxial cable is simple.

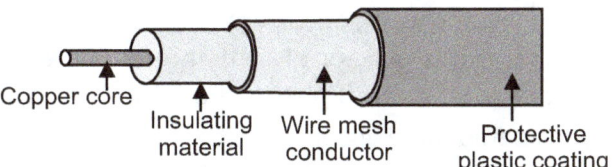

Fig. 6.24: Coaxial cable construction

- The inner conductor of a coaxial cable consists of a flexible wire which is insulated from the outer conductor by a solid, continuous insulating material like polyethylene.
- Some typical types of the coaxial cables, used for analog and digital communications are:
  - RG - 11 used for computer communication (50 Ohms impedance).
  - RG - 59 used for cable TV distribution (75 Ohms impedance).

  where, RG stands for Government Ratings.

Advantages:

- Higher bandwidth.
- Excellent electromagnetic interference immunity.
- Used for analog as well as digital transmission.
- Used for higher data rates in digital data communications for longer distances.

Disadvantages:

- Thick coaxial cables are more expensive.
- After 20 MHz frequency, attenuation increases sharply.

6.8.5 Fibre Optic Cable   [Nov. 15, May 13, 14, 16]

❖ **Important Questions Related to this Topic** ❖

1. Write a note on fibre optic cable.
2. What are the main sections of an optical fibre? Explain the function of each section.
3. Give the advantages of optical fibre link over other link.

- Optical fibre cables carry light signals instead of the electric signals. They are used for light and infrared transmissions.
- Fig. 6.25 shows the construction of an optical fibre cable. The diameter of fibre optic cables is only a fraction of an inch. A fibre optic cable can have a single fibre or a bundle of fibres to carry the information in the form of light.

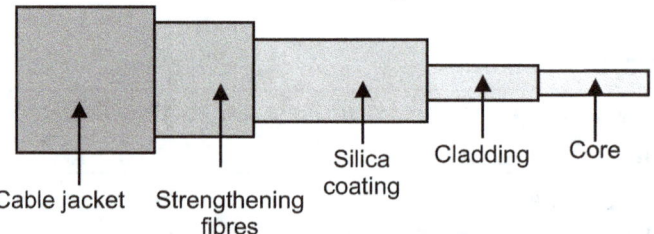

Fig. 6.25: Construction of fibre optic cable

- The inner core carries light and is made of either plastic or glass. It is surrounded by cladding material e.g. a layer of plastic or glass that reflects the light back into core. The refractive index of the core is relatively high and that of the cladding material is low.
- This entire assembly is coated with silicon oil and organic material with silica. Then it is covered with a protective inner jacket and outer plastic jacket. They provide mechanical strength to the optical fibre and protect it from mechanical wear and tear.

- The basic fibre optic communication system consists of three blocks. They are:
  1. **Optical Transmitter:** It converts the input electrical analog or digital signal into a corresponding light signal. It uses a light emitting diode, or a solid state laser diode for this purpose.
  2. **Fibre Optic Cable:** It carries the converted signal which is in the form of light from transmitting end to the receiving end. If the distance between the transmitter and receiver large, the fibre optic cables are cascaded one after the other.
  3. **Optical Receiver:** It converts the received optical signal that is in the form of light, into corresponding electrical signal. It uses photo-detectors like avalanche type or PIN type of photodiode.

Advantages of Fibre Optic Cable:
- Wide bandwidth and high data transmission rates.
- Good noise immunity.
- No ground loops and no cross talk inside the cable.
- Data losses are less.
- Light in weight with small cable diameter.
- No shock hazards hence safe and easy installation.
- They are sturdier and have longer life than coaxial cables.
- They do not interfere with adjusting cables.

Disadvantages of Fibre Optic Cable:
- The initial cost of incurred is high as compared to that of the copper wires.
- Skilled and trained operators are required to join together the optical fibre cables.
- High installation and maintenance cost.

6.8.6 Comparison of Wired Media

Sr. No.	Twisted Pair	Coaxial Cable	Fibre Optic Cable
1.	Uses electrical signal for transmission.	Uses electrical signal for transmission.	Uses optical signal for transmission.
2.	Low noise immunity.	Better noise immunity than coaxial cable.	The light rays do not get affected by electrical noise. Hence highest noise immunity.
3.	Provides low bandwidth ≈3 to 4 MHz.	Provides high bandwidth ≈ 300 to 400 MHz.	Provides very high bandwidth ≈2 to 3 GHz.
4.	Can be used for low data rates up to 4 mbps.	Can be used for high data rates up to 400 to 500 mbps.	Can be used for very high data rates up to 3 Gbps.
5.	Crosstalk is more.	Crosstalk is moderate.	No crosstalk is present.
6.	Low cost.	Moderate cost.	Very high cost.

...Conti.

7.	Power losses due to conduction and radiation are present.	Power losses due to conduction are present.	Power losses due to bending, dispersion, absorption and scattering are present.
8.	Signal attenuation is more.	Signal attenuation is moderate.	Signal attenuation is least.
9.	Installation is easiest.	Installation is easy.	Installation is difficult.
10.	Signal to noise ratio is less.	Signal to noise ratio is moderate.	Signal to noise ratio is very high.
11.	Low bandwidth	High bandwidth	Very high bandwidth

6.9 WIRELESS MEDIA

- It is also called as unguided media does not use a conductor or wire as a communication channel. Instead it uses air or vacuum as medium to carry the information from transmitter to receiver. The transmitter first converts the data signal into electromagnetic waves and transmits them using suitable antenna. The receiver receives them using a receiving antenna and converts the electromagnetic waves into data signal again as shown in Fig. 6.26.

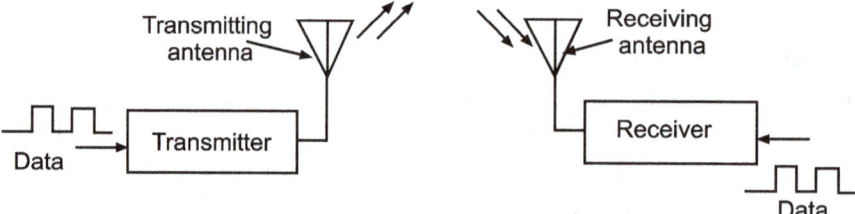

Fig. 6.26: Concept of wireless communication

Propagation Methods:

- The wireless signals can travel from the transmitter to receiver in many different ways the three most important methods are
    1. Ground Wave Propagation
    2. Sky Wave Propagation (Upto ionosphere and back to earth)
    3. Line of sight or Space Wave Propagation as shown in Fig. 6.27.

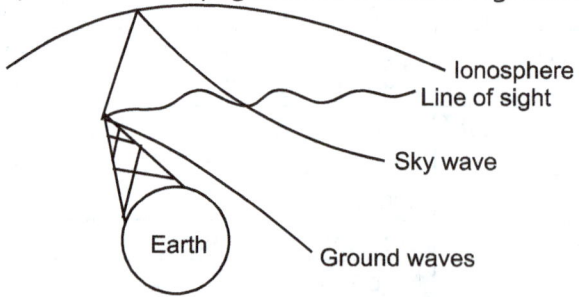

Fig. 6.27: Wave propagation

- There are three main types of wireless media:
  1. Radiowave
  2. Microwave
  3. Infrared

1. **Radio Wave Transmission:**

   Radio waves have frequencies in between 10 kHz to 1 GHz. The range of electromagnetic spectrum between 10 kHz and 1 GHz is called radio frequencies (RF). Radio waves also includes short wave used in AM radio, very high frequency used in FM radio and TV, Ultra high frequency (UHF) used in TV.

   The radio frequency bands are regulated and require a license. Unregulated frequency bands are also present but having low power. Radio wave transmission is possible in two ways omnidirectionally or directionally. The antenna used is shown in Fig. 6.28.

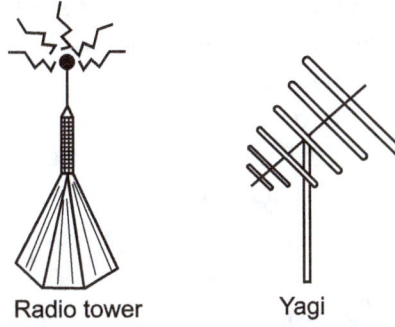

Radio tower   Yagi

Fig. 6.28: Antenna used in radio transmission

- The power of the Radio frequency signal is determined by the antenna and transreceiver.
- For computer network applications, radio waves fall into three categories:
  (a) Low power single frequency
  (b) High power single frequency
  (c) Spread spectrum.
  (a) Low Power Single Frequency: All radio frequencies are included and having bandwidth capacity of 1-10 Mbps. Attenuation is very high but at the same time Installation is simple and low cost.
  (b) High Power Single Frequency: All radio frequencies are included and having bandwidth capacity of 1-10 Mbps. Attenuation is low but the cost is high.
  (c) Spread Spectrum: All radio frequencies typically 902 to 928 MHz is included with bandwidth capacity of 2-6 Mbps. Attenuation is high and cost is moderate.

  The areas of applications of this frequency range is Paging (Tens of Kilometres), Cordless telephone (Tens of metres), Cellular phone (Few 100 km), Wireless LAN (100 m).

  Others applications of radio transmission are Cellular communication, Wireless LAN, Satellite radio systems.

2. Microwave Transmission System:

Microwave uses lower gigahertz frequencies i.e. 1 to 300 GHz of electromagnetic spectrum. Microwaves are unidirectional and propagation is line of sight propagation. The microwave band is wide (299 GHz) so it is possible to allot wider sidebands, So higher data rates are possible in microwave transmission.

These frequencies higher than the RF and they produce better throughput and performance. There are two types of data communication systems

(a) Terrestrial

(b) Satellite.

(a) **Terrestrial Microwave Systems:** These systems uses directional parabolic antennas to transmit and receive signals in the lower gigahertz range as shown in Fig. 6.29. These signals can be narrowly focused and the physical path must be line of sight. Relay towers are used to extend signals. Microwave LANs operate at low power using small transmitters that communicate with omni-directional hubs. Hubs can then be connected to form entire network. The frequency range used for this transmission is 4-6 GHz and 21-23 GHz. Bandwidth required is 1 to 10 mbps. Here attenuation is affected by frequency, signal strength, antenna size and atmospheric conditions. Line of sight requirement makes installation difficult.

Antenna

Fig. 6.29: Terrestrial microwave system

(b) **Satellite Communication:** An satellite orbits or revolves around the earth in exactly the same manner as electron revolves around the nucleus of an atom. The paths in which satellite moves are called as orbits. The orbits are of different types such as synchronous orbits, polar orbits and inclined orbits out of which synchronous or geostationary orbit is used by the geostationary satellites which requires exactly 24 hours to complete one revolution around the earth, therefore they appear to be stationary. Satellite may be used for communication, remote sensing, weather or scientific purpose.

The basic diagram of satellite communication system is shown in Fig. 6.30. An earth station transmit information signal to the satellite using a highly directional dish antenna. The satellite receives this signal, processes it and transmits it back at reduced frequency. The receiving earth station receive this signal using parabolic dish antennas pointed towards the satellite. The signal which is transmitted upwards to the satellite is called as "Uplink" and it is normally frequency of 6 GHz. The signal transmitted back to receiving earth station from satellite is 4 GHz. All these functions of transmit and receive from satellite are performed by a unit called satellite transponder. Satellite generally having two sets of transponders each having 12 making it total 24 transponders. Each transponder having bandwidth of 36 MHz, which is sufficient to handle at least one TV channel. The uplink signal received by transponder is weak and downlink signal transmitted by the transponder is strong. To avoid interference between uplink and downlink frequencies are selected to be of different values.

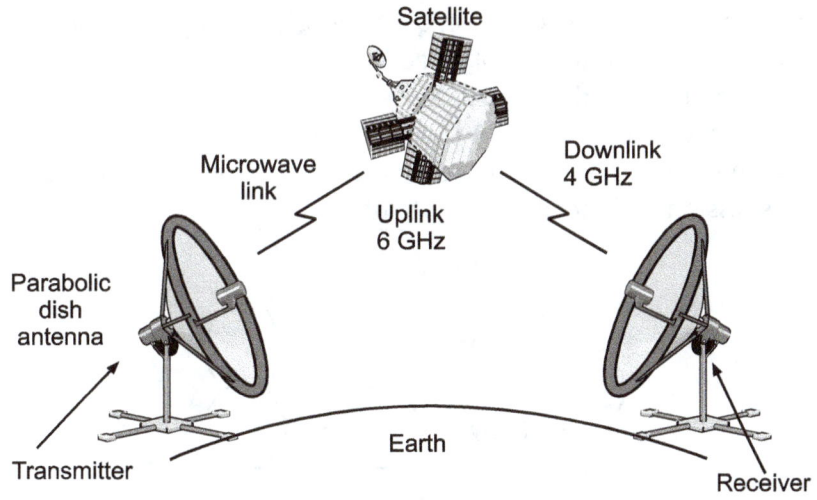

Fig. 6.30

The operation of satellite takes place at very high signal frequencies in microwave range. The typical band of signal frequencies is C band 4/6 GHz, Ku band 11/14 GHz, Ka band 20/30 GHz.

The operations of station keeping and altitude control are executed from the control room in the earth stations. The power requirement of satellite is satisfied by solar panels and a set of nickel cadmium batteries, carried by the satellite himself.

It uses frequency range from 11 to 14 GHz and having bandwidth of range 1 to 10 Mbps.

6.10 MOBILE COMMUNICATION   [Nov. 15, May 13, 15]

- A cellular radio system provides standard telephone operation by full duplex two way radio at remote locations. Cellular radios or telephones can be installed in cars or trucks and are also available in handheld models. Each cellular telephone permits the user to link up with the standard telephone system that permits calls to any part of the world.

Cellular Concepts:

- The basic concept behind the cellular radio system is that rather than serving a given geographical area with a single transmitter and receiver, the system divides the service area into smaller areas known as cells, as shown in Fig. 6.31. The typical cell covers only several square miles and contains its own receiver and low power transmitter. The cell site is designed to reliably serve only vehicles in its small area.

- Each cell is connected by telephone lines or a microwave radio relay link to a master control centre known as the Mobile Telephone Switching System (MTSO). The MTSO control all the cells and provides interface between each cell and the main telephone office. As vehicle containing the telephone passes through a cell, it is served by the cell transreceiver. The telephone call is routed through the MTSO and to the standard telephone system. As the vehicle moves system automatically switches from one cell to the next. The receiver in each cell station continuously monitors the signal strength drops below a desired level, it automatically seeks a cell where the signal from mobile unit stronger. The computer at the MTSO causes the transmission from the vehicle to be switched from weaker cell to stronger cell. This is called a handoff. All of this takes place in a very short period of time and is completely unnoticeable to the user. The result is optimum transmission and reception is obtained.

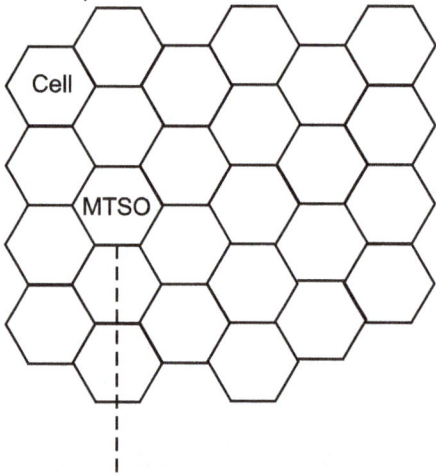

To from telephone system

Fig. 6.31: Cellular communication system

- The cellular system operates in the 800 to 900 MHz range, previously reserved for the higher UHF TV channels through 83, which were rarely used. Originally, there were 666, 30 kHz wide full duplex channels are available for communications now-a-days 832 channels are used. The cellular system also known as frequency reuse, which allows cells within the system to use the same frequency channel. Because the cells are physically small, and low power transmitters are used, and the cell sites use directional antennas, the signal does not stray beyond cell boundaries. This allows other cells within system to share the same frequency channel without interference. Another feature of cellular system is that different cell sizes can be accommodated. In low usage areas cell sizes can be large. As the number of user increase larger cells can be divided into smaller areas. This provides ease of expansion as the number of user grows. A typical system can serve up to about 50,000 subscribers and 10,000 of them may use the system simultaneously. The newer systems are digital can operate in 1.7 to 1.8 GHz.

6.11 GLOBAL SYSTEM OF MOBILE COMMUNICATION
[Dec. 12, 14, May 13, 14, 16]

- This system is widely used throughout the world. It uses the 890 to 915 MHz band for uplink signals and the 935 to 960 MHz band for downlink signals. In newer GSM systems, referred to as DCS-1800, the uplink range is 1.71 to 1.785 GHz and the downlink frequencies are 1.805 to 1.88 GHz. The spacing between the uplink and downlink signals is 45 MHz on the lower frequencies and 95 MHz on the upper frequencies. Each channel has bandwidth of 25 kHz.

- In order to achieve the uplink and downlink process simultaneously in their own 25 kHz channel. The carrier spacing of channel is 200 kHz. There are 124 channels in the lower frequency band and 374 channels in the upper frequency band.

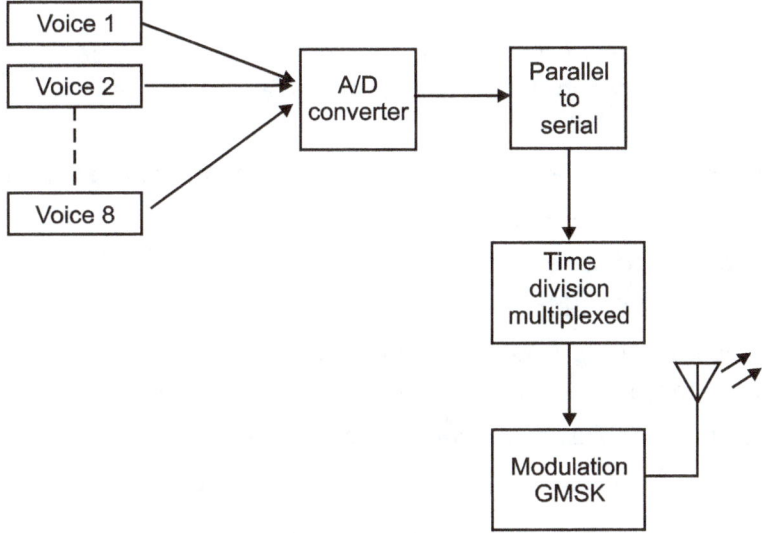

Fig. 6.32

- Basically, GSM shown in Fig. 6.32 uses time division multiplexing to allow eight simultaneous telephone calls to use each channel. This system is known as time division multiples access (TDMA). The voice signals are digitized by an A/D converter and converted to serial format. The basic digitized bit rate is 13 kbits/s. The serial voice data is time multiplexed into eight channels. Each voice channel contains one digital sample of the audio signal. Some channels may be blank if they are not being used. The type of modulation used in GSM is called Gaussian Minimum Shift Keying (GMSK). Minimum shift keying is form of frequency shift keying in which the two frequencies selected to represent binary 0 and 1 are related in such a way that their zero crossing times are same. When switching between frequencies takes place, it occurs at the zero crossing points. This reduces the number of harmonics. Therefore, bandwidth used by an MSK signal is narrower than a standard FSK signal.

QUESTIONS

1. Draw and explain the communication system? What are types? Explain the each type in brief.

2. Draw the diagram which shows various radio frequency ranges? Explain each range.

3. Write a short note on IEEE electromagnetic frequency spectrum.

4. What is need of modulation and explain its types?

5. What does modulation actually do to message and carrier?

6. Differentiate between AM and FM.

7. What are the standard broadcast frequency band for AM and FM.

8. Which two input signals are used in amplitude modulation? Explain the purpose of each signal.

9. What do you mean by FM? Write the expression for instantaneous value of FM voltage and modulation index? Explain the relation between modulation index and frequency deviation in FM.

10. Write the expression of AM? Draw and explain the frequency spectrum for AM.

11. Draw the waveforms for the following :

    (a) Amplitude modulation

    (b) Frequency modulation.

12. Define amplitude modulation and modulation index. Use a sketch of a sinusoidal modulated AM waveform to help to explain the definition.

13. Write a note on mobile cellular telephone system.

14. With different layers and frequency range used explain wireless communication system in detail.

15. Explain the communication using fibre optic cable.

16. Draw basic construction of fibre optic cable. Explain various types of fibre optic cable.

17. Draw and explain construction of fibre optic cable.

18. Explain problems associated with twisted pair cables. State different types of twisted pair cables.

19. What are the main sections of an optical fibre? Explain function of each section.

20. Write a short note on Global system of mobile communication.

UNIVERSITY QUESTIONS

Dec. 2012

1. Draw and explain the block diagram of an electronic communication system. **[7]**

2. What is the need of modulation? What are the different types of modulation? **[6]**

3. Draw waveforms and explain amplitude modulation technique. Write the expression of AM and define modulation index. **[7]**

4. Draw and explain the block diagram of GSM. **[6]**

May 2013

1. What is the importance of modulation index. Draw the AM waveform for **[8]**

   (i) Linear modulation

   (ii) Over modulation

   (iii) Modulation index = 0

2. Explain the basic structure of mobile phone system. **[5]**

3. With respect to FM explain.(08)

   (i) Frequency deviation

   (ii) Modulation index

   (iii) Deviation ratio

   (iv) Frequency spectrum of FM

4. Write a note on co-axial cable and optical fibre cable **[5]**

Dec. 2013

1. Explain the elements of communication systems with the help of block diagram. **[7]**

2. What is baseband communication. Explain limitation of baseband communication and explain need for modulation. **[6]**

3. Write the expression of Amplitude modulation. Define modulation index and draw waveform of AM. **[6]**

4. Draw and explain block diagram of GSM system. **[7]**

May 2014

1. Give advantages, disadvantages and applications of Co-axial cable. **[6]**

2. Explain the block diagram of GSM system. **[7]**

3. Define Modulation index with reference to AM and FM. Draw AM waveform for overmodulation case. **[6]**

4. Write a note on Optical Fiber and explain how light travels through a fiber. **[7]**

October 2014

1. Draw and explain the electromagnetic of IEEE frequency spectrum.   **[7]**
2. Compare AM and FM.   **[6]**
3. Draw and explain the block diagram of GSM.   **[7]**
4. A carrier of 10 V peak and frequency 100 kHz is amplitude modulated by a sine wave of 4 V peak and frequency 1000 Hz. Determine the modulation index for the modulated wave and draw the frequency spectrum for AM wave.   **[6]**

May 2015

1. Draw and explain the electromagnetic spectrum or IEEE frequency spectrum. List its applications.   **[7]**
2. Compare : AM and FM.   **[6]**
3. What is modulation? Explain AM technique in detail and write AM expression. **[7]**
4. Explain the basic structure of mobile phone system.   **[6]**

Nov. 2015

1. What is need of modulation? Explain frequency modulation in detail.   **[7]**
2. Draw and explain block diagram of mobile communication system.   **[6]**
3. Draw AM waveforms for :   **[3]**
   (i)   Modulation index = 1
   (ii) Modulation index > 1
   (iii) Modulation index < 1.
4. Write short notes on :   **[6]**
   (i) Twisted pair cable
   (ii) Fibre optic cable.
5. Compare amplitude modulation and frequency modulation.   **[4]**

May 2016

1. Define AM, Derive expression for AM. Write expression for modulation index. Draw waveforms of AM.   **[7]**
2. Write short note on :
   (i) Coaxial Cable
   (ii) Fiber Optic Cable.   **[6]**
3. Draw and Explain block diagram of GSM system   **[6]**
4. With respect to FM explain
   (i)   Frequency deviation
   (ii) Modulation index.
   (iii) Deviation ratio
   (iv) Frequency spectrum of FM.   **[7]**

SAMPLE QUESTION PAPERS
End-Sem. (Theory) Examination

Time : 2 Hours   **Max. Marks : 50**

Sample Question Paper I

Q.1 (a) For the clipping circuit shown in the Figure Q. 1(a).

Draw : Output waveform for the given input voltage waveform shown in the Figure Q.1 (b). Assume V_F for Silicon diodes = 0.7V and R_f = 0.   **[4 M]**

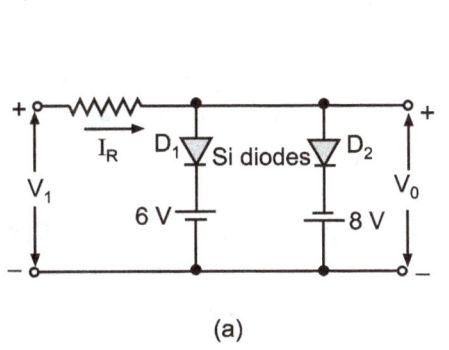
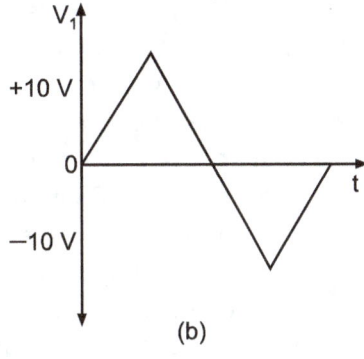

(a)   (b)

Fig. 1

(b) Draw diagram of ideal and practical equivalent circuit of Zener diode.   **[2 M]**

(c) Draw constructional details and explain operation of P-channel MOSFET. **[6 M]OR**

Q.2 (a) Draw neat circuits diagram of a Bridge Rectifier with Capacitor Filter and also draw the waveform across output terminals.   **[3 M]**

(b) Write short note on Voltage Tripler.   **[3 M]**

(c) What is DC load line? Give its significance and derive its equation for CE Amplifier.   **[6 M]**

Q.3 (a) Draw the neat circuit diagram and explain the working of an non-inverting Comparator.   **[4 M]**

(b) Give the typical values of following parameters for IC741:

(1) Input resistance (2) Bias current (3) Slew rate (4) CMRR.   **[2 M]**

(c) What is MUX? Give the relation between number of input and select lines. Also write applications of MUX.   **[6 M] OR**

Q.4 (a) Explain with neat sketch, the working of IC555 as an Oscillator.   **[4 M]**

(b) Compare positive and negative feedback.   **[2 M]**

(c) Draw and explain block diagram of Microprocessor.   **[6 M]**

Q.5 (a) Explain constructions working and V-I characteristics of TRIAC.   **[7 M]**

(b) What is Piezoresistivity? Explain the operation of transducer working on piezoresistivity principle. State its advantages and disadvantages.   **[6 M] OR**

Q.6 (a) Mention the factors to be considered while selecting a transducer for an application.   **[6 M]**

(b) What do you mean by active transducer? Explain any two type of active transducer.   **[7 M]**

Q.7 (a) What is need of modulation? Explain. Give comparison between AM and FM.   **[6 M]**

(b) Draw and explain block diagram of Global system of mobile communication. **[7 M] OR**

Q.8 **(a)** Write a short note on Global system of mobile communication. **[6 M]**

(b) What do you mean by FM? Write the expression for instantaneous value of FM voltage and modulation index? Explain the relation between modulation index and frequency deviation in FM. **[7 M]**

Sample Question Paper II

Q.1 **(a)** A Fullwave Bridge rectifier is supplied from 230V, 50Hz and uses a transformer of turns ratio 15:1. It uses load resistance of 50Ω. Calculate Load voltage and Ripple voltage. Assume value of Ripple factor and Ideal Diodes. **[3 M]**

(b) Draw and explain voltage doubler circuit using p-n junction diode. **[3 M]**

(c) Draw common base input characteristics of a transistor. What is Early effect? How can it account for the CB input characteristics? **[6 M] OR**

Q.2 **(a)** What is clipper? Describe the operation of positive and negative clippers with the the help of circuit diagrams. **[6 M]**

(b) Describe the construction and operation of a MOSFET in enhancement mode. Draw its characteristics and equivalent circuit of the device. **[6 M]**

Q.3 **(a)** Write a short note on IC voltage regulators. **[4 M]**

(b) Give the applications of IC555. **[2 M]**

(c) Implement following function using two 4:1 MUX F(A,B,C) = Σm(0,1,5,6) **[6 M] OR**

Q.4 **(a)** Draw the circuit diagram of integrator and explain its working. Draw the output Waveform for square wave input. **[6 M]**

(b) What is shift register? What are modes of operation in a Shift Register? Explain the operation of 4-bit PIPO shift register. **[6 M]**

Q.5 **(a)** Compare SCR and TRIAC. **[4 M]**

(b) What is RTD? Draw its construction diagram and explain. **[3 M]**

(c) List different pressure transducers. Explain the working of any one in detail. **[6 M] OR**

Q.6 **(a)** Explain the following characteristics of transducer:

(a) Accuracy. (b) Ruggedness. (c) Linearity. (d) Repeatability. **[8 M]**

(b) What is load cell? What is it use? **[5 M]**

Q.7 **(a)** Write the expression of Amplitude Modulation. Define Modulation Index and draw waveform for AM. **[7 M]**

(b) Draw and explain block diagram of Mobile cellular communication system. **[6 M]**

OR

Q.8 **(a)** Explain problems associated with twisted pair cables. State different types of twisted pair cables. **[5 M]**

(b) With different layers and frequency range used explain wireless communication system in detail. **[8 M]**

◈ ◈ ◈

Chapter 1

1. Compare performance of half-wave rectifier and full-wave rectifier with respect to following parameters.

   (1) I_{DC}, (2) V_{DC}, (3) I_{rms} (4) Rectifier efficiency, (5) TUF, (6) PIV of diodes used, (7) Ripple factor. **[6]**

Ans. Refer to Section 1.8 on page 1.30.

Chapter 2

1. Draw constructional details and explain operation and characteristics of n-channel MOSFET (enhancement type). **[6]**

Ans. Refer to Section 2.22 on page 2.36.

2. Explain with a circuit diagram a single stage common emitter amplifier. State the function of each component in the circuit. **[6]**

Ans. Refer to Section 2.9 on page 2.13.

Chapter 3

1. What is op-amp? Draw and explain the functional block diagram of an op-amp.

   [6]

Ans. Refer to Section 3.2 on page 3.1 and Section 3.4 on page 3.2.

2. With the help of block diagram of IC 555 explain its operation in astable mode.

   [6]

Ans. Refer to Section 3.20 on page 3.36.

Chapter 4

1. State and prove the De-Morgan's theorems. Use De-morgan's theorem to simplify

   the following Boolean expression. $Y = \overline{\overline{A}B + A\overline{B}}$. **[6]**

Ans. Refer to Section 4.4.1 on page 4.9.

2. Give a comparison between the microprocessor and microcontroller. **[6]**

Ans. Refer to Section 4.16 on page 4.35.

Chapter 5

1. Draw construction diagram and explain the working with the help of transistor equivalent circuit of SCR. Also draw its V-I characteristics. **[7]**

Ans. Refer to Section 5.1 on page 5.1 and 5.1.2 on page 5.2.

2. Draw construction diagram and explain the V-I characteristics of a TRIAC. What are the applications of a TRIAC? **[7]**

Ans. Refer to Section 5.3 on page 5.5 and 5.3.1 on page 5.8.

3. With a neat diagram explain the construction and working of LVDT. Give its advantages and disadvantages. **[6]**
Ans. Refer to Section 5.12 on page 5.27.
4. Explain with a block diagram an electronic weighing machine. **[6]**
Ans. Refer to Section 5.17 on page 5.33.

Chapter 6

1. Draw and explain the block diagram of an electronic communication system. **[7]**
Ans. Refer to Section 6.5 on page 6.10.
2. What is the need of modulation? What are the different types of modulation? **[6]**
Ans. Refer to Section 6.8 and Section 6.5.2 on page 6.11.
3. Draw waveforms and explain amplitude modulation technique. Write the expression of AM and define modulation index. **[7]**
Ans. Refer to Section 6.6 on page 6.10 and Section 6.6.1 and 6.6.2 on page 6.11 and 6.12 respectively.
4. Draw and explain the block diagram of GSM. **[6]**
Ans. Refer to Section 6.11 on page 6.37.

May 2013

Time : 2 Hrs. **Max. Marks : 50**

1. **(a)** Sketch I_R and V_0 w.r.t. time for the network shown in Fig. A. Assume both the diodes are silicon type with $V_f = 0.7$ V **[6]**

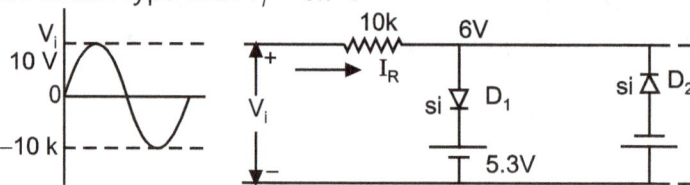

Fig. A

Ans.

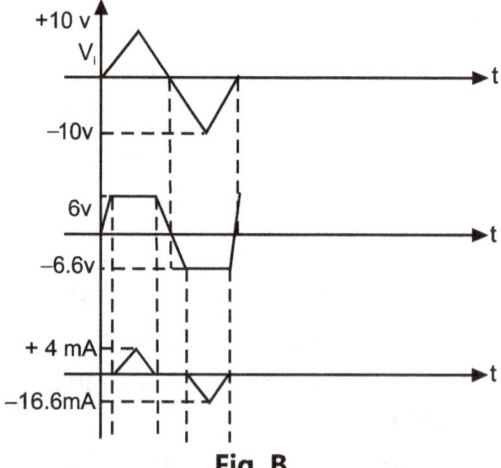

Fig. B

(b) For a BJT as a switch why CB and cc configurations are not preferred.   **[2]**

Ans. Please Refer to Article No. 2.19 on Page No. 2.32.

(c) Explain how R_i and R_o affect the performance of the BJT voltage amplifier.   **[4]**

Ans. Please Refer to Article No 2.18 on Page No. 2.31.

OR

2. **(a)** Explain with V-1 characteristics the working of zener diode as voltage regulator. **[6]**

Ans. Please Refer to Article Nos. 1.12.1 & 1.12.5 on Page Nos. 1.57 & 1.60.

(b) In the voltage amplifier shown in Fig. B, V_S = 100m V R_S = 50 Ω   **[6]**

    (i) Calculate input voltage V_i if the input resistance R_i is 600 Ω

    (ii) What should be the value of R_i to get V_i = 75 mV

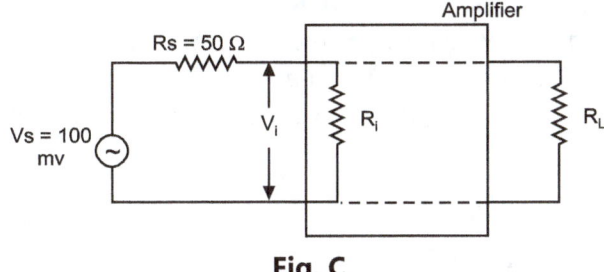

Fig. C

Ans. Vs = 100 mv, Rs. = 50 Ω

    (i) Vi = ?

$$V_i = Vs \times \frac{R_i}{R_s + R_i} = 92.5 \text{ mv}$$

$$V_i = 100 \text{ mv} \times \frac{600}{600 + 50} = 92.5 \text{ mv}$$

    (ii) R_i = ? , V_i = 75 mv

$$75 \text{ mv} = 100 \text{ mv} \times \frac{R_i}{50 + R_i} = 150 \text{ Ω}$$

3. **(a)** In Fig. C if V_a = +2V V_b = + 4 V   **[4]**
$R_a = R_b = R_1$ = 1k Ω and R_f = 3 k Ω
determine the voltage V_1 at non-inverting terminal of OP-AMP and output voltage V_o

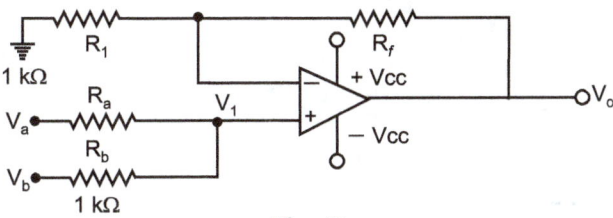

Fig. D

Ans. $V_a = +2V$, $V_b = +4v$

$R_a = R_b = R_1 = 1\ k\Omega$ & $R_f = 3\ k\Omega$.

$$V_1 = \frac{V_a + V_b}{2} \text{ for non inserting summing amplifier.}$$

$$V_1 = \frac{2+4}{2} = 3v$$

$$Vo = \left(1 + \frac{R_f}{R_1}\right) \times V_1 = \left(1 + \frac{R_f}{R_1}\right) \times 3\ V$$

$$V_o = 12\ V$$

(b) Draw the block diagram of full adder using two half adder, explain its working with proper expression for sum and carry. **[6]**

Ans. Please Refer Article No. 4.7.2 on Page No. 4.16.

OR

4. (a) With neat waveform explain IC555 in astable mode. **[6]**

Ans. Please Refer to Article No. 3.20.1 on Page No 3.35.

(b) Implement the following logic expression with minimum number of NAND gate. **[6]**

(i) $y_1 = B(\bar{D} + \bar{C}D)$

(ii) $y_2 = AB + CD + B\bar{C}$

Ans.

(i) $y_1 = B.(\bar{D} + \bar{C}.D)$

            $= B.(\bar{D} + \bar{C}).(\bar{D} + \bar{C}) = B.\bar{D} + B.\bar{C}$

            $= B.(\bar{D} + \bar{C})$

Total = 03

Fig. E

(ii) $\bar{\bar{y_2}} = \overline{\overline{A.B} + \overline{C.D} + \overline{B.\bar{C}}} = \overline{(\overline{A.B}).(\overline{C.D}).(\overline{B.\bar{C}})}$

Total = 05

Fig. F

5. **(a)** Explain in detail, the selection criteria for transducer.   **[6]**

Ans. Please Refer to Article No. 5.8 on Page No. 5.12.

(b) Explain in detail.   **[7]**

(i) Construction of TRIAC (ii) Characteristics of TRIAC (iii) Modes of operation

Ans. Please Refer to Article No 5.3 on Page No. 5.6.

OR

6. **(a)** Explain with block diagram an electronic weighing machine.   **[6]**

Ans. Please Refer to Article No. 5.17 on Page No. 5.33.

(b) Explain the construction of DIAC w.r.t   **[7]**

(i) Characteristics (ii) Application

Ans. Please Refer to Article No. 5.2 on Page No. 5.5.

7. **(a)** What is the importance of modulation index. Draw the AM waveform for   **[8]**

(i) Linear modulation

(ii) Over modulation

(iii) Modulation index = 0

Ans. Please Refer to Article No. 6.6.2 on Pages No 6.12.

(b) Explain the basic structure of mobile phone system.   **[5]**

Ans. Please Refer to Article No. 6.10 on Page Nos. 6.35.

OR

8. **(a)** With respect to FM explain.   **[8]**
(i) Frequency deviation   (ii) Modulation index
(iii) Deviation ratio   (iv) Frequency spectrum of FM

Ans. Please Refer to Articles No. 6.7 (5) on Page No 6.20

(b) Write a note on co-axial cable and optical fibre cable   **[5]**

Ans. Please Refer to Articles Nos. 6.8.4 & 6.8.5 on Page Nos. 6.29 & 6.30.

Dec. 2013

Time : 2 Hrs.   **Max. Marks : 50**

1. **(a)** Draw the circuit of series negative clipper and explain its operation along with the waveform.   **[6]**

Ans. Please Refer to Article No. 1.10.3, Page No. 1.45.

(b) Explain working of transistor as a switch.   **[4]**

Ans. Please Refer to Article No. 2.19, Page No. 2.32.

(c) Define current amplification factor for CC, CB, CE configuration.   **[2]**

Ans. Please Refer to Article No. 2.8, 2.9, 2.11, Page No. 2.9, 2.13, 2.17.

2. (a) Draw the waveform across R_L in clamping circuit. **[6]**

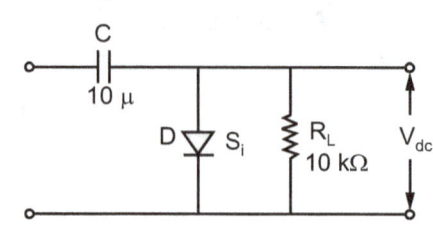

Fig. (a)

Ans. Please Refer to Article No. 1.10.2, Page No. 1.44.

(b) Explain drain and transfer chara. of Enhancement type p-channel MOSFET. **[6]**

Ans. Please Refer to Article No. 2.23, Page No. 2.38.

3. (a) Draw and explain Internal block diagram of IC 555. **[6]**

Ans. Please Refer to Article No. 3.20, Page No. 3.34.

(b) Draw the schematic diagram and explain working of 4:1 mux and 1:4 demux. **[6]**

Ans. Please Refer to Article No. 4.8.2, 4.9, Page No. 4.19 and 4.20.

OR

4. (a) Find output voltage V_o of op-amp circuit shown in Fig. (b) below: **[6]**

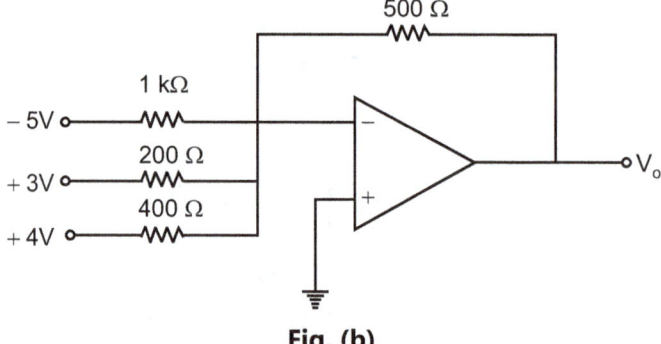

Fig. (b)

Ans. Please Refer to Example No. 3.4, Page No. 3.22.

(b) State different types of counter and design 3-bit negative edge triggered asynchronous down counter. **[6]**

Ans. Please Refer to Article No. 4.13, Page No. 4.29.

5. (a) Draw and explain operation of SCR using two transistor equivalent circuit. **[6]**

Ans. Please Refer to Article No. 5.1, Page No. 5.1.

(b) Draw and explain block diagram of instrumentation system. **[7]**

Ans. Please Refer to Article No. 5.5, Page No. 5.9.

6. (a) Draw constructional diagram and explain working of V-I characteristic of Diac. **[6]**

Ans. Please Refer to Article No. 5.2, Page No. 5.5.

(b) Draw and explain the construction and operation of LVDT.   [7]

Ans. Please Refer to Article No. 5.12, Page No. 5.27.

7.   **(a)** Explain the elements of communication systems with the help of block diagram. **[7]**

Ans. Please Refer to Article No. 6.1.1, Page No. 6.1.

(b) What is baseband communication. Explain limitation of baseband communication and explain need for modulation.   [6]

Ans. Please Refer to Article No. 6.3, 6.5, Page No. 6.5, 6.7.

8.   **(a)** Write the expression of Amplitude modulation. Define modulation index and draw waveform of AM.   [6]

Ans. Please Refer to Article No. 6.6, Page No. 6.10.

(b) Draw and explain block diagram of GSM system.   [7]

Ans. Please Refer to Article No. 6.11, Page No. 6.37.

May 2014

Time : 2 Hours   **Max. Marks : 50**

1.   **(a)** Explain Voltage tripler and quadrupler circuit.   [6]

Ans. Please Refer to Article No. 1.11 Page No. 1.55.

(b) Explain input output characteristics of CE amplifier.   [6]

Ans. Please Refer to Article No. 2.9 Page No. 2.13.

OR

2.   **(a)** Explain working principle of photo diode with characteristics. Why photodiode is operated in reverse biased mode when used as a optical detector.   [6]

Ans. Please Refer to Article No. 1.15 Page No. 1.72-1.73.

(b) Explain Drain Characteristics of an n-channel enhancement type MOSFET.   [6]

Ans. Please Refer to Article No. 2.22.2 Page No. 2.38.

3.   **(a)** Explain Daw the circuit diagram and write the output equation for   [6]

   (i)   Inverting summer with three inputs

   (ii)   Ideal differentiator

Ans. Please Refer to Page No. 3.21 and 3.31.

(b) Explain the operation of multiplexer and Demultiplexer.   [6]

Ans. Please Refer to Article No. 4.8 and 4.9 Page No. 4.18-4.20.

OR

4.   **(a)** Draw three pin IC voltage regulator. Define load and Line regulation.   [6]

Ans. Please Refer to Article No. 3.21 Page No. 3.39.

(b) Implement the following with minimum number of NAND gates.   **[6]**

(i)   y = AD + CB

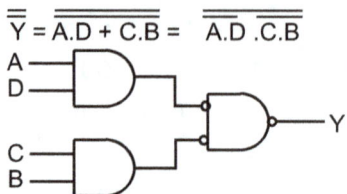

$$\overline{\overline{Y}} = \overline{A.D + C.B} = \overline{\overline{A.D} . \overline{C.B}}$$

(ii)   z = A($\overline{B}$ + CD)

$$\overline{\overline{Z}} = \overline{\overline{A(B + C.D)}} = \overline{(A.\overline{B}) . (A.C.D)}$$

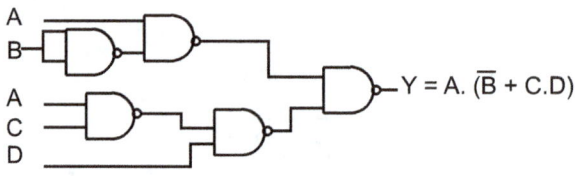

Y = A. ($\overline{B}$ + C.D)

5. (a) Explain with block diagram Digital Thermometer.   **[7]**

Ans.   Please Refer to Article No. 5.16 Page No. 5.32.

(b) Explain construction of SCR.   **[6]**

Ans.   Please Refer to Article No. 5.1 Page No. 5.1.

OR

6. (a) Explain various criteria used to select a transducer.   **[7]**

Ans.   Please Refer to Article No. 5.8 Page No. 5.12.

(b) Explain Characteristics of DIAC.   **[6]**

Ans.   Please Refer to Article No. 5.2 Page No. 5.5

7. (a) Give advantages, disadvantages and applications of Co-axial cable.   **[6]**

Ans.   Please Refer to Article No. 6.8.4 Page No. 6.29

(b) Explain the block diagram of GSM system.   **[7]**

Ans.   Please Refer to Article No. 6.11 Page No. 6.37

OR

8. (a) Define Modulation index with reference to AM and FM. Draw AM waveform for overmodulation case.   **[6]**

Ans.   Please Refer to Page No. 6.22 and 6.25

(b) Write a note on Optical Fiber and explain how light travels through a fiber.   **[7]**

Ans.   Please Refer to Article No. 6.8.5 Page No. 6.30.

Oct. 2014

Time : 2 Hrs.   **Max. Marks : 50**

1. (A) Compare performance of half wave rectifier and full wave rectifier with respect to following parameters : (1) IDC, (2) Irms, (3) Rectifier efficiency, (4) Ripple factor, (5) PIV, (6) TUF.   **[6]**

Ans.: Please Refer Section 1.8 on Page 1.30.

(B) Explain how transistor can be used as an amplifier with the help of D.C. load line approach.   **[6]**

Ans.: Please Refer Section 2.14.1 on Page 2.21.   **OR**

2. (A) Explain the operation of n-channel enhancement type MOSFET with its characteristics.   **[6]**

Ans.: Please Refer Section 2.22.2 on Page 2.38.

(B) Determine the O/P waveforms for the circuit shown in Fig. 1.   **[6]**

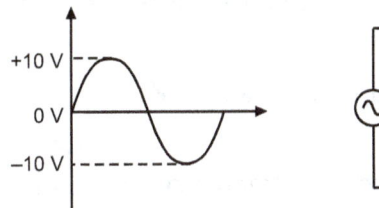 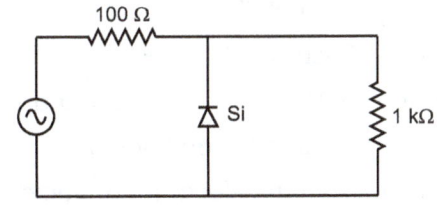

Fig. 1

Ans.: Please Refer Example 1.17 on Page 1.51.

3. (A) Explain the working of inverting summing amplifier with two inputs along with its waveforms.   **[6]**

Ans.: Inverting summing for two inputs

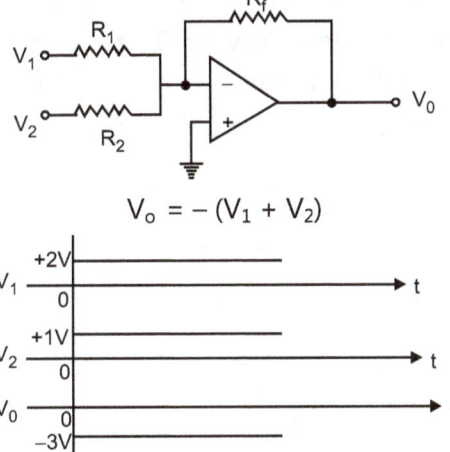

$$V_o = -(V_1 + V_2)$$

Fig. 2

(B) State and prove the De-Morgan's theorem. Simplify the following Boolean expression: $\overline{\overline{A}B + A\overline{B}}$ **[6]**

Ans.: Please Refer Section 4.4.1 on Page 4.9.   **OR**

4. (A) With the help of block diagram of IC555 explain its operation in Astable mode. **[6]**

Ans.: Please Refer Section 3.20 on Page 3.34.

(B) Compare Microprocessor and microcontroller. **[6]**

Ans.: Please Refer Section 4.16 on Page 4.35.

5. (A) Explain the operation of SCR with the help of V-I characteristics. **[7]**

Ans.: Please Refer Section 5.1.2 on Page 5.2.

(B) Explain the selection criteria of a Transducer. **[6]**

Ans.: Please Refer Section 5.8 on Page 5.12.   **OR**

6. (A) Define 'Dark current'. Draw and explain the characteristics of photo transistor. **[6]**

Ans.: Please Refer Section 5.14 on Page 5.30.

(B) Explain the construction of DIAC and draw its characteristics. **[7]**

Ans.: Please Refer Section 5.2 on Page 5.5.

7. (A) Draw and explain the electromagnetic of IEEE frequency spectrum. **[7]**

Ans.: Please Refer Section 6.4 on Page 6.5.

(B) Compare AM and FM. **[6]**

Ans.: Please Refer Section 6.7.6 on Page 6.25.   **OR**

8. (A) Draw and explain the block diagram of GSM. **[7]**

Ans.: Please Refer Section 6.11 on Page 6.37.

(B) A carrier of 10 V peak and frequency 100 kHz is amplitude modulated by a sinewave of 4 V peak and frequency 1000 Hz. Determine the modulation index for the modulated wave and draw the frequency spectrum for AM wave. **[6]**

Ans.: $E_c = 10$ V, $E_m = 4$V, $f_c = 100$ kHz, $f_m = 1000$ Hz

$$m = \frac{E_m}{E_c} = \frac{4}{10} = 0.4$$

$$f_{USB} = f_c + f_m = 101 \text{ kHz}$$

$$f_{LSB} = f_c - f_m = 99 \text{ kHz}$$

Amplitude of each side band $= \dfrac{mE_c}{2}$

$$= \frac{0.4 \times 10}{2} = 2V$$

Frequency spectrum

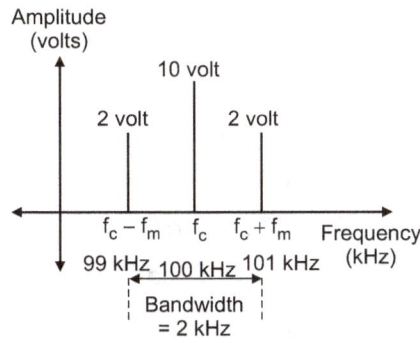

Fig. 3

May 2015

Time : 2 Hours   **Max. Marks : 50**

1. (a) Explain the working of positive clamper with its waveforms.   **[6]**

Ans. Please Refer Section 1.10 on Page No. 1.48.

(b) What is dc load line? Explain the role of Q-point on dc load line.   **[6]**

Ans. Please Refer Q. 1(b) of Dec.-2014.

OR

2. (a) Explain the working of positive biased shunt clipper with its input and output waveforms.   **[6]**

Ans. Please Refer Section 1.10 on Page No. 1.45.

(b) Differentiate between CB, CE and CC configurations.   **[6]**

Ans. Please Refer Section 2.12 on Page No. 2.20.

3. (a) In shown in the following Fig. 1 let R1 = R2 = 1 kΩ. R3 = 5 kΩ, Rf = 10 kΩ, V1 = −1 V, V2 = 2 V and V3 = 4 V. Calculate Vo.   **[6]**

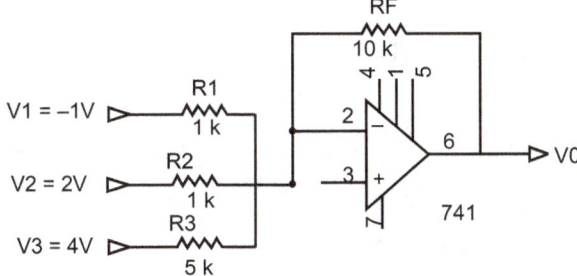

Fig. 1

Ans. Please Refer Example 3.4 on Page No. 3.22.

(b) State the IC number for the following two input logic gate :   **[6]**

(i) AND   (ii) NAND   (iii) OR

(iv) NOR   (v) EX-OR   (vi) NOT

Ans. Please Refer Section 4.3 on Page No. 4.2.

OR

4. (a) Define the following parameters of op-amp :   **[6]**

(i) BW   (ii) PSRR   (iii) CMRR.

Ans. (i) Please Refer Section 3.6, Point 4 on Page No. 3.4.

(ii) Please Refer Section 3.9, Point 6 on Page No. 3.7.

(iii) Please Refer Section 3.9, Point 7 on Page No. 3.7.

(b) Draw the explain full adder using two half adder with its truth table.   **[6]**

Ans. Please Refer Q. 3(b) of May-2013.

5. (a) With a neat diagram explain the construction and working of LVDT. Give its advantages, disadvantages and applications.   **[7]**

Ans. Please Refer Q. 3 of Dec.-2012 in Chapter-5.

(b) Draw a neat block diagram of a digital thermometer and explain its operation.   **[6]**

Ans. Please Refer Q. 5(a) of May-2014.

OR

6. (a) Write a short note on selection criterion for transducers.   **[7]**

Ans. Please Refer Q. 6(a) of May-2014 and Q. 5(a) of Dec.-2013.

(b) Compare :   (i) SCR and TRIAC (ii) DIAC and TRIAC   **[6]**

Ans. Please Refer Q. 5(b) and Q. 6(b) of May-2013.

7. (a) Draw and explain the electromagnetic spectrum or IEEE frequency spectrum. List its applications.   **[7]**

Ans. Please Refer Q. 7(a) of Dec. 2014.

(b) Compare : AM and FM.   **[6]**

Ans. Please Refer Q. 7(b) of Dec. 2014.

OR

8. (a) What is modulation? Explain AM technique in detail and write AM expression.   **[7]**

Ans. Please Refer Q. 8(a) of Dec. 2013.

(b) Explain the basic structure of mobile phone system.   **[6]**

Ans. Please Refer Q. 7(b) of May 2013.

Nov. 2015

Time : 2 Hours   **Max. Marks : 50**

1. (a) Compare half wave and full wave rectifier.   **[6]**

Ans. Please Refer Article No. 1.8 on Page No. 1.30.

(b) Explain operation of n-channel enhancement type MOSFET with its characteristics. **[6]**

Ans.   Please Refer to Article No. 2.22.2 on Page No. 2.38.

OR

2. (a) Determine output waveform for the circuit shown in Fig. 1 :   **[6]**

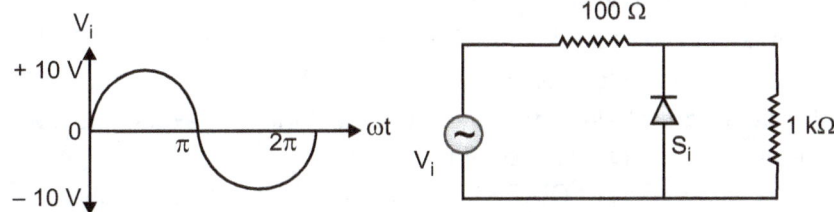

Fig. 1

Ans.   Please Refer Example 1.17 on Page No. 1.51.

(b) Draw the output characteristics of BJT in CE configuration. Indicate all the three regions of operation on it. Explain the operation of BJT as a switch.   **[6]**

Ans.   Please Refer Article No. 2.9.2 and 2.19 on Page No. 2.13 and 2.32.

3. (a) Draw the circuit diagram and write output equation for :   **[6]**

   (i) Non-inverting summer with three inputs

   (ii) Ideal differentiator.

Ans.   (i) Please Refer to Article No. 3.16.2 on Page No. 3.23.

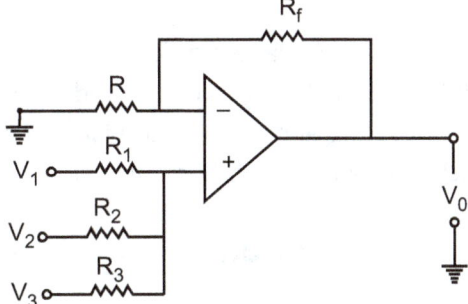

Fig. 2

   (ii) Please Refer Article No. 3.18 on Page No. 3.29.

(b) Compare microprocessor and microcontroller.   **[4]**

Ans.   Please Refer to Article No. 4.16 on Page No. 4.35.

(c) Prove the following using De Morgan's theorem.   **[2]**

$$\overline{(A + B) \cdot (C + D)} = (\bar{A} \cdot \bar{B}) + (\bar{C} \cdot \bar{D}).$$

Ans.   Please Refer Example 4.9 (ii) on Page No. 4.71.

OR

4. (a) For inverting amplifier using op-amp if R_f = 100 kΩ, R_1 = 10 kΩ, V_{CC} = $\pm$10 V, V_i = 2 V d.c. : **[6]**

　　　(i) Calculate output voltage

　　　(ii) Is the result in part (i) is practically possible? Justify.

Ans.　Please Refer Example 3.2 on Page No. 3.13.

　(b) How to implement full adder using 2 half adders and logic gates? Explain. **[6]**

Ans.　Please Refer to Article No. 4.7.3 on Page No. 4.17.

5. (a) Draw block diagram of electronic weighing machine and explain its operation. **[6]**

Ans.　Please Refer to Article No. 5.17 on Page No. 5.33.

　(b) Explain the construction of DIAC. Draw and explain its characteristics. **[7]**

Ans.　Please Refer to Article No. 5.2 on Page No. 5.5.

OR

6. (a) Explain digital thermometer with block diagram. **[6]**

Ans.　Please Refer to Article No. 5.16 on Page No. 5.32.

　(b) Define the following terms for SCR : **[5]**

　　　(i) Holding current

　　　(ii) Latching current

　　　(iii) Forward breakover voltage

　　　(iv) Reverse breakover voltage

　　　(v) Turn ON time for SCR.

Ans.　Please Refer to Article No. 5.1.6 on Page No. 5.5.

　(c) List applications of SCR. **[2]**

Ans.　Please refer to Article No. 5.1.6 on Page No. 5.5.

7. (a) What is need of modulation? Explain frequency modulation in detail. **[7]**

Ans.　Please Refer to Article No. 6.5.1 and 6.7 on Page No. 6.8 and 6.20.

　(b) Draw and explain block diagram of mobile communication system. **[6]**

Ans.　Please Refer to Article No. 6.10 on Page No. 6.35.

OR

8. (a) Draw AM waveforms for : **[3]**

　　　(i) Modulation index = 1

　　　(ii) Modulation index > 1

　　　(iii) Modulation index < 1.

Ans.　Please Refer Example 6.1 on Page No. 6.12.

　(b) Write short notes on : **[6]**

　　　(i) Twisted pair cable　(ii) Fiber optic cable.

Ans.　(i) Please Refer Article No. 6.8.3 on Page No. 6.28.

　　　(ii) Please Refer Article No. 6.8.5 on Page No. 6.30.

　(c) Compare amplitude modulation and frequency modulation. **[4]**

Ans.　Please Refer to Article No. 6.7.6 on Page No. 6.25.

May 2016

Time : 2 Hours   **Max. Marks : 50**

1. (a) Draw and Explain full wave rectifier with capacitor filter.   **[6]**

Ans.   Please Refer to Article No. 1.9.2, Page No. 1.38.

(b) Explain CE amplifier with the help of DC loadline.   **[6]**

Ans.   Please Refer to Article No. 2.9, Page No. 2.13.

OR

2. (a) Explain with V-I characteristics the working of Zener diode as a voltage regulator. **[6]**

Ans.   Please Refer to Article No. 1.12.1, Page No. 1.57.

(b) Define α and β in cast of transistor. Derive the relationship between them.

If α = 0.98, calculate value of β.   **[6]**

Ans.   Please Refer to Article No. 2.10, Page No. 2.16.

3. (a) Draw a neat diagram of 3-input inverting summing amplifier and obtain expression

for its o/p voltage.   **[6]**

Ans.   Please Refer to Article No. 3.16.1, Page No. 3.21.

(b) Compare synchronous and asynchronous counter.   **[4]**

Ans.   Please Refer to Article No. 4.13.3, Page No. 4.32.

(c) State Demorgan's theorem.   **[2]**

Ans.   Please Refer to Article No. 4.4.1, Page No. 4.9.

OR

4. (a) For the given circuit. Find V_o **[6]**

Ans.   Please Refer Example 3.4, Page No.3.22.

(b) Compare microprocessor and microcontroller.   **[4]**

Ans.   Please Refer to Article No. 4.16, Page No. 4.35.

(c) Explain how Ex-OR gate can be used as an inverter.   **[2]**

5. (a) Draw a constructional diagram of SCR and Explain its working with the help of two

transistor analogy.   **[6]**

Ans.   Please Refer to Article No. 5.1.1, Page No. 5.1,and 5.5.

(b) With a neat diagram explain construction and working of LVDT. Give its advantages and applications. **[6]**

Ans. Please Refer to Article No. 5.12 , Page No. 5.27. **OR**

6. (a) Compare : **[6]**

(i) SCR and TRIAC

Ans. Please Refer to Article No. 5.1 and 5.3, Page No. 5.1 and 5.6.

(ii) DLAC and TRIAC

Ans. Please Refer to Article No. 5.2 and 5.3, Page No. 5.5 and 5.6.

(b) Draw and explain electronic weighting machine. **[5]**

Ans. Please Refer to Article No. 5.17, Page No. 5.33.

(c) Define : (i) Active Transducer

Ans. Please Refer to Article No. 5.7.1, Page No. 5.10.

(ii) Passive Transducer. **[6]**

Ans. Please Refer to Article No. 5.7.1, Page No. 5.10.

7. (a) Define AM, Derive expression for AM. Write expression for modulation index. Draw waveforms of AM. **[7]**

Ans. Please Refer to Article No. 6.6, Page No. 6.10.

(b) Write short note on :

(i) Coaxial Cable

Ans. Please Refer to Article No. 6.8.4, Page No. 6.29.

(ii) Fiber Optic Cable. **[6]**

Ans. Please Refer to Article No. 6.8.5, Page No. 6.30.

OR

8. (a) Draw and Explain block diagram of GSM system **[6]**

Ans. Please Refer to Article No. 6.11, Page No. 6.37.

(b) With respect to FM explain : (i) Frequency deviation

Ans. Please Refer to Article No. 6.7, Page No. 6.20.

(ii) Modulation index.

Ans. Please Refer to Article No. 6.7.1, Page No. 6.22.

(iii) Deviation ratio

Ans. Please Refer to Article No. 6.7.3, Page No. 6.23.

(iv) Frequency spectrum of FM. **[7]**

Ans. Please Refer to Article No. 6.4, Page No. 6.5.

NOV. 2016

Time : 2 Hours   **Max. Marks : 50**

Instruction to the candidates:
(1) Figures to the right indicate full marks.
(2) Neat diagrams must be drawn wherever necessary.
(3) Use of non programmable electronic pocket calculator is allowed.
(4) Assume suitable data if necessary.

1. (a) Draw and explain the V-I characteristics of a Zener diode. What are two breakdown mechanisms in a zener diode?   **[6]**

Ans. Please Refer to Article 1.12.2 and 1.12.3 Page No.1.61.

(b) What do you understand by a D.C. load line and Q point? Explain their significance.**[6]**

Ans. Please Refer to Article 2.14.1 on Page No. 2.22.   **OR**

2. (a) For bridge rectifier, the RMS secondary voltage of transformer is 12.7 V. Assume ideal diode and $R_L = 1$ kΩ. Find :   **[6]**

    (i)   Peak current   (ii)   DC load current
    (iii) DC load voltage   (iv)   RMS current
    (v) Peak Inverse Voltage of diode (vi)   RMS Voltage across load.

Ans. Please Refer to example 1.8 on Page No. 1.36

(b) Compare BJT and MOSFET.   **[6]**

Ans. Difference between BJT and MOSFT

Sr. No.	BJT	MOSFET
1.	BJT is current controlled device.	It is a voltage controlled device
2.	It is Bipoler device.	It is unipolar device .
3.	BJT is having bigger size.	It is smaller in size than BJT.
4.	BJT is having low input impedance.	EMOSFET is having high in put impedance.
5.	Saturation and cut off region is used for switching applications.	Ohmic and cut off is used for switching applications.
6.	Noise in BJT is high.	Noise in MOSFET is low
7.	Symbol. NPN PNP	Symbol. n-channel p-channel

3. (a) Define and give typical values of the following op-amp parameters: **[6]**

  (i) Voltage Gain

  (ii) CMRR

  (iii) Slew Rate

Ans. Please Refer to Article 3.9 Page No. 3.7

 (b) What is meant by Universal Gate ? By using any universal gate draw AND, OR, NOT basic gates. **[5]**

Ans. Please Refer to Article 4.5 on Page No. 4.12.

 (c) What do you mean by counter ? State different types of counters. **[2]**

Ans. Please refer to Article 4.13 on Page No. 4.30.

OR

4. **(a)** Draw a circuit diagram of an Op-Amp as an integrator and derive the expression for its output voltage. **[6]**

Ans. Pleaser refer to Article 3.19 on Page on 3.33.

 (b) What is multiplexer ? Explain one with example. Write its relation between select lines and input lines. **[7]**

Ans. Please refer to Article 4.8 on Page on 4.18

5. **(a)** Draw block diagram of Electronic Weighing Machine and explain its operation. **[6]**

Ans. Please Refer to Article 5.17 on Page on 5.36.

 (b) Explain the construction and characteristics of SCR. **[6]**

Ans. Please Refer to Article 5.1 on Page on 5.1.

OR

6. **(a)** Explain the construction and working of LVDT with neat diagram. **[6]**

Ans. Please Refer to Article 5.12 on Page on 5.29.

 (b) Compare the three types of Temperature Transducers. **[6]**

Ans. Please Refer to Article 5.10.9 on Page on 5.26.

7. **(a)** What is need of modulation ? Explain Amplitude Modulation in detail. **[7]**

Ans. Please Refer to Article 6.5.1 and 6.6 on Page on 6.9 and 6.11.

 (b) Draw and explain block diagram of GSM system. **[6]**

Ans. Please Refer to Article 6.11 on Page on 6.40.

OR

8. **(a)** Draw and explain electromagnetic spectrum. **[5]**

Ans. Please Refer to Article 6.4 on Page on 6.5.

 (b) Explain the following things about FM : **[8]**

  (i) Deviation ratio

  (ii) Mathematical representation of FM

  (iii) Advantages and Disadvantages

  (iv) Modulation index

Ans. Please Refer to Article 6.7 on Page on 6.22.

May 2017

Time : $2\frac{1}{2}$ Hours   **Total Marks : 70**

Instructions to the candidates :

(1) Figures to the right indicate full marks.

(2) Neat diagrams must be drawn wherever necessary.

(3) Use of electronic pocket calculator is allowed.

(4) Assume suitable data, if necessary.

1. (a) Draw the construction diagram and explain working of LED. **[6]**

Ans. Please Refer to Article 1.14.1, 1.14.3 on Page No. 1.67, 1.68.

(b) Explain with a neat circuit diagram, function of each component in single stage CE amplifier. **[6]**

Ans. Please Refer to Article 2.9, 2.9.1, 2.9.2 on Page No. 2.13, 2.14.

2. (a) In a centre tapped FWR, the rms half secondary voltage is 10V. Assuming ideal diodes and load resistance of 2 kΩ, find : DC load current, ripple factor and efficiency of rectification. **[6]**

Ans. rms half secondary voltage = 10 V = V_{srms}

Given Diodes are ideal

$$R_L = \text{load resistance} = 2 \text{ k}\Omega$$

$$\text{DC load current} = ?$$

$$\text{Ripple factor} = ?$$

$$\text{Efficiency of rectification} = ?$$

$$R_F = R_S = 0$$

Peak current (I_m) : $I_m = \dfrac{V_m}{R_S + R_F + R_L} = \dfrac{\sqrt{2}\, V_{srms}}{R_L}$

$$= \frac{\sqrt{2} \times 10}{2 \times 10^3} = 5\sqrt{2} \times 10^{-3} \text{ mA}$$

$$= 5 \times 1.41 \times 10^{-3} = 7.07 \text{ mA}$$

$$\text{DC load current} = I_{Ldc} = \frac{2 I_m}{\pi} = \frac{2 \times 7.07 \times 10^{-3}}{\pi} = 4.5 \text{ mA}$$

$$\text{DC load voltage} = V_{Ldc} = I_{Ldc} \times R_L$$

$$= 4.5 \times 10^{-3} \times 2 \times 10^3 = 9 \text{ V}$$

$$\text{RMS load current} = I_{L\,rms} = \frac{I_m}{\sqrt{2}} = \frac{7.07 \times 10^{-3}}{\sqrt{2}} = 4.999 \text{ mA} \approx 5 \text{ mA}$$

$$\text{Ripple factor} = r = \frac{[V_{Lrms}^2 - V_{Ldc}^2]^{1/2}}{V_{LDC}}$$

$$= \frac{[I_{Lrms}^2 R_L^2 - V_L^2 \, dc]^{1/2}}{V_{Ldc}} = \frac{[(5 \times 10^{-3})^2 \times (2 \times 10^3)^2 - (9)^2]^{1/2}}{9}$$

$$= 48.4\%$$

$$\text{Efficiency} \cdot \eta = \frac{8R_L}{\pi^2 (R_S + R_F + R_L)} = \frac{8R_L}{\pi^2 (RL)} = \frac{8}{\pi^2}$$

$$= 0.8105 = 81.05\%$$

(b) Draw and explain drain and transfer characteristics of enhancement type P-channel MOSFET.   **[6]**

Ans.   Please Refer to Article 2.23 on Page No. 2.38.

3. (a) Define Op-Amp. Draw and explain the functional block diagram of an Op-Amp.   **[6]**

Ans.   Please Refer to Article 3.4 on Page No. 3.2.

(b) Write law of commutation, law of association and law of distribution for AND and OR logic function.   **[6]**

Ans.   Please Refer to Article 4.4 on Page No. 4.7.

OR

4. (a) Calculate output voltage 'V_o' of Op-Amp circuit shown in figure Draw I/P and O/P waveforms.   **[6]**

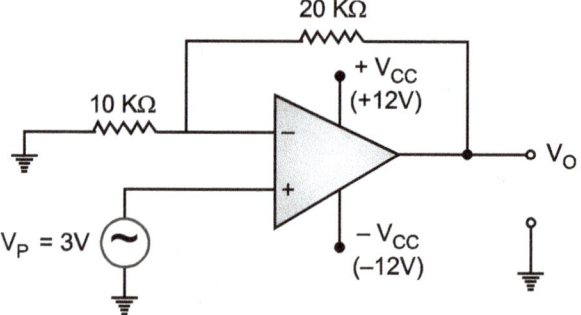

Fig. 1

Ans. $V_o = ?$

Input and output waveforms

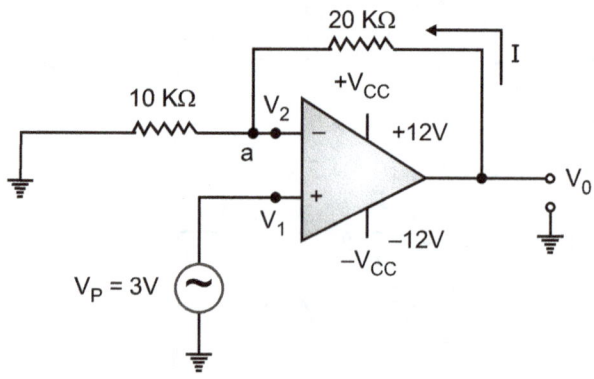

Fig. 2

This is non-inverting amplifier

∴

$$R_1 = 10 \text{ k}\Omega$$

$$R_F = 20 \text{ k}\Omega$$

$$V_{CC} = 12 \text{ V}$$

$$V_{in} = V_p = 3V$$

Output voltage V_o = ?

$$A_{CL} = 1 + \frac{R_F}{R_1} = 1 + \frac{20}{10} = \frac{30}{10} = 3$$

∴

$$\frac{V_o}{V_{in}} = 3$$

$$V_o = V_{in} \times 3 = 3 \times 3 = 9V$$

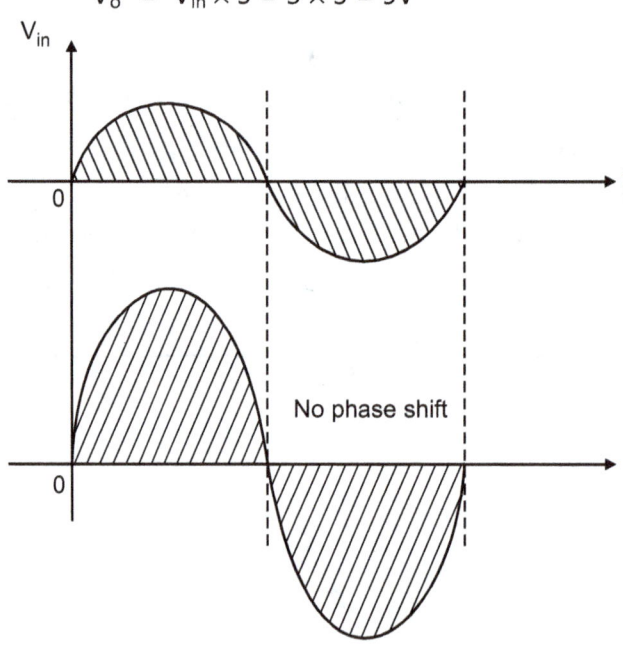

Fig. 3

(b) Draw and explain the block diagram of Microprocessor.   **[6]**

Ans.   Please Refer to Article 4.14 on Page No. 4.33.

5. (a) Draw construction of DIAC and explain working with V-I characteristics.   **[6]**

Ans.   Please Refer to Article 5.2 on Page No. 5.5 and 5.6.

(b) What is electronic weighing machine ? With the help of neat block diagram explain its working.   **[7]**

Ans.   Please Refer to Article 5.17 on Page No. 5.33, 5.34.

OR

6. (a) Define transducer. What are the selection criteria for a good transducer? **[7]**

Ans. Please Refer to Article 5.6, 5.8 on Page No. 5.9 and 5.12.

(b) Draw and explain the block diagram of basic instrumentation system. **[6]**

Ans. Please Refer to Article 5.5 on Page No. 5.9.

7. (a) What is electronic communication system? Explain the elements of communication system with the help of neat block diagram. **[7]**

Ans. Please Refer to Article 6.1, 6.1.1 on Page No. 6.1, 6.2.

(b) Explain different types of cables used in communication system with neat diagrams. **[6]**

Ans. Please Refer to Article 6.8, 6.8.1, 6.8.2, 6.8.3, 6.8.4, 6.8.5 on Page No. 6.26, 6.27, 6.28, 6.29, 6.30, 6.31.

OR

8. (a) Draw neat block diagram of GSM system and explain its working. **[6]**

Ans. Please Refer to Article 6.11 on Page No. 6.37, 6.38.

(b) Define modulation index with reference to AM and FM. Write equations of modulation index. Draw AM waveform for 100% modulation case. **[7]**

Ans. Please Refer to Article 6.6.2 Fig. 6.8 (b) on Page No. 6.12, 6.13.